THE 1ST GUNMAN

DON HARVEY

authorHOUSE®

AuthorHouse™
1663 Liberty Drive
Bloomington, IN 47403
www.authorhouse.com
Phone: 1 (800) 839-8640

© 2017 Don Harvey. All rights reserved.

No part of this book may be reproduced, stored in a retrieval system, or transmitted by any means without the written permission of the author.

Published by AuthorHouse   05/23/2017

ISBN: 978-1-5246-9372-5 (sc)
ISBN: 978-1-5246-9371-8 (e)

Library of Congress Control Number: 2017908172

Print information available on the last page.

Any people depicted in stock imagery provided by Thinkstock are models, and such images are being used for illustrative purposes only. Certain stock imagery © Thinkstock.

This book is printed on acid-free paper.

Because of the dynamic nature of the Internet, any web addresses or links contained in this book may have changed since publication and may no longer be valid. The views expressed in this work are solely those of the author and do not necessarily reflect the views of the publisher, and the publisher hereby disclaims any responsibility for them.

CONTENTS

Chapter 1 1
Chapter 2 16
Chapter 3 21
Chapter 4 49
Chapter 5 82
Chapter 6 99
Chapter 7 115
Chapter 8 141
Chapter 9 175
Chapter 10 206
Chapter 11 216
Chapter 11 293
Chapter 12 337
Chapter 13 414
Chapter 14 481
Chapter 15 575
Chapter 16 583
Chapter 17 594
Chapter 18 610

Josh's Playlist in order..655

CHAPTER 1

"Joshua, there is a breach." The quiet voice wakes me. I open my eyes with the thought of how much I hate 0-dark-thirty. To me it just seems like insanity to leave bed before dawn. My wife Sophee is curled up against me, which always makes me smile, and I quietly slide out from under the sheet. The room is in complete darkness, but I easily walk to the washroom connecting the bedroom to the main lodge, and softly close the door.

"Illuminate please, Vicky." The lights turn on with a snap. "Status of breach?"

"One breach in the coastal plain at coordinates 48 degrees 36'01.94 North by 93 degrees 29'41.05 West," Vicky answers.

"I am sorry, but do I look like a frigging GPS or Holomap?" I ask, with a hint of amusement as I wait for my eyes to adjust to the light.

"Sorry, sir," she replies. "There is a breach on the coastal plain near a rock."

"Is it a big rock?" I ask, shaking my head as I walked naked toward the shower.

"Somewhat." Vicky answers.

Never teach your personal Artificial Intelligence device sarcasm or wit, they get it.

"Notify the boys and have them meet me in the main bay within thirty minutes."

"Yes, sir."

I have instructed Vicky to call me by my first name, but I do like the *sir*-bit when she gets all formal and such. Having an A.I. is a very convenient luxury; I always try to be polite to her, but get a little annoyed with her adaptive personality center which ensures she knows my personal limits and how to activate me. Vicky plots and analyzes everything, then comes up with plans to provide assistance when I need it. It also makes her a great sounding board.

I walk into the shower which is already warmed up to the correct water temperature; maybe Vicky has saved my preference in the home system. Maybe the home comfort system saved my last setting without Vicky's help. I don't really care enough to ask. Since I was planning on having a day off, Sophee and I had a rather late night that, of course, makes me wish we had more sleep. I slowly turn in the jet stream until the hot water almost melts my brain. Maybe a cold shower would shock you awake, but a great hot shower wakens you nicely. Thinking about my sleeping wife, I smile. Bonding does have a way of changing a man's outlook on relationships and life; maybe tonight would be a good BBQ night with friends and family.

"Vicky, let Sophee know where we are when she wakes up, and then notify me so I can call her." I finished my shower and dried off before heading to the closet situated directly off the washroom. The light snap on as I enter.

I look at my work clothing, all the different camouflage and khaki items, and say, "Vicky, what should I wear?" I know it is a needless question but I enjoy her occasional zingers.

Vicky quickly speaks up. "The marauder is a class five. If you need camouflage or body armor you will already be dead, so why don't you wear something pretty?"

I mumble to myself that tossing her little ceramic ass into an ear of NewCoRN ™ and throwing it in front of the marauder will give an unpleasant view of a pig colon. I grab some digital-camouflage body armor and toss it on; it will help me if I am being banged around during the kill shot.

"How much damage is there?"

Vicky doesn't answer. I forgot I set a law that she could only speak when addressed directly. The law was due to her always trying to explain random things even if I was asking someone other than her.

"Vicky, new law. If I am alone and speak, you can assume I am speaking to you even if I don't say your name. End law." I ask again, "How much damage is there?"

"Not much. The marauder appears to be a boar; it took down the auto-post and is rooting around in a recently harvested field of NewCoRN ™"

This would be the same field that had the malfunctioning stasis generator, so there is a lot of salvage. "Why wasn't it cleaned up?"

"Cleaners 2 & Omega 3 were busy on the NewGraIN ™ fields."

"Ah," I answer.

Some staff has asked why I had cleaners named something as different at Cleaner 2 and Omega 3. There is a simple reason: when I order the units from Mars Colony they come painted with their names on them. Understand? Okay, then think of it my way, life is boring without doing little things to make other people shake their heads. I know the staff thinks I am a little out to lunch and refer to the machines as Cleaner 2 and 3 when speaking to each other, but when I get reports to my implant, the staff refers to them by the machine names not the Service Groups callouts.

"Vicky, at the next service please have the cleaners' names changed to the Service Group's names, and have the service bots repaint them all John Deere green."

"Yes, O weird one," she answers.

Bet they wonder about that, I think with a laugh. The crop harvesters are big, but to harvest something the size of NewCoRN ™ you will need it to be huge. NewCoRN ™ grows over ninety feet tall. The stalks alone are almost three feet thick. Each cob of corn weighs about two hundred pounds. A single kernel would weigh half a pound, corn flour and meal has replaced wheat as a main food ingredient. Lately we have been turning tons of kernels into popcorn which then can be sliced like bread or go to a movie and buy a single kernel of popcorn dipped in butter to feed the family. The stalks are used for wood products and the leaver are plowed back into the soil or transported off planet for biomass when the orders are received. You guessed it: I am a farmer. Well, farm operator/planet owner.

My great-grandfather's grandfather's discovery of our planet New Harvest came about two-hundred and seventy years ago, just before old Earth died. That might lead to a question of how a planet can actually die. Bio-war and nuclear war, the most evil of all wars, the kind of war that makes angles cry.

God, can I wax poetic.

At the beginning of the twenty-second century there were battles and open warfare everywhere but in North

America. Since the war on terror was lost, the Americans and the Canadians decided to form a single government which they called The North Americas. What was adopted under this government became known as the Fortress America Strategy.

Combining the two countries was really the only way to survive when things were falling apart around the rest of the world. With countries running out of money and energy, invasions to steal your neighbor's resources were commonplace. The North Americas had a missile shield, which was a phased shield that worked like a huge force field. It worked great for North America, but not so well for the rest of the world. The North Americans knew that with the wars continuing to escalate, earth would most likely become uninhabitable. An exit strategy was formed and plans were made.

Fortress America had been pissing off almost everyone else by hoarding its wealth, resources and technology. The North Americans felt that the final war was going to happen and had started allowing skilled workers get to the head of the immigration line. If you were an Engineer, Scientist, Doctor, or Agriculturist from a friendly country like England, Germany, Australia, Japan, or Korea you were in.

If I had to guess, I would say the population went from four hundred and fifty million to five hundred million in about a year. The good thing about acquiring so many skilled citizens is the amount of talent you have at your disposal. The world was going to hell, and even the most patriotic people from other countries were willing to gamble everything for a chance to live.

In the twenty-year build up of technology during the start of Fortress America, all automotive and aviation manufacturing were gearing up for mankind's survival. Space probes from Voyager to the Enterprise—hey, I didn't name it—were exploring the galaxy and finding habitable planets. Mars was in the process of being terrifomed for about forty years already. People in the North Americas got to work building starships before the balloons went up. Anyone with big money either built their own ships or formed groups to join government ships. GM, Ford, Boeing, and others were producing ships at quite a pace. It seemed every week or so a new ship was being readied.

My great-grandfather's grandfather was major shareholder in General Motors and that gave him enough clout to buy a small ship; small being a relative term. From bow to thrusters the ship was fourteen-hundred yards long, basically the size of fourteen football fields. It was nothing more than a massive barge with life support.

Creature comforts were minimal. The sleeping quarters had low gravity for comfort and were placed near a large theater area for classes and meetings. There was no skimping on the science labs and livestock holding pens. Whatever was in the ship was all they were going to have; it would be years before trade could be set up with the other colonies. It's amazing what ten billion will buy. Great Great Grandfather blew his entire fortune building and stocking the vast ship.

The best thing about these ships was the technological changes created at this time to power them. The power to lift the ships was antigravity, which uses the power of the earth's magnetic fields to lift the ships. Once you formed an antigravity bubble around the ship it would lift from the surface of the planet, move the bubble's focus to one section of the hull and it would propel the ship. Sure, the gravity-bubbles were slow and had to be formed on a planet, but they were the only way for humanity to leave Earth. The faster-than-light drive was not invented until years afterward.

Then the war started with Great Britain getting hit first. London was attacked with bio-agents, and the death toll was approaching one hundred percent. Then Paris was targeted. The bio-agents decimated the Parisian capital too, and then the diseases spread quickly to other cities and countries.

As soon as the first attack started, Fortress America locked completely down and no private ships or planes could make it through the barriers. There was a fairly long lead-in to these events, so it came as no surprise when the shield came fully down. The only people who were able to get in after the lockdown were on military ships or submarines with phased-shield nullifying generators which would allow them to pass through into the fully shielded North American security zone.

The second London was hit with the biological agents, boarding protocols for the starships were initiated. After years of packing and ensuring everything was ready, everyone in the North Americas was loaded into thousands of ships. Great-granddad's granddad packed up his family and his closest friends, along with some of the best technical people and including some biologists with their families.

He took twenty-five hundred people from Earth and gave them chance of a new life on an unpolluted planet. This gave him a group of very dedicated colonists. Maybe it was loyalty to the family, maybe knowing that earth was effectively poisoned and would be uninhabitable help to create the dedication. Either way we had awesome people to start the colony with.

At the same time as the shield fully locked down, China decided to invade Australia and Korea. Of course India and Pakistan got into the fray. It got a bit nuclear, with India making their point with a bunch of mushroom clouds and Pakistan answering back with their own nuclear tipped missiles. By then it had got very ugly with huge armies massing to invade each other's countries. It would have been quite the war if the biological agents had not got them too; four hundred million dead Pakistanis and around five hundred and fifty million dead Indians within the first day.

China got nuked a few times and threw millions of souls away in the taking of Korea, and then Japan thought that was enough of a threat to launch twenty nuclear missiles at them in order to ensure that would be the end of this leg of the domination play. The Chinese never did get off the cost of Australia either, because the plague that destroyed the Indians was in atmosphere. It found their ships and killed almost all of the crew in a few weeks.

Unfortunately for the Australians, who stayed home and thought thousands of miles of oceans would protect them, it was already on their shore. Toxins and bacteria were carried on the wind, by birds, or anything else alive. I am sure somewhere there could have been a survivor, but no one ever heard from them.

Did I mention Saudi Arabia? Well, the house of Saud decided to use their military might against the People's Republic of Iran. Of course Egypt and Syria hated that, so they attacked Israel—guess it made sense to them. Egypt didn't have nukes or good bio-weapons; no one could figure out why but Syria was more than willing to share. As a result, Israel nuked the supreme piss out of the Middle East in order to protect themselves, but it was too late because even Jerusalem was nuked in return. Nuclear fire destroyed some of the oldest cities on the planet; it was a very sad thing to watch.

Vatican City was destroyed with a small nuke even after Rome was hit with bio-weapons. With exception of Moscow and Berlin which burned under a nuclear fireball, the rest of Europe was biologically attacked. The bio-weapons were not recognizing borders and neither did the fallout from the Middle East. Most of the planet died either in a blast wave of nuclear fire or when the bio–agents took hold. The new plague was a fine combination of smallpox and anthrax, with mortality rates in the very high ninety percent range. I guess it lost some of its toxicity due to the radiation, but the radiation levels were high enough that it was killing the other few percent—though it took a little while longer.

The world took less than fourteen days to go from eight billion to five hundred million.

Faced with a planet that was basically screwed up everywhere but under the shield, mankind had only one option. Leave quickly. From the high radiation areas that wouldn't be habitable for 10,000 years to the bacteria infested areas without so much as bug left alive, there wasn't anything even the best minds could come up with to bring the planet back from the edge of darkness.

North America couldn't drop the shield without letting in the manmade plagues and radiation; plans were made for a mass exodus. Everyone had been buttoned up in ships since the London attack, and it was just the right amount of time needed to synchronize the many thousands of launches that delayed the departure. Radiation counts were getting higher around the shield and earthquakes were becoming comonplace. It wouldn't be long until the shields could not protect North America from this new harsh environment.

Scholars still discuss the changes that could have been made to clean up the planet and provided enough renewable clean energy to stop the fighting. Of course religion had *nothing* to do with the wars.

Yeah. Sure.

It would not have mattered how much free power from the anti-gravity there was because by the time the Fortress closed and the war ended there was no one alive. Except for North America, there was nothing left. Animals died, people died, religion died. Christianity survived but they were not fundamentalists or fanatics like Islamic jihadists who created the bio-weapons.

The shield dropped and the simultaneous exodus began. Granddad Chandler decided not to go in the same direction of the rest of the fleet; he went east, maybe because he was a Mason or maybe because he wanted his own planet without having to share it. Either way, after four months of travel he found what he was looking for.

It was a rather small planet with no moons. Very green and blue, the split between land and water was very defined. One giant land mass filled about forty percent of the planet in a thick band around equator and a two oceans covered the rest of the surface. The terra firma was stable with no active tectonic activity; it had large boreal forests, huge plains, and nice weather. It was a great place for a farm, and Chandler Garvie knew that supplying food would be a great business.

New Harvest, as our planet became known was actually named by one of the kids on the ship. Great-Great Granddad was like that, putting kids first and always making sure to include them. At least they didn't name it Earth the Second or something else equally ridiculous. The ship landed with little problems, and the scientists confirmed the test probe's readings for a week before the doors opened. The long journey had made everyone ready to work and survive; because everyone on board was either family or an employee the pecking order was established.

Chandler Garvie's vision of supplying food to the galaxy allowed the people of New Harvest to set up the farm quickly, taking only a few years. During that time, it was discovered there was something a little odd about the way the old earth's biology grew. It took several months for the biologists to figure out why everything, including the people, was growing larger. It wasn't just due to the planet having a gravity that was about 0.19gs higher than old earth and, as a result, caused the New Harvesters to be a little heavier muscled than anyone else in the galaxy. No, it was biological and in the air and water everyone breathed and drank every day.

Once the natural enzymes that caused the growth were figured out, a vaccine was quickly synthesized and administered. It is safe, with little to no side effects, and it became procedure to vaccinate babies shortly after birth, as well as to anyone staying on the planet for more than a week. Who wants to be nine feet tall in high gravity? It was not like we had time to start a basketball league

Some of the animals we imported turned out better with the additional size. Cow's got the vaccine because the beef got very stingy and tough when they grew too large. Deer, chickens, and pigs didn't require the shot and this is what caused issues. We did not know what kind of predators were hiding on New Harvest when we were making our plans, so we assumed we needed some tougher animals.

The deer we brought in were Canadian Whitetails and their meat was delicious even at two tons. Yes, the deer could weigh as much as two tons, and reach approximately fifteen feet tall. Since our plants and seeds grow freakishly large, there was enough food for the larger animals. We merely air dropped teams of robotic planters all over the Great Plains to keep the vegetation plentiful.

The deer acted like deer and were not an issue, but chickens ended up growing about twice the size of the old birds from earth called ostriches. They still had decent flavor and produced ten-pound eggs and while this made for bitching omelets, the birds were quite unpleasant to deal with and had to be separated from people with their eggs being collected by remotely operated vehicles.

The really stupid decision was bringing Russian wild boars instead of domestic pigs. They foraged well and generally stayed away from settlements, but their size and intelligence made them a concern. They became known as Marauders as the boars would continually probe the fences to look for openings. A mesh shield would only phase itself about thirty-six inches into the ground, and while it would go hundreds of feet into the sky marauders don't fly. Ditches and ravines get flooded in heavy rains and the washouts get a little deeper each time. The marauders, continually in search of an opening, find one and with a bit of routing they get in. Marauders treat other animals and people like they are just another food source.

We tried to figure out why they want in, and realized the corn and grain must be the draw. We attempted to sow more crops outside of the shields in order to feed the pigs and discourage them from coming into the settlements, but it was not enough apparently. They could smell the amount that had been planted and wanted the easier, more dense food source; not sure if it was the amount of feed or the fact they could mix up their diet with animals at the livestock pens and town sites. I must protect my crops from this, sure I can grab a railgun and blast the crap out of whatever is crossing the line, but one important thing though, and wild boar meat doesn't get stringy or tough. No matter how large they get, a Marauder always tastes good. Rich, sweet meat that's finely grained and juicy is always in demand.

The boars are huge with a live weight between five and nine tons for a Class 3 which when cut and put in stasis is three and a half to four tons. At the prices paid in the open market, four animals and a load of corn would pay for a new bulk carrier. Needless to say, railguns were not good to use on the pigs, too much damage and waste, however enjoyable it is to blast them to little pieces

Big boars were very unpredictable and smart, add huge crops to the mix and we have problems. We had to put shield generators around the entire farm and settlement after a couple of oversized boars savaged two small towns. They came into town at night like bulldozers, hungry bulldozers. New Harvest lost a full third of our people and six months worth of crops.

It was then decided by Grandpa Chandler that the loss of one life by a five-ton pig would never happen again; the same shield technology that protected mankind could be adapted to protect the farm. Okay, at around one hundred and seventy-five thousand hectares, it's a rather large farm with two-thirds of the land for crops and the other third for beef and chicken. Great-Great Grandpa's head research scientist was one of the smartest people mankind produced. It was his life's work that made the vaccine to stop the growth problems. Tim also came up with a twist to the shield technology used on earth. Instead of having a non-permeable phased shield, he was able to cross-link quantum strands to create a mesh version: rain, sun, and wind could go through it like a chain link fence. However, if you drove a hover tank into it at high speeds you would smear yourself all over the shield without ever getting in.

After several generations the farm is stable with great crops, a lot of beef and chicken, as well as venison and pork when we sent teams outside the shield to hunt. I ensure the proper resources are in place to plant and harvest the crops. It was such an easy job; nanites and technology worked well. The boars of freakishly large size are the worst issue we have on New Harvest.

Funny that everywhere else in the galaxy they could produce great machines and services, but not vast amounts of food. I mean, sure, Mars Colony has huge greenhouses and domed animal pens, but they require so much money to maintain that they're not cost effective or efficient enough.

Sure, there were a lot of planets with decent atmospheres, but either they had soils without natural nutrients or they had pests. The bulk mass from our corn and other plants that we sent off planet allowed for some colonies to create a better soil make-up, but it was a long process. New Harvest is great, and has only a couple of beasts on land that will eat a man. The ocean is quite a bit more dangerous with creatures that could swallow any fair sized ship. Near the shore, various pests will try to pull you into the water, but we can deal with them.

Within ten years of landing, the crops and meat were able to pay for an elaborate planetary defense system. This was necessary because having planetary wealth could make you target. Good thing our founders hadn't run powerful species bent on war. Pirates do exist, and who wants to lose a crop or people to slavers?

You had to work, but pay was generally really good, and health care was also free to all citizens. I guess that was the Canadian in Great-Great Grandfather that set that up.

CHAPTER 2

When I decided to head off-planet for the first time there were about 8,900 people living on New Harvest in two major settlements. I was young and really stupid; I felt the need to leave New Harvest and the farm to join the People's Free Force. I wanted to make a difference with my life instead of being trapped following my grandfather's path. Yeah, I know it sounds like a communist army, but it was the opposite. So many planets were settled in a short time without a thorough investigation and soon they found out things can go bump in the night. The P.F.F. bumped back.

I turned eighteen and was not happy with life on New Harvest. Programming planters and service bots felt like it would kill me in a long, slow agonizing manner. My family name ensured that I always had to be working and setting a good example. Granddad was a strict humorless man with me who thought of nothing but the crops, how much product could be shipped off planet. I thought it was his personal goal to suck all joy from my life by making me act just like him. Since my mom spends all of her time in the bio-engineering labs working on plants and seeds for less than ideal growing conditions found on other planets, my grandfather was tasked with making me into a version of himself that the farm could use. My boredom with the farm put me into a stupid state of mind where it did not allow me to see him as the leader of our people and protector of New Harvest.

My father, before he died, had a completely different way of raising me. Dad had a few problems with authority and broke rules when he thought they shouldn't apply to the son of the man who owns the planet, but his generally quiet demeanor and sense of humor was a kinder way of teaching than Grandpa's hard way. Dad would show you that the right way was easier in the long run by often doing something poorly or taking shortcuts on specific tasks then laughing about it later. I was never sure if he purposely did things wrong just to prove that or he really didn't care, he was the ultimate teacher. At least I was smart enough to see what was happening and adjust my work so the same thing didn't happen to me.

Either way, Granddad was always riding Dads ass and was not impressed with his teaching style. I think this was what made me want to leave after dad passed away. My father liked to get outside the shield and ride an old all-terrain vehicle he rebuilt, and thought being chased by an angry boar was quite a thrill. The problem with old machines is they sometimes break down, which is not a good thing to happen when a marauder is chasing you. So when I was twelve, I lost the only positive role model that I thought I had. Mom hardly left the labs, my granddad was a hardass, and my life sucked. The next six years were very difficult because I was restless, and then finally I turned eighteen.

That's when I jumped on one of our freighters and took off for Mars Colony. Granddad didn't pretend that he was happy with my decision. He and I walked through the busy loading port with all its smells and activity. It looked like a very large shipment of meat and biomass was the load of the day. We paused just before the passenger gate to watch the loaders put containers on the roller beds to be drawn into the ships hold. It was then he quietly offered up his years of wisdom in a rather paternal manner.

"Josh," he started by saying, "You need to find out what you want to do. Take the time to learn something that will make you happy. Find yourself a good woman to marry and bring yourself home. New Harvest will be here for you when you have found what you need. Remember you're the only heir."

I got kind of choked up and told him I would be back when I could, and to send a message if I was ever needed. I put out my hand and looked him in the eye; it was rather startling to see him looking back at me with watery, tear-filled eyes. He ignored my outstretched hand and hugged me.

As I walked on the companionway I looked only at my feet, if my gaze landed anywhere else I too would have cried. Granddad's emotion made me realize that he did care and maybe just maybe my own feelings were wrong. It took me a frigging hour to find my cabin because I was would not ask anyone where my cabin was on the ship named after me. Yeah, the starship carrier/freighter I was on was called the "Boy Named Joshua". Guess granddad was a bit proud of having a grandson and heir. There was a two-month journey ahead of me that I thought was going to be a drag, little did I know what good old granddad had planned.

I had a poor night's sleep and woke up hungry and decided I was going to embrace the journey. No way was I going to have my meals served to me or make them from the Autochief in the cabin. I opened my cabin hatch and decided to head to the crew mess. As I strolled towards the mess I noticed that a few of the other passengers were standing near the hatchway to the mess. I tried to squeeze between them with a simple "Excuse me" when a large hand grabbed my throat. He pushed me back into one of the other guys who grabbed my arms, and that is when the beating really started. I took quite a few punches to the face and kidneys as I was being choked by the first guy. Before a fight there should be some tough talk, yet they didn't say a thing. I guess they decided there was nothing to say.

I must admit, no matter how many times I got hit I didn't go down—hard to fall when you're being held up by the throat. A grayness started cloud my vision from the choking; they seemed intent on either killing me or kidnapping me. Maybe it was the shock of being attacked that delayed my reactions since I had never been in a real fight. The martial arts training I had taken did kicked in and those first few seconds made me realize I was not successfully putting up a good defense.

Then something just went click in my mind and the grey started to change to red. I turned my head and bit into the arm holding me by the throat. The warm saltiness of his blood filling my mouth and the scream ringing in my ears woke me up even further from the fog that had fallen over me. The hand fell from my throat; I spat the chunk of arm out and started to fight back effectively. Mr. Big Hand took a thumb in the eye and I slammed a few elbows into his face before he went down, and then I was then left with Mr. Kidney puncher. He must have been getting tired as his hits didn't seem to hurt anymore. I grabbed his face and tried to push his head thru a bulkhead. It didn't work, but he did hit the floor with Big Hand. Bob the Kicker tried to score a field goal, which I swept aside and stepped into striking range as my palm strike smashed his face in. As he fell too, a slight noise behind made me turn quickly. A steward was standing in the now open hatchway, a little pale, and looking at the mess I created.

"Are you okay, sir?" he asked.

I think I'll be pissing blood for a while, I thought. "Call medical please," I said with a raspy voice before falling forward to my knees, then on to my face as I passed out.

CHAPTER 3

I woke up surround by a warm light green liquid. Floating face down with a scuba style mouthpiece in my mouth I rolled over and tried to stand. A very bright light turned on and I could see that I was in a rejuvenation tank, I was feeling like a million credits, no pain in my face or neck and my body did not feel like a punching bag anymore. I spit out the mouthpiece when my feet hit the bottom of the capsule and I could lift my face out of the fluid. It felt good not to be breathing thru a tube.

"Could you please dim the lights?" I asked.

"Yes sir," was the slightly metallic sounding reply. The lights grew dull and I was able to look over the side of the tank and get more than a glimpse of the room I was in. The light green gel was receding from my body and a spray of warm water was rinsing me off. I did a quick survey, and everything seems healed.

"Who am I addressing?" I asked.

"Mark II."

"Who's A.I. are you?"

The Mark II responded, "By the command of Chandler Garvie the 1st males in line get their personal A.I.s when they turn eighteen. Your health issues activated me when you were tanked; I am you're A.I. sir."

"Mark II you are now Vicky-save," I instructed. "Download a new voice accent: earth British female-save," I order.

"Orders saved sir," she answers.

"When do I hatch Vicky?"

Vicky's quiet voice says, "Now, sir!"

The tank slowly opens and standing outside are two people waiting for me, by the uniform and rank insignia one is the captain, the other one is wearing a white lab coat and can only be the ship's doctor. I look briefly down realizing that I am naked, oh well.

I step out of the tank and speak in a clear voice, "I want those pricks charged."

The Captain nervously smiles and hands me a towel. "That will not be necessary, Mr. Garvie. The crew has tossed them out the airlock. "

This startled me. Sure I was a Garvie, but to die like that for giving me a beating? Even I thought it a bit excessive.

"How exactly do you get away with killing them? My god, Captain!" I say in a fury.

The Captain looks at me without blinking and informs me for the reason behind his actions. "My crew had nothing to do with their deaths." He takes a breath. "They were dead before you made it into the tank sir."

Crap, I thought. "Am I under arrest?"

"There will be no investigation, sir. They beat you in a poorly planned kidnapping plot. Once they had you unconscious you would have been taken to a shuttle and then taken away. Surveillance cameras picked up the assault and by the time security got to you the fight was over. There was evidence in their cabin that this had been planned for awhile"

I take the clothes offered by the doctor and proceed to dress myself.

"Why did security take so long to respond?" I questioned.

The doctor spoke up. "Actually it was all over in less than two minutes. Your nose was broken and one kidney was crushed, you also had a partly collapsed windpipe. If your nanites had not kicked in and boosted your adrenaline levels, you would have died."

"Yes, sir," the Captain agreed, "their identification cubes let us track them while you were in recovery. These guys were very hard hitters from Rockfall. Your kidnapping would have allowed them to get freighters of goods rerouted."

"Am I free to go back to my cabin?"

The Captain smiled. "Sir, I am putting an escort with you. It would be our pleasure to have you at my private mess for dinner with the Officers. "

"No, thanks," I said. "Unless you want to include the whole crew, I'll take my meals with them." From my viewpoint I was a working man who was in training to be a soldier.

The Captain shook his head and said, "I don't think the ship's crew would take an invitation from me; they are rather standoffish and strictly observant of protocol."

"I take they know who I am?" I ask.

The good doctor replied. "Yes, and they are rather embarrassed about the kidnappers and your injuries."

"Vicky, do they have a mess large enough for a banquet?"

"Yes, sir," she answers.

Granddad wants me to act like a leader so I will lead,

ran through my mind. Being the well known grandson and namesake of this ship comes in handy I thought.

"Captain, please park the ship in the next orbit you can find and send a flash back to Harvest informing them of the delay. May I have the honor of supplying the meal and refreshment? Granddad will allow the delay, and I want all spacers present. Please have a piglet removed from stasis and prepared Harvest method. Remove a couple of kegs of beer as well please."

"May I address the crew?" The Captain nodded and I asked Vicky to go ship wide.

"Attention on deck for an announcement from our namesake."

I smiled at the Captain's introduction and then began my announcement. "This is Joshua Garvie. Sorry for the blood in the hallways of your fine ship. Captain Grey is going to park the ship in orbit around the next planet so we can have an evening off watch. Since I seem to be causing the problems here, I will be supplying a piglet and some beer. I would appreciate it if the whole crew was in attendance. Close com, please, Vicky."

The Captain and doctor both trade a look as the Captain asks "Church Key?"

"Yes, why?" I asked.

The Captain smiled before saying he had never had the spare credits to actually have it on the ship. I see the doctor grinning and nodding as well. Well, since I am in Granddad's will and his only heir I guess I can get away with it. With a nod I turn and head out of the infirmary.

"Vicky, am I going in the correct direction?"

"Take the second passageway on the right, third hatch, sir."

"Thank you. Vicky, what do I have to do to send a flash to Harvest?"

Vicky answers with "Direct me to send it whomever you wish and I will route it through the ships systems."

I think for a minute, a Captain of this ship can't afford Church Key? Either the price off Harvest is too high or their wages need to be reviewed. "Vicky, post the ships wage rates on the bulkhead please." I sit down on the lounge and watch the numbers slide across the wall. "This ship has good transit times and never gets less that a 4 star rating, so why have they not been rewarded for service?"

"Sir, your father's responsibility was to take care of the people of Harvest. Unless there were complaints that reached the Chandler some of the crews would most likely be waiting for it. It would seem that having a position on the Boy Named Joshua and being well fed is more important than cash."

I sit back for a minute and think that this ship is raking in the profit for good old granddad so why not act the way he wants me to be and deal with this little problem. Even though I am leaving New Harvest behind I am still a Garvie.

"Vicky, flash to Granddad, live conversation,"

"Opening flash, sir."

"What now?" Granddad grumbles, as he answers the call.

"Hey, Granddad, I got beat up."

His avatar looks me over. "How bad?"

I smile back and say "I was only tanked for a couple of days."

"Okay then, thanks for letting me know."

"Granddad, I didn't call you to tell you I got beat up. I

wanted you to know that this crew is grossly underpaid yet loyal, and we should do something about it."

"Listen, Josh, I don't care what you do, pay them what you think is right. Anything else?"

"No. Thanks for the Mark II Granddad, Joshua out."

"Well, you're old enough now," he finished, "Garvie out!"

That was simple, I thought. I hang out in my cabin listening to music and talking with my A.I. to get to know her/it. It surprised me to find out that four hours of tank time healed the injuries I had and the other forty four were to have nanites install her in my chest cavity against the spine. The adaptive personality programming is quite impressive with her explanations about how things were more tailored to my likes which were data and not speculations. My firm instruction told her if I want an opinion I'd ask for it. Vicky's program also modulated her voice in volume and frequency or tone while monitoring my responses until she found out what relaxed and was accepted best by me.

Only once did she ever ask me why I chose Vicky for her name, and if an A.I. could be amused she would have been. I did not know anyone named Vicky. If she was named after anything that I had preconceived notions about, then I may not treat her as something new. Makes sense to me and she didn't have any issues with that. Makes me wonder if she thought I was over analyzing things, though.

We were in the middle of our little marathon get-to-know-you talk when Vicky informed me that dinner was ready. I opened the hatchway to armed men that greeted me with a salute.

"We will take you to the mess, sir."

The 1st Gunman

"No salutes. I have not earned them yet." Even as I said that, I realized I didn't mind being called "Sir" one bit. We walk into the mess hall to find it loaded and everyone waiting for me. I went around some tables over toward the bar to grab a bulb of Church Key's Northumberland Lager which is the greatest beer in the universe. Ships don't use cans, or glass for drinks because the way they could become projectiles when they ship maneuvers or is in a braking pattern, instead they use recyclable bulbs which are made of a very light weight polymer and of course shaped like a flower bulb with a flat on the bottom for standing them vertical. The Purser quickly slid up next to me.

"The officers would like you to join their table," he said. The crew's eyes are on me as I walk to the opposite end of the mess sipping on my beer and stop in front of the Captain and the senior officer's tables.

"Captain, please grab some bulbs of beer and join the crew with me." I hoist my lager towards the crew.

With a smile at Joshua the captain stood up. "Gentlemen, Mr. Garvie requests we join the crew. Everyone please grab a tray of bulbs and serve the crew the first round of drinks."

This caused a few murmurs among the crew because officers didn't usually serve the enlisted. *"We do now,"* I think. There was a division between the crew and the officers that is like a wall in the mess, officers at one end and crew at the other end. On New Harvest we treat each other very respectful but you will find workers and managers breaking bread and enjoying each other's company. When I see someone who doesn't believe they are good enough or not worthy of being with others because of job titles I get annoyed. Sure the officers have rank and need to give orders but they don't need segregation. I patiently waited until everyone got a bulb and the Captain raises his bulb.

"Spacers, a toast to the Garvies and to our namesake."

Spacer or Officer, it didn't seem to matter, when they had a beer and someone to toast. The look on the spacers and officers' faces was pure joy at having Church Key beer. The deep, full taste and moderate alcohol level was... how should I put it? In the words of Granddad, "It was like the tears of wee angels crying on my tongue."

Since it was only made on New Harvest and an all-natural product, the taste was more than a little better in comparison with the garbage produced on Mars. Sure, we had the money to build a much bigger brewery, but why bother? If you go into one of the watering holes back on New Harvest and ask for a draft, guess what you get... a Church Key Northumberland Lager.

Everyone stood and raised their bulb with a hearty "*JOSHUA!*" before enjoying their drink. Having the captain raise a toast to you and being welcomed in this manner almost brought a tear to my eye, almost; I am not that sensitive. I nodded to the group and raise my bulb.

"To a damned fine ship and crew! Get a plate and fill up please" I say.

I moved to an empty spot to join a table of crew members and see the officers doing the same and sit for a bit while waiting until everyone is eating and, of course, drinking before I stand back up. The group goes silent without any prompting—darn polite this crew is. I take sip of my Church Key before starting to speak.

"I recently spoke with Grandfather about your pay grades. Since my father passed there has not been regular scale reviews for any New Harvest crews, and for this I am full of regrets. Each member of the crew will get a one-cycle cash bonus plus a twenty-five percent raise. As these are wet ships, I am also instructing the Purser to ensure there is Church Key on board for the crew and it will be priced correctly, not for import. Cheers!"

I lowered my bulb and departed from the party silently. As I walked to my cabin I could still hear the cheers and yells. Since I am not really a member of this crew, it's not my party.

"Vicky?" I ask quietly.

"Online, sir."

"File the bonus for two cycles and increase the rate by thirty-five percent. Send a message with each pay stating the Captain made good argument that his crew was worth more than we offered, and after thorough review it was agreed upon."

Not only did I show the crew that officers are humans when they brought them drinks and sat with them, but I forced the officers to see the crew as equals in the greater scheme. I may be popular now, but the Captain will have even more respect from the ship's compliment after they discover he "convinced" grandfather to increase their wages further. Of course, by giving him the credit I will have his loyalty.

"Please upload pay scales to New Harvest and ensure it passes."

"Done and approved, Sir," Vicky replies.

This took less than five seconds. Odd that an AI... assistant would have that kind of speed and uploading ability rolls through my mind.

"Vicky, explain your speed," I order.

"Sir, your instruction was relayed to New Harvest and Billy Jean, who is New Harvest's Mark V A.I., accepted the instruction on your grandfather's behalf. She filed it with central storage, and the bonus plus the message about the increase are to be included in the crew's next pay."

"Vicky, how do you have this much ability?"

"Sir, I am a Mark II, full military processors and protection ability. I am created to be a full support unit, protection, assistant, and a class one healer."

I sit back for a minute. As a class one healer she will be programming nanites for enhanced healing and physical upgrading, the military processor will give her full access to any systems period, plus the intuitiveness of a personal assistant.

"Vicky, how many Garvies have an A.I like you?"

If an A.I. could smile I was hearing it in her reply. "Only one sir."

I rolled my eyes and said, "Explain?"

"I am the only one of three of the generation Mark IIs. The cost of a Mark II is far too much to be viable product and the possibility of one being used for conquest or war is too much of a burden to my creators. Since every male Garvie gets a military level A.I. when they come of age, it was decided to give one to the Garvies.

"Why the Garvies?" I ask

"We are created on Asthran with is rich with heavy and exotic metals. Their entire population was in danger of starving when your great-grandfather sent several heavy freighters of supplies to save them. Since he personally delivered it and supported them getting back on their feet, a pact was made. Asthran supplies high level A.I.s across the galaxy for the military mostly."

"Mostly?"

"There is one set of exceptions: you, your father before he passed, your grandfather, and most likely your son when he gets to be of mature age."

"My son?" I ask with a laugh. "You know something I don't?"

I make it to my cabin without running into any other passengers. The hatch opens silently without having to palm the keypad. Knowing that Vicky is a Mark II full military package makes me wonder what settings she has.

"Vicky, please list base operating parameters and duties for the Mark II, and have them projected on the wall."

I walk across the cabin to the washroom… Okay, *head*. I am not a spacer by trade and don't have to use the proper lingo. The lights turn on as I walk into the spacious room. One of the benefits of traveling on a huge star freighter is that they have all the amenities, like a real shower. Smaller transports usually don't have the space for extra water recyclers. There is nothing wrong with sonic showers except they leave you feeling itchy—clean, but itchy. There isn't anything better than a hot shower to clear your head. I dry off and walk into the main cabin to see my instructions have been carried out.

Rules

1. Safeguard primary's life.
2. Active scan at all times unless ordered to passive by primary.

3. Ensure primary's nanites are at level one.
4. Scan nanites and program for deviations.
5. Assistant level one ensures primary's comfort and ease.

"Vicky?" I query.

"Online," she answers.

"You don't shut down?"

"No, I am programmed never to shut down; I use active and passive scans at all times." "What are you scanning for now?"

"I am scanning the cabin for electronic bugs, checking the life support systems and records of this ship, as well as reviewing engine maintenance records. Sub routines are checking the passengers manifest and crew records and I have locked out the cabin hatch to everyone but you. Your damage repair nanites are being monitored, and general health nanites are checking your system for cancers. I am inspecting the galley's supply list and scanning for poisons. I also examined the plot for our destination and suggested an improved route to the navigation system."

"That's kind of presumptuous of you, isn't it?" I ask with a smile.

"No, I have more processing power than every system on this ship. I could simultaneously run all systems on this ship and several other ships without any loss in performance."

Holy crap!

"Vicky, please continue your scans and answer this: "What are you worth?"

She answers. "You could buy forty-two freighters

with what I cost; Quantum processors and triteirene base materials are expensive, but I like to think I am worth it.

"I figured that out when we were having our little talk this afternoon. Would you have caught those kidnappers if you had been active?"

"Yes, I would have been able to warn you or security before you left for the mess."

"If Rockfall needed food why not ask? We'll sell to anybody with credits," I said.

"The people from Rockfall are a lot like the old pirates from Somalia on Earth back in the twentieth century. They would have held you hostage for a while, getting a bunch of shipments of food to sell, and then they would have killed you." Vicky said.

Security is good, but I don't want babysitters. Nice that she could have saved me from the beating but as a soon to be soldier my personal defense should not be left up to an A.I.

"Vicky, who do you report to?" I ask.

She answers, "You."

"No one else gets reports or updates?" I carefully expand the question. "No other systems; no reason for you to update Granddad or the people who built you?"

"No, I communicate with your nanites and other systems to ensure your safety, but the personal assistant programming will not allow me to share any information unless I have your direct authorization. Your privacy is part of your personal security," she concludes.

"New rule, Vicky. I will turn on my own lights and open my own doors. Please let me live without the assistant until I ask for it, but stay active unless I instruct otherwise. Should you see something that may be important tell me first? Also, do not contact security *ever*, unless I am incapacitated. Am I clear?"

"Yes, Sir."

Can an A.I. sound sad? She seemed to be almost mournful at my instructions, as though I did not want her working for me and it made her sad.

"Can you take sub-vocal commands?" I ask. Being able to communicate without talking will be very handy in combat or situations where stealth is a necessity.

"Yes, and I can communicate the same way."

"Great. Another directive: please stay sub-vocal unless I request otherwise," I command, and then add, "Vicky, can you access AutoChef here?"

The response is an immediate yes and that she had already downloaded all my favorite foods from my home's unit. That makes me smile because whenever I get homesick knowing my mom's best meals were programmed in will give me some small level of comfort.

"Have a small pizza made for me with another bulb of beer, please," I order. "And I have one more question. If no one knows where I am and what I am doing, would you contacting my home back on New Harvest let the cat out of the bag?"

"Sir, I am a Mark II. Nothing can trace me."

Lovely, I think to myself, I wanted to get away and be my own person, having a Mark II protecting my privacy might be a truly good thing. The pizza was remarkably good and the beer cold; exactly what I needed after the long day I had. I crawl into my bunk, quite full and comfortable, and then realize I forgot to shut the lights off. I suck!

"Vicky, please wake me up at Oh five hundred…and please kill the lights".

I guess having an assistant is good when I need it. As I lie on my bunk in the dark, listening to the gentle hum of the air circulation systems and the odd thump or bang, more than a few thoughts about Vicky and my future spin around in my head. Will they accept me having a Mark II when I join up for the People Free Force?

The ship slides like a wraith through space with the faster than light drive is running at 100%. Unfortunately there were no wormholes anywhere close to New Harvest to provide a quick trip to Mars Colony.

* * *

Vicky reads and assesses her primary's condition and starts to perform a complete scan. The scan results immediately start coming in, healing complete, pre-cancer cells detected in lungs.

Command -

-Nanites created and programmed for repair.

Study mission assignment - infantry, sniper, Gunman.

New scan - parameters vision, reflexes, and strength.

Report - pre-cancer cells repaired, nanites searching and replicating.

Vision 20/20, reflexes 82%, Strength 115%.

As that is not optimal for Joshua's chosen profession, Vicky makes an instant decision to ensure the primary is at top level.

Command

-Nanites created,

-Program for deeper sleep-,

-Focused and dispatched target, brain-.
Command
-Nanites created,
-Program-,
-Focused and dispatched target eyes and neural pathways-.
Command
-Nanites created,
-Program-,
-Focused and dispatched target muscles-.
Continue monitoring primary.

A lengthy period of time passed as Vicky scans and makes adjustments in the same manner. Nine hours later, total scanning and upgrades are complete.

Command;
-Nanites created,
-Programmed for current DNA configuration-,
-Maintain-, -replicate- and dispatched.
Command
-Shut down sleep control nanites-.

* * *

I open my eyes and look up at the ceiling; everything is a bit darker than normal, but I can see the glow strips on the ceiling even when they are turned off. My stomach rumbles, and I realize I am really thirsty and hungry. I flip the cover off and stand up. My body seems to be moving quicker, as though I am feeling no resistance to the ships artificial gravity.

"Vicky! What the hell have you done?"

"Enhancements and upgrades have been made to make you better, sir."

"Better? Screw you. Remove them!" I command.

"No, sir, they tied into your DNA and, since you are my primary, I need to make sure you are able to perform at a top level," she finished.

"What about free will?"

"There have been no commands against upgrades or enhancements, sir."

"Lights on please, and provide a list on the bulkhead of what you did." I sat down on the bunk and watched the words scroll by. "Pre-cancer?"

"Yes, Sir, those four cells have a hundred percent likelihood of turning to full blown terminal cancer in less than twenty years."

"Oh." I feel deflated. "Stop list please and give me an overview."

"Sir you have full medical nanites inside your body that repair any known illness or damage. If the damage to your system is very severe they will stabilize you until medical can throw a full regeneration suite into you. Your eyesight was decent, but now it is perfect with the ability to detect heat and improved night vision. Your body had good muscle mass; the muscles have been made stronger, and the neural pathways and responses have been better mapped to greatly increase your speed and reaction times."

I take a second to look in the mirror across from me. I look mostly normal.

"Okay, why am I bald?" I ask.

"I didn't want to wake you up to take more nourishment

for the energy for fueling the nanites to make the upgrades, so I had the nanites use your hair as fuel."

"Will it grow back?"

"As soon as you have enough food energy in your system I can send nanites to regrow it."

"As primary do I have total control and commands on any upgrades or changes?"

"Yes sir."

"Vicky, new command: you may scan and repair damage, you may scan and fix cancer or any diseases, and you may not make any other changes without my consent, save command."

"Accepted sir," Vicky confirms.

"Do you have any combat training modes that can be downloaded in my sleep to help me in the future when I am in the P.F.F?"

"Already done sir."

Now I realize that good old granddad has used his considerable influence to equip me with a Mark II to ensure my safety at great cost. Average soldiers get Mark X versions that are simple communicators and very simple medical trauma nanite programmers. Vicky's ability to talk audibly through any sound systems or interface with systems was amazing alone, not to forget that she was also class one healer. I had never heard of a class one anywhere but in a medical facility.

"Vicky, I met physical requirements for entry into the Peoples Free Force before today and now thanks to you I greatly exceed them. I passed the mental aptitude tests on my own. However fit and intelligent I may be there is still a need for person defense; does the law in the outer worlds and Mars Colony allow for personal arms?"

"Yes" She answers

"Please have a selection of personal arms sent to this cabin," I say.

"Sir this is a Garvie cabin. Just lift the bunk and look under it."

"What's so special about a Garvie cabin?" I ask.

"Do you think all crew and passengers get food synthesizers, med scanners, and a cabin as nice as this?" Vicky asks. "You have been raised in a rather cushy environment and because of that your views are somewhat limited to the harshness of the galaxy. Did you think your Grandfather would not have you in a decent or well appointed cabin? In the outer rings of this solar system things are nowhere near as polished, and I feel I should warn you that these standards of living and luxury are rare.

"New Harvest is the best place in the known universe for quality of living and there are applications for employment in the thousands submitted weekly by those who desire a better life. Your grandfather only allows the most qualified people with desirable skills to come to New Harvest. Most planets struggle with having enough good food and I calculate New Harvest to be the second richest planet in the known universe, right behind Asthran."

I smile and think, *Wow. Granddad owns one of the most economically rich planets, and I am the only heir. I didn't realize we were that well off.*

I push the lift button on the bed controls, and the bed silently rotates upward. The gleaming panel under the bed covers the storage area and is blank with a recessed hand outline. I put my palm on it and there is a short beep before the panel slides away.

Inside storage area is an amazing array of weapons and a holographic unit. I pick up a holo-base and toggle the on switch. My granddad's face appears above it and I hear his voice sub-vocally through my implant.

"Josh," he begins speaking, "I received a flash from the Captain stating you were hurt and instructed him to give you the Mark II while you were stasis. I hope you are now feeling better. Mark II's have a stealth mode that will appear when you are scanned for a new implant at basic. It will appear to them that you bought your own military implant so the surgeons at the base will not have to install it, they will want to make sure the Mark X you have has the proper programming. Your Mark II will appear to be a Mark X and fool them; no one will know that you have it. This should give you an advantage if you are smart enough to use it properly.

"Another thing," my grandfather continued, "is that you should carry a weapon with you at all times, the bigger the better. From reports I have seen ninety-nine percent of the threats are mutated from Old Earth or alien, and only one percent would be crime. I am going to insure that your would-be kidnapper's employer is dealt with in a very harsh method. This is a little crime that we need to cut it out like a cancer. Remember not to take any dumb risks during your training. Find a woman and come home as soon as you are ready! Garvie out." He finishes and blinks out of existence.

I put the holo-base back into the trunk and pick up a sweet 10mm Sig Sauer—*nice piece*—to slide it out of the holster. I grab a box of the gun's ammo and start to open it to load the magazines.

"Sir," Vicky begins speaking, "use the light blue box of ammunition. It is a high shock round that will not pass thru a fleshy target."

I open an ammo box of the right color and load up the sig. I then pick up a smaller automatic handgun and ask, "Vicky, what's this?"

"It is a .17 caliber rail gun," she informs me.

Yeah, baby! I have never seen one that small before, as all the ones at home are rifles.

Vicky informs me, "This is for personal protection at short ranges in very harsh conditions with maximum firepower."

"Sweet, how does it load?" I ask.

"There are fifty .17 caliber darts in each clip that are charged with negative ions, and the clip itself is a miniature generator that completes the pistols firing circuit when inserted. Once you pick the weapon up and seat the first clip providing power to the gun it does a bio scan and the gun can never be fired by anyone else as it is personally locked"

Ultra cool, I think to myself. I put safety on the weapon and put a magazine onto it, to see lights glow briefly along the barrel for a second or two before the gun goes dark.

Vicky says, "The weapon is now personally locked should you lose it in a fight it cannot be turned on you."

I smile to myself because I don't plan on losing a fight. I remove the mag, and add the railgun to my pack with a dozen more. I zip up the bag and throw it by my shoes, when I leave the ship at Mars Colony it will be with me. When I strap on the holster I feel silly, like a cowboy gunslinger, and leave for the mess. I stroll casually down the deck and am greeted by several armed security guards at the end of my section.

"Morning!" I greet them.

The leader looks at me with a bit of an odd look on his face.

"Is everything okay, Mr. Garvie?"

"Why?"

He looked down and mumbles, "Nothing."

"No, seriously, pal. You are here obviously to watch out for me, so why do you ask?"

He looks at me and says, "You have no hair and it looks like you have put on some weight."

"Fat?" I ask.

"No, sir. Solid."

"Oh, well, I guess I should have bought looser clothing, eh?"

I am somewhat amused. I walk past them and Vicky pipes up into my implant, "Sir, they are asking the bridge if they should be accompanying you everywhere?"

I laugh. "Vicky, please contact the Captain and tell him I don't want or need security now that I have an active A.I. per my instructions."

"Done, sir," she answers.

I walk into the mess and realize that it must be morning meal as the place in almost full of diners and get in line at the buffet. The girl in front of me looks back with a gasp and steps out of line with a "Sorry, Mr. Garvie."

"Crap, get back in line, please. We all have to eat," I say. I look at her and she is wearing a pilot's uniform, and the name tag above the pocket shows her to be Ensign Summer. I hand her a tray as she steps back into line.

"What's good?" I ask.

She must have got her game face on because she smiles coyly back and says, "I could be."

Well, crap. I turn a hundred shades of red and stammer for a minute.

"Please excuse me." I say as I walk to the other side of the serving area to grab a coffee. She was cute enough and had a nice figure, but was a bit to forward. So of course I tucked my tail and ran like hell.

Now that my body is enhanced I should maybe start eating better.

"Vicky please scan buffet and tell me what would be better before I get to training or set up some nanites to convert food to a better nutrients."

My implant softly beeps and Vicky says, "it is part of the general bio-med nanites functions, however fill up on meat and fruit. It will help."

So I grab some Asian pears (New Harvest grown) and pile up some chicken slabs on a plate. I also take a bulb of some vitamin water and look for an open table. I spot a table with only one guy sitting at it, so I head over to him.

"May I join you?" I ask. The man looks up and nods, so I sit down.

"Thanks." I stick my hand out. "Josh."

His grasp was pretty tight with one single shake. "Jay," he says with a nod. I make a quick appraisal of him and presume he is in his forties; hair starting to thin and grey a bit, hard features. I don't see any rank or badges on his well-worn camo. No pretty rejuv going on here I think.

I dig into my food. It's funny how things change quickly, from struggling and being alone to having an AI and nanites.

I realize that being bored and unhappy isn't really a struggle. From what Vicky tells me I have had a really easy life to date. Not like the guy across from me, he looks like he has been thru a few scraps. It makes me wonder why he would be wearing People's Free Force camouflage without rank though.

The chicken is great, and the pears are fresh and crisp. Jay is watching me devour my dinner like a hungry pig. I feel his scrutiny and slow down a bit, but continue to eat. When I get up from the table to get seconds, he follows me to the buffet. Looking me over, he then says, "Try red meat; it will help with muscle mass."

What does he know? I think to myself, but I grab some more meat anyway because Vicky told me to not because of his advice. As we return to the table I look at look over at Jay. "Do I fit a profile?"

"You look heavier than you did when you bought us all dinner," he answers without looking up. "Since I heard there was an attempted kidnapping, it stands to reason that you got hurt and have nanites doing some repair work. Now that I am sitting across from you my A.I. is telling me I am within a meter of active nanites."

I smile as it starts to come clearly in my mind and ask, "Why do you have an A.I. that can scan?"

Jay finishes swallowing his bite and looks me in the eye. "P.F.F. semi-retired. I now work for New Harvest as a security advisor."

"You've met my Granddad?"

Jay looks at me very calmly and honestly to say, "Yes, I have never met a better man."

"How about my Dad?"

He shakes his head. "No, I came to work on New

Harvest at the time he died, and I was part of the search party that found remains of his all terrain vehicle."

"Really? No one told me they found it. Where was it?"

Jay shrugs. "Not my place to tell, ask your grandfather." He then returned to his meal.

"Maybe I want to know from you!" I start to rise out of my seat. I am unsure why he won't answer me and even more so surprised that I am allowing my temper to cloud my judgment. All I knew was my father died and I never found out if they recovered his body.

"Kid, don't get your panties in a bunch," he says.

"Kid?" I ask, narrowing my eyes. "Maybe you want to rephrase your comment."

Jay looks up from his food again, and stares at me openly. "Josh, you seem like an intelligent young man, but I answer to your grandfather not you. So F-off!"

I sit down in shock; no one ever told me to F-off before. Time to learn from my mistake, I can cool off and quit acting like a child or continue on this wrong path. The poor path is not how I was raised and I am not bringing respect to my family.

"Why are you going to Mars Colony?" I ask to break away from the direction I was heading.

"You're a quick learner, Josh, to go from pissed off, to realizing you were acting like a goof, to instantly taking your anger out of the equation shows that you have maturity."

I grin. "Maybe I was afraid you were going to kick my ass, and I don't need another beating this trip."

Jay smiles at me and I realize this is the first time he had done so. It seems smiling is not something he does often, and I make a mental note, this is a serious man who is very sure of himself. He could be a dangerous man in a fight comes to mind in a split second.

"Josh, I know you are not afraid of me. I have reviewed your psych profile and, win or lose; you would not have backed down because you were afraid of any man. You have no fear. Inside your own mind you were drawing on some reserve logic that is a rare commodity. From what I know, you were probably just surprised I had to audacity to speak to you in such a manner."

He has read my psych profile and he is semi-retired? Did Granddad give it to him or did the Peoples Free Force use him as an advance-screening agent? Either way I am not too surprised.

"You will get to know me very well in return, as I am going to be your constant companion for the foreseeable future. Your Grandfather hired me when I retired from the P.F.F. to set up training for you, and then to ensure you don't end up like your father. Now that you are going for basic training, the P.F.F. is more than happy to welcome me back as one of your trainers."

"Were you a trainer before?" I asked.

With a shake of his head he answered, "No, I was a tier one shooter."

That raised my eyebrows a bit. "A Gunman, huh?"

"Gunmen's Element," Jay answers. "1st Gunman."

Holy crap! Those guys are known as the super soldiers. A few hundred years ago they would have made Navy Seals look like girl scouts. I remember watching some old historical entertainment videos from back before the exodus, and one stuck out in particular. The movie was called *Star Wars,* and it had these guys called Jedi who were supposed to be the ultimate good guys/police/samurai. Well, the Gunmen's Element was known for being the most frightening fighters on any planet. When humanity had security issues they called in not an army but a squad for the worst situations, the Element. Normally one or two Gunmen would solve most issues. I can't believe Granddad hired a retired P.F.F. soldier, let alone hiring one specifically to watch over me. The skills I can learn from this guy!

"So are you to be an advisor, trainer, Drill Sergeant or what?"

"Consider me a personal trainer. How is the interface with you're A.I. going?"

"Vicky is a peach; I can only be amazed at what she knows and how fast she is." I tell him.

"An A.I. is only a tool. Learn to trust your instincts, and only use her to provide information or data. Your physical enhancements and A.I. are better than any I have ever heard of in military and you should be active in a year or so."

Jay pauses for a second to take a drink before continuing. "You will find that training in Gunmen school is not class based but individual performance. Your fitness level was damned good before and your weapons skill was on average for Gunmen. You will learn more weapons and tactics, and then when you show proficiency you will advance. Most of the training will be direct neural downloads with real life scenarios afterwards; training that used to take years can now be done in months."

I turn my attention back to my meal and continue to eat. *One year, ha! 9 months if they grade fairly,* I think to myself.

Jay finishes his plate and stands up about the same time

as I do. I pick up my tray and walk with him to the recycling chute and deposit my tray.

"Good, a Gunman cleans up after himself; he only leaves solutions, not work for anyone else. Remember this, Joshua, everywhere you go and everything you do will reflect on not only yourself but the Gunmen's Element."

I look him in the eye and ask, "I guess that the game is on?"

"Oh, there is no game. Why don't you grab skin armor and lose the popgun? Meet me in the gym in ten minutes and let's train in some unarmed combat."

"I have had some training," I say.

Jay shakes his head. "And didn't you almost die a short while ago?"

"Maybe, but now I have combat mode… right?" I query.

"Karate and Ju-jitsu are nice, combat modes are good, but brutality is better," Jay says as he walks away. All my life I have held back, never giving my absolute best until I was blindsided by those kidnappers. Sure they are dead, but I almost died. *Now that I can be brutal, wait until he gets a load of me*, I think.

CHAPTER 4

I look up at Jay as he leans over me with dripping blood from his nose.

"Nice nose!" I say with a painful gasp.

"How's your chest?" he asks, ignoring my verbal jab.

"Not so great." I slowly start to rise from my back without ever breaking eye contact. There is no way I am taking my eyes off him during training or I will end up unconscious.

"Good, good," Jay says, "even when you were hurt you never took your eye off me."

I laugh. "I was concerned that if I did it would be swollen shut like my other eye."

Jay extends a hand and pulls me the rest of the way up off the floor. "You're doing much better, next time do not let me up when you have me down and you would have won."

"Noted," I reply. "Show me your combo again, if you would?"

I rotate my neck and shoulders while slowly turning in a circle to keep Jay in view as he continues to circle me. "Not much point in it," he said as he stops in front of me and points over to the bulkhead screen which is showing the replays of our previous bout. I turn my head toward the screen and pretended to avert my gaze, because I knew

I could not trust him. Misdirection is a very common tool in fighting and since Jay is a Gunman he is going to use every tool at his disposal to win. Maybe I am a far better actor than I thought because out of the corner of my good eye I saw Jay frown at my trust and lunge forward at me. I causally stepped into his charge and delivered a vicious roundhouse kick to the side of his head right behind his ear. Jay's eyes glazed over as he was thrown sideways into a heap. I jumped into the air and started to follow thru with a heel to the face until I realized he was out like a light.

"Vicky?"

"Online," she replies.

"Please call medical."

"I was scanning the training sequence and notified medical that your trainer was unconscious before he hit the deck." The hatch slides open and Doctor Cliff walks in followed by a tech with a gravity gurney.

"Morning Mr. Garvie" he says with an irritated look on his face. Why he is annoyed is beyond me. He has obviously been told that we are training in hand to hand and I mean it is not like he has not been notified every time we get hurt over the last few days. To save energy and resources, Vicky has had base medical nanites here from stores and is using them on me daily. Jay on the other hand needs to go to see the doctor on a frequent basis since his A.I. is a Mark VI and not a Class One healer like my Vicky. Cliff opens his scanner and starts his evaluation. A hypo spray is applied to Jay's neck to add the appropriately programmed nanites to jump start the repair as Jay groans and struggles to sit up.

"Easy," Doctor Cliff cautions him. "You have some vertebrae damage and need to come for a short tank."

Jay eyes me and said, "Nice!"

"Be glad I didn't kill you when you went down," I reply. "I feel that my control is getting better, had my heel of actually hit your face we would not be having this conversation." I said feeling a bit relieved but not wanting to show it because he is supposed to be training me, not be my punching bag. I know he was fighting very hard and experience is the best trainer. It stills bothers me to injure someone who I don't call a friend but an ally. The tech that came in with the doctor lowers the gravity gurney and helps Jay to sit on it for a moment then helps him lie flat.

"How long will Jay need to be tanked?" I ask seriously.

Dr. Cliff's reply is less friendly. "Twenty hours, sir, and then you can continue on with your attempts to kill him."

"Doc, I attacked Mr. Garvie to see if he was learning, he would have been the one laying here if he wasn't."

The doctor shakes his head in resignation, "Gunmen... and they wondered why I left Mars Colony."

As they slide out the door Jay instructs, "Cardio-Cardio-Cardio."

I smile and head to the shower thinking that he is probably not too happy with me at the present because even he hates being tanked.

* * *

Weeks pass by as the *Boy Named Joshua* flew toward Mars Colony. Captain Grey knew that he would be much happier when their namesake is off the ship and under someone else command. The ships medical reports show Joshua taking less and less damage and the trainer taking less now as well. He shakes his head at the thought of what the Chandler would think if he actually read the reports and would hate to be held responsible for Joshua's injuries. Even the pay increase that Joshua authorized would not be worth the wrath of the Chandler if things went south. *Three days is all I need*, the Captain thought after getting the last plot from the navigation A.I. Captain Grey turns away from the view screen, looks to the First Mate and says; "ship wide please." The First Mate hits a key and nods. "Ship wide comm ready, sir."

"This is the Captain we have exited into to normal space and have plotted a course to Mars; estimated arrival will be three days from now, that is all." *Three Days….*

Across the ship the crew smiles, some for the possibility of shore leave on Mars with a little extra cash from their bonus, others for relief because of who is traveling with them.

* * *

After hearing the announcement I have to grin, don`t get me wrong training with Jay has been awesome but I am ready to continue my training on the base. I lie on my bunk and wonder how training will start, will it be decent or like those old videos show with someone yelling and trying to intimidate us?

"Vicky" I start the questions; "Does the combat mode include weapons?"

"Yes, you have the knowledge of ballistics and theory and when you shoot a few practice rounds on any weapon to familiarize yourself you will be able to use it well. Your records indicate that your basic shooting skills were of an acceptable level before you left New Harvest, but now you are going to be exposed to a plethora of new weapons and systems. I think Jay said it best when he told you that practice makes perfect."

"All the shooting I did was for creeper defense in the scouts when I was a kid. I never thought it would be so important." I said, Sure she is an AI but I do enjoy talking with her.

"Yes, and you received your Marksman Badges every year." She said. "Do you know why?"

I think about what she said for a few minutes, and realize that learning to shoot at a higher skill level will benefit the farm, I could provide additional support in case of shield failure. *Benefit the farm*; I was planning on having a life away from Harvest and learning some skills that would make my life more interesting. I never thought that my deep routed reason for leaving was to teach me skills for going home. It makes me wonder why Vicky was asking such a direct question.

"Enlighten me please."I order.

"After your father died the Boy Scouts on New Harvest were tasked with creeper defense when the mesh shields were changed to larger openings. There had to be a reason for this besides airflow. Since Jay ordered it and all scouts went thru firearm training, it stands to reason that the entire program was orchestrated to provide you with this training. You psych profile may have showed a trend on you leaving to join the military and your grandfather wanted to ensure that you were prepared so you would survive and come home."

"I wonder why they went through all that." I ask out loud.

"You were a rather stubborn young man from your

reports and it was easier to challenge you this way then send you for shooting lessons."

I continue to rest on my bunk thinking of what a pain in the ass I was to my family. There is a point in everyone's life where you either change or slip back. This is the change point for me. I will be less of a burden on everyone I meet.

* * *

Basic training was not too bad; learn weapons, learn more fighting, learn some biology, learn tactics. It was funny to me that I signed up the Peoples Free Force and was preselected to become a Gunman. Everyone who ever signed up hoped to be accepted as a Gunman. Granddad's influence would not have helped me here, psychological testing decided what your role would be. Out of nine hundred recruits, three Gunmen were selected. The trainers were not like any of the military videos; we were never yelled at or treated poorly by them. If all Gunmen were anything like me the drive to succeed took away the need for that mode of teaching. We didn't speak to each other, not for any reason other than training was individual one-on-one with the instructors. We did nod at each other in passing. Gunmen were sort of envied and hated by the rest of the recruits; the Element didn't make our lives any easier by ensuring that Gunmen wore different pattern from all other recruits, it was a digital pattern loosely based on green and black tiger stripes. I thought it looked pretty cool but the shirts had Gunman Recruit on the back in white letters. Regular navy and general security operators took every chance they could to make our lives miserable. Once they saw Gunman

Recruit on a shirt they tried to either bully or harass us in some manner.

After a particularly rough week, the Element gave us a three-day pass. I decided to spend some additional time at the rifle range on my Saturday morning. We draw our own weapons, so I had picked a Model 700 Remington Sendero in .300 Winchester magnum, synthetic carbon fiber stock with stainless titanium barrel and action. The holographic sight could zoom up in magnification fifty times. I stayed away from stabilized weapons and thought that shooting should depend on ability not technology. With the new battle ammo this was a serious weapon; adjustable warhead rounds had the ability to change a bullet from armor piercing rounds to explosive warheads. By noon I had fired enough rounds that I was told by the range officer to get the hell off base. I decided to do a bit of wandering around, and try to find a place to get a few drinks and a good steak.

Eighty percent of the population from the North Americas decided to stay on Mars, and the population eventually spread over most of the terrifomed surface. The town I was currently in grew to support the base with the usual kind of entertainment for servicemen. Close to the base there were only two options: fast food or stripper bars. I asked Vicky to scan them and see if any had steaks or a decent reputation for food. Her answer was quick.

"Try the Dirty Monkey." I laughed at the name and asked why that venue was preferable when it had such a filthy name.

"No health code violations and they buy meat from New Harvest."

It was what I thought a typical stripper bar would look

like. I had spent all of my off time in the last nine months on base, yes there was passes off base but I somehow felt that my time would be better spent on the range or studying. The bar was dimly lit and smelled like beer, meat and sadness. I found myself a table in an out of the way corner and sat down facing the stage. Service was quick with a waitress appearing almost like magic in the dim light. Only by yelling could she hear my order over the pounding music. I ordered two steaks and some beer. Within a few minutes some of the almost naked girls were over to ask me if they had anything I would desire; apparently "your absence" was not what they thought an appropriate answer.

Tough luck ladies! It's not that you're ugly; it is just that I don't think you would be interesting to play with and I am busy eating steak.

I look toward the stage because the girls dancing were naked and, let's face it, they were naked. I notice two other Gunman recruits sitting up front cheering on the girls and drawing the ire of a bunch of spacers across the stage. There are no bouncers in view and I realize the other recruits are on their own with the spacers. It may be the Gunman shirts or the fact they are totally falling down drunk. I start to eat faster because I knew they are going to be in trouble.

Too late!

All of the spacers get up and move on the drunken recruits. I stand leaving my half eaten meal and walk casually toward the back of the gang of spacers. They are wearing P.F.F. navy uniforms. The leader of the spacers slugs one of the trainees in the side of the head with no warning and knocks him over. The second recruit staggers to his feet and gets his arms pinned by another spacer, the leader of the thugs is

The 1st Gunman

yapping at him about him being a useless princess and that he was going to kick his ass. I spoke up from behind the group.

"Not while I am on my feet!"

The leader of the group of spacers turns toward me, "Take him too." It wasn't really much of a fight; I deflected the first punch with a sweeping block and broke his jaw with a palm strike. I rotated slightly and with a low sidekick to the second guy's knee his leg buckles with a snap. Then I wade into the group swinging and jabbing. To be perfectly honest, they were a mob of bully assholes and I never broke a serious sweat. Eventually I made it to the two Gunmen, only one of which is conscious while the other was out cold on the floor.

"I'm Mike," lucid one says, and stuck his hand out. "Let's help Steve and get out of here before the M.P.s come."

As we half-carry, half-drag Steve toward the door, the girlfriend of one of the spacers comes over and starts punching me. I can be a decent guy and she was pissed off, so I block a few punches without hitting her back. By this time Steve is starting to come around, so Mike helps him to his feet. Steve and Mike thought it funny that this chick is trying to punch the crap out of me and they start laughing. This of course makes the girl even angrier, and she starts hitting me harder and faster. Good thing she was a dancer I guess and not a body builder I thought, as her punches were only stinging.

All I could do is cover up and wait for the M.P.s, because I was not going to hit a girl. It just wouldn't be right. She threw a punch that hit my forehead and, by the clear snapping sound, she broke her wrist. By the scream and the way her wrist was bent backward I did not have to be a doctor to diagnose the break. Thank god the M.P.'s showed up to arrest us dangerous Gunmen recruits. We got to spend a whole night and most of the next day at the crowbar hotel until Jay bailed us out, by that time we were becoming good friends.

Once we got back to the base late that afternoon we were called into our Commander's Office for a royal raking over the coals. We walked into his office together, stood lined up before the Commander's desk. The Commander said nothing at first while looking at a sheet of paper on his desk; he had absolutely no expression on his face. I smile inwardly as he must have printed it out special instead of just reading in on a holo-screen, the lack of a totally pissed off expression and visible anger means we are here because he has to make an example of us and not because we are in any great trouble. His eyes look up from time to time to look at us as he reads the document. Not sure if Steve and Mike picked up on the show he was putting on but they were standing at rigid attention like me. The Commander picks up the sheet off his desk.

"Thousands of dollars in damaged furniture, broken jaws, one knee, and a few noses. Care to explain?" He barks out with his very loud command voice.

"Sir," I began, "My brother Gunmen and I were under the influence and I made a bad judgment call. I made the mistake of not covering them quicker." Sure it was stretching the truth a little, but we are friends now.

"Then you should know better, goddamn it. That's a lot of injuries."

I grin briefly and say, "Well, that's what you train us for Sir."

"And what is this charge that you broke a woman's wrist?"

That caused Mike and Steve to crack up, and they could not stop laughing. The Commander looks at them like they were something he scrapped of his boot.

"Explain!" He growls.

Steve and Mike instantly stopped laughing at the tone of the Commander's voice and resumed standing at attention. Mike kept his gaze slightly above the Commanders head and spoke. "Sir, one of the spacers that started the whole assault on us had a stripper as a girlfriend. She decided to get revenge on Josh for knocking him out. She was laying a beating on Josh like you wouldn't believe and Josh would only block punches until she hit Josh's forehead and broke her own wrist.

"He's a good guy and wouldn't hit her back," Steve said. "You should see if there is a video from the security feed because it is so freaking funny, sir!"

The Commander looks at me for a second, a bit impressed but trying to hide it. "You learned a lesson yesterday, Gunmen always help each other. Forfeit one weeks pay. Get out of here." He waded up the sheet of paper and tossed it on his deck. We quickly saluted him and turned to get out of his office before he changed his mind on the punishment.

Steve and Mike exit the room first, and I follow. As they are walking in front of me, Mike says, "We should get a copy of the video; it would be freaking funny to see it again."

"Not sure I could watch it without pissing myself," Steve answers.

I have to laugh at their unconcerned attitude; they must have read the Commander like I did.

"Let's go out for supper… I hear Mike is buying," Steve

offers with a grin, "After all he feels guilty for letting me get punched."

Mike laughs. "Jerk-wad!"

We exit the Gunman's building and head over to one of the base's diners. It is a couple of blocks away and it is staring to get dark out. The dinner isn't very busy when we get in so we take a table near the back of the room. Steve leans back in his chair and looks to me. "The cook here had a Gunman for a brother and treats us well."

Mike explains: "Well as in no spit or pubic hairs."

"Good to hear." I say with a smile. They have obviously been having dinner together while I was either at the range or studying, it's too bad I didn't get the time to get to know them sooner as they seem like really good guys.

"You guys think the Base Commander took it easy on us because he expects Gunmen to always kick ass or because we stuck together?" Mike asks.

Vicky accesses the implant in my head and sub-vocally communicates with me to say, "I have reviewed his reports and he knew you were a loner and didn't know the other recruits before the fight. His report indicates he knows you lied to protect your brothers in arms and by showing loyalty towards them at your own peril and taking the blame for not covering them sooner."

I look at Steve and can see him pretending to study the menu. We are getting along fine but I think they are most likely wondering why I would put myself in the line of fire with the Commander on their behalf. Both Mike and he really don't know me, sure they think that I am trustworthy but are curious to the reason. Odds are they don't know my family name or much about me.

"Well, guys, I bet the Commander knew we were not even acquaintances yet and let us off the hook because of us working together. I am a bit of a loner nature, but since you two have seen fit to treat me as a normal asshole much like yourselves I am going to buy you both the largest steak you can eat tonight.

"After that I think we should be able to have a few beers in peace, get drunk, should spacers decide they want to bully anyone with a Gunmen Recruit's shirt on I think it should be our duty to correct this notion they have. Then we shall precede punch out some of the guys who like to make our lives miserable and destroy some more furniture. Since I saved almost all my wages we should be able to make bail… that is if we can't break out of jail. Are you guys with me?"

Steve looks at Mike with a smile. "Nice speech. What do you think?"

Mike is quick to reply that my idea is okay because there are no hockey games on, but there had better be shrimp on the steaks. Steve just nods in acceptance.

* * *

A couple of hours later I am standing in the bar with over half a dozen regular enlisted types groaning at our feet. I have blood dripping from a split lip and look to Steve who is just finishing off his last brawler. Steve seems to have fared a bit worse than me and I can see his shiner from across the room, his nose looks a tad mashed and is leaking blood on his shirt.

"My one guy is bigger than your largest guy," Steve says with a happy grin

Mike laughs out loud and finishes throwing his last guy

over the bar. The M.P.s pour into the place, and start waving their little shock sticks at us. I move over to stand with my friends as the M.P.s try to encircle us. They have black uniforms with white lettering which make glow in the dim light. The M.P.s are uniformly large guys who look like they enjoy cracking heads. They are armed with shock wands, which can deliver an incapacitating amount of voltage I remember them from weapons training; they hurt like hell and make you lose all control of your extremities.

"Move back toward the wall," I say, and we slowly move, stepping over the enlisted to stand with our backs to the wall. The M.P.s are not happy with us taking a defensive position and pause for a minute when they realize we are not going to allow ourselves to be encircled.

"On the floor, on the floor!" The head M.P. yells at us

"But it's dirty," Mike complains, and that causes Steve to laugh. I don't take my eyes off their leader, knowing they are trained military cops they will react with overwhelming force to control us. I hate shock wands and several of them are also armed with handguns in covered holsters as well.

I motion to the obvious leader of the M.P.s and say, "We will go with you, but no handcuffs or lying on the floor. We are Gunmen." I lied as we are only Gunmen recruits but we are close to graduation and no one ever tries to harass full Gunmen. The M.P. has more far more brawn than common sense. He actually threatened to shove his shock stick somewhere we would not like it. I decided then and there that I would never submit to these clowns, we didn't start the fight and he knew that before he tried to arrest us. Gunmen are known as fighters and it is only his ego that requires him to man-handle us.

"Watch their sticks boys." I said as the M.P.s start to move in on us.

The M.P.'s face turns into a mask of anger as he raises the shock wand and tries to drive it hard into my chest. In a flash I step forward with a high left forearm block, to deflect the contact tip away from me and reach under his arm to grab his wrist to lever him backwards. The M.P.'s shoulder and arm dislocates as I grab the shock wand from the M.P. and turned it on him. The voltage must have been set at max because he crumpled, and the rest of the military police force charged at us.

I parried a few sticks and shocked a couple more M.P.s before I saw one fumble to open his holster for his gun. Battle reflex mode kicked in and I battled through the rest of them like a screaming banshee. Steve and Mike stopped their fighting in amazement, as my attack speed allowed me to finish off the rest of the M.P.s before the pair could do much more than take drop a M.P. each.

I look around to see military police lying everywhere on the bar floor. By my count there has to be at least sixteen inert forms. There is no escaping what we did; the Commander will not be impressed I think.

"Fortune favors the bold" I muse.

We left the bar to see a silent crowd of spacers and navy personal watching us. We looked a little beat up but our heads were high and everyone could see we were ready if there were any more problems. We walked past them without a word and round the corner to getting out of their sight. We broke into a quick jog and made it to the Gunman's building back entrance, it was locked and I did not have the code for the key pad. Before I could ask Vicky to crack the code the light turned green and the door opened.

Sub-vocally I said, "Thanks Vicky."

The hallway that led to the Commander's office was empty so we sat down on the floor directly across from his door. Scraping with a bar full or navy personnel and then with the military police is very hard work. Made me feel a bit hungry and thirsty so I sub-vocally asked Vicky to have a pizza and some beer delivered to us. If they throw us back into the crowbar hotel the food quality will just plain suck.

We were sitting there for several minutes nursing our injuries before Mike asked, "Wouldn't it be better to head back to our billets and pretend we did not know anything about what happened?"

"I don't think I could keep a straight face while I was lying about not being there," Steve replied with a wry grin.

"If you are sleeping in your beds and they send in a couple of dozen more M.P.s with shock wands, how do you think each of us will fair?" My question gave them something to think about as they realized it could have a much worse outcome for us in close quarters alone. Steve nods in agreement, while Mike stares at the ceiling wondering why he is always getting in trouble.

About twenty minutes later a server bot wheels into the hallway with an extra large steaming mushroom pizza and a cooler loaded with Church Key covered with ice.

"Vicky, you rock," I say sub-vocally.

Mike looks at the pizza and beer appreciatively. "We are definitely keeping you around." Steve looks at me with a quizzical expression because their A.I.s don't act like lock pickers or can take orders for food. I will give him points for self-control.

We all grab a bulb of beer and relax for a minute to let the pizza cool. Since the beer was very cold it tasted like nectar from the gods. From the smiles I saw my guess would be that neither of my friends had ever tried beer from New Harvest before. Our little calm was broken by the sounds of thudding feet coming down the hall. The Commander came storming around the corner, but stopped when he sees us camping out in front of his office drinking a beer. The look annoyance on his face changed to one of astonishment as he checked out the slightly mauled Gunmen recruits sitting on the floor.

The Commander's voice was loud but calm, "I just got a call that some of my Gunmen beat up a bar full of navy recruits, and then knocked the crap out off the entire shift of M.P.s," he then roared. "Explain what the hell you're doing here?"

Mike grins. "Beating the morning rush, sir."

"Saving Captain Black bail money, sir?" Steve adds.

I look at the Commander and add my own suggestion. "Looking for a good man to share our pizza and beer with, sir?" Mike holds up a Church Key and gives it a wiggle.

The Commander takes a quick breath to deal with the situation. "Get the hell off the floor and into my office." He steps past us and palms the door open and walks in. We limp in after him, and he motions us to the chairs across from his desk. I can tell now he is not even upset a bit with us by his demeanor. The Commander steps behind his desk to pull the chair around in front of his desk and sits down.

"What's on the pie?" he asks.

"Pep, bacon, and mushrooms," I answer.

Mike opens a beer and hands it to the Commander.

He looks at the Church Key and asks, "How did you get this? I was unaware it was available on base." He smiles and takes a long pull from the bulb.

"It was from my billet and another box is on its way, sir." I answered back and I sub-vocally told Vicky to send my last case of beer to our location.

The Commander's face relaxes making it apparent to us that our actions were not going to be thought of too harshly. He looks almost happy or content before he speaks. "Ten years ago, I was an active Gunman," he told us. "Back in the old days no one messed with the recruits and I was unsure why and when it started. It is really nice to see that everyone is going to start respecting or fearing the Element again." The Commander takes another long pull to finish his beer. "I don't think having people afraid of the Element was what I meant, having a healthy respect and knowing boundaries is more of the mode. A Gunman should be the toughest, meanest, son of a bitch out there. I think you have shown the spacers and the M.P.s just that. Be glad you didn't kill anybody and that I am not deducting the cost of their medical bills from your pay."

We had a good talk, a decent pizza and some really excellent beer until the M.P.s found us. From the sound of their footsteps in the hallway they must have brought several squads of M.P.s. Hate to figure out what that was costing them in overtime to call that many men into work this late at night. The highest ranking officer barged into the Commander's office and was rather pissed when he saw us having beer with the Commander. He told the Commander to release us to their custody.

I grinned as I stood up and turned to Steve and Mike.

"I don't believe staying another night in their jail is on the table, shall we?" The two Gunmen are on their feet in a second with serious looks on their faces. There is no thought of the numbers of M.P.s that wait for us.

The Commander stops us with. "Not tonight, boys. They may be assholes, but we are on the same side." The M.P.s leader looks furious and stomps out of the office. The Commander smiles briefly at the three Gunmen who are ready to deal with the M.P.s who now are in full bully mode. "I don't take orders from junior officers and they need an alignment." He walks out into the hallway to rip a strip off the M.P.s. Knowing the Commander has everything well in hand I open the cooler and dig for four beer. I toss one to each of the boys and place one on the Commander's desk. It is not long before the Commander returns. "They want you charged and held back from the Gunmen's Graduation, it is of their Lieutenant's opinion that you three lack self control and maturity." the Commander told us. "They feel that longer training and some punishment would make you grow up." Steve and Mike look a little annoyed about this. I smile at my friends and address the Commander; "Maturity is not the issue sir! The spacers and M.P.s need to get off the confrontational attitudes with not only Gunmen trainees but other citizens as well. It would be a shame if we ended up needing to address their behavior. Maybe they need some training in sensitivity and teamwork to help them to develop a proper relationship with civilians and armed forces personnel." I look down at my now empty bulb of beer. "Sorry for the preaching Sir."

The Commander grins like he is pleased about

something. "I told them to get stuffed anyway. How long before more beer gets here?"

We had a few more beer and quite a few laughs, the Commander seemed pleased enough that he brought out a bottle of scotch and we all took time to make some toast at every sip. The Commander's wife must have missed him, because she showed up looking for him. She stopped short when came thru the door and saw us casually drinking with her husband, After a moment she then proceeded to give him proper hell for getting us poor young men drunk. We did not know what to do; Mike was very subtle and stared at the ceiling and whistled softly. I stared at my boots and did not make eye contact because as she walked in the door Steve whispered, "Shh, stay still, they hunt by sound and movement." If I looked up while the Commander was getting chewed out by his superior I would have broke out laughing. I was impressed that she did not drag him out by the ear. The Commander finally gave enough "yes dears" and, "I will make sure they get back to the billets safely dears", to satisfy her so she left. I took the opportunity to hand him another beer quickly. The Commander levels a firm eye on us before speaking.

"I expect no gossip or rumors regarding the dressing down I just took."

Steve puts a serious look on his face, "Sir, I had too many beers to pay attention properly but I did think I may have heard a Generals voice, and since any discussion was above my pay grade I disavow any knowledge to any conversations spoken in this office."

It was well after dawn when we headed back to our billets. M.P.s were standing around outside the building and watching our every move, to which I decided to speak with their Lieutenant. I motion for Mike and Steve to stay back while I approach the M.P., Mike watches with a grin wondering if we are going to need to fight again.

"How did he move so fast last night? Higher gravity training and enhancements maybe?" Mike asked Steve.

Steve smiled at Mike's question because the same thing has been rolling around in his mind and said, "Don't know, but at least he is on our side!"

I stopped directly in front of the Lieutenant of the M.P.s, "Gunmen will not be harassed anymore, period!" I said to the M.P., "Spread the word that we are here to help and protect humanity and will tolerate no crap from anyone."

The M.P. doesn't look me in the eye which shows his disdain for us. "Laws are for everyone; you're not special."

I wait till I catch his eye then ask, "Do you really want see how special we are? Try to attack someone innocent or us again. Keep the peace and control your men or we might actually get angry at your behavior." I turn my back on him and walk away. Our previous dealings with the MPs were not emotional, but the time has come to let the military police and the spacers know that we are here to fight for humanity sending them to medical to get tanked after defeating them is getting kind of old.

* * *

The Commander waited until he felt better from his hangover, which was the next day to call the training officers in for a meeting and including the base's A.I. He had reviewed the marks and scores and now had first hand data about the Gunman recruit's attitudes.

The Commander was waiting until everyone was sitting at his meeting table and then hit a key to link in Monitor. "Gentlemen, we have full reports on the trainees. We will start with the psychological profile first, Monitor?"

Monitor was the base's training A.I. whose job was to select candidates for the Gunmen's Element. Performing psych evaluations on students using all known data completed this task. Younger people choose direct downloading of data while they were in stasis as opposed to classrooms for sixteen years. AIs had complete neurological records of most students because everyone learns in a different manner and they had to tailor education to an individual's profile. Monitor was a Type V A.I. that automatically stored this information without ever telling anyone unless they applied to the P.F.F. Once they applied, applicants were either assigned a specific duty or reanalyzed for further duties. The class this year had three acceptable candidates which was the most they had seen in one year for over a decade. The three men in Gunman training this year were very highly rated by Monitor.

"I have handled all Gunman acceptances for the last twenty-three years and have a few things to note. One recruit has a depth of resolve with abilities that sets him apart from the other sixty-eight Gunman recruits I have seen.

"Joshua Garvie has one of the most complex minds I have ever scanned. During the first day of orientation we motivate the recruits by playing videos of the 9/11 attack on the USA, the death of Osama, the invasion of Kuwait from Saddam Hussein, and the beginning of Earth's last war. Most of the P.F.F. soldiers or navy personnel use symbolism to motivate themselves. Joshua Garvie does not; he holds his emotions and passion in check. His inner self knows what right and wrong is without having to be motivated. He truly is the best qualified person to lead the Gunmen's Element.

"Watching how Joshua conducts himself and the way he deals with the harshest things we throw at him sets him apart from the rest. His skill in problem solving allows him to look deeply into many complex issues in order to solve them before they reach an excessive level. He tempers the hard decisions with compassion, but doesn't shy away from difficulties to get the required results. Often the outcome of his decisions greatly exceeds the expectations.

"Look for example of what he did with the M.P.s; he defeated them easily, got acceptance from his Commander. How many recruits would even think of waiting by your office after what they did? He took responsibility for the fight and thinks of the other trainees as his people. Joshua then explained to the Lieutenant how he was going to conduct business with them in the future. Nothing questionable is left unanswered."

Jay smiles at Monitors review, he has seen Joshua do this kind of thing for years on the farm.

Monitor continues "The M.P.s were very unhappy, so he took the personal element out of their defeat by telling them that Gunmen are there for humanity and to not to be fighting them. If the M.P.s don't like it they can react, but he warned them about the consequences and gave them an option not to fight. Odds are that the M.P.s will leave Gunmen alone." The other training officers nod in agreement with Monitor. Jay's rare smiles light up his face because he knew that Joshua would develop into a good leader and his opinion has just been reported on by an impartial machine. The Commander looks up from his data screen and across the table at Captain Black. "Jay, I hope you are ready to give up the 1st Gunman's position, I am promoting Joshua to the position of 1st Gunman."

Jay nods, "after six years I think less stress will make me feel relieved. I will still have my job on New Harvest."

"I think you should give them a week or two to solidify their friendship before graduation." Monitor advises. "Their profiles suggest that the fights and similarities in their beliefs will allow them to create lifelong bonds.

The Commander looks at the rest of the training officers for a minute then addresses them. "We are all agreed that they have exceeded the training requirements; Jay, lighten up on the schedule for the next two weeks."

Jay nods again, "Monitor, please provide daily reports on their activities and interactions."

* * *

Running is not a sport, in the Element it is a way of life. Mind you I never run from a fight. I did practice running at normal rates and at battle reflex speeds. The normal rate is fast enough but at reflex rates I was three times faster than Steve or Mike. It was funny to watch those two run together as they were very competitive. My enhancements made me quicker naturally and I did not feel the need to be in front of them. I did laugh at them when one of them would fall back saving energy then move past the other near the end of the run to be in the first position. They teased me on never winning a run until I told them that I didn't think their fragile egos could take such a savage beating and that there would not be enough beer on the planet to wash away their tears.

Since our schedule had lightened up after our night with

the Commander we got to train together. Knowing that we all had the same basic skills gave me more faith after we drilled together. Steve and Mike seemed to need more unarmed combat training and I was happy to assist them and got continually bruised by them. I avoided laying any hurt on them. Since our time was freed up we only split up at range time. Mike and Steve love lasers and railguns. Me, I hated them because they were just too easy to use and applied overwhelming force.

Lasers were not too bad at closer ranges like under a few hundred yards but after that in atmosphere they lost the intensity required to be effective. At short range you could set them to wide beam and use them as flamethrowers, very handy when knocking out a swarm of vampbirds. Railguns were overkill in almost all situations unless you wanted complete and utter destruction of your target and anything behind it. Don't get me wrong power is good, but it should judiciously applied unless collateral damage is not an issue. I think my friends were a tad jealous of my shooting skill and the surgical way I could drop something at long range. At short ranges they were as good as me but as I always told them; "Long distance is the next best thing to being there."

Today my friends thought they would like to train edged weapons so I left them to their own accord and went to the extended shooting range for super long distance practice. With ramjet rounds I was scoring hits at three miles.

Vicky's chime interrupts the tight focus I have on my distant target. "Sir, you have orders to attend the Officers Mess in full dress uniform at 17:00 hours." As I look through the scope at the distant target I can feel my heart start to beat a little faster with excitement from the news, it has got to be graduation or maybe a court martial in full dress uniforms. I snicker at the thought and will my heart to slow down before taking the shot.

* * *

The instruction said 17:00 hours so I take my time dressing and enjoy the walk to the Officer's Mess. My walk was timed perfectly because I got there about five minutes early. The Mess was in a fairly busy section of the base, pedestrian traffic was high but not impeding my walk. I stepped into the lobby area and saw Steve and Mike waiting by the entrance to the mess. They are dressed pretty as well, pretty being defined as Gunmen's full dress uniforms.

We wait until a one minute before the hour and walk into dead silence. Everyone in the room is standing to attention facing us. It seems odd to me to have everyone dressed like us including the bartenders because the Gunmen's Element never has formal events and this was the first time I was wearing this uniform.

The Commander is near the back of the room beside Captain Black with a smile on his face. We march up to them in single file and salute. Jay smiles, returns the salutes to Mike, Steve, myself and then offers me his hand, which I step forward to shake. Thinking back on it later it was more of an honor because he recognized I was worthy of the position I was going to be given. Steve and Mike had already moved to my left in front of the Commander to salute him. As soon as I finished shaking Jay's hand I stepped sideways and saluted the Commander.

"Tonight three Gunmen join our hallowed ranks," the Commanding Officer announces loudly. All the Gunmen present hit the tables or walls with their closed fists seven times. I vaguely wondered if they practice beating tables as every hit was done together. The Commander waits until the seven hits were done then announces "Gunman Mike Earle" and pins a small silver lightning bolt on his collar which denotes a Lieutenant's rank in the Gunman's Element. The entire group less the Commander and Jay beat three more times in sync with their fists as Mike shakes both the Commanders and Jay's hand and steps to the side.

"Gunman Steve Burton."

The Commander pins the same rank on Steve's collar. Again the group beats three times as Steve shakes his hand and joins Mike off to the side.

The Commander looks directly at me. "For the first time in the history of the Element we are raising a new recruit past Gunman. 1st Gunman Joshua Garvie"

I am stunned, me the 1st? No wonder Jay looks so pleased. The Commander adds the silver and red lightning bolts to my collar. The fist banging starts again but seven times for me, I hope that doesn't hurt Steve and Mike's feelings. I shake the Commander's hand and then Captain Black's.

"Does this mean I get paid more?" I quietly ask Jay with a smile.

This causes a chuckle from my friends who were still in hearing range. The Commander looks around and nods at the group on men standing around, almost in sequence they all return to their chairs and tables. Jay asks us if we would join them for drink in the company of the rest of the active and retired Gunmen present now that the ceremony is over. I laugh inside because Gunmen don't generally parade around and have huge social events.

To have this many Gunmen having a drink together is amazing. Since I only know a few of the trainers it is either a big deal having three new Gunman or they are here because Jay is retiring.

Jay points to the bar. "Steve, Mike, we need a couple of minutes with Josh, get us all a scotch if you would be so kind."

As they move off quickly towards the bar the Commander addresses me.

"You're replacing Captain Black as 1st Gunman, are you aware of your extra responsibilities?"

I shook my head and answered; "no sir!"

* * *

Over at the bar Steve and Mike get their drinks and the bartender asks them to take a few minutes before going back. Mike looks at him and puts his hand out.

"Mike."

The bartender smiles and shakes his hand.

"My name is Edwards, Gunman retired, if Jay sent you for a drink they will want to have a little discussion with our new 1st Gunman."

Steve shakes his hand as well and asks; "Steve, is it a big deal that he made 1st right out of training?"

Edwards nods and says; "that it's never been done before. Jay was the 1st Gunman for the last six years near the end of his career. The Commander was for three years before Jay." He thinks for a second, "I have seen four men become 1st Gunman and the Commander that promotes them always talks to them privately for a couple of minutes before cutting him loose on the universe. I think they are telling him about a few extra duties he has. They will ready for drinks in a few minutes."

Steve looks at his drink on the bar and doesn't pick it up, Mike still is chatting with Edwards as he looks over the group of Gunmen in the mess. It would appear that some were active too long as the Gunmen near him look weary. Steve continues to look at the group and thinks he can see maybe a dozen Gunmen who look like they are still active. Mike finishes his conversation with Edwards and turns back to Steve. Seeing him watching the crowd he studies them for a few minutes.

"What do you think, twenty-three active Gunman?" Mike asks. Steve nods his head because Mike most likely asked Edwards how many Gunmen were active and was going to bet a beer on the number. Mike is a good guy but a bit predicable.

* * *

"When there is a problem in any sector or on any planet you are near the call will come directly to you." The Commander said.

"Gunmen can call for other Gunmen for support in situations that are dire." Jay says.

"You, being an officer who is in second command of the Element will have the power to call for an armed cruiser. Be smart, and be brutal in the defense of humanity. Instruct you're A.I. to contact Monitor for the rights and responsibilities of the 1st Gunman. Know it inside and out." The commander finishes.

The Commander then broke eye contact and looked toward the bar. I took this as a dismissal and turned toward the bar. Quite a few Gunmen shook my hand as I threaded my way around the tables to get to the bar.

"Vicky?" I start to sub-vocally instruct her to download my responsibilities when she says, "download complete!" "Review it and prepare an overview for after this gathering please," I command, as a glass of very old scotch is put into my hand. My mind is spinning through the things I have learned from classes and by direct download during training, but it all comes back to leadership and commitment. Leaders lead by example and have total commitment to their people and responsibilities.

"Is anyone in this room not an active or retired Gunman?" I sub-vocally ask Vicky.

She answers back with "no, everyone is."

All the Gunmen are watching me and Jay gives me a little nod. I raise my voice. "May I have everyone's attention?" Even both the retired Gunmen behind the bar need to be included. "You gentlemen behind the bar, please make sure everyone has a drink including yourselves and join us." I wait only a minute until everyone has a drink and is ready.

"To those I have not met yet, I am Joshua Garvie." I motion to Mike on my left, "This is Gunman Mike Earle and on my right is Gunman Steve Burton. Today we join your ranks, and we will work our asses off to be worthy of your legacy. A toast to the Gunmen's Element!"

I raise my glass and then take a sip and everyone in the room follows suit. I walk past the bartenders who have stepped out from behind the bar and take their place behind the bar. I nod to them, "You guys sit and socialize and we will pour drinks for you." Steve and Mike join me, and we proceed to serve the rest of the Gunman drinks until the

Mess empties a few hours later. When the last Gunman leaves we take a few minutes to clean the bar up, and then grab some beer before sitting at a table. Sub-vocally I tell Vicky to pay for all of the booze we served tonight and not to access anyone's accounts for payment.

Mike decides to ask me if I am going to be all bossy-like now that they report to me.

To this, I laugh and say, "Damned if I know." We give each other a tap with our glasses and finish our mugs. We were so busy serving the Gunmen that we didn't get much time to have any drinks ourselves and the calm quietness of the empty mess is refreshing. It is easy to see that Mike is wondering how we will work together and what the dynamic will be. Steve is really enjoying his beer and is trying to act casual but his mind is on the exact same thing.

"Most Gunmen are only active between five to ten years or so, then they are either mentally tired of fighting or just want to start a family so they retire. Do you guys have any idea what you want to do when your time is up?"

Steve shakes his head. "I don't want to be a bartender for current Gunmen it would be far too boring."

Mike nods in agreement. "I would rather not stay here on Mars either."

"When our time is over I will be going back to New Harvest. Think about coming out for a visit because there will always be work available. Steve and Mike look stunned for a minute and then grin. "Are you going to take us pig hunting?" Steve asks. It makes me think that even though we haven't been friends very long they have taken the time to research where I was from. It also means they know who my family is. Shows how good of guys they are not to try and use that data. I couldn't imagine living somewhere without friends, and they were most likely thinking the same thing. The speed in which I made friends with these guys surprised me because back on New Harvest I had a lot of acquaintances but no real friends. I guess my name had something to do with it, or it was the barriers I put between myself and everyone else as I was growing up. Granddad seems to have friends and deals with it; maybe he isn't the hardass I remember.

Deciding to take it easy on the liqueur until I have reviewed the regulations would be a better choice than getting pissed up with my friends.

"Gentlemen" I address my friends, "I am going to read up on the duties and responsibilities a bit more so I am heading to my billet. The tab here is paid so have a few and relax, I will see you in the morning." I stand and they both hold up their beers in salutation when I leave the Officer's Mess. As I step out of the door I almost run into a couple of M.P.s who quickly salute me when they see my rank. I return the salute, "Would you watch the two Gunmen who were having some drinks and get them safely to their rooms afterwards? If they get tanked up or if they get out of hand to call me."

The younger of the two M.P.s gives me with a quizzical look. "You would trust us, sir?"

"Unconditionally," I answer. "What has happened in the past is nothing; we are all on the same side!"

This got a smile and a second salute from the M.P. as he realized there was no animosity from me at all. I turn and walk out of the lobby leaving the M.P.s to communicate via radio that I had given them new orders. The 1st Gunman is a Captain in rank, which means I outrank all M.P.s and even their officer in charge which isn't too bad considering I am a few months shy of my twentieth birthday. Giving the M.P. the order from my new rank to assist Steve and Mike ensures it will be obeyed,

It is bright and clear evening as I take my twenty minute walk to my quarters. I decide that waiting until I get there is dumb and say, "Vicky, go active, please and tell me about my new duties."

"Leadership is the key item with quite a bit about responsibility." Vicky voices lowers. "You have been doing everything listed since the day I came online with you, now it is formalized. You already lead by example and always ensure that everyone around you is taken care of." Vicky finishes off leaving me feeling that she thinks the document is rather dumb.

"Thanks Vicky I will read the document in full when I get to my room."

CHAPTER 5

A Gunman has a busy job; there are many creatures that need dealing with. Seems that most of humanity has lost its taste for fighting, or even effectively protecting themselves, and the Gunmen's Element was kept pretty busy during my tenure. After the first six months with us being dispatched to various parts of the galaxy, I decided we needed more work time and less travel time. It would benefit anyone who needed us if we were nearer to the Outer Rings of planets.

I strolled into the Commander's office for a meeting and said, "We are doing no good sitting here, I think we should take turns visiting various trouble spots and just show up in different places to show settlers and miners that we are thinking about them. Maybe we can solve little problems before they get larger and we would be a lot closer for faster response time."

I had it all planned out and was ready to defend my views to the Commander when he said; "Okay."

How anti-climatic was that?

I looked at the clusters of planets that had typically more problems than others and drew up a loose schedule for us to follow. Maybe we would follow it, but if something changed or we got a call we could be pretty flexible. I got to meet a lot of nice colonists and miners who were usually happy to see a Gunman, so I was always getting invitations for dinners and parties.

I would go for dinner sometimes, but it always seemed that they were looking for decent men for their daughters as most colonies had limited gene pools or simply not enough men. It was safer just to eat alone and leave after taking care of business, at least that was my feeling. Since we traveled alone in WarHawks we always had a private place to eat and sleep. There was no way to hold the other active Gunmen to that standard, and from all accounts there was no reason to. I did hear reports that for all their talk Mike and Steve were not as wild as they pretended to be. Steve was a bit of a player with the ladies but had not got caught yet.

I was between assignments travelling towards a small outpost to make a courtesy call when a request for help came from the planet Dorene; apparently they were having issues with something called a stumbler. It took a few days at high sublight speeds to get to Dorene. Once I was close enough to see it clearly on my screens I could see brown land masses volcanic in origin fairly evening spaced oceans or seas laying blue and deep in-between them. I checked the report on Dorene to find out the fishing and mining town of Borne is their working capital. The mountains and hills appear to stretch from shore to shore with high cliffs and steep rises being the common feature. The ground and rocks seem to be the same color as the sparse foliage. Vicky took command of the autopilot and ploted a course towards Borne's landing site. It was quite easy to see why their town is placed here because it is the only reasonable slope and beach on this side of the continent. The automated landing beacon guided Vicky to a pad near the administration building.

We landed and I waited a few minute for the outside skin of the ship to cool before opening the hatch and walked into the sunlight fully outfitted and ready to battle. A nervous young woman met me, she was dressed in poorly tailored suit which did not hide the fact she was very good looking. Her brown hair was wavy and shoulder length. High cheek bones gave her an almost a regal look. Her nervousness showed in her posture and the way she was shaking before she spoke.

"I am 1st Gunman Joshua Garvie," I say to introduce myself. She doesn't meet my eyes and continues to look at the ground between us.

"Sir, we need your help. A Stumbler has destroyed several fishing villages, and we are having a hard time catching enough food to keep the miners fed."

"Are you the planetary head?"

"No sir, I thought a Gunman would be less likely to kill a woman. I am asking for help on my fathers behalf."

Gunmen killing innocents? They obviously do not know our mandate and a smile crosses my face as I now know why she is so nervous. "Why would a Gunman kill someone he has come to help?" I ask with an honest open expression on my face.

She looks confused and says, "Because you are a Gunman and we are not getting our quota."

I wonder at that for a second, if their bosses are killing people because they don't get quota I will have more than stumblers to deal with here.

"What's your name?" I ask.

"Bethany."

"Please take me to your father, Bethany."

She sighs in resignation knowing control is out of her hands and leads me to a small-fortified building at the edge of the town next to the landing site. The building was fairly new, and looked like it was made to survive earth quakes with diagonal bracing on the exterior. The windows were small and very thick.

Bethany stops before she opens the door, and asks me what I am going to do with a cracking voice that sounds like she is on the edge of hysteria. I don't answer and walk thru the first door leaving her outside. I open the second door and every nerve is on edge as I walk thru expecting to be shot or stabbed. You never know what people will do when they are scared. The room is well lighted and full of manned workstations. A rather short, pudgy and scared looking gentleman is standing in front of the first desk. He looks at me a moment before speaking. "I am responsible for the loss of life by not calling sooner for help." The rest of the women at the workstations are ignoring us and pretend to be working.

I hear Bethany open the door and come into the room to stand behind me. I pause for a second sad at the thought someone would be so afraid of dying they would endanger a loved one. I wanted to grab him by the neck and scream, "You protect your kids not use them as a shield"

"Is this your daughter?" I ask with a serious tone.

"Yes," he answers.

"The only misjudgment I see is sending your daughter to meet me because you're afraid to die. You should have left her where she was safe and sheltered and went out to deal with your own fate. However, I am the 1st Gunman and I think you have a poor opinion of us. We don't kill people unless they are killers or pirates; if you're not performing well that is a business matter with whoever governs your planet. The P.F.F. and the Gunmen's Element only care about safety for humanity, nothing else."

I watched a small change come over the man as he gained some hope from what I said. Bethany took a few steps to be closer to her father; she smiled in relief as well. "I never gave my father the option to go meet you at the landing pad. He was not acting like a coward and did not send me!" I nodded to her signaling that I understood but still thought he should have been man enough to be the greeter.

I put my hand out for a handshake. "Joshua Garvie pleased to meet you."

He cautiously reaches out and shakes my hand. "Administrator Paul Jones, I am the planetary manager." He still sounds a little uncertain. "You don't punish people for poor leadership?"

I laugh. "Should that be the mandate of People's Freedom Force and, specifically, the Gunmen's Element no one would want to be a Gunman. We protect humanity from alien life forms and the occasional pirate. How can I help you?"

Bethany hugs her father with relief then turns to ask; "Can you really stop a stumbler? We have tried, but our weapons are ineffective."

"Do you have any videos of the stumblers?" I really wanted to know what exactly these creatures are, and start making plans on how to get rid of them. "What kind of weapons have you been using? Where do stumblers come from?"

Paul reaches back to his desk and keys a button to raise a monitor out of a cabinet against a wall. "Watch the monitor," Bethany said, and she hits a few keys on her wrist band to start the video.

A pale white slug with hundreds of legs comes out of the water and crawls thru the village. It is about a hundred feet long and maybe thirty feet wide, and approximately twenty feet high. It walks on land awkwardly and stumbles frequently. The slug-like creature doesn't seem to be eating anyone, just walking and crushing everything in its path. Building and vehicles get smashed and flattened as the creature crawls over them. The stumbler continues on its path, and eventually moves up toward the mountains before disappearing from sight.

A second video starts and shows the same creature returning on the same path of destruction. A man with what looks like a laser drill is standing in the stumblers way and starts firing at it. The surface of the stumbler glows orange where the laser hits it, but doesn't burn thru the exoskeleton. The massive creature continues toward the water with smoke rolling off its surface where the laser tried to burn thru it. I will give the miner points for guts but none for intelligence as he continues shooting ineffectively until the stumbler reaches him and crushes him into a paste. I shake my head at his stupidity.

"Anyone follow it up the mountain to see what it is doing?" I ask.

Paul shakes his head negatively, "People are too afraid and it moves up slopes to steep to drive."

I turn for the door and, on my way out, I say, "I'll look into it."

I head back to my shuttle, and when I reach it I open the cargo hatch to access my ATV. After unhooking the hold-downs bars from the chassis, I get into the cab to run the pre-checks. Once the green light is given by the on board computer I quickly fire up the engine. The dual tracks propel the squat machine up to a hundred clicks, and I tear through the path of destruction winding through the town toward the mountains.

As soon as I clear the town site and approach the hills I can see why the vehicles would not be able to follow it. The steep slope and occasional crevice would not stop a hundred foot long walking slug but it would greatly impede a wheeled vehicle. My vehicle runs on two high speed tracks with hooked studs that allow me to perform almost vertical accents. Good thing because there was over a dozen steep sections I had to cross.

It doesn't take very long to find the reason behind the stumblers journey through the village: it was nesting. I drive the ATV over the last ridge to find a small basin in the middle of the summit. Steering around a few larger boulders I see open pits with long skinny pale green eggs heaped on each other. I pull the ATV to a stop and get out to check the eggs. They are almost as tall as I am, and narrow, not quite cylindrical. I reach out to touch its leathery surface and am surprised to find it tough looking but as smooth as silk and warm. There had to be at least forty eggs heaped into this shallow nest in the rocks. I look around, but there are no adults in sight and nothing protecting the nest.

"Movement at your six," Vicky warns me.

I spin around as a stumbler hatchling breaks free of a buried nest; the creature's antennas are waving around scanning for a threat or maybe food. As I move to the side, slowly shifting away from the stumbler, its eyes start to track me. I pull my rifle off my shoulder into the ready position and wait for the stumbler to make the first move.

Slowly the stumbler approaches me with its narrow antennas bobbing from side to side as I gradually back away even further. The creature's head comes up and its mouth opens until I can see row after row of short pointy green teeth that drip with either venom or saliva. Since I don't plan on getting bitten it really makes no difference. The teeth appear to me to look like they were created for crushing and chewing shelled creatures, which makes sense because they are not fast as an adult.

It lunges at me and falls short of where I stand twelve feet away. Good to see that it is as graceful as its parents are. Maybe we should rename the stumbler hatchlings to awkward face planters. Before it can regain its footing I put a rifle round into its head, and it rears backwards showing me the bloody hole in its head. Not that being shot stops the damned thing, it continues to get up even as I dial the next bullet to armor piercing and fire again.

The bullet goes completely thru the creature from head to ass, and it drops in a heap. This leads me to believe either the brain is in the body cavity or it must require a lot of damage internally to kill it. Without thinking twice I walk over to my ATV, drop a homing beacon, and leave before more of the eggs start to hatch. I could have sat on a rock and shot them all day long but why be stupid and endanger yourself without good reason.

I follow the same path back to the village, and all the way back to my ship. After putting the ATV back in the cargo hold, I jump into the pilot's seat and take off. I don't stop to talk to Bethany or her father because if the eggs are starting to hatch the village and the mine site could be swamped with hungry young stumblers.

"Vicky, please use the scanners and tell me how big the nesting site is or how many nests are there," I ask as I steer the shuttle directly toward the beacons signal

After a minute Vicky throws a bunch of red circles up on my heads up display. "Seven nests sir, the oldest nest is where the beacon is, and two more stumblers are hatching from that same nest."

"What do you thing would be more effective Vicky, a railgun or implosions?" I ask.

"Vacuum missiles will be faster."

* * *

I fly up to about a thousand feet and pull my shuttle into a hover directly above my beacon. At this height I can watch the attacks on the nests and stay out of harm's way. I could manually target each nest but using my A.I. is faster.

"Vicky, target each nest and fire with two missiles to each."

Vicky doesn't bother to argue that one missile should be enough and releases the weapons. The missiles streak downward, silently propelled by their anti-gravity drive systems. The missiles implode with a blue flash on impact, creating huge overlapping holes in the mountain about a hundred feet across. There is no dust, as the anti-matter implosion pulls everything into clumps about the size of your fist.

"Scan for eggs and nests please," I say.

"Nothing, sir."

"Take control of the shuttle and fly a search pattern looking for more nests and adults on this land mass please."

Gunmen do not only deal with the immediate threat but ensure possible future threats are dealt with as well. Ensuring a hungry horde of walking slugs doesn't kill more humans is personal plan of the day. If there was one stumbler there could be a dozen, one nesting site could be several.

I decide to take a nap in my chair since Vicky will be flying the search pattern for at least a few hours. I awake to Vicky's chime three hours later, and sit back up with a yawn as I stretch.

"Pattern complete: three more nesting sites," Vicky announces.

"Do we have enough missiles?"

"Only if you use one for each nest sir," she said.

I get out of my seat, and walk few steps over to the small galley to grab a coffee. A cup of steaming coffee appears as if by magic on the Autochef pad. I smile at it and say, "Thank you Vicky." Vicky's personal assistant mode recognizes patterns and behaviors which allow her to do things like make coffee when I wake up. *I do love my coffee.*

"Plot courses to nests and one missile to each please, Vicky."

I sit down and watch Vicky pilot the shuttle to each nesting site and then blow each one out of existence as I sip my coffee. Within another hour I was out of missiles, and there were no more nests on this land mass.

Vicky then returns us to town, and I go into Borne to meet Paul and his daughter again. They are waiting in his office and having heard the explosions off in the distance. I explained to them that their stumbler had been destroying their town because it was nesting in the mountains and, upon locating the site; and that I discovered the young stumblers were highly aggressive.

"I have killed all the eggs and will deal the adults," I said. "Do any small ones ever attack the villages?"

Bethany shakes her head, "in the three years we have been here we have never seen the parents or the young before this attack"

Not sure I would refer to this as an attack, but it is their planet. I think to myself.

"I do have a question about your work here. Have your employers killed people who don't meet quota?" I ask carefully. Administrator Jones is quick to say; "no, but we got yelled at last year."

I try without success to hide my smile. "It is not likely they would be sending killers then."

"I will hang around until a parent comes back, from my A.I.'s analysis it might be laying clutches of eggs days apart on a several year cycle or maybe it lays eggs here and on other land masses. If it returns I will kill it, and I will train a few townspeople on how to do deal with the stumblers in my absence. I also recommend you order shield generators on your next resupply to stop stumblers from coming ashore."

* * *

I toured around with Bethany to see a couple of the other towns and check out the mine site. The people of Dorene were a bit hesitant at first when they found out I was a Gunman, mainly from the rumors of us being baby-eating killers. Once I had spoken with several people about the nests and what was happening, I had lots of volunteers to help watch for the adult stumblers.

I spent a couple of days at the mine site and another few days at a couple of the towns, and generally made the population feel Gunman actually existed to help and not to eat their babies. Once that happened I found myself fielding lots of offers from people for dinners and lodging. Bethany seemed interested in me and was hanging around almost every second she could, so I tried to play the concerned protector and spent nights sleeping in my shuttle. Sure, she was pretty, but I was not ready to settle down, and she was hunting for a husband. I have responsibilities in the Element that I take very seriously and a girlfriend might make me less effective at my job. Don't get me wrong I want a family and kids someday, just not now.

A few nights later I was lying in my bunk having Vicky scan for stumblers when she said, "Bethany is approaching from her father's house and she is armed."

I slide out of my bunk to my feet. "With what?"

"Something that appears to be in a bottle and two glasses."

I dress, grab my rifle, and quickly leave the shuttle to wander down to the docks and up the beach.

"I think the other Gunmen would be very amused to discover you are afraid of a girl with a bottle of wine." Vicky said.

I laugh. "Not afraid, just cautious with my freedom."

"It might do you good to drink some wine and have some company." I wonder if Vicky's council is right. Maybe relaxing a bit would be good for me. Maybe Bethany is just trying to be friendly, but at midnight with wine?

Right and I was born yesterday. I stop and head back to my ship thinking I will have to show Vicky how wrong she is. I am not afraid of a girl with a bottle of wine. It would be funny if she hit me with it so I could say, "See Vicky, I was right." As I approach the ship I see Bethany standing by the hatch and say hello. She turns, startled.

"I thought you would be here resting and might enjoy some wine."

I smile. "Well, I thought my scanner had a glitch, so I checked the perimeter and there is nothing around. Let me grab some chairs."

I pulled a couple of folding chairs and a small table out of an equipment hatch. The night was pleasantly warm but I think Bethany wanted to actually go into the ship, I played dumb. I cracked the top and poured us a drink. I looked over my glass at my guest.

"May gods give us the wisdom to discover the right, the will to choose it, and the strength to make it endure." We clinked our glasses and she looked oddly at me.

"Most Gunmen always say a different toast before they drink." I inform her.

Bethany laughs and curiosity gets the better of her so she asks me just how many I know. I think about a few of my favorites and smile. There are more than a few that should not be said in mixed company.

"Hundreds," I answer.

The wine was an imported blush and quite strong. Bethany talked about how lonely it was here, and how dull the miners and fishermen were. I was pretty sure I knew what she was hinting at, but I wasn't going to lead her on when my direction in life was headed a different way. I told her that I too was lonely and missed my Caroline too, which made her go silent for a second.

"You're in a relationship?" she asked.

"Long term," I answered. "Caroline is a lab researcher on New Harvest and I miss her a lot. You would like her; she is intelligent and very dedicated to her job."

Thank god Vicky is ordered to stay sub-vocal unless instructed to go active or she might have told Bethany that Caroline was my mother. I sit sipping my wine inwardly grinning to myself, because Bethany had enough class not to try to steal me away. Bethany seemed resigned and actually looked a little more relaxed now that she didn't have to try and woo me. We talked until the bottle was gone and I thanked for an enjoyable visit before she returned to her home. I waited until she left and then put the table and chairs back into the ship. I did notice that the wine was affecting my balance a bit as I made my way to my bunk.

"Well done," Vicky said. "You didn't lie or hurt her feelings, and you had some wine with a pretty girl."

A mostly successful evening, I think to myself as I lay down on my lonely bunk. The wine worked well and I fell asleep quickly. I have to admit I did have a rather nice dream that night about Bethany's willingness and flexibility. I awoke late in the morning with a slight headache, *stupid wine*, and decided to lie in bed and watch the ceiling for an hour or two. Vicky didn't suggest any aspirin, but I knew she could sense the headache.

Shortly after noon, she told me a stumbler was approaching the shoreline. I grabbed a .50-caliber railgun rifle and walked outside the shuttle; dozens of villagers were aware of the stumbler and gathered on the hill beside the town.

The stumbler had come ashore and was already moving up its previous path of destruction thru town. Taking my time, I managed to cut across and meet the stumbler at the midway point almost in the center of town. I charged up my rifle and waited until it was almost to me. I could hear people on the hills yelling for me to be careful. Listening to their warnings made me wonder if I looked like Horatius at the Gate, from their view, although I don't feel like him. I waited until the entire stumbler was in view before raising my rifle. I put the targeting laser in the center of the oncoming stumble and pulled the trigger.

At a distance of fifty yards, the hardened bullet accelerated out the magnetically charged barrel to 12,000 feet per second. The projectile was traveling over eight thousand miles per hour and took a fraction of a second to reach its target. The projectile hit dead center of the stumbler. The three ounce bullet transferred so much energy into the stumbler that the results were catastrophically spectacular.

The stumbler blinked out of existence in a shower of red and green jelly. My audience on the small hill at close by and everything in town within three hundred yards was liberally coated in stumbler-mush. It sounded like a shower of rain when the stumbler mush was falling back to the ground. The sound of people on the hill throwing up was clearly audible over the sound of falling stumblers chunks and I had to smile, a wicked bloody smirk; *this is what I do*.

I turned and headed back to the landing pad in order to get cleaned up. When I got to my ship I opened a compartment on the side and pulled out a shower nozzle. I have to say the outdoor faucet comes in handy during missions like this when I come back covered with blood and grime. I stood beneath the showerhead in a stream of warm soapy water until most of the gore was sloughed off me. I undressed outside by the hatch and walked into my sonic shower for a better cleaning. Feeling itchy but clean I get redressed and throw my dirty clothes into the reclaimer. I spend half an hour cleaning the rail gun then decide to do something about the gore splattered shuttle. I drop my butt into the pilots chair and raise the shuttle up about mile into the sky and take it for a high-speed run to use the air friction to burn the skin clean. I circled their continent and noticed at least three more beaches where a stumbler could come out of the water. Since there is only one nesting site they should be pretty safe.

I decided to wait a while before checking on the good folks who were covered in guts to give them time to clean up. It wasn't long before people and machines were moving around, and hoses were being snaked into the nearby ponds to use fresh water to start washing down the town. I will give it to the town that most of the fishermen were fairly hardy people with strong stomachs. Most of them were still gore-covered, but manned the hoses until the buildings were as clean as they could get them.

Leaving the shuttle I headed back to the Administrator's building. The fishermen manning the hoses were now spraying down the streets and washing the gore from the buildings into the gutters. Quite a few waved at me, the ones that were not angry because they had to clean up my mess. After I knocked on the door and was told to come in Paul was sitting behind his desk, and looked up at me, displeasure was evident on his face. For people with a monumental problem they sure don't seem happy that it was just solved.

I wonder if they would have been happier if I shot it full of small holes and left it for them to deal with. All one hundred feet and twenty tons of it sitting in town for them to section and haul away, the thought of that makes me grin.

"Was that the smallest weapon you could use?" he asked.

I shook my head. "It is the only weapon I am willing to leave for your people to use in my absence. You can order more from Mars Colony, but I only carry a few with me. I am leaving tomorrow, so you'll need to send me a couple of people I can train on how to use it. I will be sure to send the manuals and maintenance requirements over to you as well."

I never saw Bethany again after that day, but I suspect it was due to the completion of my job and her barfing at the result of said job that changed her mind about the kind of guy I was. It was too bad we were not going to be friends after we had such a nice bottle of wine, but being mentally strong I will work through my feelings and just try to make it through the next few days.

CHAPTER 6

My time in the Gunmen's Element was exciting, but after six years solid years of deployment I decided it was time to return to New Harvest. Granddad and mom are not getting any younger, and maybe I could find a nice girl to help run the farm. It took several weeks to clean up my duties, there was no one to replace as 1st Gunman so I would be still in contact and working from New Harvest. I cleaned up the schedules and ensured the proper traveling protocols were loaded to Monitor. I found Mars Colony dull because my good friends had retired almost a month ago. The Commander and I had a few drinks on my last night before he proclaimed that I had put the Element back on the right track. He also tried to get me to stay on in administration or as a trainer. No such luck for them: I am going home.

Since I had never had a vacation, I was going to take a couple of weeks to hunt some snowbeast on Tertian before my return, I thought a pelt from one of the creatures might make an excellent throw rug for my home, which was already built to my specifications and waiting for me.

I sent a flash to New Harvest about my plans, but that I would return afterward to take my place in the family. The two weeks on a snowy planet would be good way to refresh myself after years of back-to-back missions. Sure, when I get home I would still be active reserve for our quadrant in case of trouble and I would also retain the title and position of 1st Gunman, but only until someone else could replace me. No one stopped me from taking my shuttle and ATV when I left, so I guess they thought a reserve position might still need it. It made me pleased I would have great equipment but I was slightly sad that I had to have it. *Oh suck it up whiner.* I smiled at my thoughts as my career in the People's Free Force was not totally complete. This was what I signed up for.

* * *

The Arctic-like weather on Tertian does not hide the smoke from my burning ATV. The smoke was a thick toxic cloud that I was able to avoid by moving upwind. Guess my luck hadn't totally run out as I was uninjured and was not pinned in the burning wreckage. Spending two weeks alone hunting in Arctic-like weather on Tertian may not be the smartest thing I have done. Actually, it is one of the dumber things I have tried to do. Lady Luck is a fickle bitch.

My ATV was lying in a very steep valley after the snow bank on the top of the ridge caved in causing an avalanche that made my vehicle to roll to the bottom. If I was designing these machines I would have rupture proof fuel cells because the spilling the fuel was the catalyst for this smoke.

Most of my camping gear is smoldering, but I did manage to pull my rifle and pack from the ATV before the fire became too large. As I am dressed well in a standard Gunman's battle suit I will be dry and warm even without the rest of my things. I wade thru the deep snow towards the shelter of some blown over trees and set my rifle carefully against a stump. The rifle is fine for this weather as it is stainless and synthetic, which was why I chose it for my trek. My thinking has gone into survival mode, and I open my pack to start taking stock of what I have. Extra ammo for the pistol, rounds for the rifle, a rail pistol and ammo, a water bottle, filtration straws and pump, survival blanket, fire starter, knife, trail mix, coffee, and Kcal rations. Right outside pouch on the pack has chute wire and a saw. Left pouch has power cells.

I sit back with a relieved smile. I can hike out of here without too many problems since my clothes are battle skin-suits that are waterproof with an onboard heating and cooling system. I will be fine. I just have to walk thirty-five miles a day and I will be back to my shuttle within a week. I consider leaving immediately, but decide to wait a while longer to see if the fire burns down enough for me to salvage anything. Maybe the snow shoes survived. I lean back against a tree trunk and close my eyes. After years of active duty I can fall asleep quickly, while still being aware enough of my surroundings to sense any danger should it approach.

* * *

The retrieval globe moved with a casual pace, branches and trees seem to flow thru it like smoke. A mouse of some sort moved in the snow, and the globe suddenly shot over to cover it, and then without a pause it continued. The mouse was no worse for the globe's action and continued on its way, mostly likely to become dinner for some predator.

The globe then moved on until it found the smoldering ATV. A brief pause, and then the globe expanded until the entire ATV disappeared inside it. There was a significant pause while the ATV and its contents were analyzed. The globe rose up into the air about seven feet and then popped.

The ATV quietly fell back into the snow filled gulley, and the globe—now back to its original size—went directly down the trail following a set of footprints. The analysis of the smoldering ATV and its technology showed promise but the weaponry showed a one hundred percent - MEETS CRITERIA- status. If the globe was alive it would be buzzing with excitement. Its scanners pinpointed a heat source so it accelerated to its target. The life form ahead is humanoid and had a weapon, the globe expands larger and moves into acquisition mode. The side of the sphere dissolves and then reforms when it covers the target. Once the target is securely inside and acceleration dampeners are active the globe takes off at the speed of light leaving nothing but an echo from its passing.

* * *

I awoke with a start, opening my eyes to see nothing but blackness; something isn't right as the cold now gone. I started to feel around the stump I was resting against for my rifle. Once I found it I used the barrel as a poker. I did not have to reach far to touch something hard. I pulled it back and raised it upward about the same distance before hitting something hard again. I reach upward with my hand until my fingers encounter a warm surface that was smoother than glass. It is slick, but after feeling it with my fingers I realize it is dry.

It's time to try to push my way out I think as I get to my knees, then feet crouching to press up with my back to the smooth surface. I strain with my legs and back trying to force my way through to no avail. I sit back down breathing heavy and grab my pack and open it, feeling around for my flashlight. Once I have my light in my hand I turn it on, the inside of this thing looks like I a black eggshell. I then pull out my combat knife and give surface surrounding me a hit with the pommel. The surface feels solid but doesn't make a sound which make we wonder if I am in some sort of damping field so I open my mouth to speak and nothing comes out. My mouth is moving and air is coming out yet it is silent. I sub-vocally try and access Vicky with no success, either she is being blocked or is not functioning for the first time since I have had her.

So this thing I am in absorbs sound. This would be fascinating were it not for the fact I was stuck inside some strange sphere with no knowledge of how I got there or why. I look at my rifle and contemplate trying to shoot my way out but tossed those thoughts away. Trapped and wounded from a ricocheting bullet or dead would not be cool. I try stabbing at the wall with my knife, yet it doesn't even make a scratch. I take a drink of water, eat a handful of trail mix, and contemplate my predicament. It makes me wonder when I will run out of air or water. If the air holds out I can survive a week with the water I have. Knowing it is out of my control, I calmly wait.

Without being able to speak with Vicky and the fact I knew the dampening field was messing with my perception of time I really had no idea of how much time was passing. I had just taken my last few drops of water when the black sphere I am sitting in pops. Three things come to mind instantly:

1. I am free,
2. It is a very bright place.
3. I am falling.

Before I can even orient myself for landing I am lying on the ground. The height of the fall was minimal because I am unhurt and don't even have my breath knocked out of me. I am looking straight into the grass, well not grass, but some odd kind of multi-leaf clover which carpets the earth under me. The sun is quite bright and the temperature is in the low 80s. My skin-suit is still working just fine and has changed to cooling mode, which makes me quite comfortable. I have no real idea where I am and how I got here, a situation that intrigues me. I joined the P.F.F. for adventure, right now I am in a situation that I have never been in before.

I stand up to scope out my surroundings and discover I am at the peak of a rolling hill. Looking around me I see more rolling hills with very minimal vegetation, coloring seems normal, *yeah, totally lost*. There is the lack of snow that would indicate I'm not on Tertian, and the atmosphere is very humid but not excessively hot. It is most definitely a different place than where I fell asleep. Maybe even a different planet, yes definitely a different planet because Tertian is in a winter cycle.

"Vicky, where am I?" I ask, hoping I am once again connected with my A.I.

"Sir, I was taken off line for twenty minutes judging by internal data gaps," she answers, much to my relief. "Scanning finds no satellites or beacons. We are not on Tertian anymore."

"You may be wrong about the amount of time you were off line as I ran out of water while in the sphere." I inform her.

I pull my Tilley hat out of my back pocket and drop it on my head. This is somewhere I have never been. I shoulder my pack and pick up my rifle. The bolt opens easily and, after checking the barrel for obstructions, three rounds go into the magazine and one in the pipe. I could carry a lighter rifle but having Thor in my hands makes me feel a lot more secure if I run into any dangerous creatures. Why would I name my Remington rifle Thor? Most Gunmen see firearms as tools like shovels or axes. Not me I love this rifle, it is a thing of beauty with exceptional workmanship and when you look past the pretty factor it is one of the most accurate chemical weapons ever created by man. I never nicknamed anything else but this weapon deserves a name.

There are higher hills or mountains off in the distance, so I will head in that direction hoping it will lead me to a settlement or at least to somewhere I can find shelter. Walking through the gently rolling hills is fairly easy but water will shortly be a concern in this warmth, so I had better watch for a stream.

After several hours of walking without seeing a water source I crest a hill, and the land flows away to dirt and sand. Desert plains all the way to the mountains by the look of it, and not a plant or stream in sight. I turn back down into the clover-filled valley and walk to the deepest part. With a little bit of work I am able to dig a shallow hole through the dry soil until I get to the wet stuff; a few more minutes and water starts to trickle into the hole. I use my water purifier to fill my drinking bottle and the hydration pouch in my pack, so the journey to the mountains should not be too bad.

I continue walking. The miles passed slowly as the sun beat down. Studying my surroundings, a few things did not seem right. Sure a semi arid plain is normal enough, but there were no clouds. Not one, being used to terrifomed planets and places that have humidity like this place normally there are clouds. Being not sure of the significance I will need to keep my eyes on the weather in case I need to get to shelter quickly.

Watching the ground ahead of me I am sure I see something move. After hours of walking the first sign of life is significant so I pause to dig through my pack and pull out my binoculars, raising them to look a good two hundred yards ahead. Scanning in the vicinity I'm sure I noticed the movement, I finally pinpoint what I was searching for.

A rock seems to be moving.

As I focus on it, legs appear at the bottom of a small stone I estimate to be the half the size of a human head. From what I presume is a rear view, I notice there are three legs on either side of the rock; there is no head or tail that I can see. The grey chunk of stone moves slowly, almost the speed of a turtle. This gives my heart a jolt. I don't pretend to know every animal species on the planet of Tertian, but this is most certainly not one of them. Maybe Vicky is right.

I laugh out loud because my A.I. is always right. Being unsure if the rock-creature is dangerous or not, I have to decide if I am going to go around this area or check them out closer. There is no way to tell if the rocks that are above ground are plain rocks or these creatures and there is a lot of them scattered across the arid plain. The animal's camouflage is excellent, if I had not seen it move I would have thought it was just a rock. Not knowing if it is venomous, able to fire stingers or shoot laser beams out of its eyes makes me continue to watch the creature and, as I do, a shadow passes over me. I look up expecting to see a bird, and realize once again that I am not on Tertian.

I have to laugh at myself for thinking the obvious over and over, because all of Tertian is in the middle of their winter cycle. Wherever I am, whatever planet or place this is, it could not by any means be mistaken as covered with snow and ice. By my guess, this terrain is currently in a late spring to early summer phase, which could put me on any one of a thousand different planets.

The flying lizard appears to be about two meters long with half of the length being tail and is a very bright green. The wings span a distance longer than its body and are slightly lighter in color as the sun shines through the membranes. If it could shoot fire it would be a dragon.

The lizard swoops down to hit one of the rocks at random, trying to find a rock critter. Since the rock field is not a herd of the spider-rocks but mostly plain rocks, the dragon-like animal has to hit a lot of rocks before finding a spider. There must be a different feeling between a rock and a spider because the dragon quickly turns in the air after hitting the one I was watching and grabs it with its mouth and starts to fly away the legs of the spider wiggling from the lizard's jaws. I scan the sky with my binoculars looking for more of the flying lizards, maybe they can grow thirty feet long and have a taste for Gunmen. Not seeing any more of them flying around I resolve to keep my eyes on the sky a lot more.

Well, the immediate need in my life is to look for civilization and to get shelter and then I could check the creatures out later. Deciding the fastest way will be straight through the field, I step into the rock-covered plain while keeping a wary eye for lizards and moving rocks. I move quietly but cautiously toward my goal. I see no other odd occurrences and wonder if I am hallucinating, or perhaps I am still asleep and having a really strange dream. That would be the easy explanation and I wish I could believe it, but life has never given me the easy explanations and I have never dreamt in such clarity

I take a sip from the hydration pack and continue on my merry way. After another three hours I figure I am at the midway point to the hills and can easily make it by dark where I am sure to find a place to take refuge for the night. That is, of course, if it gets dark I think with a smile. There is always the possibility that this is a planet of eternal sunshine, and wonder how apex predators would hunt. It would be interesting because they could charge out of the ground or sky at any moment. If they did it would at least break up the monotony of my trek.

Walking allows me to think about my life, about what I know. I am a Gunman from the Gunman's Element in the People's Free Force. Seems like a lonely life but I go where I want, when I want, and pretty much do whatever I decide is right. Being a Gunman for six years was a lot of fun, the short break to Tertian for a hunting trip before returning to New Harvest was a self-indulgent luxury that just burned my ass. Now that I am here I can either wallow in self-pity or treat it like another adventure… Oh, well, maybe I'll get stressed out later. One of my good personal traits is that things out of my control do not tend to worry me much.

As I get closer to the mountains I can see some smoke. Good, maybe there will be people, *and hopefully said people are not two-headed, mutant cannibals,* I think with a laugh. Deciding the best course will be to stay hidden and maybe scout out the location of the smoke rather than head straight for it, I break far to the right and head up a valley between two higher peaks. The temperature difference in the shade of the trees is a nice change from the plain's heat. The trees look normal, but of course I don't have a clue what they are. At least they are not attacking me. No worrisome biting insects yet, either. This place would be nice if I wasn't lost on a foreign planet. I remove my pack and sit down so I can take a few more sips of water, and then I open the rations pouch and eat a tube of Kcals.

I put the pack back on; slowly and carefully I move up the valley. The trees are absolutely still due to the lack of a breeze, or they could just be watching my every step. I can see lots of movement from small flying creatures that might be birds or smaller dragon-lizards in the tops of the trees. Another thought hits me, with all this walking, carrying my pack and rifle, I am not getting tired. I feel very light on my feet, which makes me think the gravity must be quite a bit lighter than I am used too.

The trees thin out a bit near the top of the valley. I pull my binoculars out of my pocket and check out the crest of the hill. Seems safe enough, so I move up beside a small boulder to check the other side with the hope it is a real rock not one of those really big spiders. As I move, I pull my rifle off my shoulder, and crawl to the peak.

To my surprise there is a town. The buildings are similar in shape to the yurts from old earth except they are much larger. There appears to be solar panels covering every roof, and the roadways are natural stone with lots of green areas interspersed between them and the buildings. The layout of town is roughly circular with another large green area about the size of an average soccer pitch in the middle. A rough count gives me approximately a hundred buildings.

There is a fortified wall circling the end of the cove, and the town is inside its arc. The main gate is open toward the water. I can see the inhabitants moving about, there are some in the fields and others in town moving around in small groups as they go on with their daily lives.

What the heck? I think they look Asian in appearance by their skin color; there are no adults in sight, only young teenagers and children. The average person there is about four and a half feet high. As I study the town more I realize they have regular features: arms have hands, legs have feet with toes, faces have only the requisite amount of eyes. The females have very long black hair, and the males have mostly short hair; all of the youths present are uniformly slender. *No one has two heads and they don't act like cannibals.*

As I study their interaction I can see they work well together watching the younger ones, they seem very calm and supportive of the smaller children. Odd behavior for teenagers I think, as there is no animation in their movements. Kids being kids chase balls and generally move around, but these children talk to each other with no hand gestures or raised voices. Often you see the teens touching hands or putting a hand on a shoulder when they are having conversations. And where are the adults? There isn't a one in sight, so perhaps they may have gone through the gate to spend their days fishing.

I slowly move back from the hill and take some time to drink more water. Doing an inventory of my supplies, I know they will not last more than a couple of weeks. Do I wait for the adults to return or go down and meet the kids? Maybe the adults will sell me some supplies or help me contact the

P.F.F. A slight breeze flows over the ridge and provides a bit of relief from the heat as I debate what to do next.

Soon I hear yelling and rattling noises off in the distance, so I raise my binoculars and look back over the crest. At the north end of the village, the farthest from gate, there are several large cultivated fields with what appears to be huge spiders being chased from the crops by several young people. I drop back to my original position and decide to rest up a bit until dark. I can now tell that darkness or twilight will be approaching by the way the sun is much lower in the sky. I imagine they will close the gate at night, and then I can see when the adults get back.

I sit there a moment with my eyes closed, but it is too bright to nap. *Oh well.* Maybe I will do a sweep around the village and check out the gate before dark. I take one last peak at the children through my binoculars before creeping far enough away that I will not accidentally be seen when I stand up.

Moving down the tree-covered valley, I cross through a small marshy area. The ground in front of me is fairly flat with a lot of small puddles. I look down at the puddles to realize they are footprints of some sort. I stop and crouch down to investigate them, there are two impact points in each track several feet apart. Maybe the larger spiders made these during foraging. I raise my binoculars to scout the area in front of me. Nothing moving, so time to leave the marsh before I get eaten or have to make so much noise that everything and everyone knows I am here.

I cross over the ridge in front of me so I can see the village wall after an hour of walking. My placement is on the water side of the wall. There is one young person on the beach pulling a fishing line in with some sort of hand winch mounted on a small frame. The cove in front of the wall is closed in on the sides with a very narrow opening out to main body of water.

With the breeze in my face it smells like fresh water rather than a salt-water ocean. From the angle I am looking from no shore is visible through the opening to the main body of water. On either side of the opening are large stone pillars that don't seem to be used for anything. The pillars are not quite as high as the rocky ridges that surround this little cove there is no marking on them and if I had to guess they might be huge gate posts. The only beach section is where that person is currently pulling the line in.

As the young girl, now that I am close enough to see, is continuing to winch in the line with a fish on it the end of it thrashing about. She pulls it up on the shore, picks the fish up by the gills to remove the hook, and gently pries it out. It's a nice fish of about two feet long. She then turns toward the gate and, as she does, a bulge in the water appears about thirty yards from the shore. Her back is to it so I am all business instantly because gate equals something to be kept out, I move my rifle over and seat the stock it into my shoulder to cover the shore.

Through the scope I see the water boil up, and a long shape breaks free from the water to lunge for the girl. It reminds me of some kind of pike like fish with the addition of rear legs only. The tail sways from side to side as the legs propel it up the sand on its belly; the large mouth starts to open while the fish-like creature slides effortlessly across the sand. As the pike clears the water entirely, I realize it is at least forty feet long. To most people it would seem like a monster. I've seen worse.

The range to the attacking creature is less than three hundred yards from my vantage point. I peer through my scope and line up the cross hairs on the area below a huge right eye. The beast's jaws are opened wide enough to swallow the girl with one bite. The mouth is ringed with rows of dagger like teeth that must be over a foot long. The head of the creature rears back a bit in preparation to pounce, and the girl has now realized she is in danger and drops her catch as she tries to get away from the predator.

Whatever this thing is it can outpace her easily. I thumb the safety off my rifle, take a quick deep breath, and release the breath just as fast then caress the trigger. The two hundred grain bonded warhead round leaves the barrel at 4960 feet per second, and at three hundred yards the drop is about .050 inches. With 4100 lbs of force, the bullet passes through the eye and into the brain of the beast.

Coming off the significant recoil from my rifle, I see the animal nose into the sand only a few feet from the girl. She stops and looks at the creature as its tail thrashes its deathblows. She then turns and looks around, including up the ridge where I am sitting, trying to find out what made the noise. I don't move and she continues to search the ridge; I guess my camouflage still works well even in this strange terrain. Thank god for smokeless gunpowder or she may have pinpointed my location anyways.

I hear an electronic gonging, and she turns to walk back over to her dropped fish. To collect it she has to walk by the beast and does so without a second look, before she heads thru the slowly closing gate. She was pretty brave—no panicking or nervousness—just grab the fish and walk away.

No adults have come back yet; there are no boats or docks in the cove.

Once the gate fully closes I see the entire wall start to shimmer and can discern little flashes of light at various spots. It appears as though there may be a low-level force field or electrical field of some sort. I'm in a good place to watch the gate and think my spot is high enough to stop anything that might want to crawl up the ridge which would be good because I would rather not make any more noise until I have more information on these people.

I lean back against a rock and palm my bolt open and take another round from my belt and push it into my Remington. I love this rifle. I could use a railgun rifle or laser, but they use power sources that can die while a simple rifle with a cartridge cannot be shut down. I hope there are not too many of those critters or I might run out of ammo before I can get off of this planet.

Where are the adults? Are they dead, or did they merely leave the kids in a safer area than they must traverse? These people obviously have decent technology, so why don't they deal with the sea creatures? Why did the girl catch just one fish instead of a dozen? How many kids live in this village? I have more questions than answers, and if I want to discover the truth I will have to study the village some more tomorrow. I will also need more food and water soon, because I won't live on kcals and trail mix long, at least not by my choice.

CHAPTER 7

Sophee takes her fish into the village and briskly walks toward her family's home. Being alive is good. She could sense that someone was there on the ridge, but was rather phlegmatic. Not in the lazy way, but unexcited by events. Calmness radiated from the ridge and whoever her protector was he did not broadcast emotions at all. Her father has warned her many times not to check lines before the darkness fell as the eels always hunt near shore in the late day. Sophee knew she would have died without the thunder from the rocks, and realized she should tell her father about it. Not that dying from being eaten would be as bad as being rendered. Only she would pass, and not her entire family if it happened quickly. When she opens the door to her home her father's displeasure is evident as he starts to scolds her.

"Catching a fish this time of day is dangerous. You were lucky. How many of our people have died from the eels? What are you thinking about, my daughter?" he asks with firm voice. Sophie stands holding the fish by the door with her eyes downcast for a minute, and then she approaches her father before speaking.

"Father," Sophee begins to say, "I do not wish to eat the little crawlers. I am tired of them. You and mother are tired of them. I risked pulling the line at dusk, because there is never anything on the lines during the day."

Hyun turns from his daughter to look at his mate for support. Mere who is standing in the prep room cleaning greens nods briefly at her mate, Hyun taking her ascension turns back to his daughter and calmly asks, "Do you not think an eel might have gotten you?"

"Yes, father, an eel came out of the water but thunder from the hills struck it down."

Hyun looks into his daughter's eyes to ask. "Truly?"

"Yes father the eel was fully out of the water when it was killed. I couldn't outrun it, and that is when it happened. The thunder saved me. I looked at the hills and could not see my savior; whoever made the thunder was very calm and still. This was all I could sense."

Her father turns away with watery eyes and takes a ragged emotion filled breath. "Mere, we must make some plans for a visitor."

His wife comes over to join him with a gentle smile and says, "Maybe it will finally be time?"

Mere wonders what the odds would be that their last retrieval sphere would bring someone that could help. For the last ten years they had used up their highest technology to create the spheres at a rate of one every few months. They were out of the raw materials to make anymore. What would happen if the sphere returned someone or something more harmful than their foes? Her fear and concern would have to wait, for her daughter was alive and well and maybe, just maybe they would get lucky this time.

"Sophee, please run the fish through the processor. We

will save it for tomorrow." Mere instructs as she goes back to finish cleaning the greens.

Sophee removes her sandals by the door and takes the fish over to the processing device sitting on the counter. It is half a black sphere similar in design to the retrieval sphere only about a foot high. She pushed the input key and the side of the sphere opens silently so she can feed the fish head first into the opening, a green light blinks to inform her that the finished meat will be held in stasis until needed. Sophee smiles at her mom, and heads to the sanitary room to clean the fish off her hands.

* * *

"Sir?" Vicky chimes.

"Yes Vicky?" I answer back.

"I have analyzed the source that shut me down, and I have done a reboot. I also was able to ensure that type of tachyon field will no longer affect me."

"Good, do you know where we are yet?"

"No, but I can send sub-light requests to the P.F.F. for retrieval as soon as I figure where we are."

"How will that work now that I am semi-retired?" I ask.

"The Gunman's Element will send a scout ship for you as soon as they receive the request regardless."

"Vicky, continue to scan for dangerous life forms, and wake me if needed."

* * *

After the long walk, the fresh air and warmth of this planet tired me out or I was in that sphere longer than I thought, either way again I sleep like the dead until late morning and wake instantly to my AIs warning.

"Sir, there are two life forms clearing the ridge directly behind you, so be ready."

I roll right springing to my feet, draw my pistol, and to my surprise I find myself looking at a couple of teenagers. One of them appears to be the girl who I saved yesterday. She can't be more than an inch or two within four-and-a-half feet tall, and even though she is really short it is proportional. She has a very slender body, and is most likely about fifteen years old. Did I mention very pretty?

The other person, and I use the term person loosely because they are humanoid, is male and slender with a slightly—and I mean *slightly*—older looking face. Their facial structure makes them look like young Asians. They are both dressed in white pants and what looks like Gi tops.

"Vicky, do they have weapons?" I ask sub-vocally.

"None," comes her answer.

I lower my gun and holster it. The look on the boy's face is absolute hope mixed with caution as he steps forward slowly. Either they don't have strangers here very often or the sight of me drawing a weapon on him scared him. I feel bad because I like kids and they should not have to be afraid. To my surprise the boy says "hello."

Guess that they are not aliens because they are speaking English.

"I will be translating what you hear and say," Vicky says sub-vocally.

Translating? I didn't know Vicky could recalibrate my voice. I will have to speak to her later about this.

"Where am I?" I ask.

The boy looks nervously at me and says, "We call our planet Sooule."

"Never heard of it," I say.

"We summoned you here," the boy says. "Please come to our home. We will feed you and tell you everything. I am Hyun, and my daughter is Sophee."

Daughter? Shit. I wonder how old he is? How old she is? They look like teenagers and yet were actually father and child, so there must be something odd about the way they age. I send a sub-vocal command: "Vicky, would please you scan them and give me an update?"

I pick up my pack and shoulder my rifle to follow them. We walk at a leisurely pace without speaking; Vicky makes an announcement through my implant. "I know where we are, sir. We are outside of the Outer Rings, six light-years from Tertian. Now would you like a targeted burst to the P.F.F.?"

"No," I sub-vocalize, "let's see what is going on first."

It takes a couple of hours to reach the beach with the route they took which wound along the top of the ridge and then angled back toward the water on a steep slope. It eventually brought us down to the beach. As we walk past the semi-devoured beast, Sophee raises a cute little eyebrow and with a very subtle palm raised gesture alludes to the condition of the dead animal as if to say "Your work?" I nod, so she gives me the nicest smile I have ever seen before stepping to the side of the trail to allow her father lead the way toward their home. I can only guess that more of those pike things were eating the dead one, as it now lay partially devoured.

"Technical scan complete class five tech level, no powered weapons, solar power charges the gate and wall, which has a simple electrical shocking field, and battery cells charged from each of the homes roof systems—one building has much more electronic signatures in several different wave lengths. It would appear that these people have a have a database and a network," Vicky reports.

As we enter the town people start coming out of homes, some of the mothers are holding babies, most of the women are crying, a bunch of smaller kids break away to start trailing us. The sight of an armed Gunman in a camouflage battle suit is enough to keep the older ones back, but not the very little kids who are curious by nature and see Hyun and Sophee with me.

Sophee turns to address the children with a very kind and soft voice to say, "Let's try not to scare our visitor."

"Yeah, because you are all so very frightening," I said, with wide eyes.

My attempt at humor fell on deaf ears because the kids just looked at me. *Tough crowd* I thought.

Sophee looks at me with concern and takes my hand. I don't know why, maybe she is trying to comfort me or maybe she wants to show the kids I am okay. The feeling that ran through my hand from her touch was like being shocked; the buzz traveled up my arm and into my chest. I stopped dead in my tracks on the road wondering what heck was that.

"Vicky, what was that?" I ask sub-vocally.

She returns with, "What was what?"

"Please give me a quick med scan update on myself."

"No changes other than heart rate, why?"

I quietly think about it for a second and come up with no answer as to why I felt this way after touching Sophee's

The 1st Gunman

hand. Hyun continues to walk away absorbed in his own thoughts. Standing directly in front of me, Sophee stares at me as if I am some kind of freak show; her green eyes were looking intently into mine. What was she trying to see there? *Man, she has nice eyes.* They look right through you, almost to your soul, which makes me a bit nervous because my soul had some dark spots. A girl who is as kind to others and compassionate as her would make an excellent wife someday. Too bad she is not older. The thought made me laugh as I carefully pull my hand from her warm grasp.

"I was joking. I don't really think the people of Sooule are frightening, so please accept my apology if I was out of line." I apologize while trying not to smile.

The buzzing in my chest still wouldn't stop and my heart was hammering like I had just ran twenty miles, so I step back away from her and continue walking behind Hyun who was completely oblivious to our moment. I take a sip from my hydration tube and wonder if my bizarre reaction was because I am dehydrated. There is no way the sensation could be caused by a girl so young; I refuse to believe that.

* * *

Sophee smiled to herself. *He is the one,* she thought as she hurried to catch up to her father and guest. Finally the bond! Sophee had always wondered if she would ever bond and had hoped, but with their declining population and lack of men her age it seemed unlikely.

She knew her father could sense her joy, but he probably would attribute it to having a warrior here. He would have no idea that her pulse was pounding so hard it was all she could do to keep walking. Her joy was so intense Sophee never even noticed they were approaching her family's home or that every person in the village was out watching the stranger.

It was obvious he was armed with strange weapons, and that though his clothing stood out in the town it would make him all but invisible in the forest. His height and posture made him appear to be very inflexible, yet his smile was genuine and his nodding to the people made him a bit less intimidating. The fact he struck down an eel the day before to save one of their own filled the village with hope. More than a few people were wishing he were the solution to their problems and the hero they needed.

Sophee was watching him walk and was enjoying when he turned his head to nod at some of her people, He had a little smile that hinted at his amusement or general happiness. He was not nervous or even on guard and that calmness radiated off him. It could be felt by all the Sooul. Would he want to bond with her? She would be the only Sooule ever to bond with an outsider. She has many questions about this man, did he come from a large family or was he a single child? Surely someone as brave as a warrior would want a family. She then had a thought, what if he is already bonded to someone else and he triggered the bond in me but doesn't actually want to bond. Sophee has never heard of that before but decided to remain positive because what will happen, happens.

* * *

I follow Hyun as he walks up to a larger hard shelled yurt-shaped home with Sophee trailing right behind me.

The 1st Gunman

The door disappears as he walks through it. Nice force field, *tech level five my butt, seven or above is more likely.*

I step up to the small platform in front of the door and enter their home. Sophee follows me through the door before going over to another female to give her a hug. This is not just a house, but a home. The inside is has warm soft colors and a very intimate interior that makes it feel very cozy. The entire place is open concept with another door off the kitchen or prep area. There is a counter in what could be a kitchen but no table or major appliances that I can see.

I look down at my boots, and decide to remove them; tracking dirt in their home would be rude. Just as I bend to unsnap the clasps, Hyun said, "No, keep comfortable and do not worry."

I feel kind of like Gulliver around these small people, so I remove my boots anyway and take off my pack. The boots only added a couple inches to my six foot two inch frame, so their removal didn't close the gap between our heights difference all that much. Nevertheless, my parents always taught me to respect other people's homes, so I was more comfortable with removing my footwear before stepping further into the house.

I unload the rifle so it can stand safely by the door, it is obvious that these people are not the danger. It will help keep them at ease if I am not fully armed. I then punch a sequence into my sleeve keypad and my camouflage morphs into a non-threatening off-white coverall. The father smiles again nervously, and motions to the large pillows in a sunken living area. I walk over and sit down on one of the thick comfortable cushions.

The other girl or woman comes into their gathering room and she carries with her a pitcher of liquid and some small glasses on a tray. The female is smiling like it is the best day in her life; my presence is a good thing for these people.

Hyun points at her. "My mate, Mere."

I find myself smiling, and nodding to her, "Ma'am."

She looks almost identical to her daughter, with her delicate features, green eyes and slim build. If I had to guess, there are maybe a couple of lines around the eyes and, between that and the shorter hair, it was the only thing that would allow me to tell them apart.

"Would you like a cup of refreshment?" Mere asked, still smiling.

"Please," I answer.

Vicky comes through my implant. "75% Human DNA; Korean with another species I cannot identify. The man and woman are in their late thirties, and their daughter is twenty.

"Why do they look so young?" I ask her staying sub-vocal.

"It would appear they have a longer than usual life span from a small amount of alien DNA."

I think for a minute. "How did you scan DNA, Vicky?"

"When the girl Sophee took your hand, I transferred some nanites onto her so that I could scan them," she said.

Okay, then. They only appear young, but they are obviously mature adults with families. This would make Sophee an adult so I guess I shouldn't feel too when bad talking to her. When I came into their village I did not notice any older people, do they stay young looking until they die?

"From their demeanor and the way they speak, you will need to talk softly. Otherwise your voice will likely intimidate them because of your greater size."

"Good thing to know. I am not going to whisper, that

would be too strange, but I will tone things down so they are not afraid."

I take one of the small glasses and Mere fills it; I nod and say, "Thank you." Mere proceeds to give a glass to Hyun and Sophee as well. Taking a tentative sip, I discover it is very cold water. I lower the glass to study my hosts as Hyun and his mate sit across from me. Sophee sits between them.

I wait for them to start and they wait until I am ready. I do not think they are playing games, but want me to take the lead and start asking questions. Throughout my life I have learned that questions can put people in the defensive state where they will lie sometimes, but the truth generally comes without prompting. I take another sip and watch them study me; it feels weird to be the object of their close inspection, but I calmly wait. Finally Hyun gathered enough courage, took a deep breath, and started to speak.

"Who are you?"

* * *

Mere and Hyun traded a look as they studied their guest. He was an incredibly tall man and very muscular. Mere noticed that, although he is quite a nice-looking, he has no airs about him. The patience he shows is odd. As they study him and are studied in return, they sense his calmness; his light blue eyes scan them and seem to be taking in every detail. Instead of questioning them, he waits for them to speak first. When Hyun asks him who he is, his rich voice washes over them.

"I am Joshua Garvie, the 1st Gunman of the Gunmen's Element in the People's Free Force. I am very pleased to meet you."

All Mere and Hyun could do was cry at the overwhelming relief that struck them, finally a warrior who may be able to help them. Even though they do not know anything more of this man that he is calm and polite, he did save Sophie from the eel. Sophee put an arm around each of her parents and tried unsuccessfully to control her crying. Making a good impression on Joshua would be what she is trying to do now. Sophee thought about Joshua's name, it was strong and she had never heard it before. He has a last name, which too is something to be proud off.

* * *

What happens then was surprising, because Hyun and Mere start sobbing. Even Sophee is crying a little. They were so emotional I thought they were going to lose their sanity. I take a breath and look at the cause, my presence, they might not know what a Gunman was but they know what a soldier is. This is what is making them cry. It makes me fell feel like I should wrap my arms around them. That would be weird, comforting these strangers. It makes me wonder how they would react.

I go to take another drink from my cup, but realize the glass is empty. Sophee notices this through her tears and jumps right up to refill it. Before I can even say thank you, she drops to her knees and throws her arms around me in a huge hug. I wonder if her parents saw a look of shock on my face, at least this time it didn't almost knock me off my feet when she touched me.

As though realizing she was crossing some invisible line, Sophee gets up quickly and goes back to sit against her mother. I see Mere smile through her tears at Sophee, and then looks very intensely at her daughter.

Sophee beams me the happiest smile I have ever seen, and she is either missing or ignoring her mother's scrutiny.

Why they are crying must have major significance, so I look at them with compassion while trying not stare. They take their own sweet time to regain their composure, and that makes me wonder why their reaction is so extreme. Whatever their problem is, I decide instantly to try to help. A smile crosses my face, because I do not care what their issue is; I just want to solve whatever problem causes so much emotional reactions.

The girl, Sophee, has her arms around her mother and Mere's arm is over Sophee's shoulder. Hyun is holding Mere's other hand. Looking at them I can see what a close family they are. If I had been a better son or grandson my relationship with mom and granddad could have been this strong, not that we would fall into a sobbing huddle though.

As I watch and wait for my hosts to calm themselves it becomes more apparent to me that Sophee is not just pretty, but drop dead beautiful. The term that suited her best would be breath-taking. Her mother is about the same size physically and is also pretty, but my eyes are continually drawn to Sophee for some reason.

Man, is she beautiful.

Sophee's looks are about all I could think of until I realized that I should be focusing on their problems and not their daughter's beauty. I have to force myself to look at Hyun, who has to be within an inch or two of the women's height and not nearly as interesting to look at. What could possibly upset this family so much?

Is it these eel things? Are they the issue, with minimal weapons that could be remedied?

It takes all of ten minutes for the crying to stop, and still I wait. Eventually Hyun is able to speak. "Our people have been on this planet for a long time, we do not know the exact duration."

"Then the unthinkable happened. The Gham attacked us for the first time, we lost many people. We worried that our previous explorations had brought us to the Gham's attention, so we stopped traveling. We tried to hide, but the Gham always found us, even though we went underground." He stopped speaking and was holding his hands clasped tightly together. The anguish in is voice showed as he shook.

I decided to break this train of thought which caused him so much pain so I spoke evenly to him. "You have two separate DNA signatures; one is human from Asia on old Earth. How did that happen?"

Hyun "About six hundred years ago one of our exploration ships made it to a planet very far away. Our scientist took DNA samples from the humans we found and grafted it to our species. What you can't see is the difference in our bodies and that we had great results, the species we took samples from allowed us to have these larger and healthier bodies."

I wonder if the larger bodies were to breed fighters. How could eels find them in caves? If they had starships why not leave to a place without eels. There are a lot of questions that needed to be asked and I was forming them into a large list. I study Hyun and his family; if this is bigger, then how small were they before the influx of Korean DNA?

"Yeah, you're monsters for sure," I quip.

The confusion on their faces is apparent. I guess they don't get irony or humor but in my own defense I am on a strange planet and I did warn Sophee about my humor during our walk here.

"Sorry, my sense of humor sometimes gets the best of me," I said "Where I am from you would be considered rather short. If the DNA from Earth helped you to attain larger frames, than you must have been quite small."

"Although you are very nice looking as a people, I honestly thought you were children when I first saw you." I shook my head; this was not what I wanted to say, or how I wanted to say it. Hopefully they are as forgiving as Sophee is pretty because they might take offense otherwise. "I mean absolutely no disrespect; it was a simple visual call at a distance."

Mere smiles; "You are a very different type of person than the Sooul. There is no worry in your heart about how you got here. You are very calm but I do detect a stubborn streak."

"Me? Stubborn?" I laugh aloud. "Am I that easy to read?"

Hyun meets my eyes and says, "We are all empaths. My mate and daughter are very perceptive. I see no evil or malice in you; only a very firm belief in what is right and wrong. Mere on the other hand looks deeper and sees more of what you would call your soul. My daughter is even more sensitive than we are."

"I see your humor," Mere starts, "and a dark place as well that you try to lock away."

"My belief is such that I think laughing is better that anger or tears," I reply. I then look to Sophee and raise an eyebrow. "Your review?" I ask curiously.

A flush of embarrassment crosses her face, "You are kind, but still look at us like we are children. You would have waited indefinitely before you asked why you are here. You have a solid belief of who you are and what you can do." She took a breath before continuing.

"When you saved me from the eel, it was with no extra effort in your mind. You strive to be more than what you are, but you have been changed by what you have seen. The dark places that my mother sees are well controlled or suppressed, which seems odd because there are no evil thoughts or bad intentions in your emotions." Sophee stops because if she continues her parents will figure out she is bonding and it would be better if they learned to like Joshua before having him possibly in the family.

I look at Sophee for a few seconds. "You may be the first person ever to call me kind, thank you. I always try to be courteous, but in my line of work it is not something I am called." I take a sip of my water before I address the rest of Sophee's comment about me. "Okay, then, since you think I will never ask, why is it that I am here?" I pause for a moment, and then grin. "See, I am not *too* stubborn."

Hyun stands and walks to the prep area to get more water for the pitcher. As Hyun returns he starts talking. "The one hundred and ninety people here are the last of our kind. Within a year, we will all be dead. By casting out our last retrieval sphere we hoped to bring someone back that might help us leave this planet; we do not care where we go, only that it is safe. We have some rare metals to help with the costs and are willing to sign ourselves as servants to leave."

"You have decent technology, so why not just kill the eels?" I ask.

"If you are able to kill an eel more will come to eat it, and then the new eels will stay in the area. But they are not the issue, the Gham are. They come and kill people every ten days; usually an entire family group dies."

As I am listening to their story, I sub-vocalize instructions to Vicky. "Find out all you can about Gham, including strengths and weakness."

I ask Hyun again, "Why not take them out? Are they that powerful?"

Mere is looking intently into my eyes and says, "You do not understand. As empaths we bond for life, and the killing of a sentient being, even if we were doing it to save a life, would drive us insane. If you were bonded, the insanity would also affect your mate. When the Gham comes, they usually take one person and slowly render them so they are in the most pain. They collect the emotional energy from the dying person and family. They then take off in their ship with the bodies only to return again in ten days."

"So you can't fight back?" I ask with surprise.

"Not against a sentient life form," Sophee informs me.

Vicky chimes in thru my implant. "I have scanned for the Gham and found various references to them in this sector, but no one knows where they are from."

I wonder why the P.F.F. has not heard of this yet. Had these Gham attacked anyone under our protection there would have been something done. If Vicky knows where we are we have to be on a fringe of the outer worlds. It could be that humans have not just run into the Gham, space is big. "Vicky, access the Sooul's database and get me as much information about the Gham as they have."

Within a few seconds she said, "Downloading."

I ask my hosts for a minute and I sit back and close my eyes as the data is downloading directly to my cerebral cortex. I can understand it would be odd to them and will have to explain about Vicky afterward. My primary responsibility is to find out what a Gham are and why they are harvesting these people. I know they are watching me sit with my eyes closed and it doesn't feel very odd, maybe because they are empaths and understand people better it seems more normal.

The data shows this was an older civilization. Records are spotty with gaps of time almost like they have had to merge damaged files. The population is down to one hundred and ninety people from five hundred million. Genocide, clearly the Gunman's Element needs to be involved. As I access the more recent data of the people of Sooul, I see that Sophee is un-bonded and there are no other males of her age left alive on the planet. It is very funny how Vicky thought to show that to me.

I check the data on the Gham and there a recounting that once in the very distant past a ship had landed on the beach and one of the Gham died from an eel attack. The other Gham returned to its ship and left. Ten days later another ship landed in the town with four Gham, and ever since it has always been four of them.

The Gham are bipeds, and stand at least seven feet tall. They have large upper bodies, arms that are almost ape-like, and very narrow legs and hips. The face is vaguely insectoid with small beady eyes and what looks like mandibles covering the mouth and nose area. Their entire bodies are dull brown in the torso and shiny black for the extremities.

"Vicky, what is a render?" I ask being unsure I really want to know, but knowing that I need to.

"There is a recent video on their database sir, but it is ugly." Vicky informs me.

"Show me," I order.

The video starts with four Gham stepping off the walkway of their ship. The ship is rather plain and boxy. It is a dull brown and less than thirty meters tall and the only feature on it that I can discern is the hatch and walkway. The ship actually looks like a rounded bullet with its motors hidden from view on the ground.

The Gham are walking around the kneeling Sooul, it appears to be more than a thousand of them who have spread out across the field in the center of this town.

As I am watching the video Vicky says, "Large families split up because the Gham always want the maximum kills for the minimum effort."

One of the aliens is carrying a metal staff which it pushes deeply into the ground, once the alien moves away from the staff I can see a dull yellow orb on the top of it. Once the staff is in the ground I notice that none of the other Gham is carrying weapons.

The Gham randomly pick out a young woman from the Sooul and grab her, each Gham grabbing an arm or leg. She struggles to get free but the Gham are huge and strong by Sooul standards. I notice that her family is crying and screaming even if the woman is remaining silent. I can feel the bile rise in my throat as this beautiful woman struggles with the Gham.

They lift her so she is stretched out, horizontal to the ground, and level with the Gham's' waist. They hold her with one talon as start clawing at her with their other talons until the woman can no longer keep quiet as the claws shred her clothes. The tattered material scatters on the ground until there is nothing left remaining on her body, and she is nude. Gouges and shallow slashes appear on the girl's skin as the Gham continue to claw at her, and she screams relentlessly.

I feel myself getting angry at what I see and wish to stop the video, but as a Gunman I must have all the data I can get in order to know what they do and the level of retribution I will inflict upon them. This pour woman was being killed in front of her family and by shutting it off I feel I would be lessoning her ordeal if I did not know everything about it.

The young woman is a bloody mess with deep lacerations all over her body and her screams are turning into frantic shrieks of pain. The five others in her family, who appear to be parents and sisters, are echoing every sound and seem to be in equal pain as they thrash around on the ground.

The staff's yellow orb begins to glow ever brighter as a pale mist seems to leave the dying family. The orb absorbs their energy like smoke into a vent. The rest of the Sooul have turned away from the suffering family not wanting to have to watch how they too will eventually die. The Gham's bug-like faces are expressionless and their actions are robotic as they work the poor woman.

The aliens then begin to pull hard on their victim's extremities, and the poor girl gives an even louder shriek as her arm comes off at the elbow. I do not really need to explain how they finish her off, but let us say a more miserable way of dying would be hard to find. I wouldn't even call it a rendering or killing. It was torture pure and simple.

Gham cause as much pain to an individual as they could by torturing them to create pain for the rest of the family. They all die, the whole family dies. The video was singularly the nastiest thing I have seen.

The Gham then collect the dead up into their arms, and carry them to the ship. What they need the energy for is unknown and the bodies were likely food for the soldiers. The video ends with the ship taking off; from the lack of flames they must be using a reactionless drive. The ship disappears quickly while the families reunite. There is a lot of tears and hugging.

* * *

Hyun, Mere, and Sophee sit quietly while their guest closes his eyes, and watch his face for any reactions or hints with what he was doing. They can sense his decency and are willing to give this man time to absorb or think of what he needs. Sophee takes a minute to read the man she has started to bond with, she is able to sense him far better than her parents.

Sophee looks at her mother. "Joshua has been having one-sided conversations with something that invokes emotion. He is full of disgust at the moment and I don't know why."

Mere is totally surprised at her daughter's ability to read the stranger, either he is an easy mind or something is going on. Sophee's hand goes to her mouth with a gasp; she was reading his sorrow when something ugly and feral flashed across Joshua's mind. The emotion he projected was so powerful when it touched her mind that the impact of it brought her to tears again. The absolute strength of conviction and the depth of resolve that radiated from Joshua was like a tidal wave. One that was calming because it was absolute, instantly she knew what the resolve was about. Death is coming to the Gham.

Her mother and father reached for Sophee to calm her when they saw the tears pour out of her eyes.

In a very soft voice Sophee said, "*We are saved.*"

Mere accepts that as the truth and continues to try to read her daughter's emotions. Unless Sophee is bonding she should not be able to sense so much from a man.

Sophee slowly pushes away from her parents to approach the still motionless Joshua. She knelt beside him, and put her hand softly on his cheek, for Joshua's sorrow tugged at her heart. Hyun watched Sophee with increasing concern; she was showing signs of bonding.

"Sophee," he said quickly, "this man is not of our world. His ways are not ours, and he is an unknown person. We even don't know whom the Gunmen work for."

Sophee speaks in almost a whisper, as she continues to gaze at the man before her. "It doesn't matter now."

Her mother is smiling as she quietly addresses her mate. "It will work out Hyun. The bond is well on its way." Hyun shakes his head in disagreement but stayed silent.

* * *

I open my eyes to see Sophee moving her hand slowly away from my cheek. I look over and see Mere smiling and Hyun not looking happy at all. I sub-vocalize to Vicky. "What just happened?"

Vicky sounds almost smug, "Sophee was reading your emotions and now feels that her people will get help from you. She may also have more than generally nice feelings toward you."

I sit up straighter, take a deep calming breath to steady my thoughts, and turn to speak to my hosts. "I have a personal artificial intelligence device that can communicate with me sub-vocally. Her name is Vicky, and she knows where we are." From the lack of surprise they must have known something was going on.

"These Gham creatures need to be dealt with!"

As soon as the words leave my lips, Sophee and her mother could see that my emotions were flat and calm from which was a very quick change from what I was feeling when watching the video in the previous minutes. Neither said a word about my control and how my emotions could lock down like that but would probably talk about it later.

"When is the next ten-day?" I ask.

"The Gham will not speak to you, they never speak just kill," Mere said.

"I never said that I wanted to speak with them." I said with a firm expression.

* * *

I shivered when Joshua said that he did not want to talk to the Gham. The tight smile was almost as menacing as his emotions when he was reviewing data on the Gham. My dad is still looking at me with a worried look because he is sensing that a bond is forming. Neither mom nor dad realizes what this big man is. Sure my Joshua looks like a huge scary warrior but his heart is filled with equal parts of good and darkness. That darkness has a mortal enemy now. There is no telling if it is confidence in his weapons or in himself that he feels. One thing is for certain, the Gham have a foe, someone who will not be a victim.

* * *

Hyun has not taken his eyes off his daughter the entire time. Guess I had better be careful then.

"May I call you Sophee?" I ask formally trying to show respect and manners.

"Of course you may Joshua." Sophee said with a beautiful smile.

Weird, when she said my name it rolled off her tongue so softly and slightly seductive I actually liked it. Sophee is looking into my eyes, which makes me think about how perceptive they are with their gifts. I know her father is watching her like a hawk. I figure that trying to screw up her name so she would be annoyed and stay away from me will not work.

Seducing a young woman into my bed was not my style anyway, good thing as she would see thru that as well. The thoughts of both these things made me smile even when I knew she could read my amusement.

Sophee smiles at me too, which is rather odd to see with tears still on her face.

"What is the flash of humor about?" Sophee asks.

There is no way I am going to open my mouth to put my foot in it, being empaths they would know an untruth so I clam up.

I have to ask again about the Gham's next visit before I get and answer from Hyun.

"Seven days. Can we leave before they get here?"

"Vicky," I say, "Go active vocally. How long before we can get a ship here?"

"Four to six weeks depending on what ship gets the request for pick up, the ship's schedule and where the ships currently are now."

I decide that without having a ship within a close distance to either move the Sooul or fight the Gham it will be totally up to me. Four Gham should not give me much of a problem. I wonder though what will happen when they don't return home or to where ever they go. Will another Gham ship come in another ten days or will one be back right away? Minimum time to get a P.F.F. ship here is twenty-eight days. There is no way to get the Sooul off planet before the Gham come. Hiding the Sooul from the Gham is out of the question based on what they told me. I don't run either because it would only make you die tired. Even if we could run the Gham will still be a danger to humanity.

"It is better that I deal with these Gham now," I said. I look to my hosts and ask, "Is there a place nearby where I can stay while we wait for these creatures show up?"

Hyun looks a little happier that though I am leaving their home, I am not going too far. It is obvious that he does not want me around his daughter. Mere on the other hand looks like she was about to offer something, but stayed silent.

"Most of the homes in the town are empty, pick any dark home," Hyun tells me.

I had a strange feeling that Sophee and Mere don't want me to leave, but are not going to say anything to disrespect Hyun or counter his instructions to take any home.

I stand up from my cushion on the floor, and thank them for the refreshment. I move to the door quickly to leave. I put my boots back on. I grab my pack and rifle before saying my good-byes, and slip out of the house. I stand for a minute on their porch in the warm evening before leaving.

I look past a few of the lit homes at one that was dark and realize that I could not bear going into some murdered Sooul's home. I don't know if it is out of respect for the dead or that being in such a place would not be mentally relaxing knowing how they died. Tomorrow I will at least find some better food since I left Hyun's place before they fed me.

CHAPTER 8

I start walking through the town and head toward the wall that surrounds the cove. Without thinking about the direction I am taking I am slipping into back into Gunman mode and automatically go towards the threat. If there is a wall, there has to be something bad on the other side. Even if it was, half-eaten and not a present threat there could be others.

I key the buttons on my sleeve and turn my battle suit back to green digital tiger stripe camouflage. I sit on the ground cross-legged and lean against a planter that holds a single tree. It is a fairly small bushy tree that I have never seen before in a hard plastic type planter. My eyes continually switch from watching the gate to watching along the wall. Maybe two hours until total darkness, I figure.

"Well, I have slept in worse places Vicky." I say aloud.

"You should have gone to an empty home and slept somewhere comfortable." Vicky scolds me like my mother did when I was young.

I grin at Vicky voice, "Passive scans please."

So here I sit watching the wall with no supper, no adults around to talk with, I guess it is lucky that I am more of a loner, but it would have been nice to have a little bit of dinner and a nice conversation. The Sooul seem like easy people to talk with as I could just speak my mind and their empathic abilities would allow them to know I was sincere.

Of course, I would have to try to hide my growing infatuation with their daughter. This causes me to smile because she is unlike any girl I have ever met. The way she softly talks and looks at me like I'm the most important person in her existence makes me want to get to know her better. The fact the Sooul can still function after losing hundreds of millions of citizens amazes me. I also realize that because the Sooul do have a semi normal life they have to be strong mentally.

I make myself comfortable by removing my pack, cradle my rifle in my arms, and look up at the gate. I am surprised they do not have a sentry on duty with these eels being such a problem. The Sooul will have one now, and for the next week if they like it or not. I was getting a little hungry, but would wait until later to have a Kcal. Leaning back a bit I study the gate. It doesn't look very strong, but the electrical field must work well enough to stop your typical eel.

* * *

Back in the house Sophee rises from the cushion she sat on to address her father who was still standing by the door after Joshua left.

"We told Joshua that we would feed him father! One of us should have showed him where he could sleep as well afterward. Sending our savior away unfed is very unkind; you have raised me better than that."

Hyun looks at his daughter with surprise. She has never been as forceful, but now she was very different, almost like Mere when they bonded.

Sophee heads for the prep area, she then keys a few buttons on the food processor. A couple of pounds of raw boneless fish fillets appear on the pad inside the device as they are recovered from stasis. Sophee is quick to retrieve the meat and start cutting them up into strips for cooking.

Mere wanders past her surprised husband to the prep area and puts her arm around Sophee to give her a warm hug. "Let me help you."

The mother and daughter cook the meat on a small grill and, once it is cooled, they slice it further before adding some vegetables. Then the pair rolls it with rice-like material in a seaweed wrap.

Hyun watches this whole process with trepidation, it is not normal for Sophee to speak like a bonded woman. Sophee has got far more meat out than they will eat. Mere seems to be very understanding of their daughter's attitude. Mere sensing the changes that her daughter is feeling tries to draw out Sophee's thoughts in a conversation. When the older woman asks her daughter what she is thinking, and Sophee smiles rather uncertainly Mere knows she is in the right track.

"I don't know if he will like me," her daughter said, "but I sense he is a really true person. He is kind, and that lack of fear in his heart that you could sense is only the top layer of his personality.

"Whenever I think about Joshua my heart feels odd. My goal will be to get to know him better, and find out if I can be the one he chooses." Sophee looks at her mother a moment, to see her reaction. "That is provided Joshua bonds like the Sooul do and if we live through the next ten day."

Mere can sense Sophee's reserved joy and opens her arms to hug Sophee again without saying a word before turning back to the food. They finish making the rolls of fish and vegetables. Sophee divides it in half so her parents can have dinner.

"Mother, Father, I am taking dinner out to my Joshua." Sophee fills a small jug with wine and puts it in a basket with plates, the food and a couple of glasses. Sophee is surprised that her father said nothing when she left.

"He is a good man," Mere states to her husband. "I sense it too, and am never wrong."

"Have you seen the size of him?" Hyun asks. "He must weigh at least three times what we do. Those muscles make him very frightening, not to mention the weapons he carries. Can a warrior be a good choice for our daughter to make? He appears dangerous, but looks and ability can be very different things. What if he cannot come through for us? Are we getting our hopes up, just to be let down? Does Sophee deserve to be hurt or have more unfulfilled things in her life?"

Mere, seeing that Hyun was pretty wound up let him finish venting before replying. "Sophee is not afraid of him, and she has more skills than you or I will ever have. Her choice is made; we will have to wait to see if Joshua chooses Sophee in return." Mere smiled at Hyun. "The absolute worst thing that can happen is Sophee will have seven good days before the Gham come back, and she deserves to have that happiness."

"I still don't like it," Hyun grumbles into his cup of wine.

"Neither did my father with you!" Mere reminds him.

* * *

Sophee paused outside her door to look around,

searching for Joshua. She stood there for a few minutes, uncertain, until a child heading home pointed toward the gate. With a smile Sophee shooed the child towards his home in hope he would hurry along. She did not want an audience when she took Joshua his dinner.

Walking quickly towards the gate, Sophee wondered if Joshua went outside of the wall. She hoped he didn't, because it is a bad time of day to be near the water because of the eels. As she passes one of the planters, Sophee notices Joshua sitting motionless, cross-legged, with his thunder weapon resting on his lap. His eyes are watching the entire wall and gate which, to Sophee's surprise, makes her feel very warm and safe. *Here I worry because my father let him leave and he is already protecting us.* Sophee is unsure why, after the insult of not feeding him and allowing him to leave she worried if he would be here still. The strong purpose filled heart she sensed would never do that and she should have had more faith in him. Feeling bad and standing there quietly in the dark gives her a minute to study her Joshua and read his emotions. He looks relaxed but ready for anything with that big weapon on his lap. Reading is emotions is easy, he is happy and content which is so odd knowing what is coming and the fact he has to deal with the Gham.

The is a slight questioning part in his mind that lets Sophee know that either he heard her coming or his Vicky machine told him. Sophee takes a step toward Joshua and quietly clears her voice.

"Excuse me Joshua?" She says as she approaches.

Sophee moves into Joshua's sight line. "I have brought you some supper, there is a lot here. Is it okay if I join you?"

"Be careful you do not upset your father," he replies. "I

am not empathic, but I can only imagine how fathers may feel about their little girls."

* * *

At my words, Sophee's eyes damn near set fire to me.

"Is that how you look at me?" she demanded. "Like a little girl?"

Did she just stamp her foot in the sand? She is a fiery little thing, the thought made me almost laugh. I made sure not to let her see my amusement, though, for fear of how she might react.

"Well, I don't want to hurt your feelings, but yes," I answer somewhat honestly. She is beautiful and seems quite sweet, but *damn* does she look young.

She lowers her eyes and asks, "May I talk with your Vicky machine?"

That's odd I thought, let's see what she really wants. "Sure," I answer. "Vicky, please go active."

"Hello, Sophee," my A.I. says thru the speakers built into my pack. "How can I help you?"

"Can you answer a few questions from your scans?"

"Continue," Vicky says.

"How long is a Sooul day?"

After Vicky answers that it is twenty-four point six hours, Sophee asks another question. "How long is a Sooule Year?"

"Three hundred and fifty two days," is Vicky's reply.

"Can you scan me and tell me how old I am?

"Twenty of your years, Sophee." Apparently Vicky knew where Sophee was going with this and I suspected where she was headed too.

"Joshua already knew this Sophee."

Sophee then looks directly into my eyes and says, "Most of my people bond and mate when they are seventeen or so, and I am twenty. Do you think a child could have made you this meal?" She stands holding out a plate and a jug for my inspection. With an expression of exasperation on her face, she continues to look into my eyes awaiting my response.

On immediate retrospect, I am acting like a jerk. Yes, she looks young to me, but she a mature adult. I am not narrow-minded about most things. Just because she looks young, should I be treating her like a kid?

Little steps, Josh, I think to myself. I really need to smarten the hell up. Maybe some of my people skills have backslid while I was in the Element. I certainly could use more interaction with people. I can fix this; I know I can if I just put some effort into it. Taking a breath, I say; "Sophee, thank you for bringing dinner and most certainly, join me."

A smile crosses her face and I can see her relax for the first time since approaching me. I hadn't realized how uncertain Sophee had been until she smiled.

"Okay," she answers softly as she dropped to her knees across from me. Reaching for the jug, she pours me a cup of wine. The taste is light, but the alcohol content could impair my reflexes or judgment and that would not be a good thing. Not when you have a pretty girl who may need protection sitting with you.

"Vicky," I say sub-vocally, "Remove the effect of the alcohol as I drink it and then go inactive."

Vicky goes vocal and says; "Goodnight Sophee," and then goes passive.

Sophee asks if Vicky is sentient and to that I answer, "I

do not think so but I try to treat her with respect as if she is. This way I have done nothing but treat her kindly even if I am wrong."

Sophee hands me a small plate and uses some tongs to put several of the rolled things on my dish. I do not really care what they are; not eating a Kcal supplement already has me pleased. I am pretty open to trying any kind of food, and this plateful looks and smells good. Before I try a bite, I look into Sophee's eyes and apologize for treating her like a child. I explain to her that in my society hitting on a girl as young as she looks would be considered pedophilia.

"Why would you hit me, is the food that bad looking?" She innocently asks.

I start laughing at her question until tears roll out of my eyes. "Where I am from, if you are trying to get a girl in bed we call it hitting on them, we don't actually hit them."

Sophee still looks confused for a second, then asks; "why would you want a girl that you are not bonded with in your bed?"

Damn, is she serious? "You know... for sex?"

Sophee looks down and says; "We know about love of course, but can you mate with someone who you are not bonded with?"

So here I am having a talk with a very beautiful girl who obviously looks very young and she is asking questions about my love life. Sure, she is not a teenager maybe I should treat her like the adult she is, but I still am a little uncomfortable with the situation.

I am a Gunman for god's sake. Why should I be uncomfortable?

Maybe the walls I have put up don't allow for

relationships. During training I went to peeler bars with some of the troops, but was there for the beer. Girls, while desirable, are the only thing that scares the shit out of me. I do not seem nervous around them and I don't hit on them, instead I act all *Gunman*. Quiet, dangerous, away on missions... pathetic really.

"Sophee, in most of the galaxy that I know, being bonded has nothing to do with mating. I do not engage in casual mating because, honestly, I have not found the right girl yet. Making and keeping close relationships has always been difficult for me because the direction my life has taken." I pause for a minute then whisper to her, "Please don't tell anyone you meet that I told you that. I have my tough guy reputation to consider."

"Is this tough guy reputation important to you?" Sophee teasingly asks.

"Actually, I would rather my actions define who I am rather than a reputation. Being the 1st Gunman usually is enough of a reputation."

Sophee Looks down at my untouched plate, "You have not tried the food yet," she said.

"It looks great. You made this?"

She smiles and nods again. "I used the fish I caught when your thunder weapon stopped the eel."

I take a bite to be pleasantly surprised by the flavor. "This is good," I say as I take another mouthful. The slices of the fish rolls were absolutely delicious. Wow, She's a good cook and beautiful. Sophee waits until I have eaten a few before she draws me back into our conversation. "When you said you do not hit on girls, you were embarrassed. Truth rings out in your words, as well as your emotions."

"Are you going to have some?" I ask as I point at her untouched plate.

"Don't change the subject," she says, ignoring the fact she had done the same just moments earlier. "What is a pedophilia?"

"It is when bad people sexually abuse children. It is a foul crime that I would arrest a man for." I answer back.

She doesn't look upset by my casual statement, but she doesn't smile at it either because I know she can read the seriousness of my emotions when I spoke.

"Have you decided to treat me like an adult now?" Sophee asks quietly.

"Without the sex, yes, we can be adults," I causally claim.

"No one on Sooule does that anyway," Sophee says with a soft laugh. "We only share love after bonding."

This makes me grin and allows me to quip; "Someone must sell a lot of white dresses."

Sophee pauses from taking a small bite to ask; "What is a dress?"

Before I can answer, I hear a splash and then a thump at the gate. I spring to my feet pulling my pack on before the gate starts to buckle in. The breeze carries a wet fishy smell to me as I realize whatever came to feed on the carcass is too big to be concerned with the semi-electrified fence.

A quick visual scan reveals there are no children or people in sight and I realize is it starting to get quite dark. Sophee was surprised when I jumped up and had not started to move yet when I reach down to pick her up like a sack of potatoes. I run like hell for higher ground up by the wall for a better shooting position and to get Sophee out of immediate danger. I gently lower her to the ground and

The 1st Gunman

see her eyes go wide with fear when the gate collapses into a hundred pieces as the eel pushes through the gate.

It is easy to surmise that a creature this size is hungry, wither it could smell people when it came ashore or it was just searching for food I do not know.

"Vicky, go active," I instruct. "How many eels are there?" I ask. In the growing darkness it is hard to see what is approaching.

Vicky says "one on shore and two more large ones coming into the harbor."

I palm open the bolt on my rifle to remove the armor piercing bullets and reach back to my belt pouch to pull four out unset warhead rounds. "Vicky, set the yield at fifty percent." Variable explosive ammunition works like a programmable bomb.

"Done," she answers.

I reload the rifle and step over to the edge of the hill. The eel has completely pushed through the gate and swings its massive head back and forth, looking for a target. This sea creature is huge; at least twice the size of the now missing dead one. It is darker in color than to one that I previously killed and seems to be moving easily despite being out of water.

I shoulder my rifle and quickly sight in on its eye and let loose with a round that penetrates the head and detonates with the force of fifty lbs of hyper-explosive. The eel's body flops to the side when most of its head vaporizes and leaves its body in a spray of gore. "I am death and I have come for you," escapes my lips.

In full Gunman mode now, I turn to see Sophee standing just a few feet from me looking ashen. "Please stay up here where it is safe" I tell her as I maneuver for my second shot. The eel that followed the huge one is smaller and faster I take a quick snap shot that blows the eel in half about six feet behind the head.

Vicky yells in my head; "Sophee!"

I turn and see that the gate's destruction has destroyed the electrical field and now eels can come over the wall. Above and behind Sophee, another eel was just starting to rise up to pass over the wall and Sophee would be the meal of choice. I cannot take a shot with a warhead round without possible hurting or killing her, so I do the next best thing I can think of. I don't have time to sling my rifle so I drop it, as sprint back towards her I draw my .40-caliber sig to start firing rounds into the eel above Sophee's head. When I am four yards from her and still firing, I launch myself into the air to put myself between the Sophee and the eel.

* * *

It is funny how a man like Joshua blushes and stumbles over his words when he talks to me. It is a good feeling to see him enjoying the dinner I made him. There is a splash in the water from behind the gate and in a flash Joshua picks me up and runs up the hill near the wall. His emotions are calm but I can feel that he is not running away. Joshua set me down very gently and pulls the big thunder weapon from his shoulder to check it. He works fast to replace what must be the projectiles. The eel that smashed the gate is the largest one I have ever seen. Joshua moves forward and I can tell he is totally focused on the eel. He is not even breathing hard after carrying me up the hill. His weapon thunders once and the eel just exploded. I can sense no excitement which is odd. Joshua quietly said something about death when the eel blew up. When Joshua looked back to check on me he smiled. His voice was calm but commanding when he told me to stay put. When he pulls his weapon to his shoulder again it strikes me that this is as natural to Joshua as breathing, every motion is smooth and fluid like he has done it thousands of times. Another eel dies and Joshua's head snaps back to look at me as he is pulling out a smaller weapon. This one is not as loud and he is shooting up high above me. It only took him three strides to reach me and he jumps over me into an eel's open mouth. The eel was coming over the wall silently and would have eaten me in another second. There is no sound from Joshua when he drops that weapon too and pulls out a large knife to stab the eel in the eye. The small weapon hits the ground so I grab it quickly as Joshua lands with a thump on the ground. I toss his weapon to him and he actually thanked me. I can feel he is in pain but he just keeps fighting. His weapon sounds like one long bang as he shoots up at the wounded eel. I scream, "Joshua" as the creature collapses on him. He is not dead I can still sense him and see the eel move a bit and my Joshua pulls himself free from under the eel. He gets to his feet quickly for someone who was in an eel's mouth and almost crushed. I am surprised to hear him speak so calmly when he asks me to please stay close to him. How can he even walk? Blood is running down his legs and pooling on the ground yet he picks his big weapon up, checks it and then starts shooting again. Are all humans this tough?

* * *

As I passed by Sophee's head with my leap the eel struck at me, grabbing my left leg in its toothy mouth. It is very unpleasant to feel the teeth grate against your thigh bone; the pain is something good because it made me focus tighter on my chore. I lost my hold on the sig and dropped it when the eel tried to get a better grip on the tasty morsel hanging out of its jaws. I pulled my combat knife out of its sheath with my right hand as my left got a tenuous grip on the eels head. I stabbed forward burying the knife into the huge unblinking eye as fast and any many time as I could thinking if I mauled it enough I might be able to push through to the brain.

The eel reacts to the pain and loss of its eye by opening its mouth and shaking its head so violently it threw me to the ground. I land hard on my side and quickly bounce to my feet trying to ignore the wounds in my leg. Sophee seeing me get to my feet tosses me back my sig. Blood is splashing down around us from the eel shaking its head to try and relieve the pain from its ruined eye. I reload the pistol quickly and limp closer for a better shot.

"Thank you," I say to Sophee as the eel's head rears back like a snake about to strike. Ensuring Sophee is safe makes me stand between her and the eel. I raise the sig and then proceed to blast the living crap out of the eel from my position under its jaw. The bullets went directly up into the eel's brain. The pain from my wound is a constant companion now and my leg is throbbing badly as I unload every round into the eel. During the last two shots I could see the head of the eel start to sway and wobble slightly to the side.

I drop the empty clip as I try to scramble to the side to reload, but my injured leg gives out as the dying eel collapses. I hear Sophee scream my name in a warning as it lands on me knocking the breath out of me. Thank god, it was not a giant; I have a difficult time breathing as I push at the slippery mass of flesh. I push more on the ground with my good leg and shrimp my body sideways until I clear the eel. As I slowly struggle to stand, Sophee points at the open gate and I turn to see a more eels sliding over the first two. I don't know what is drawing them here so fast. If three can turn into a several how many are going to come. First one, then three now a bunch, to me it looks like a swarm.

I limp, mostly dragging my left leg, over to my rifle and pick it up. I blow the dirt off the action and check the scope and barrel for obstructions. My Remington is a tough well built rifle and shows no sign of damage.

"Please stay close behind me, Sophee," I request.

I reach for my ammo pouch and say, "Vicky, all rounds fifties." Rather than having to set the basic bullets from amour piercing to explosive by hand Vicky can scan and program them as they come out of the pouch.

I fully reload my rifle as Sophee points toward her parents place. An eel slides toward it looking for its next meal. Knowing how they could take out the gate the house would not be a safe refuge. The look on Sophee's face says it all; she is scared to death for her parents.

Oh yea of little faith. Moving closer to the edge of the hill was very painful with my leg throbbing incessantly; I concentrate on my task at hand and push the pain to the back of my mind. If I avoid moving too much more it will not bother me until Vicky can get the nanites into full repair mode.

Seating the rifle stock into my shoulder gives me purpose. Everything instantly goes into slow motion. The low light scope brings the eel approaching Sophee's parent's home clearly into focus, the crosshairs line up with an eye. With a simple caress of the trigger I end the eel's existence in a cloud of pink mist and then address the next creature attacking the village. The sixth eel also tried to come thru the gate over top of the dead ones and lost its head in the same manner. I reload the rifle as I watch more eels break free from the water. Five more shots with explosions and it is over, nothing is moving for the time being.

"Sophee can you call everyone into one area?"

"Sure, but why?" she asks in a daze.

Either she is in shock from the attack or the sound of the shooting has affected her. She seems like she is concerned or preoccupied.

"If everyone is in the same area it will be easier to protect the village, because I will know what places to specifically defend."

"Can you still walk?" Sophee asks, the concern in her voice is evident when she puts a gentle hand on my arm.

"Oh, yeah, I will be fine in a while. Right, Vicky?" I say somewhat trying to minimize her worried expression.

"Sophee can you get more food?" Vicky asks through the speaker on my pack. "Joshua will need fuel and water for his body to heal."

Damn, my leg starts throbbing again as I limp slowly down the hill with Sophee. Good thing the wounds were caused by dagger like teeth, punctures will heal quicker than a slash. Pushing the pain further back in my mind to focus on the mission is a chore. Protection, no bloody eel is going to harm anyone. I stand a little straighter as I move back down to the ruined gate.

* * *

We get closer to Sophee's parent's place I see can see their eyes peering thru the doorway.

Sophee yells "Mom, Dad" and runs to them. Her father and mother grab her in a tight embrace happy to see her safe.

Sophee says; "Come father we must call the rest."

"Vicky, are you scanning any more eels yet"

"Nothing of size yet in the harbor, but more are coming," she answers.

"These eels emit and very high pitched sound wave in the 150 kilo-hertz range before they attack which draws in other eels, from the sounds that are being returned there is a lot more eels heading this way." Vicky warns me.

I finish reloading the sig and holster it. The rifle is slung over my shoulder and I take a sip from the hydration pouch in my pack. It tasted good so I continued to drink until it was empty. The nanites must be working overtime replacing blood and sealing the leg wounds. It would explain why I am so thirsty.

As the people start arriving they are all talking rapidly, without Vicky translating for me their voices are just a buzz of noise.

"Vicky, amplify," I instruct. My voice booms out over the crowd. "You lost your gate to a large eel and several more made it through. There are now a lot of smaller ones in the bay and they will be coming ashore shortly, drawn by their calls and blood of the dead ones. Stay inside these first groups of homes tonight I will know what area to defend. It doesn't matter if eels can come around the outside of the gate or through it, you will be safe.

Sophee and her parents quickly led the rest of the crowd

to their house and the three other that are beside it. The crowd quickly splits up and goes inside the homes. Sophee returns out of her parent's home with another small plate of food and is looking a bit scared.

Amusing as it is to see her eyes so wide I said "please go inside with your parents they will need you to help keep your people calm."

These people don't know who is on their side I think to myself. Sophee puts her hand on my chest for a second and then walks quickly to her home and disappears inside. To conserve rifle ammo I decide to get out my .17-caliber railgun from my pack. I really hate it, but long gun ammo will not last forever. I finish the small plate of food. Opening my pack I find the railgun and holster. I remove extra ammo from the pack as well before putting my sig inside for storage.

"Vicky, give me a damage update please." I ask.

Vicky responds; "Twelve deep puncture wounds; they will be sealed within a half an hour. You need to eat more and drink at least a gallon of fluid to replace the blood you lost. By your elevated blood pressure you must be in a fair bit of discomfort. Would you like the pain receptors turned down?"

"No, I will live with it. How low is the gravity here?" I ask.

Vicky immediately replies, ".78 normal."

I think of old Earth normal, which is the lower than New Harvest by about twenty percent. I knew I felt light on my feet but now understand why I could jump so high. Good thing too because that eel would have eaten Sophee as a snack. It made me wonder if the higher gravity makes my skeletal structure stronger as well. It did surprise me that the eel didn't actually bite my leg off.

"That jump must have been impressive to Sophee," Vicky says.

"Why do you think that?" I ask her.

Vicky doesn't respond right away and I know what she is doing. I see the personal assistant rearing its ugly head try to play matchmaker. I guess I should not be too surprised as Vicky has told me I need a girlfriend or companionship for years. Vicky gives me a minute or so to think about what Sophee saw before saying anything

"Odds are that you did look like some kind of superman to Sophee," she says.

"Stuff it Vic," I say with another smile.

"You have been on this planet for a little more than two days and yet, by my count, there have been at least thirty smiles revolving around one person. Other than the wound, your blood pressure has been low and relaxed. It is funny that your heart rate increases only around that one girl too. If you live through this little adventure it might end up being a good vacation for you."

"My smiles are usually on the inside," I quip.

"Sure, Joshua," she says with a skeptical voice.

I put a magazine into the railgun and drop another four into my pocket. It is a slow painful walk back to the gate. I squeeze past the dead eels and move into the opening where I can see the entire beach.

"Vicky; scan behind me at the town, inform me if any eels make it inside the gate," I said.

* * *

Back in the crowded house Sophee was telling Shoran how amazed she was with Joshua's attitude, here he was talking about his belief and about love and then he turns into this fearless killing machine. He was wounded and still is fighting. It's enough to leave a normal person in shock, but not him. Sophee is watching Joshua thru the open door, he limps toward the beach and she speaks out loud to her father.

"Did you notice how he reloaded his weapons and moves to protect us without any thought of his own safety even though he is wounded?" Sophie then gives a small sob. "My Joshua has blood still running down his leg and he is hurting."

Shoran and the other close by could see that Sophie was upset by tried to give her room which was not easy in the crowded house. The sunken living room had children laying everywhere and the adults stood in small groups wondering if they would live thru the eel attacks tonight.

Hyun says; "His A.I. is probably blocking the pain for him."

Mere smiles at her husband and slowly gives her head a shake. "I can feel his discomfort from here in the house, he is in a fair bit of pain yet he accepts it. I can also sense amusement and I don't know why. What I find really odd is the fact there is no hesitation in his actions. Joshua has no fear, only purpose. Remember what you said, my dear, about a warrior's appearance and ability? I feel his ability exceeds his appearance."

Hyun is quick to nod to his wife's view because she was the second strongest empath or reader of all the Sooul. Even if he can't sense at that level the women in his life can.

Sophee turns to her friend who had just come from the prep area and says; "When the eel broke thru the gate he picked me up like I weighed nothing at all and ran uphill to defend the town. My Joshua killed several eels and jumped over me into the eel's mouth. When he dropped his small weapon he was still fighting with his knife. He is incredibly fast and strong!"

"Well," Shoran says, "You would expect him to be strong have you had a really good look at him? He is a huge man, all those muscles!"

"I wonder if he could live with one of the people of Sooul." Shoran gets a smile on her face at the thought.

Shoran, a year younger than Sophee is her best friend and is in the same situation. No men of mating age that are not already bonded live on Sooul. Since it is unlikely she will live long enough to bond her and Sophee have become best friends, sisters, confidants.

Sophee turns scarlet and Shoran notices immediately. Wait… Sophee called him "My Joshua." Sophee's reaction was a definite sign, are they bonding so soon?

"Oh, Sophee, are you not afraid of him?" she asks breathlessly.

Sophee looks down embarrassed to meet Shoran eyes and was afraid to raise her face for fear that her father will show his disapproval. Everyone has gone silent and is listening to their conversation. In a home so small and full of people it was like a public display.

"I don't know how I feel," Sophee admitted. "We have only known each other for a day. He is kind and funny, but I think he is uncertain about me."

Shoran's face looks upbeat as she hugs her best friend. "I know that you will be who he will want."

Mere is standing in the prep area listening with everyone else as they studiously ignore the mini-drama taking place.

Even though they hear everything they look away and pretend the family has privacy.

Hyun touches his wife on the shoulder, "My dear, I will be more understanding as I now see our daughter's bond is already forming. I will treat our Joshua with the utmost respect and kindness from this time forward. I think he has no idea of the bonding process, and he did save my daughter for the second time."

Hyun then turns to the rest of the Sooul in his home and says; "Please treat Joshua like a Sooul and not like he is only a warrior here to save us. When we cast the last of our spheres we had hoped to escape this planet and we had no idea that this might happen with my daughter."

Sophee's embarrassment was lessened by her father's truthful announcement. Mere and Sophee both could tell that even if he was unsure about Joshua personally he trusted Sophee's instinct. Sophee felt totally safe and secure when she was with Joshua outside but her father could not sense things like she did and was no here near as comfortable with Joshua.

Joshua had left so quickly to deal with the eels there was no time to bandage his wounds, and Sophee was concerned that the bleeding would weaken Joshua or make him ill. He was endangering himself for all of them, without a second thought. His AI said he needed food and water to help him heal so she decided to broach the subject of food with her father.

"Father, his A.I. asked me to ensure he got enough food to help the healing process for his wounds. I am worried that because of his size the small plate I gave him may not be enough. May I take him some more?"

The 1st Gunman

"No, I brought him here it should be me." Hyun said seriously.

Sophee could feel her father's love and relished in the warmth of it. Even if Hyun were scared to death of the eels, he would not allow his daughter to take his place. Both Sophee and Mere could sense Hyun's fear and were impressed that he would endanger himself taking the food to Joshua.

The sounds of rapid-fire bangs can be heard from behind the wall and instantly everyone knew that Joshua was shooting again.

Sophee dials up all the fish from stasis to make a lot more dinner. Sophee, Shoran, and Mere start cooking and rolling the fish into the same type of seaweed rolls Sophee and her mother had made for Joshua earlier that evening. Sophee concentrated on making the first large plate of food for her Joshua. Mere and Shoran continued to make more seaweed rolls for their guests that had not eaten yet this evening.

Mere is quick to point out, "If we survive this eel attack there will be lots of meat available tomorrow."

"Hopefully we can get to them before the scavengers start feeding." Hyun muses.

"Mother, with my Joshua protecting us we will all be fine in the morning," Sophee said as she hands her father the larger plate of food she made with a jug of water.

"Go carefully please Hyun." Mere requests looking worried.

Hyun takes a deep breath and walks thru to the door that dilates open. Sophee looks to her mom and says; "Dad is being very brave going out there, if he could believe what I know he would not have to be so brave."

Mere is amazed at her daughter's positive outlook. She knows that Sophee ability is much more sensitive than her own to subtle nuances in personalities, but to have this level of faith in a person she has only known for a day?

"My Joshua is not afraid at all," Sophee continues. "When he was walking toward the gate he was not worried about his leg or the eels, he was just in some kind of battle mode where he knows what he has to do and does it. His only thought was a protective emotion. I am not afraid of the eels anymore because of my Joshua but I am worried about the pain he might be feeling and ignoring. Seeing him wounded bothers me, because he was saving me when he got hurt."

Mere smiles at Sophee and can sense the amount of faith she has in Joshua's ability to keep Hyun safe which of course makes her feel so much better. Mere is happy with her daughter's assessment; because she is bonding and will have a much deeper understanding of his thoughts and emotions.

"Despite his injury, I hope he is still able to protect your father," Mere says calmly, in her heart she knows Hyun will be safe but worries regardless.

* * *

Vicky gives a little beep and, staying sub-vocal, says "Hyun approaching from the house."

I don't turn to look at the other man because eels in the twenty-foot long range are converging on the shoreline. Eels have identical heads and move together like a school of fish as they converge in the shallow water. The only warning from these smaller eels is slight ripples before they surface at the shoreline.

I use the holo-sight and target each of them as their heads break free of the water. Rail guns are accurate, but the kinetic energy they share with the target is excessive. Accelerated to hyper-velocities by the railgun, the .17-caliber dart that hits an eel pretty much turns the entire creature to very small fragments. This makes for a very messy shoreline.

Maybe if I can continue to shoot enough in the water the larger ones will be happy with the food they can reach. It is my theory as I shoot the ninety-fifth eel and the sight flashes green to warn me that there are only five rounds left in the magazine. I get a fresh magazine from my pocket. The amount of eels appearing is slowing down at the moment; I take the final five shots and reload quickly.

Hyun clears his throat and says; "My daughter said you need food and liquids to help you're A.I. with the healing process." Hyun holds the food up so I can see it.

The food and drink is appreciated because I think that I look stupid bald and then I answer; "Thank you, it will help."

I have not had to fire a single shot from this clip as the water churns around the dead eels. The chunks of blown apart eels are feeding the new arrivals as I hoped they would.

"Let's take a load off," I say and walk over to a piece of the broken gate facing the water.

Hyun asks; "Off what?"

I chuckle "My feet, is Sophee all right?"

Her father is silent for a few seconds, and then totally ignores my question by asking a question of his own. "Can you hold the eels back until morning? We can clear the beach and town then, as it is safer."

Well at least he is taking to me. I can tell he is not too happy with me being around his daughter. This I understand without being empathic, still I am not a bad person and … I wonder why I am defending myself?

"Yes sir I can," I say deciding that straight forward honest answers would allow him to get to know me best.

Hyun passes me the plate which I happily take from him. "Would you like some sir?" I ask. Hyun shakes his head and sets the pitcher of water down beside me. I waste no time and start to eat. The texture is soft outside and a bit crunchy when you bite through the fish and rice to the uncooked vegetables. The meat and rice is slightly sweet while the vegetables are tangy similar to a radish. Together they complement each other, bet it would be good with a glass of beer. Hyun sits quietly keeping an eye on the water while I eat the food he brought.

Two more eel's heads appear, so I snap two shots off to stop their advance to the shore. I take another bite and ask; "this is very good, is it a family recipe?"

"It was my mother's; she shared her recipe with Mere when she was fourteen years old."

"You have been married that long?"

"What is this married?" Hyun asks in return.

"Bonded or mated or however you call it." It would be odd to me married at that age. Hell, I am not really ready now at twenty-six years old.

"Yes. Normally Sooul wait until we are older to bond, but with the continuing decline of our population would have been unfair to deny Mere happiness. She may not have lived to bond out of her family if we hadn't done so at a young age. Our bonding process can take many years or it can take mere days; it is only the depth of the people's soul that can speed it up. Mere and I took about a year for our bonding process to complete, and in that time she became like a second daughter to my mother."

"The Gham took your parents?" I ask tentatively.

"No, eels took them, no suffering and the impact on our family was minimal. Since I was bonding with Mere it sped up the process. Mere and I mated at fifteen when our bond was complete.

I think about it as I eat and have more questions but don't want to ne nosey so I change the subject; "How do you plan to move the dead eels?"

"We will take as much of the protein as we can, and then herd some crawlers over to clean up the leftovers."

I think about it for a second, before saying "You mean those things that look like rocks with legs?"

"No, those are the babies. I mean the big ones that we have to chase from the fields."

"To me they seem like crabs and could hurt you." I state.

Hyun has a blank look on his face.

"A crab is an aquatic spider from my planet, New Harvest. They will eat anything, dead or alive, that they can catch." I explain.

"Oh, ours are slow enough that a child crawling could be safe. They only eat greens or carrion; crawlers normally stay away from the beaches because of the eels."

I finish off the last of the dinner, "Please thank Mere for the meal."

"Sophee made yours; apparently it was her duty." He said with a sigh of resignation.

"Vicky," I say out loud, "Using the materials we have on

this planet and some of the Sooul's tech, can we fabricate a small phased shield to protect the mouth of the bay?"

"Yes sir I can get the processor in Hyun's home recalibrated and have different materials fed into it. Two of your power cells from the pack should be enough. It will take a few hours but since they are all networked it can be done. Someone will have to place the anchor points." She concludes.

"Vicky, make it happen," I give the order and look briefly at Hyun before watching the water again. "Hyun, if I am not crossing a social or theological line, may I ask what religion you practice?"

Hyun laughs out loud and says, "I will tell you this: as a people we tend to believe in what is real, like our relationships, because any god who over a period of five hundred and sixty years would allow the death and the suffering we continue to endure would not be a god I wish to serve." He paused to consider my expression, but I showed no surprise since I felt in a similar way

"I hope I have not offended you with my views."

I smile. "I would like to believe in a higher power, but with the wars that almost destroyed humanity it seems less than believable. My Grandfather and Mother go to church regularly, and I used to go with them before I joined the People's Free Force. I don't serve God, but mankind… or maybe I serve God by serving mankind. I am not sure. However, I do respect a person's right to worship a higher order."

"Will you tell me your surname or family name?" I ask.

He slowly shakes his head and says; "I don't have one because of the Gham. We were afraid they would search our databases. Once they had the family data they could match families up to have larger groups to kill. Our people decide random deaths were better than group slaughtering."

Our people stopped exploring space when we encountered the Gham. We thought relocating to this planet might hide our people, but they found us. We also tried to hide in caves and underground, but then they destroyed our cities with weapons we have never seen before." Hyun was starting to get panicky and wide-eyed as he relayed his history. "You have to understand Joshua that the Sooul have never had a war or fought anyone."

"Hyun please quit being afraid of the Gham. I will help your people, on my word as a Gunman and as a man." I said trying to show firm resolve.

Hyun paused and looked like he was taking a second to calm himself. After a few moments when he looked less shaky he smiled. "Could you explain to me what the Gunmen's Element in the Peoples Free Force is?" Hyun asked. "It sounds important, but before we can be fully comfortable in your presence we would like this answered."

I smiled back at Hyun and notice some movement by the gate as a couple of six foot eels are sliding toward the opening. I limped over and crush their heads with a boot heel and then limped back to Hyun. He appears shocked that I would deal so casually with the creatures.

"Saves ammunition," I said. "When mankind left our home world of earth they spread over a vast area in the known Outer Rings. We had to leave earth without a lot of investigation to other planets that have either dangerous creatures like your eels or other creatures that had to be dealt with. Since most humans don't bond like the Sooul, some can fight and be unkind to each other or prey on the weaker populations. Few people live outside of accepted behaviors and it is only a problem when they attack innocents.

"The Gunmen's Element is made of people with special training and abilities who have a calling to solve problems caused by dangerous life forms—whether they are animal or human. Our motto is "Peace and Safety for all Humanity…" I stopped, not saying the rest, as I hate making long speeches. Peace and safety for all humanity, Peace by superior firepower, Peace by the total destruction of our enemies, I think there was peace by two or three other things but really hate trying to remember it all.

"What if we are not totally human?" Hyun quietly asks.

Again I smile. "If it walks like a duck, sounds like a duck and looks like a duck…you and the rest of your people have more humanity than most other humans I know. I tell you this as a great truth; if you had nine arms and were green your people would fall under our mandate."

Hyun nods at my comment and then asks; "you said that you are the 1st Gunman. Why that title?"

A flush of embarrassment made my face feel warm. "We have positions in the Gunmen's Element."

Vicky, sensing Joshua's embarrassment, goes active again and asks; "Sir if I might interject into this conversation?"

"No Vicky you may not," I reply curtly to shut her down. "I was a supervisor."

Hyun very easily senses Joshua's embarrassment, so he leaves the subject alone. Hyun knows that there is more to him just being a supervisor, because there is also some pride in Joshua's emotions.

"These Gham either will go away, or they will die, and then your people will be safe!" I inform Hyun bluntly.

Hyun is surprised at the absolute honesty and faith that Joshua has in what he just said. A spark of hope runs thru him. "We have precious metal. Will we be able to buy our passage off this planet? I speak for all of the people here." Hyun asks.

"Simply, yes. With your knowledge of farming, most colonies would be grateful to have you. What precious metals do you have?" I ask.

"Gold! I saw it in the database; they call it by a different name." Vicky informs me out loud.

"If we can purchase our way off this planet," Hyun asks, "how long is an average service to be held too?"

I put my hand out and grasp Hyun's shoulder in friendship. "Sir, you will be taken from this planet because it is the right thing to do. Your gold is yours to purchase whatever you need in order to relocate to a safer planet; most places don't allow that type of bondage you refer to." Josh paused a moment to let Hyun adapt to the idea. "Hyun, would you like a list of planets that have agriculture and would accept immigrants?"

Hyun looks like he has seen the light for the first time in years. It doesn't take an empath to see that the possibilities of his family and people staying alive have him encouraged.

"Vicky, please download a list of planets and send it to their database. Rate them from one to ten please based on economy and life style." I feel bad for the Sooul because they are so desperate, but maybe the planet listing will give them a little something to look forward too.

I open my pack and hand Hyun two of the power cells

for the shield. "Vicky will let you know when to add the batteries to the processor units. Please return to your family, and ensure they are safe and calm."

Hyun stands and looks up into my eyes. He looks a lot more at ease and clasps his hand on my forearm. "I sense nothing but truth and honesty; we may have to keep you."

I laugh as he walks away because I will be going home to New Harvest as soon as the Gham are dealt with.

* * *

Hyun heads back to his house wondering if he was being sent back to really calm the people or just to ensure he is safely out of the way. Since his ability is not as strong as the rest of his family's he will have to accept it at face value.

Vicky patches herself thru their network and instructs Hyun to put the power cells into the processors and which other base materials to add to the units. Shoran's father took the second one to their home and got it started as well.

Hyun's family was not surprised to see him return safely and asked for updates on Joshua's leg. Vicky, after monitoring the conversations decides that these people need some reassuring.

"Hyun!" Vicky calls through the homes system. "I am not breaking any of Joshua's privacy rules by telling you this, but I will inform you of things that may set your mind at ease. The People's Free Force is a galactic navy, and the Gunmen's Element is comprised of their elite soldiers. The 1st Gunman is the best of the best—not just because of his ability to fight, but his higher level of intelligence. Joshua has been the leader of the Gunmen's Element for six years and has helped too many people to list. I have been his A.I. for seven years and I have never known him to brag or be boastful, so he would not tell you this."

Sophee smiles at her mom with a raised eyebrow. "Can I pick them or what?" People not used to her being so open look at each trying to figure out the pride she is feeling for Joshua. Shoran starts to smile when she reads Sophee's acceptance of the A.I.s report tempered with her own feelings.

Hyun smiles at Sophee's uncharacteristic humor. When the bond starts to form some personality traits can be shared, and her Joshua said he likes to use humor. When a bond as strong as Sophee's is forming it is natural that she would start using humor like Joshua does.

The Sooul present in the home start to visibly relax now that they have a better understanding of the man outside. Talking about how lucky they are to have him here defending them and speculating about how effective their Joshua could be against the power of the Gham keeps them occupied for the better part of the night. Hyun told them about the smaller eels and how Joshua just stepped on them like bugs even though they were large enough to provide a nasty bite.

As the night progresses the sound of the shooting slows as the eels ranks thin out. All at once there are four or five shots in quick succession when a newly arriving group of eels gather and try to come ashore. The Sooul jump at the renewed gun shots and most of them look at the doorway wondering if he is okay until the next shot happens. Sophee doesn't bother because of her ability to sense her Joshua's mind.

"He is tired and not concerned with the eels, not even a little bit," Sophee says to her mom and best friend. "The pain in his leg has almost completely faded away."

The amount of stress Hyun's guests were feeling at the start of the evening slipped away. Kids slept and the adults spread out started to relax and find places to lie down and sleep. Even Hyun's family managed to grab some sleep.

CHAPTER 9

Down at the water heads start to pop into the open as more of those damned eel-things start to come ashore. The amount of blood and gore in the water must be attracting them from a long way off.

"A large group is now entering the cove," Vicky warned.

It's time to go to work again. I start shooting as the swarm of eels starts to surface. The group of eels is huge. Several times eels actually made it partially on the beach before I could shoot them during the rush to shore. A magazine and a half later, nothing is moving in the bay. I walk down toward the shore and look at the water's edge, which is red with blood; there are chunks of dead eels bobbing in the small crimson waves. God, I hate the smell of fresh blood. It always depresses me to think of how much carnage I have created.

Yes, these are just animals without higher brain functions, but they are still innocent of malice. It is not their fault they are hungry; it is instinct for them to prey on other creatures for food. I know that human life is more important, I believe this in my heart, but that doesn't mean that I like the fact I am required to do this. Still sentient life's protection requires hard actions by people like me and whether I like it or not.

After seven years in the Element, maybe returning home will allow me to recharge my weary soul. I realize that deciding to take the time to hunt after I left the P.F.F. was selfish, mom and granddad deserve better. I also know that if I hadn't Sophee, her family and people would be dead soon. That alone makes my decision a good one, even if it was by luck or chance that I ended up here.

"What would it take to speak real-time with Granddad?" I ask Vicky.

Her answer is immediate. "An F.T.L. power system from a starship or cargo ship. I have scanned for one and it does not exist on this planet."

Well, that is not going to work unless the Gham decide not to leave and then I will have one. That is presuming that the Gham are using a faster than light drive that Vicky can access. It does seem logical to assume the Gham would have one on their ship.

It ended up being a very long night with shooting eels and trying to stay awake. Vicky had to dump adrenaline in small amounts into my blood stream to help keep me awake and shooting. Dawn came slowly at first with the sun creeping over the ridge that surrounds the bay. No eels are trying to come ashore since it started to grow lighter in the early morning. I am standing close to the water wondering when the blood will dissipate in the surf. The eels and small fish have cleaned up most of the bobbing chunks of dead eel.

Vicky has worked all night programming the processors to build the shield generators and she had them complete shortly after dawn. She then pulls me out of my tight focus on the shore by saying the shield generator is complete.

"Vicky, would you please ask someone to bring the generators out here?" I request.

As I shift my weight I realize the pain in my leg is virtually zero, and looking down I see that the nanites have even sealed the holes on my pant legs. I rub the top of my thigh where the teeth had punctured through my muscle, and it was only a bit tender.

"I guess the food had enough nutritional value, eh, Vicky?"

She answers back; "maybe with the quantity you ingested, rocks would have worked."

"I thought it was tasty and did not want to hurt their feelings"... I try to defend myself even though I know I did eat a lot. By Vicky's silence she either agrees with my defense or doesn't want to allude to me being a pig. I continue to stare at the water while the people of Sooul leave the group of houses they stayed in overnight. The adults look tired and kids being kids treated last night as a campout. Hyun is leading the way with Mere and Sophee are following close behind. Sophee looks very happy when she sees me and is carrying a shiny volley ball sized metal sphere in her hands while another girl—*crap*, woman most likely—is carrying the other one.

As they reach me, Hyun hands me a pitcher of water that I gratefully accept. A long drink of cold water is just the thing my body needed after being worked on by nanites all night. I pour the rest of the water into my canteen to refill it, and clip it to my belt. This I will save for my walk to place the generators.

The whole crowd is staring at the bloody water at the shoreline; I wait for their negative reactions and am surprised to see none at all. I know they are smart people who are aware what this bloodied bay means, and there is no doubt that they heard well over two hundred shots. Put two and two together and a few hundred plus creatures died here. For sensitive people they are remarkably indifferent about the carnage.

Hyun looks at me and, with a small wave of his hand at the crowd, he says, "We thank you for our safety."

I decide to leave my opinion about the blood covered shore alone and not apologize for mess I made because, *this is what I do*. I just smile and nod to accept their thanks.

"Eels do not like the dawn, and they have already gone to deeper water," Mere informs me after noticing my weapon. "They will not return until later, around dusk."

I follow Mere's gaze down to my hand and realize that I am still holding my railgun. I change the magazine to a fully loaded one and holster it. Because of my sense of humor being what it is, I give a quip back to her. "I sense the truth of your words."

Mere doesn't smile, though Hyun actually does and that surprised me that he is picking up on my humor so quickly.

Sophee touches her mother's arm to get her attention. "This is the humor I told you about. He is not being rude," Sophee says.

Crap, I did it again. "Sorry, Mere. Please understand that due to my not being empathic I was cracking a joke at my personal expense."

I hold my hands palms upward in a sign of supplication, so that she can see that I am opening myself honestly to her. She smiles backs and nods making me realize that she accepts my apology.

I pick the fifteen pound spherical generator from Sophee's friend. "Thank you," I said. Each of these self contained generators will burrow into the rocks at the entrance of the cove. When initiated they will link together to form a shield to block the entrance from any large creatures that try and swim in. They will provide security against any more eel incursions.

I reach for Sophee's sphere, and she shakes her head. "I have it," she says, and then walks past me toward the ridge. Either she thinks I can't find the trail to the entrance of the cove or wants to be with me, interesting.

I look to Hyun with caution for I don't know what he will say about Sophee going with me. Getting no reaction from Hyun, I look over to Mere who has a tiny knowing smile on her face. It must be okay with them. "I will return her safely home sir, after we place the shield generators." I say with honesty.

I turn and take a few quick steps to catch up with Sophee. As we walk together towards ridge Sophee turns right and leads towards the furthest pillar with the generator firmly in hands. I admire her verve as she walks with me. I shorten my stride to match hers as we walk so she does not have to run to keep pace with me.

"I can carry that for you if it is heavy." I offer.

Sophee stands a little straighter, showing her determination by saying, "I will be okay."

We circle the bay and start climbing the ridge. There was not much of a path, if anything it would be a goat trail. *I wonder if they have goats here?* Sophee leds and really doesn't take the best route but I follow her anyway. A few hours pass by as we climb the ridge and walk the small trail along the top, I can hear Sophee's breathing start to get a little harder so I decide to sit and rest.

"Let's take a couple of minutes to rest," I offer. Sophie gives me a weary smile and nods. It takes her no time to put the heavy generator down. I sit down on a flat level rock and Sophee sits beside me, and I pass her my canteen. After a few small sips she looks at me, then away. Sophee keeps making those small glances, and it seems like she wants to say something but cannot find the words to do it with. Finally, I raise an eyebrow at her in question.

"Can we talk?" she asks softly. Sophee waits for my nod, and then continues speaking. "I was very worried about you last night. We could sense how much your leg hurt, and you were limping pretty bad. We never had time to treat or bandage your wound before you left. I felt awful about your situation."

I shrug. "It's just pain, it goes away eventually."

To me the pain in my leg was a very small thing compared to the problems the Sooul have been enduring. If I made any kind of a big deal out of it I would be a wimp or selfish to take anything away from their suffering. The Sooul have been through much worse as a people. I would like to explain this to Sophee but it is almost frigging impossible to talk to this beautiful girl, as I feel myself being drawn closer to her than would be prudent. It is bad enough that I hang on every quiet word she says, without me developing a worse crush on her.

Sophee is holding her hands on her lap very still and without having her skills I am unsure of her direction.

"Last night I told Shoran how brave you were when the eel almost ate me. She wonders how I can talk to you without being afraid of how dangerous you can be. When I think about what Shoran was saying it makes me unsure how to answer her."

For some reason I can't quit grinning like an idiot around her, no matter what the topic of conversation is. She could be telling me anything because I really have to concentrate on what she says or I would lose my train of thought to stare into her beautiful green eyes.

"Your friend needs to know that you and all of the Sooul have nothing to fear. I mean from me or any other creature."

I wanted to tell Sophee I'm a tier one shooter and list what my accomplishments were so they would know who and what was willing to die to defend them. I will not show off or brag to her, I would rather let my actions speak for themselves. The people of Sooul are all going to be safe because I want to keep *Sophee* safe. No wonder her dad doesn't like me around her, he is probably sensing my crush on her. I try to wipe the smile off my face; the one caused merely by her presence, but just can't seem to do it.

Sophee continues, either ignoring or not seeing my stupid grin. "It is just that I am not thinking of you as a stranger or someone who would ever hurt me, I think of you as someone very special to me. I really like you."

This gives me a pause. Learning that she really likes me makes me feel like a schoolboy with a crush. Crap. Should I tell her I like her, too? Or should I wait? Yes, she looks young, but is older than she appears and more mature mentally than most people my age. It is completely acceptable for us to like each other. I need to just calm it down, and play it cool.

"I am glad you're not afraid of me, it must be because

you can sense that I am sincere." I take a few breaths; *I'm special to her, she likes me.*

"Have you eaten this morning?" I ask.

Sophee shakes her head slightly. I notice everything she does is subtle, like the way she nods, smiles or moves. Sophee's skin is a very light olive, her features are very delicate with a cute little nose, her lips are full and always shaped in a smile—which is hard to believe because of what the people of Sooule have had to endure. Her almond-shaped eyes stand out, as they are a very vivid green.

Crap, I am staring at her again. Busying myself to prevent further gawking, I open my pack and grab a pouch of trail mix. I open the pouch with slightly shaking hands as she watches me and offer her some. She holds her hand out so I pour some into her palm. Sophee takes the small handful of the snack and looks quizzically at it.

Pointing, I label each item of food. "These are nuts and that's bran. Both are from my planet, and when we combine them together like this we call it trail mix. I like to munch on this when I don't have much time or when I am somewhere I am unable to make meals. It is very healthy for you." Trail mix is much better than Kcals, I would not want to subject her to them.

She raises her hand to her nose and smells the granules she's cupping in her palm. "Do I eat it all at once or individually?"

So there I sit watching her and thinking about how she will eat it, I never even heard her question. I watch her smile a bit more and hold her hand out to me. I open my hand and she puts the mix in my hand. She then takes the package from me and removes some more. We sit in silence until I clue in that she is waiting to see how I eat it.

"Sorry," I say. "I was zoning out."

Smooth, Josh. Way to make a good impression.

I grab an almond and pop it in my mouth. After chewing, I say, "Almonds are nuts that grow on some of the trees on my planet, and are one of my favorite things to eat."

Sophee picks one up and smells it before taking a delicate bite and then slowly chews it. If she were from back home I would think that she had more class than anyone else alive just by the way she eats. No smacking of her lips, chewing with her mouth closed, and enjoying every little bite. I've never seen anyone eat an almond in several bites, it was fascinating.

"This is excellent," she says with a genuine smile.

We share the water with the trail mix for a few minutes. When we were rested I pick up both the generators and stuff them into my pack, it's a bit of a tight fit. I don't care because I am not letting Sophee wear herself out carrying things when she is much less than half my size. Sophee starts to protest about me carrying both of the spheres, but I just give her a grin. "Do you actually notice Sophee that I am much bigger and heavier than you?" I ask in a light voice.

When she nods, I continue. "I come from a planet that has a much heavier gravity, so I have a more dense muscle mass. Because I also have nanites in my blood stream to help me be healthier and stronger I don't tire as easy."

"Oh, all the women in town have noticed the muscles and were commenting about how strong you looked," Sophee says with a blush. "They believed me when I told them you jumped into the eel's mouth and, if we were not empathic, they would not have believed that you could stop the eel from crushing you, let alone and then push it off you."

Now it was my turn to blush. "Jumping into the eel's mouth was not the plan," I told her. "I only wanted to block it from hurting you until I could kill it. I really didn't push it completely off me. I sort of pushed it to the side so I could squeeze out from under it." I explained.

* * *

I give my Joshua a huge smile; I know that the blocking the eel comment is a great truth layered with protective emotions. Those emotions that radiate from him instantly let me know that although Joshua may not say it, he is bonding. It was also rather surprising that he could say with absolute conviction "until he could kill it" with no questioning if he could or not. He knows his own abilities and is sure of himself. I will have to inform my parents that he is the warrior that Vicky claimed he was. If the night before had left any doubt in anyone's mind it would be erased after she had let them know this little tidbit of information gathered from him.

Vicky speaks through Joshua's pack and says, "Sophee, Joshua has been awake for a long time. When he finishes the shield he must sleep for awhile because he will not be able to function well without rest." It worries me that Joshua thinks so little of his health when he believes he has a mission. I give him a stern look that makes his smile larger. Since he will not take it seriously I reach out and take his hand. They are warm and calloused but gentle when he gives me a squeeze back. I blink my eyes rapidly as I look down at my sandals or he would see the tears in my eyes from the emotions I am feeling.

* * *

"Thank you. Go passive until I need you, Vicky," I order. Turning my attention to Sophee I make a comical face. "I swear Vicky is worse than my mother."

Getting to the old pillar at the entrance to the cove's mouth took less time than I thought. Since I was carrying both of the generators, Sophee was able to move faster than before even though she appeared rather tired. I looked at the pillars closely and realized they are damaged, as though at one time there had been a fence or net across the entrance to the cove that had been ripped away.

I quickly climb down from the top of the ridge to the top of the pillar and place the generator against the stones of the old ruins. Opening the sliding cover over the panel, I hit the initiate button and climb back to the top where Sophee is waiting. I look at the water that lies between the two pillars to try to decide if it is worth the risk to swim across the mouth of the cove. It will take the rest of the day to make it over to the other side if I have to walk around. Sophee either senses what I am thinking or uses a woman's intuition and grabs my hand.

"Eels are not the only things that bite in the water," she says.

I turn back with a simple; "Alright Sophee." We start hiking back; I can drop her off at her home before continuing to the other side. Unless the hike is worse on the other side the shield should be on before the eels return.

As I walk behind Sophee on the narrow trail, the

realization she is petite and not a teenager finally works its way slowly into my mind. *Cute butt,* as she walks along the path ahead of me sort of make an impression to solidify that. Their years are as long as ours, Sophee is twenty years old, and she likes me. I keep watching her butt as we walk until I realize what I am doing.

Idiot, quit being a pig!

Vicky hears the thought and sub-vocalizes back to me. "I do not think of you as an idiot or a pig sir."

To keep myself from staring at Sophee's backside all the way back to the village, I decide to talk with Vicky sub-vocally. "Why are you off passive?"

"I am off passive because, for some reason, you are using sub-vocal communication instead of keeping your thoughts to yourself."

"Weird."

An hour passes with Vicky and me discussing the eels and their behavior. Vicky believes they live in schools based on their ages and size. We are about a third of the way to the base of the hills and Sophee looks just about done in. Her breath is ragged and I see her steps are starting to wobble a little bit. It is obvious to me that physical exhaustion is taking a toll on her.

I ask Vicky sub-vocally "Why would Sophee be so tired from walking, she looks in decent shape?"

"The nutrients they get here are low, because they don't get enough proteins since the eels keep them from fishing late in the day. Sophee was risking her life to get the fish you ate; it would have provided her family with good nutrition. For some other reason, the crops that are growing here are lower in nutrients as well."

I pull my canteen off my belt and get the trail mix out of my pack. "Sophee, could you hold this please." I ask as I hand her the items. Sophee's weariness shows but she stops walking and turns to reach out for them anyway. I pick her up and cradle her as we walk. She starts to complain about me carrying her. "Drink water and eat some nuts, you will feel better." I said in a tone that was firm but gentle.

I hope she will listen to me, as I am larger and stronger, she is tiny. Sophee can't weigh more than ninety standard pounds and since she doesn't struggle in my arms it is a rather pleasant experience for the last four miles. Sophee relaxes and puts her right arm around my neck.

I move slower than usual because it is so enjoyable walking in the sun with this lovely girl in my arms. As she nibbles on the bag of trail mix and sips water, Sophee can see my smile and realizes that having her so close is making me happy. Every once in a while Sophee's finger would touch my lips as she fed me an almond but, after the first few times, I tell her I am not very hungry yet and for her to enjoy them.

What I am unaware of is the fact that the closer we are physically the faster the bond strengthens. Obviously, Sophee knew, and that would explain why she allowed me to carry her.

The beach appears far too soon and, upon reaching it, Sophee doesn't try to jump down. If anything, she seems content and happy to be in my arms, not caring what people think. I am okay with her in my arms as I stroll towards her home. A Sooul woman runs up to us and asks if Sophee is all right. Sophee could not look any more right with the smile on her face. There was no way I was setting her down yet, so I had better explain myself.

"I took a poor path to the mouth of the cove and she is exhausted so I thought carrying Sophee would allow me to walk faster." I said. I take a few seconds to look in Sophee's eyes; "and I am enjoying Sophee's company."

The woman smiles at me carrying her best friend. She is pretty but not as breath taking as Sophee. "My name is Shoran and I'm pretty tired, too."

"Sorry, this one is taken!" Sophee says matter of factly.

I just grin at Sophee's simple response and continue to Hyun's house. Her parents are pushing a cart loaded with slabs of eel meat towards the door. Hyun's mouth drops open in surprise when he sees Sophee's position and her arm around my neck. Mere just nods at us as I carefully set Sophee on her feet.

"Home safe and sound like I promised," I said.

Looking at the cart Hyun was trying to maneuver, I estimate that it had to weigh at least two hundred pounds. It was filled with freshly butchered eel fillets. The Sooul must have been working hard harvesting the eels from last night. This much meat would be a welcome addition to the Sooul's diet.

Turning to Sophee's father I said, "Excuse me sir."

When he steps out of the way, I lift the cart up and carry it to their prep area. This, of course, impressed the hell out of Mere and Sophee. After I set the cart down beside their processer, I turned to leave. Her father is looking oddly at me, so I return the look with innocence. If I was a father and some stranger was carrying my daughter around I might look oddly at him too. I think a second about the meat they have harvested and turn back toward Hyun.

"Sir, my A.I. informs me that the nourishment your people need is sadly lacking due to your shortage of good animal proteins. From her scan the eel meat may not have everything you need either.

I peel my pack off and start pulling out all eleven tubes of the semi-hard Kcals. Each tube is seven inches long and two inches wide and dull in color. "Each tube contains enough advanced nutritional supplements that, when taken daily, they will keep me alive and healthy when there is nothing else to eat. Put it in your stasis unit on the meat you are processing. I will have Vicky reprogram the units to convert these into basic vitamins and mix it with your food supply. Spread them around if you wish."

Sophee holds out the pouch of trail mix to me. She had hardly made a dent in it.

With a shake of my head, I say, "Please keep it to share with your family, I hope they enjoy it as much as you did." I want to pick her up again and hold her but the other pillar is waiting for a generator. I resign myself to leaving, "Thank you for your company Sophee, I had a wonderful morning." Mere is watching our little exchange with that tiny knowing smile again while Hyun still looks a little shocked after seeing me with his daughter in my arms.

I walk out into the bright sunlight trying to clear my head a bit, when I am with Sophee I lose a bit of focus. I begin to jog back across the beach. When I reach the ridge at the other side of the cove's mouth I practically sprint up it.

After I get to the top Vicky sub-vocally informs me, "Hyun's stasis processor has accepted the programming and the Kcals will be converted to vitamins. The supplements will be added for everyone's meals across the network. It is my opinion sir that you should have kept the Kcals to make sure that you had enough good fuel to keep your nanites at top condition."

She then changes the subject after scolding me; "the first generator has burrowed to the proper depth and is awaiting the signal from the second one."

I thank her for the information and keep moving along the rough path at the peak of the ridge. The jogging and climbing have been keeping my thoughts occupied until I reach the second pillar. The trip took only about an hour with the pace I set for myself. Had I have been walking with the Sooul it would have taken over three times as long. I remove the second unit from my pack to set it in the proper position. The unit starts to vibrate when I key its initiation switch and uses high frequency vibrations to sink itself into the rock. I wait until it is fully finished burying itself to the proper depth which takes little more than an hour. While I wait, I sit in the warm sun and think about Sophee. This bond thing they talk about is odd but I don't mind it one bit. She is such a good soul; I lose myself when I look into her eyes. The only thing I would change about this developing relationship is I would like to know what she is thinking. Her reaction when I picked her up was surprising; I thought there would be more of a fuss. Her arm around my neck touching me was hard not to focus on. Sophee did enjoy the close contact as well, that was noticeable to me without their gifts.

"Vicky, how deep will the shield penetrate into the rock?"

She replies, "Three feet into the rock and one hundred feet into the air.

"That concerns me because the power to run that level of shield can only last a couple of months."

"It will be a couple of safe months," Vicky says.

This gives me more to think about like where do the Sooul want to go? Maybe I will get lucky and they will like New Harvest. Maybe I can talk Sophee's family into trying my planet because I don't think I could stand her going away.

"You are still sub-vocalizing. "Vicky states.

"*Crap!* Sorry, Vic!"

Before I can say anything further there is a bright white flash and a huge pop as the shield slams into existence.

"Modulate screen to a six inch opening," I order and, with a soft hum, the screen slowly breaks apart to divide into strands, and then into a mesh.

"Shield status?" I ask.

"Shield holding firm." Vicky replies.

I feel a sense of accomplishment with this shield now operating. Since there is no chance of eels making it through the shield now I should ensure the bay is clear. So I take off at a fast jog to get to the beach before dark. *Splendid*, I think to myself as I am jogging, *this shield should provide a decent break from their nightly problems.*

"I have more information about the Sooul if you wish to hear it." Vicky says after I have been jogging for a half an hour.

I slow down to a walk to catch my breath. "Where is it from?"

"I am monitoring several of the homes in town, and some interesting conversations are happening."

Maybe I should tell her not to spy on people, but she never informs me of anything that would disrespect people's privacy. She has from time to time helped me by giving me an edge when people are dumb enough to vocally discuss plans that are not pursuant to peace. "What makes them interesting?" I ask.

"They all are processing eel meat into their stasis units and creating programs for foods that they haven't had in awhile. They are also discussing the Kcals you have so graciously provided," Vicky began. "Some of the men thought they should accompany you to the other end to the cove, but by the time they were ready to leave, you were already out of sight. They could not believe how fast you were gone. Sophee has shared the trail mix with her parents, and they have told others to come try it. Mere particularly likes the walnuts."

I smile at the memory of Sophee trying an almond for the first time.

"More than a few Sooul have commented that you make them feel safe, and they hold you in the highest regard for saving them from the eel swarm last night. Sophee has spent considerable time explaining your mindset when you were battling the eels. Having someone to help the Sooul through these difficulties is a new thing to these people. Their only sure thing the Sooul had before was their love for each other. Having you here, with your strengths and honesty, is a catalyst for some serious discussions."

"People should be safe." I say aloud, "The Sooul think that safety is not their right, I hope to alter that thought."

"As they watch the review on agricultural planets, everyone is so impressed with New Harvest the most, but don't believe you will take anyone there except maybe Sophee."

"Well, they are wrong," I say. "All the Sooul would be welcome on New Harvest." *Let her chew on that,* I think to myself.

Vicky responds again, "I can't chew!"

"Vic, please theorize why I am going sub-vocal with my thoughts rather than only when I want to speak to you."

Vicky's adaptive personality allows her to know when it is time to help or when it is a time to offer opinions. She can do this based on data that also allows her to know what tone to take in order to ensure the primary's comfort and ease. In this case her voice and tone reminds me of how my mother spoke when I was a kid.

Vicky softly says, "I have scanned you repeatedly and see no fresh injuries or chemical imbalances that would cause this alteration, so it has to be environmental… And by this I don't mean air or water.

"It is obvious that the Sooul can bond outside of their race, and for some reason Sophee's thoughts and actions are drawing you in. Your lack of concentration is because you are mentally enthralled with this new relationship. My opinion is your brain is adjusting to the strong feelings of the bond and not controlling other aspects as well. I can find no reason why you would be so drawn to her except that she is truly beautiful by human standards, and very kind. In my so very humble opinion you have needed this for years, because the lack of female companionship has caused a void in your life. For some reason Sophee is as drawn to you as you are to her… it's quite fun to watch."

"Thanks Vicky, I find your opinions interesting." I try and interrupt because having an A.I. deep dive your life is just plain odd.

"I'm not done." Vicky says, "From Sophee's side, which you don't understand, you are like Hercules to them; it is not just that you are larger physically. It is because you don't lie to them and easily solve problems that have been insurmountable to them. For the first time in hundreds of years, these people are starting to have hope—you have done this in two days." Vicky goes silent when she was done.

"I know that I like the Sooul and, yes, Sophee especially," I say out loud, not daring to test my misfiring sub-vocalization. "When the eel came over the wall all I could only think was *not her*. Vicky, please stay in assistant mode. If you see me acting like a jerk, not behaving in a manner befitting Gunmen or even a possibly a future husband, please tell me."

Deep in thought, I decide to walk back to the beach. Will Granddad allow me to bring two hundred or more people to settle in New Harvest? Certainly he will if I ask. Will my mom like Sophee? Absolutely, she would… after I finish speaking to her and she understands I am not robbing the cradle. *Damn*, I am going to take a bunch of ribbing from my two best friends. Why couldn't she be beautiful *and tall*? Well, I can always shoot them!

Laughing to myself at my thoughts, I then address Vicky aloud. "Do you have any more information from their database on bonding?"

"No, sir, the Sooul has absolutely nothing logged as data in case the Gham would access it. Would you like my speculative observations and theory?"

I never have asked for Vicky's theories before today, only wanting data, but what the hell.

"Please?" I ask.

"By monitoring the people of Sooule, I can tell you that they love deeply. Watch how they treat each other and the children. There is no misbehavior or misunderstandings, because of their gifts. From my observation, Sophee loves deeply and this would be my assessment of you as well. Even though you stay away from relationships with females up until now, you likely wondered if you were ever going to meet the special one. Since she thought, she would die before meeting her special one both of your thought patterns were already in sync. All you had to do was meet because saving her already put you on her good person radar, your respect and calmness amplified it. This bond allows total understanding of the emotional complexities in relationship that is forming between a pair."

"Thank you Vicky, now I do know that the way I am feeling is because of the bond and that makes it easier to understand." I realize that Sooul call it a bond and humans call it love.

Instead of feeling trapped or odd because of the speed of bonding or falling in love, I simply feel happy. Sophee is kind and soft-spoken, but last night when she brought me dinner she got annoyed with me, saying I looked at her like a child. She can be rather firm when she wants. It will be interesting to see where this leads and great if I end up with a wife. I can picture the look of happiness on mom and granddad's faces right now.

I have almost reached the beach when someone in town

notices the shield. Word spreads like a wildfire, everyone is leaving their homes and they are clapping and cheering.

"See, the legend of Joshua the 1st Gunman grows," Vicky said out loud.

"Yeah, but you're the one who built the shield."

Vicky agrees; "but you gave the order and installed the shield."

As my feet hit the sand I realize how weary I feel, so I try to ignore it. I still have work to do. As I walk to the shore, I draw my railgun and then stand loosely focusing on the water. Hyun and Mere leave the growing crowd and walk quickly to me and ask if there is a problem with the shield.

Without taking my eyes off the water I answer. "Eels are now outside the shield."

"It has been on for quite a while, am I correct Joshua? Hyun asks.

"Yes, for a couple of hours." I reply.

"The eels are only now appearing, is the shield not strong enough to stop them?" Hyun wonders aloud.

"There is no way of knowing if there are any caves or tunnels that will allow them access to the cove. Due diligence demands that I watch for eels and prepare for the worst case scenario." I said as I continue to focus intently at the water for signs of eels.

There is silence for a minute while they digest my words.

"No one has ever taken care of us before, and this is a great feeling for the Sooul. How long will it take to be sure?" Mere asks with a kindly smile.

"I don't know Mere, but I want to give it a bit of time before I rest."

Vicky sub-vocally says, "If you fire an explosive round

into the center of the bay I can scan the echoes and map the bottom to let you know if there are passages."

"Thanks, Vicky," I sub back to her. I holster the railgun and remove my rifle from my shoulder. The crowd goes dead silent and starts backing up thinking it must be serious if I am pulling out the big gun. I can't blame them for being cautious.

"Hyun, please tell them that there is no new problem, merely that I am going fire a round into the water so my AI can listen to the echoes. This will allow us to know if there are tunnels or passageways that might let eels get past the shield. It will likely stun some fish, so you will have more food available shortly." I said with a calm smile.

The crowd of Sooul stood back; they had heard my shooting last night but had not seen it done. I am betting they were curious.

"Vicky, are they still fifties?" I ask needlessly. It was not like she would have reset the ammunition back to armor piercing without telling me.

"Yes, sir they are." She replies out loud.

I flip the safety off my rifle and, in one smooth motion, pull up the rifle into firing position. I wait until a small wave crosses the midpoint of the cove, and target the base of the wave. I pull the trigger and the bullet drills into the wave and deflects downward.

The sound of the shot makes most of the Sooul jump. A second later a soft thump well below the surface happened before a fountain of water lifts into the slightly darkening skies when the warhead round exploded. I palm the bolt open and chamber another round in case I trigger an attack with the first shot.

As I ignore the crowd who are still standing a safe distance from and watching the shore, Vicky goes active and says loudly so the Sooul can hear as well. "Per your command, I have scanned the base of the cove using echo analysis and there are no openings to the sea. Also, nothing in the water is over three feet long. Going passive sir."

"You're a ham Vicky, but I love you anyways." I reply.

In return she says, "No more energy boosting for you. Eat something and get some sleep, out!"

That puts me in my place. I can only guess that she said that out loud so the Sooul would feed me. My tiredness seems to be a bit less now that the Sooul's cove is safe. I keep looking over at the Sooul but don't see Sophee.

The people of the village are now crowding around the shore, looking at the dead and stunned fish floating from the explosive round's shockwave, but they're not going into the water. Perhaps, after all these years of avoiding the eels, they have forgotten how to swim. Maybe the Sooul have never learned to swim, that sucks, kids and water go together on New Harvest. This is another thing that they need to feel secure with to give them a better quality of life.

I know they like to eat fish and they are most likely wishing they had boat to retrieve them. I make an instant decision to help them. I unload my rifle, and put my holstered sig and railgun into my pack with the ammo. I lock my pack and lay it down some distance away from the water so it doesn't get filled with sand or need drying out. I see that some men don't always wear shirts in the warmth so I figure it is okay for me too. I then hit the seal release, and step out of my boots and one-piece battle suit.

Why the hell is everyone looking at me?

The Sooul stop looking at the fish and all are staring at me. Either they have never seen a man in shorts or they have to be wondering what the hell I am doing. These people are treating me like a show,

"Hercules, remember?" Vicky sub-vocally reminds me.

I don't care if they are curious about my physique. Under my battle suit I wear long shorts, they don't hide the cords of muscles on my legs but at least I am not hairy as I think that would scare them. Sports, hard work growing up, training and missions in the Gunmen's Element have sculpted my body. There were good base muscles on my frame from living on New Harvest because of the higher gravity, but eating right and hard work enhanced the definition of my build. I am a fairly modest man, but I am not embarrassed to take my shirt off either.

I turn away from my equipment and walk back to the shore. In one day the blood has pretty much dissipated. I shallow dive into the water and swim over to some of the stunned and killed fish. I grab several, sidestroke to shallower water, and then hand the fish off to some children who were at the shore watching before heading back out. The parents joined the children and were taking the fish from me as well to take home. I found it amusing that no one came in deeper than his or her ankles.

After I have retrieved a several hundred pounds of fish, I decided to grab one last fish and slowly paddle my way over it. The light reflected off its scales in blue hues, when I got closer I could see that the torpedo shaped body ended in a toothy mouth. It was not dead or stunned as much as the others had been, as it turned quickly and bit me on the chest when I grabbed its tail. The jolt of pain from the quick bite almost made me swear. The damned fish swam away without even saying it was sorry. *Stupid fish.*

Vicky instantly says, "I can't heal the bite without using all your hair! You need food and rest, so let the Sooul treat your wound. I will recharge some nanites in case of infection after you eat. Out!"

I swim to the shore, dragging one arm over the other through the water. As I stagger onto the sand, I realize that I am so tired it is a chore to stand. When the crowd of Sooul saw me bleeding, they rushed to provide aid, asking me if I was okay. I laugh and hold my hands out to stop their advance.

"I am okay," I tell them as I walked to my gear. This I know because Vicky would have told me if the fish had passed on any toxins. The onrushing Sooul stopped in their tracks when I smiled and headed toward my gear.

I still have not seen Sophee yet. But I am going to see her before I rest come hell or high water. Hyun is standing by my gear, he reaches down and picks up my rifle carefully while two other men take my pack and clothes. Motioning for me to follow him, Hyun just walks away. Mere and Shoran walk beside me, Shoran is smiling widely showing her pleasure at the days events while Mere seems to be annoyed with something, beats the heck out of me, maybe she hates fish.

"Sophee and others are making a large meal, so come to the house and rest until it is ready," Mere says, shaking her head at the sight of the blood on my chest. "I will clean that up for you as well. Some of our people will want to stop by either to thank you or they will want to ask questions about where we can go when we leave here."

As I walk to the house, I notice there are more young

girls and women around me than there are men. This amuses me because, if I have my choice, I might end up being off the market girls. I continue to smile because for the first time, the realization hit me that I actually want to be with someone possibly for the rest of my life. This bonding thing does change the way I feel, it's funny that I am so relaxed about this whole situation.

As we reach the front of the house, Sophee came out, gave a quick impish smile and darted back inside. She comes back out with a towel for me and then disappears again. I sit on the porch for the last few minutes of daylight while Hyun and the other gentlemen take my gear inside. The Sooul who followed us here waved and left for their homes. I decide to take a few minutes to gather enough energy before going inside to face everyone that is left.

I do feel a bit naked without a gun, but it is not like there is any more danger from the water so I just suck it up and enjoy the brief solitude.

Hyun comes out of the house holding pair of drinks and sits beside me on the bench. He hands me the glass, for which I thank him. I raise my glass for quick cheers before taking a sip of the wine. I would much rather had a cold beer. Mere came outside as well and knelt in front of me to push my arm to one side. I feel a little like a wuss. *Just let me bleed.*

"It is just a scratch." I protest.

"Teeth don't scratch," she chides me as she spreads a salve over the bite marks. She continues to cluck her tongue at me as she administers to my wound.

"Everyone around here would certainly have better sense

than trying to grab a live sillfish!" Mere nicely reminds me that I don't know all the creatures here.

I detect a note of joking in her voice, and I reply similarly. "Sorry, whoever would have thought it could be dangerous here?"

Hyun was taking a drink and started to choke as he laughed. Mere shakes her head, mumbles something about men, and walks back into the house. I grin at Hyun until he stops choking. It takes him a few minutes before he finally gets control and says; "She doesn't know what to expect from you."

"Mere?" I ask.

"Yes, Mere is having a difficult time with your humor and carefree attitude, she never knows what you're going to do or say. She does however enjoy the way you make Sophee feel."

I lower my glass and look Hyun directly in the eyes at the mention of Sophee's name. Her dad is talking about his little girl and I need to respond in the correct manner so he knows what kind of man I am. How to explain my feelings to a father when I am only just learning what they are is no simple task.

"I worry about Sophee's expectations and hopes." Hyun says cautiously.

I am glad he could actually tell me this; to see him laughing and choking on wine to honestly admitting his worse fear means he feels secure enough around me to talk. Hyun is worried because his only daughter is bonding with a virtual stranger and a warrior to boot. I can easily understand that his love for his daughter has him so concerned.

"Sir, I have nothing but respect for your daughter and would die before allowing anything to happen to her. I really care for her already and, while I don't completely understand the bond and why I am feeling this way so quickly, I will not push or otherwise coerce her. I feel very protective of Sophee. Please believe that although I have done hard things to bad men, I have never done it out of malice."

Then it hit me, I will do it with malice at the Gham. I have seen the video of the crime these monsters have committed against the people of Sooule, and I plan to ensure it will be paid back in spades. I start to open my mouth to say this, but am interrupted by Hyun.

"We bond quickly or slowly, and sometimes never at all." The other man states calmly. "But my people always know right from wrong, and Sophee's choice is you. In this, Mere and I will never interfere. As her father I will tell you that I accept your word and intentions."

I could see Hyun was a little more visibly relaxed after my declaration to protect and care for his daughter. This is the way he should feel. We sat together on the small porch and watched as different people went into their house. They all nodded and smiled as they carried in dishes of food that smelled terrific. My stomach rumbled constantly and I am not too proud to admit there was a bit of drool.

Finally Sophee steps out the door with a white garment held folded in her hands.

"This is for you; we would hate to see you catch a chill." Sophee eyes shine as she hands the folded shirt to me. I catches me off guard because I am so used to wearing battle suits I never thought the Sooul would think I didn't have any other clothes. Of course it was true that other than my suit everything else I own is sitting on Tertain in a frozen shuttle under four feet of snow. It also strikes me odd that they would either have something in my size or be able to program a replicator correctly so fast either.

I take the clothing and look up to meet her eyes as I say "Thank you."

As I unfold the shirt Sophee says, "My mother and I made it this afternoon."

I put it on and it is more like a gi than a shirt, loose and comfortable. The material is very light and feels almost like silk. It fits well to my surprise and I am honored they would take the time to do this. Other than my mom when I was younger no woman has ever made me anything. I was touched by their kindness. I wonder if this is a normal thing or if Sophee and her mother want me to fit in better with the Sooul.

I guess Sophee can feel my gratitude because she kissed the top of my head. "The food will be ready shortly Joshua." Sophee said before heading back inside with Mere. I sit back and give her dad a raised cup. Hyun regards me for a minute or two then says; "You are a very social but quiet person, are all Gunman like you?"

I chuckle at his question; "Gunmen are fairly serious individuals, my two friends are very similar to me, I do not know the rest personally so I honestly can't say." I figure that since he is talking with me I can find out more about the bond. I take a deep breath and ask Hyun; "How do the Sooul marry, is it after bonding? Is there a ceremony that couples have to do? Just for curiosity's sake, of course."

"Marrying? I don't know what that is, but it is pretty simple. A couple talks and begins to form a relationship; if they bond the male will declare he has bonded to the mother. The daughter will then be escorted by her mother to her new home and is presented to the bonded male," Hyun answers.

"That it?"

"That's it." Hyun looks keenly at me to try and figure out what I think they should be doing. "The father usually stays homes and drinks a lot while his daughter mates." Hyun says. "It helps us cope with losing our daughters."

Now I am blushing, probably at the thought of Sophee and mating or in embarrassment that her father will be staying home drinking. "Really, you don't mate for fun and never have more than one partner?"

He lowers his glass to look seriously at me and asks; "do you?"

"No, sir" I answer quickly. "Some men do, but I do not. I had not found the right girl yet, and I feel a little different about these things." I look openly at Hyun; "I swear this on my life."

"Truth and truth" Hyun says with a sigh. "I am growing to like you even if you plan on stealing my daughter." He smiles, and then takes a final drink from his glass. "Please join our family and friends for dinner to celebrate that we have no worries for a few days."

Hyun gets up and wobbles slightly as he moves toward the door. *A few days?* More like the rest of your life I think with resolve. I stand to follow him and realize that I have passed a milestone; Hyun is growing to like me. I can tell Mere doesn't hate me already. Oh happy days, hope there is a lot of food ready.

CHAPTER 10

When I walk into the house there is one heck of a gathering going on, as quite a few Sooul have decided to hang around. The atmosphere is cheery with people talking and laughing, and Sophee almost dances over to me. Her eyes are wide with excitement when she grabs my hand and leads me over to a section of pillows. I sit down and off she goes again without a word before I can tell her of the conversation I had with her dad. I see her over in the food prep area, god I hope she will bring me something to eat. I don't have enough time to think before another cup of wine is put in my hand by Shoran. A quick sip and I realize I can slightly feel the effects of the wine; Vicky is not going to help me by cleaning out the alcohol level apparently.

"Nope" she answers, "the sleep will do you good, out!"

Stupid non-vocal blip, I will have to work at keeping my thoughts to myself.

Sophee helps her father over to a cushion beside me and near Shoran's parents, and then takes off again to the prep area. Once Hyun was seated a few other people joined us on the cushions, most however waited near the prep area for the delicious smelling food.

Hyun nods at his cup and says; "watch this wine, it has a good kick."

I nod in acknowledgement while thinking; you're a third of my mass and probably didn't eat much today. Soon a platter, not a plate but a huge serving dish, was brought over by Sophee. She sits very close to me on the same cushion and says; "try this," as she points to a slice of meat in batter. I realize there is no cutlery or tongs, so with a shrug I pick up a piece with my fingers and eat it.

She looks at me for a reaction and I said "sorry, I was really hungry. I will slow down and enjoy the next bite." To my surprise she then took a different looking piece and held it up for me to bite. There was no hesitation with her offering it and none with me eating it. I didn't even wonder if it was fish or eel. When I look up and see everyone in the house grinning and watching us, I shrug. What the hell they probably don't have Gunmen sitting and sharing a meal with one of their girls very often.

"Are we now a social experiment?" I ask Sophee.

She blushes and replies in a halting voice. "A bit of one, they can read my emotions and know that I am bonding. They all sense your decency and are hoping it will work out for us."

"Me too," I say while looking in her eyes. "I hope it works out for us."

With a smile she gives me a kiss on my lips, and then adjusted her position to lean against me. I put an arm around her and, with my free hand, continue to eat slowly. Every few pieces, Sophee is quick to feed me one of the choicer or different cuts. Sophee actually told me what meat I was eating; a stupid sillfish did not taste as good as the eel.

"Are you going to have any?" I ask.

Sophee laughs out loud and her voice is musical with her happiness. "I already ate as I was making most of this. You enjoy your dinner."

Looking around, I have to smile at my good fortune. I am sitting in a nice home with a beautiful girl who really likes me, with her parents and friends who also seem to accept me. I can't help but wonder if they would be that way with any stranger? Would Sophee bond with anyone? Was I just the first human here?

Vicky interrupts my thoughts and, staying sub-vocal, tells me rather firmly; "smarten up." I had forgotten about the unfortunate change in our communication that some of my thoughts were no longer private. When I have some alone time with Vicky we will have to discuss what we need to do to either fix or bypass this little glitch.

"Because of the way the Sooul bond and their being empathic," Vicky continues, "you're the primary focus of Sophee and it is only because of the level of mental connection with her that you alone have. Give her more credit than you are currently."

"Yes, Vicky," I said sub-vocally without any emotion in my voice. Of course she is correct. I tighten my arm around Sophee as I admit that Vicky is correct. Again I have been aligned by my A.I.

Shoran is the first to come to actually sit with us rather than eat with her parents, and quickly brings up her point. "We have looked at all the places your Vicky sent us, and we would like to go to New Harvest. Our gold should get us there if the boss of the planet will allow it. Is there servitude on New Harvest to be a citizen?"

I laugh aloud at this question. "There is no servitude, period. Everyone is free, so you would be paid to work. Chandler Garvie is a good man, and I think he will be open to your people joining New Harvest."

Shoran looks at me quizzically. "Garvie?"

"Yeah, he is my grandfather."

"You could have told us," Shoran said slightly miffed that I did not come forward with the information earlier.

I pause for a moment to think about it, maybe I should have told them about my family. Then again I have been kind of busy and haven't had much time to actually talk to these people. "I would far rather have people I meet judge me from by my actions rather than who I am. My family owns the planet and I am cautious in that regard. As soon as I get a star drive I will speak directly with him about the Sooul."

After I say it, that it is how I should be treating the Sooul. I should be judging Sophee and our relationship for what it is, not wondering if it could happen with anyone. *Crap, I am such a tool.* Sophee is quick to pick up on my emotions and that I am annoyed with myself.

Sophee tilts her head back to look up to my eyes. "Relax. Every Sooul likes you—not just what you represent, but Joshua the person."

"Especially Sophee." Shoran says with a smile as she gets up, laughing, and to head for the food counter.

Sophee blushes and looks down at her lap. "But you knew that," she said quietly.

Before I can explain how I am feeling, a man with his mate joined us. He is a bit shorter than his mate and they both are well tanned. When I shake his hand I notice that his hands are rough and calloused like a farmer's hand. He introduces himself and his mate. "I am Lim and my wife is Hyo." I nod until I swallow my mouthful of food; "I am very pleased to make your acquaintance." I say as they both plunk themselves down across from Sophee and me.

"We can talk while you eat." Hyo kindly offers. I don't have to be told twice and take another bite. Lim regards me for a second looking me up and down. "If all of your people are as large as you the farm you have must be very successful. What exactly do you plant and raise on New Harvest?" He asks candidly.

I start of explaining about grains which they have a good knowledge about. Soy then and corn are two main crops that they have never heard of. I find myself enjoying his surprise when I tell them about the size of the NewCoRN™. Their eyes are huge as they take in the enormity of New Harvest's operations. I explain vaguely about mammal livestock and that we are the single largest producer of food in the known galaxy.

"I can only imagine how happy your people are to produce such wonders," he says.

"It's a big job feeding half the galaxy," I reply. "You would like it."

Shoran arrived back with another plate of food for me, which I gratefully accept as there is still a little room left in my stomach.

"Are there single men there?" Shoran asks before letting go of the plate.

This causes me to laugh aloud. "What you want, a big goofball?"

Sophee's face is puzzled; "I am not entirely sure what a

goofball is, but I think she would." She ends her statement by giving me a hug.

"I have a couple of true friends that would make excellent mates, as they are still single. But as a direct answer yes, there are single men on New Harvest."

Different people stop and ask questions about New Harvest. Their questions run from farming to technology. As I am sitting there, a little girl of maybe two-years-old crawls over to me and up on my lap. I pick the giggling child up into my arms and give her a kiss on the top of the head. She continues to chuckle and squirm, as she climbs all over me like I am a jungle gym. It is nice that the kids don't think that I am scary right away because the parents are only just starting to feel more relaxed after they talk to me.

Sophee opens her arms to collect the little girl, because I was having a hard time carrying on a conversation as the child mauled me and I laughed. The little girl's arms wrap around Sophee's neck as they across the room. Sophee carries the child back to her folks. *She will make an excellent mother to my kids.* Wow, that thought came out of the blue. Still I find myself hoping the bond is hitting her as hard as it is hitting me. Sophee finishes sharing a short conversation with the mother of the little girl and practically runs back to sit against me.

Another young woman with a newborn stops in front of me a bit later and shyly nods a greeting. When Sophee introduces the other female as Sung her only living cousin, I put my hands out to hold the baby. She is very tentative when she hands the tiny infant to me, as if she is wondering if I would be gentle with the baby. I lift the wee baby up to my nose, and inhale deeply. Everyone is looking at me holding the baby and wondering what I am up too, which makes me feel as though I am a troll who might eat this kid.

I hold her for a few minutes more, and the baby girl starts to get restless. Rather than handing her back to her mother, I rock her gently and softly sing a few lines of an old song from back home. I used to do to do this for my cousins when they were little, so I wasn't at all uncomfortable with the situation.

"Dreams are like angels that keep better faith.

Love is the light scaring darkness away……"

The baby calms, and falls back to sleep within the first two lines of the song. I smile and carefully hand the child back to her mother who smiles at the care I exhibited with her baby. This sweet little child alone would be a reason enough to knock the crap out of the Gham.

Sophee is looking up at me in amazement, her green eyes are watery.

"I love the smell of babies," I say with a shrug.

"The smell of a baby is a good thing that makes you happy? Mere asks curiously, when I had returned the baby. "That's a very odd thing for a warrior." Mere shakes her head in disbelief as she walks away toward the prep area.

I grin at Sophee. "Not that odd, I am pretty normal compared to my friends."

* * *

Sophee and Shoran were very amazed that a fighter would take time to hold a baby, let alone sing to one. The words Joshua softly sang were interesting and were very honest. Both of the girls could sense Joshua meant every word and truly loved the baby. Sophee's pleasure at Joshua's

The 1st Gunman

love of babies was strong enough that Shoran and everyone around could sense it. It seemed that the more relaxed Joshua got, he was broadcasted his emotions. While Sophee was always an open book to the rest of the Sooul this big man who saved them was becoming less of a mystery. Shoran could see every time Joshua looked at Sophee his emotions were extraordinarily tranquil.

Sophee's arm is around Joshua's waist as she closes her eyes and relishes in the way Joshua's emotions show the deep love and commitment he is feeling. Sure they had not had enough time to have any deep discussions but that time was coming. Joshua moves and his arm lifts off my shoulder as he carefully stands up.

"Please excuse me Sophee," he says and he turns leaving me sitting alone on the cushion. Joshua nods to some people as he walks out the door. No one knows where he is going or what is happening. I scramble to my feet and run out the door after him not caring if I look pathetic chasing after him. I've only just found him and there is no way he can leave me. Joshua is walking quickly toward the outer fields and stops when he hears me running toward him. He turns with a smile at me which makes me realize he may not be leaving.

"Have I done something to upset you?" I ask with sad expression.

"I didn't know where the facilities for waste management were so I thought I would go into the brush for relief." Joshua said with amusement.

Joshua's ability to lock down and control his emotions causes Sophee to wonder if he is just placating her. At least she wondered that until he picked her up with a hug and gave her their first adult kiss. When Josh sets her down

Sophee is breathless. She can sense the love and respect he has for her and Sophee's fears disappeared in the blink of an eye. *He is no longer treating me like a child,* came to her mind with stunning clarity.

"Come back and I will be a better host and show you where it is. You will stay with us for the nights, all of them!" Sophee said rather breathlessly.

"Won't people talk about me being in a house with an unbonded girl?" Joshua asks.

"You worry too much," Sophee says.

Josh and Sophee head back toward Sophee's parent's home holding hands. She doesn't let go of his hand but walks with him over to the single door which leads to the sanitary room.

Sophee is waiting for me when I leave the sanitary room, so I think what the hell and pick her up and walk over to the cushions again. Her mom's and friend's smile are half a mile wide now that I am showing my affection for Sophee publicly. Sophee's smile is closer to a mile wide.

* * *

As soon as Joshua starts getting visibly, drowsy most of the Sooul leave. A bunch of them decide to go out and look at the shield.

Mere smiles kindly at Joshua, "You have had a long rough day Joshua; we can only imagine how tired you are."

"I am warm with a full stomach, got snoot full of wine and a kind wonderful girl snuggling up to me. I cannot imagine a better day than this." Joshua said truthfully.

Hyun has been asleep for hours. Mere pushes a switch on the wall and a bed folds out, that is barely long enough

The 1st Gunman

for a Sooul. Joshua chuckles at the sight of it and points at the cushions on the floor. "Where does your dad sleep?" Joshua asks Sophee. She points at the folded out bunk. Joshua picks Hyun up and carries him over to lay him on the bunk. Mere mouths a silent "thank you."

Joshua returns to the cushioned area and makes himself comfortable by removing his new shirt. He lays back and takes a few deep breaths. Sophee and her mom continue to tidy up. Sophee passes by Joshua she covers him with a blanket, As soon as they are done the clean up Mere walks over to her sleeping husband, keys a switch to dim the lights and removes all of her clothes.

A bright red flush appeared on Joshua's face as he closes his eyes quickly to give Mere privacy. Mere laughs softly, "close your eyes Joshua if it makes you feel better, I sense your embarrassment but bonded people are very open around their families. Have no fear as mating will not happen because of my mate's drunken state." Now that Joshua can't see her he can laughs and said; "if you find yourself needing to mate warn me and I will go for a walk."

CHAPTER 11

Mere referred to me as family.

I am still chuckling at Mere's openness and wonder how I would react if Sophee jumped naked into my bed. Her parents are in the same room and that would be awkward to say the least.

I didn't have to wait long to find out. After leaving the sanitary room, Sophee walks over to me, removes her clothes, and slips under the sheet with me. I handled it with calm and poise; I froze up. Some brave guy I am. My heart is beating like a drum and Sophee lays on her stomach with arms in front of her and her chin is on her hands. Her green eyes are bright and search my face for any negative reactions from being this close and naked.

I don't think I checked out her body once even though she was naked because I could not simply tear my eyes from hers.

I do not touch her either as she lays beside me smiling. The desire to wrap my arms around her is difficult to overcome. It would seem I am far more cautious than she wants me to be. "Does this mean we are officially bonded?" I ask lightly.

Sophee nods. "I know how you feel; I can sense your love and commitment even if you do not say it. You are not talking about it, because you are so confused about the speed of the bond. When you do speak, you want to make sure that you clearly convey your emotions and beliefs."

Sophee has a point, I know the way I feel and it seems ludicrous to not accept it. I always worked at doing the right thing and now it is before me why should I hesitate? Softly, I tell Sophee, "I do love you." Her smile is filled with happiness and tears roll down her checks. "Joshua, I will love you for the rest of my life." Her hand right hand moves from under her chin and rests on my arm. Sophee is not sure what comes next because of my failure to touch her yet. I brush her tears away and ever so gently pull her to me. Our lips meet for a much sustained kiss. She was breathless again when we finished. "I too will love and protect you for the rest of my life." I whisper fearing Mere is listening to every word and sound. The realization that I am in love makes me think for a moment about what Sophee needs to know. Sure I can shoot a few eels but before she is too stuck on me I should tell her more about what I can be. Never before has my heart been filled with such joy, and it is not easy to inform Sophee that she doesn't know everything about me or what I do.

"I am not always a nice person," I whisper. "I have killed sentient beings, and if the Gham do not listen to reason I will kill again."

"Stop it, I know your heart and you are a wonderful person." Sophee murmurs back, cuddling all the closer. She has one arm across my chest, and her leg is arched over my hip. I am getting very aroused, and there is no way she couldn't notice it.

"Vicky, help me loose that, please," I sub-vocalize. This

woman, this goddess in my arms deserves the very best, not a stolen moment in her parent's house especially with them in the same room. That is not what I am about, things will be done correctly. After all I have waited this long, what is a bit longer…damn it. Within a minute I am calm and relaxed. With the blood rerouting back to my brain, I am able to concentrate on our discussion. Sophee could sense my calmness either by my emotions or the lack of Mr. Happy under the sheet. Her smile faltered a bit for the first time.

"Sophee, I am in love with you and I will always cherish you, only you. I do not think we should mate until this Gham issue is finished and we are at my home on New Harvest."

"Oh… Do you want me to leave?" she asks in a particularly small and vulnerable voice.

"Never," I said, I want you with me always but the second part of our relationship will need to wait a little bit longer, if you're okay with that."

She squeezes me tighter. "I knew I had bonded with the right mate. You just proved that everything I thought is true."

Sleep, *hell,* that isn't likely. I have this absolutely beautiful petite woman lying naked in my arms with her breasts pressed against my side and her legs twining with mine. My fatigue was gone and all I wanted to do is hold her tight and listen to that soft almost musical voice. If I had my choice I would never sleep again.

We talked softly about the future, and what she could expect when she gets to New Harvest. Sophee's questions let me know that she was planning a long life with me. This made me feel better because when the Gham come back I will ensure Sophee's plan comes to fruition. Her questioning was more targeted around me, what I liked and didn't like. She wanted to know fine details that I never even thought about, which made me laugh.

"I didn't plan on meeting anyone," I start to say, "So my expectations are really simple. Live a life of love and laughter with my family. I will protect and take care of you, first and foremost, and then the New Harvest people and the land. What are your expectations Sophee?"

"Pretty much the same, except I will need lots and lots of loving."

"Gee, let me think," I tease, and we both laugh.

Sophee quietly asked, "You really like babies?"

"I am sensing disbelief from an empath? Are your powers fading?"

Sophee is quick to quip. "Well I never thought a warrior would like babies, so maybe my skills really are fading."

"Good thing you're beautiful, and have that to fall back on." I wink at her so she knows I am teasing.

Sophee just hugs me tighter and mumbles, "Goofball."

I'm not sure she knows what a goofball is but with her intuition she must have figured out I was hacking myself earlier and is more than smart enough to be able to use it. That gives me another thought; this is no paper doll. Not only is Sophee kind and sweet but she is incredibly intelligent. With the Sooul being unable to kill a sentient being and living through the continued slaughtering I had not given any thought to these people's intelligence. Solar power, networks, stasis field storage, let alone the technology they use in their bathrooms prove the brains that the Sooul have. I hope now that Sophee and I have bonded I will be able to think more clearly. As the 1st Gunman I should be seeing the details and nuances that other would miss.

"Do you sing a lot?" Sophee asks.

I laughed; "Sorry If I hurt your ears, normally when traveling between missions I used the downtime to read or practice playing my guitar."

"Guitar?" Sophee asks.

I smile at how she is trying to learn everything about me. Before now I would have thought that having anyone know everything about you would be odd. At least she does not know about the dark spots.

"It is musical instrument from history that people play for fun or entertainment. Vicky; can you have the processors make one?" I ask needlessly, after all making a shield from scratch would be more difficult.

"In process sir, it will not be wooden but just a metal frame. The tone and sound will be the same as normal although the mass of the instrument will be slightly more than you are used to." Vicky explains.

Normally I play to amuse myself but I do know a few romantic songs Sophee might like. Playing for her would be okay and because of the bond I would not feel weird or self conscious.

Sophee's eyes shine as she smiles. "Would you play for us some evening?"

"Us?" I question.

"Everyone enjoyed when you sang to the baby and our people would enjoy listening to music with their families since we have never heard your guitar before."

"I am a warrior who fights for a living my love, not an

entertainer, but I will do my best." I say as I pull her tighter for a gentle kiss.

We whisper late into the night…

* * *

I waken sharply to the voice of Hyun asking Mere, "What happened last night? Why is Sophee with him?" He asked in a bewildered voice. "The last thing that I remember was Sophee bringing Joshua a plate of food." Hyun grabs his head theatrically, "bad wine, we should throw that jug out."

Mere smiles at him and says; "The bond is complete. I sense nothing but happiness from both of them. Your daughter sleeps still, but her bonded one is awake and wants to talk with you."

With these words, I carefully slide out from under the cover, trying not to jostle Sophee. After ensuring the blanket was covering Sophee, I step over to where her father is standing while I pull my shirt on. First looking at Hyun and then Mere, I whisper, "May I talk outside with both of you please?"

Thank God Mere had clothes on now. I need to focus on Sophee and our relationship and not be blushing and embarrassed because I am unused to seeing females, specifically my mother-in-law to be naked. Hyun slept in his clothes; I could not imagine having this conversation otherwise.

We walk outside on to the small porch in early morning sun. Mere is quick to take a seat on the bench and pat beside her for me to sit down. Hyun waits until I am seated and sits directly across from me. I take a deep breath because I am out of my comfort zone. Who knew that talking to her parents would be so hard? Mere sensing the turmoil in my mind puts her hand out to hold mine. I pause for a minute and then think; dude, just spit out the truth.

"No matter what you think I did not mate with Sophee last night. I will not until I have your blessing, and until we are on my own planet in my home."

Hyun looks to his mate, rather than me when speaking. "How did Sophee take this?" His question was directed toward Mere but meant for me. Either he's getting emotional data from his wife or he doesn't want to face the fact his daughter is ready to leave the nest. I wonder if his ability to sense truth is not as strong as Mere's and he wants her to mediate.

"Happily, I think." I said, "She may have been a bit surprised at my reasons but understood why I think we should wait."

Hyun's surprise is very evident by the incredulous look on his face. "Is this a normal thing for your people not to mate when you bond?" Mere is watching me intently waiting for my answer.

I don't even have to think about my reason. "Sir, most humans don't bond like the Sooul do. When we share the experience together I want it to be private, personal and her time of love. Most people off this planet would likely want the same thing. My thoughts are the Sooul don't want privacy because they need as much family time as they can get with their uncertain future, or formerly uncertain future."

When I was finished speaking both Mere and Hyun are nodding. I can tell that they are reading me well and know that respect for the daughter overrides any of my needs or desires that I may feel.

Hyun and Mere both hug me. "You're a good man Joshua." Mere wipes her eyes as she said it.

My face feels warm at the praise, "I seriously try to be, but I am a man and a flawed individual." Hyun shakes his head in disagreement, "You make the correct choices for what you think are the proper reasons. Your ways are different than ours, if Sophee can be happy with you it is not our place to interfere."

"Okay, thank you." I said, as I struggle mentally for a minute, I don't want to discuss this anymore. Mere and Hyun don't need to know all of my thoughts. My reasoning is mine alone, and they won't understand. Mere picks up on this and says; "Is there something else Joshua?"

Now is the perfect time to change the subject.

I nod, "There is an issue with your language, I can't speak it without my A.I. and you cannot speak English. All of mankind speaks English and it would benefit your people to do so."

Hyun doesn't catch the under currents of my thoughts; "We can take lessons either from you or when we get to New Harvest."

"My AI can program nanites that are able to alter your language centers in your brain. Normally a language would be a direct download which is more cost effective than nanites. We could do it here with my reserve nanites. They would be added to food and you would just wake up and be able to talk to anyone. You will find it important because most humans don't have the translators or high level AIs."

Mere says "We trust you." Hyun nods; "I speak for all Sooul, please have the nanites programmed by your Vicky."

This was a successful talk, I smile at my soon to be parent-in-laws.

Mere warmly hugs me again, "Hopefully Sophee won't be too grumpy today with all that has happened."

"She may need to get some extra sleep, as we talked well into the night." I state.

"As do you," Mere says with a gentle smile. "Go rest and we will tell our people of the language issue and how we will resolve it.

"Yes, my new mother" I answer obediently, and walk back inside.

Before I can cross back to the bed, Sophee sits up quickly with wide eyes. She must have heard the door's force field dilate, as she is looking around frantically for me. At her movement, the sheet falls away from her torso and allowing me to admire the view as I walk over to the cushions.

"Good morning, my love," I say with a kiss to her forehead.

Removing my shirt, I once again get under the sheet with her. With a huge smile she melts into my arms. To me it seems very odd her naked under the sheet with me and her parents knowing about it.

"Maybe you should tell me when you are leaving so I don't worry." She says happily.

I grin, "You were sleeping and I wanted to talk with your parents about our relationship."

"That's it?" She asks.

"Mostly, Vicky?" I say aloud.

"Yes sir?" She replies in an instant.

"Can you produce the nanites to reprogram the language centers of their brains?"

"Sir, with the amount of nutrients you are consuming I really should not do it. I should be your translator. If the Gham arrive and you are wounded in a battle with them, you will need a reserve."

"Thank you for the concern, but I am not feeling much danger from the Gham. Please program the nanites now, and add it to the Sooul's food supply. Produce milk chocolate bars. One for every person here on Sooul so they can get two treats."

"Sophee, please talk sense into your…"

"Vicky!" I interrupt. "That's an order!"

"Very well, sir. Please place your hand on the stasis unit so I can transfer your base unused nanites to the food."

I gently separate myself from Sophee's embrace and walk to the food processor. I place my hand on the input pad. There is a sharp pain as the nanites are brought from inside my body through my palm. Within a minute Vicky says, "Complete, going passive."

I rub the sore spot on my hand where the nanites passed as I walk back to Sophee.

Sophee looks a little concerned and asks, "Will you be in danger?"

"Only a little." In my answer she sees mostly the truth, and a bit of evasion. Nothing in battle is guaranteed and I won't lie by saying it is. The apprehension in her eyes lets me know that she was still worried. Damn Vicky for making her concerned.

"I am an effective fighter." I say, giving her a smile to show my lack of fear. "If the Gham decide not to leave, I will end them. It's as simple as that, so please don't worry about me."

My emotional state; and fact that I could speak in calm soft voice with absolute conviction, not to mention the fact I started kissing her helped Sophee to relax. Sophee has her hand on my bare chest. She looks me in the eye and asks, "By your state of partial undress can I assume you are changing your mind?"

"No, I haven't, but when in Rome." I say with a grin.

Sophee's ability now that we are bonded allows her to know that I find it funny to use old earth sayings. She hugs me tighter. "You are so very funny. I will need to research ducks, rome, and a lot of things you say."

"Okay, get some sleep," Sophee is still tired and snuggled into my side lying on my arm. She was sound asleep when I decided to closed my eyes.

* * *

Mere and Hyun walked around the town explaining the language issue and the decision to allow the nanites. Not a single Sooul questioned the decision, they accepted it because their leaders do but more importantly their Joshua offered it to them.

There was also a lot of faith in their Joshua. More questions were asked about Sophee's relationship and what happened last night? The Sooul that had dinner and stayed at Hyun's home could tell the couple was in the final stages of the bond. Since the people of Sooul never felt the need for total privacy they mistakenly figured the bond had happened with the usual results. Most assumed they knew rather than asking direct questions about the couple's bond. When the Mere and Hyun reached Shoran's home, they were asked direct questions.

"Where is Sophee? What happened? Why is she sleeping so late?" Shoran excitedly demanded to know.

The Sooul are always very open about all things, Mere decides that even though Joshua is a closed book, Sophee is typical Sooul and she could share the details. After all, Shoran and Sophee were best friends.

"It all started when he realized he was too tall for a standard bed. He picked up Hyun and made sure he got into our bed. Joshua only removed his shirt; I think he is quite shy. When I removed my garments to get into bed, I could sense keen embarrassment and discomfort." Mere smiles at Shoran before continuing, "I could feel his uncertainty about where he was; it was quite sweet and charming. Sophee lay with him and again I could feel unease but not as much as before. There was a lot of energy and excitement, which immediately died off. They talked in such low tones I could not hear them. Within a couple of minutes all I could sense was happiness."

Shoran eyes go wide. "Did they...?"

"No." Mere chuckles. "It is not his way. They have bonded but he wants to deal with the Gham and take her to his home before completing their bond. From his unease and our conversations, I think he is afraid of taking advantage of Sophee. I can also sense he has complete and utter dedication, almost a kind of worship for her."

Shoran is grinning ear to ear and practically hopping when she says, "I want to go to New Harvest and meet my giant man!" Hyo smiled at her happy daughter knowing she is thinking about the single men Joshua said live on New Harvest. If Shoran can meet a man like Sophee's Joshua all worry for her future would be erased.

"Your mother and I hope we live to see the day." Lian wishes out loud as turns his head to Hyun. "Is it too much to hope for?"

"From my mates view no, but we should be asking Sophee more questions." Another smile crosses Hyun's face, "Good luck getting a minute alone with her, she's all about her bonded one now."

"In my opinion you could ask her or her mate-to-be anything because he also is painfully honest." Mere simply says.

* * *

I awake to a chime and open my eyes. Sophee is still sleeping soundly; poor thing must have been beat.

Vicky stays sub-vocal and says; "You need more nutrients."

"Status of my orders from this morning?" I ask.

"Per your orders, nanites have been programmed and added to the towns bulk food supply. Chocolate will be produced at evening meals, and small bars with be issued for every person. I do not agree with your decision to possibly endanger yourself without proper healing protocols."

"I know Vicky; a man has to do what a man has to do." I say.

I really don't care if my AI likes it or not, what I think is right is what will be done. Vicky accepts what I say and leaves that subject alone for now. It is silent for one minute then Vicky opens up sub-vocally once more.

"Sir, my scans on the Sooul's data records here have pinpointed the next time that the Gham will land."

"When?" I ask.

"One hundred seven hours, and fifteen minutes." Vicky said.

That gives me four and a half days of Sophee time before I need to fight. Fighting is almost a foregone conclusion as any species that would murder hundreds of millions of any sentient species are killers. Killers don't negotiate, at least not when they think they have all the power.

"One more thing sir, I will be unable to suppress your urges due to low nanite volume. You're on your own, stud!" By Vicky's tone of voice she has accepted my decision and now is back into personal assistant mode. If Sophee had not been sleeping I would have laughed out loud.

I slowly stand and stretch, Sophee murmurs softly. I bend over listening to what she is saying and I hear my name. *I dream of you too little one.* I quietly pull on my new shirt as I go outdoors. Wow we have slept all morning and it is mid afternoon by the height of the sun. I feel hungry again, but decide to walk to the center of town and look at the Gham's landing site.

Not sure why I feel so compelled to check it out early. Maybe the Gham are the only uncertainty here and as a Gunman I know making advance plans is paramount to success. Seeing it alone without Sophee would allow me to focus more on the site than on her. Not that I wouldn't rather be with Sophee at all times.

As I walk by the people of Sooule, all eyes are on me. I have no idea why they watch me so closely, unless it is just curiosity because I am a stranger. How was I to know Shoran had all ready told everyone that I had bonded with Sophee? Hopefully my private decisions and thoughts can stay that way.

I finish my stroll at a grassy area behind the cluster of homes. Trying to imagine this area as a sports field, concert venue, or even just a kid's park is not easy after seeing the video that was taken here. I can feel the horror associated with the area when I see dried bloodstains near a section of crushed down clover grass. I walk over and look down at the rust colored stain and sit beside it. An innocent was tortured to death here. A family died. My plans start to form in my mind, the Gham ship with their F.T.L. drive will be needed to call for help.

"Vicky," I say aloud, "send a message to Granddad about what we have seen where we are for pick up. Convey my apologies: wait! Record this for transmission please: Granddad, Mom, I am sorry for being selfish by going hunting before I came home. My decision, however inconsiderate to my family, has put me in a place I needed to be."

I continued talking, trying to explain about Sophee and the Soul. About how I felt and what these good people needed. When I finished, I told Vicky to add the number of Sooul for transport and broadcast it toward home. Sure it could a while to get to them but the message would eventually get to my family

Ending the recording, I close my eyes for a minute while I think. "Vicky, how long do you think it will take to for the message to get home?"

"A week or two, maybe faster depending on where the signals get bounced from."

"Thank you."

As I sit beside this place of horror and cruelty, several questions twist thru my mind. If these Gham come, forcing me to kill them, how will the Sooul react? Eradicating a bunch of eels is not like doing battle with sentient beings. The brutality and violence required to defeat this foe may be too much for the gentle Sooul to cope with. Will I be a monster to them? Can Sophee fall out of love with me and break our newly formed bond?

I am certain of one thing, and that is I will end them. I will not allow the Gham to harm one more Sooul. Darker thoughts intrude on my mind as I make many plans to deal with the Gham. Each strategy can have several outcomes, all of them bad for the Gham. I get up from and stretch again for a minute as I look at the elevation change toward the back of the open field.

Walking slowly around the meadow, I can see the Gham craft in my mind and the way it will land. From the video they don't seem to be in a rush at all. Slowly landing and coming out in a group. If I had a ship I could take them out before they enter the atmosphere. No ship or heavy weapons are available. Should I use the railgun to vaporize them? If I do that how many more will come back, so many that I couldn't protect the Sooul from them?

Hell, if they attack again like they did the first few times everyone could die. There is no way currently to defend against aerial bombardment. The Gham could stay in orbit and drop kinetic energy weapons. They don't even need aimed projectiles. Rocks would work as well with this undefended town.

Maybe I should use the rifle, and snipe the Gham from in hiding? No, I will not leave Sophee alone or use the rest of the Sooul as bait or possibly thinking they will die because I deserted them.

Ambushing the aliens when they land is not possible in this opening. They would know something was up if the Sooul were not waiting. My guess is that they also will be actively scanning as they come down to land.

Stand up fight? I walk toward the slight rise near the back of the field and look back across the meadow at the landing site. It is a clear zone for shooting, well within range of my weapons. I wonder if I stood back and shot them if they would respond with railgun or lasers? Not a good idea if I am in front of the Sooul, collateral damage must be avoided. I cannot allow one single Sooul to get injured; my promise was they will be safe.

Should I get as close as I can to the ship, and attack when they open the hatch? With no way of knowing what defensive systems they have to repel boarders would make that option unwise.

My path is clearer now to me.

Vicky has remained silent the entire time, so either I am not going accidentally sub-vocally or she knows this is my problem to work out. It is up to me to fight for and defend the Sooul.

As I run through these thoughts and more, I set the priorities. Protecting Sophee and the Sooul is the primary priority. Killing the Gham to take the ship, and use the F.T.L. drive to call for support is secondary. Or I could use the F.T.L. drive from the Gham ship as a weapon.

I see movement out of the corner of my eye and pause for a second as my girl walks into my view. Sophee is heading toward me from the town. Since I do not want to worry her I think to myself be happy don't dwell on the Gham. Be in the moment; be happy to see my love. I walk toward her trying to think only good loving thoughts.

* * *

Sophee woke up to find Joshua gone. She actually smiled at the thought of his being considerate not to wake her up, as she slept a peaceful sleep without dreaming of the Gham for the first time in her life. It only takes a second of thought to realize Joshua is being himself and checking on the shield or something equally important. Sophee loves the fact that Joshua is so protective and yet thoughtful. My Joshua moves around so much and has a lot of energy, his business amuses me. *I hope that he retains the energy later* she thought.

Sophee gets out of the bed, and heads to the sanitary room to wash up. After getting dressed, she folds up the large blanket and reorganizes the cushion back for sitting on. Since Joshua is obviously busy at the moment she grabs a bowl and some clippers.

The processor's light glows briefly and a metal object starts sliding out on to the counter. Sophee stops to watch wondering what the dark metal thing could be for a minute before remembering last night's conversation. When the item clears the mouth of the machine it unfolds into an odd shape. There are wires that stretch almost the whole length. Sophee looks at it with wonder because Joshua is very causal about his shields and weapons. This thing has to be the guitar instrument that her Joshua told her about. It looks very funny to her even if Joshua said it made music. Sophee picked it up carefully and laid it on the cushions for Joshua to find. How something this strange could keep Joshua busy or from getting bored for periods of time was lost on her.

The late afternoon sun is bright and warm as she walks to the gardens to collect some plants for the next meal. Sophee thought it was nice to be able to cook and create food for someone with an appetite and, if she gets to New Harvest, she hopes whatever job she has to get will give her enough time to cook and care for a family.

Turning from the plants she was gathering, Sophee saw her mother rushing toward her. Her mother's emotions did not reflect the calm look on her face. Concern was the prevailing emotion that her mother had. There was no fear or any other major emotion but concern and maybe a touch of kindness. Sophee stood up and started walking to meet her mom in mid garden.

Mere reaches Sophee and puts her hand on her shoulder. "Joshua is sitting in the gathering meadow by the spot where the last rendering happened. People can see him just sitting there staring at the ground. There are serious emotions emanating from him." Mere paused for a minute as to catch her breath, but it was more likely she was taking a second to convert Joshua's emotions into word. "The darkness in his heart is in the open."

Sophee said, "He left me while I was still asleep, any negative thoughts must be directed at the Gham only. Mom, he is truly good. I know this because we talked late into the night about our thoughts and feelings. When he realized we had bonded, I thought it would be time to…you know, but he said no. I was sad for a minute until my Joshua said that he had to solve this Gham issue first." Sophee's wide eyes and emotions are imploring her mother to understand what kind of man her Joshua is. "I think his honor is making him put the Sooul first before his happiness. I know this is his first reason but something also makes him use restraint." She looks down as a dark red blush covers her entire face; "and oh how he was ready."

Mere actually blushes as well and silently holds her hands about four inches apart. Sophee who is now growing redder by the second shakes her head and holds her hand much farther apart.

Her mother gasps at the thought before regaining her composure. Mere's hand drops from Sophee's shoulder and then she says, "Go and be with Joshua while I make the meal, maybe your presence will calm the darkness." Sophee is very quick to pass her mom the basket and clippers before hurrying to calm her Joshua.

She walks quickly to find Joshua. When he fought the eels he was dead calm, if the Gham can invoke this much emotion from him how badly will it end for them? Her mother's gasp in surprise makes her wonder if mating will be difficult. Since Sophee has no knowledge about mating she had better talk about it with her mom in detail beforehand. After all her knowledge was only from what she has overheard from her parents sleeping area. If it were not for the fact that she truly knows that Joshua will be her mate for life it would be a scary prospect to mate with him.

When Sophee reaches the meadow, Joshua is no longer sitting by the blood-soaked ground. Glancing around, she sees him walking near the far side of the meadow studying the whole area. Sophee can see him mentally accessing the landing zone and the slight rise behind the last rendering area. From what she has seen when he battles he is looking for shooting areas and kill zones. Again this calms her because her Joshua is planning to keep her safe.

Pausing for a second to watch him, Sophee reads his emotional state. From Joshua she can sense the darker side of his personality, the violent intent he exudes when he is making his plans. For Joshua being such a kind and loving man, the violent intent or darkness as they see it, is a shocking contrast.

When she steps into open view, he paused and his emotional state changed or went flat again. Joy and happiness replaced his emotions. His self control is amazing. What would create such a warrior Sophee was asking herself? As soon as he calmed, he walked directly to her and picked her up in his arm to kiss her.

Sophee thinks her heart will burst through her chest. Now the dark place has gone away and Joshua's entire being is filled with nothing but joy and love. When his arms wrap around she feels everything will be all right. The protective love is so strong Sophee's eyes start to water. If lovemaking with her bonded one is anywhere near as satisfying her life will be absolutely perfect.

* * *

"Hello," Sophee said lightly when she caught her breath, "Did you rest well?"

I look at the goddess in my arms, and try to explain that it was the best rest I ever had.

"Never before have I ever been so relaxed, you complete a part of me that I didn't know was missing." I said. "This morning sleeping with you was the most peaceful time I have ever had. The only thing better was finding out you loved me last night. Singularly it was the best night of my life."

Her finger touches my lips to silence me. "It was the

best night of my life so far, and I am still waiting for the better night."

Right to the point, I like that in a girl.

Her head dips and she shyly says; "I am looking forward to it, even if my mother is concerned about that night for me."

It does not take a second to know what they are thinking about. I ask Vicky sub-vocally to scan Sophee medically and tell me about our physical compatibility.

"I have already scanned Sophee when I checked her DNA. Yes, you are compatible if you take it slowly and gently."

"Thank you Vicky." I say sub-vocally.

"Vicky says we are compatible, but I should be cautious," I tell Sophee.

"I think you are always cautious...unless you are throwing yourself at an enemy," Sophee says seriously

To this I have no defense and stay silent. Attacking something with complete abandon is not a Gunman's way. We tend to plan out our attacks, unless shit hits the fan. Been in a few of those situations, seen it, done it, got the tee shirt. I am not going to lie to Sophee and tell her it will not happen. Maybe her idea of me throwing myself at an enemy was when I jumped into an eel's mouth. *Ha...if you think that you have seen me throw myself at an enemy just wait a few days...*

Sophee has still got her arms around my neck and I decide that putting her down is not an action I am willing to take. I lift her up higher to carry her. Sophee's arm slides around behind my neck as I carry her back toward the house. We leave the meadow and slowly walk taking time to stop and kiss frequently. When I can finally tear my eyes away from Sophee I look toward the group of homes and see several people smiling at us.

"I guess it is okay to kiss you in public now?" I ask, not really caring if anyone thinks I shouldn't.

"Everyone now knows we are bonded and is happy for us," she says.

I stay quiet and just smile. The Sooul know far too much about each other. Maybe Mere or Hyun were telling people that Sophee and I had bonded or they are using their mental gifts to find out. As I walk through the town, people greet us and smile like there is no tomorrow. Either these people live in the moment and are happy for us or they are beginning to believe their ordeal may be over. If it is the later I had better be victor in the coming conflict. Hell, I hate to lose anyway but now that I have Sophee my motivation is through the proverbial roof.

Maybe Vicky was right I should have kept some Kcals.

"Sophee, I am going to need a lot of food over the next few days." I said, after all I don't want them to think I eat like a pig all the time. "I will need to have lots of energy," I say. Almost immediately her heart starts beating faster and her face gets flushed.

"Are you asking my mother to deliver me to your bed?"

I shake my head no. "Let me deal with Gham, if there is a fight I will need the energy, then we will make plans."

She is silent and I hope her feelings are not hurt. I continue to think about how I feel and hope she is sensing my emotions. Her heart rate resumed its normal rhythm and the flush slowly left her face. She still had her arm around my neck and seemed okay but I still wondered what she was thinking.

As I walk around the bend leading to her parent's home,

her father is sitting on his porch reading something. We got within a dozen steps before Hyun finally looks up and sees me, with a laugh he asks, "Is Sophee tired again?" I would have thought he being a Sooul would understand my need to be as close to Sophee and humanly possible.

Using my most respectful and serious voice, I answer. "Sir I cannot bear to set her down because I am afraid without my light of my life I would be trapped in darkness and be unable to find my way."

"Well said, Joshua," Hyun says surprised at my response. "Now, would you like to eat outside or inside?"

"It doesn't matter to me as long as I am with my Sophee." I carefully lower Sophee to her feet. From the smile and expression on Sophee's face, I am okay and not in trouble even though I am not asking her mother to deliver her for ravishment.

I sat with her father outside until our meal was ready, we did not even talk. It was peaceful to sit on the porch and just chill out. The ladies joined us outside so we could all enjoy the fading sunshine as we ate.

I of course eat like a machine, Sophee and Mere had a plate and Hyun had seconds. I think I had four plates of food. Sophee's parents did not bat an eye at the amount of food I ate. I didn't know if Sophee had explained why I was eating so much. Either they knew why or just thought a bigger person would require more food. Of course knowing how kind the Sooul are maybe they just didn't care.

"Milk chocolate has been created and there is one for every person on Sooul except nursing babies. You will find them on your stasis pads, Joshua says enjoy." Vicky announces thru the home's sound system. At this news, I get up and walk inside the house to retrieve them for my new family. There are three small bars of chocolate sitting on the output pad. I pick them up, head back out to the small porch. I feel like a kid giving a gift because I am eager for them to try chocolate and I am looking forward to their reactions. I give one to Mere, and then Hyun.

"Sophee, close your eyes and open your mouth please." I ask

Without hesitation Sophee shut her eyes and opened her lips. I carefully put piece of the chocolate on her pink tongue. Being a part of a good experience for Sophee means a lot to me, there are so many things I want to do and share with her. This is the first of many and I hope she enjoys it.

"Now close your mouth, and let it melt." I said. I lean forward to watch her expression. There was slight rising of her eyelids when the chocolate started melting and her taste buds processed the flavor. Sophee sat very still as the chocolate melted away to nothing. If I do anything else in my life I want it to be what causes Sophee to smile the way she does now.

Sophee opens her eyes. "It is wonderful, can I have more?"

I hand her the rest or the bar of milk chocolate and receive a nice kiss as a reward. I then realize that her parents were waiting to try it because they wanted Sophee to have the first taste.

Sophee looks across the table at her parents with that happy smile and says; "Maybe you will not like chocolate and I should hold your pieces."

We start laughing at her not too subtle attempt at acquiring more chocolate. Mere eats her treat in much the same way as Sophee, breaking it into small pieces and closing her eyes for the first taste. Her father is grinning as he eats the chocolate by taking a bite off the bar. As Sophee nibbles on another small piece she looks quizzically at me. "None for you?"

I slowly shake my head, "No, I speak English" I reply with a grin.

"That is not what I mean Joshua; would you like a taste of your chocolate?" Sophee asks.

"Why yes I would, thank you." I lean over and give her a really passionate kiss. When I break away her eyes are wide and her face is flush with excitement.

"Yes, it tastes good." I say with a laugh.

Sophee sputters for a second trying to speak and then giggles, "Your welcome."

Mere and Hyun watched the entire little interaction smiling. They are clearly staring to understand my humor.

"Quite the change we are experiencing this week," Hyun says happily.

Be ready for more, I think to myself. I am going to do everything in my power to make their lives better.

"Is this a typical food for your people?" Mere asks. I can tell she wants to know more about me and our people on New Harvest.

I look down at the table as I ponder the question, and then reach out to hold Sophee's hand before answering. "I have family, but since I also sit with my new family it is a hard question to answer. If you enjoy it then it will truly be my people's food."

Mere nods and turns to her mate and says; "A heartfelt truth has just been told."

"And as a direct answer this is a flavor, it is put in some

specialty foods and drinks. It is more of an ingredient or a treat than a food staple." I said.

Sophee catches her mother's eye and smiles at Joshua's "My people comment." Both can sense the amount of love and respect Joshua has for the Sooul.

"So this is what the bond does to a person?" I inquire, looking at Hyun. "I was not all sappy before meeting the Sooul. Rather than talk about the truths, I felt staying silent was my thing."

Mere laughs, "Joshua; compared to the people of Sooul you're still about as talkative as a rock."

"Maybe it is that old mankind adage that a tough man needs to be silent and filled with purpose," I said with smiling.

Hyun's relaxed and happy expression did not change "You could do anything here and not have one Sooul think you any less a warrior; we know who and what you are. The women of Sooul, who are far more sensitive than any man, were continually discussing with us the state of your emotions when you were fighting the eels. We know your heart."

"Sir, I would not argue with you, but that really was not much of a fight." I explained.

Sophee and Mere shared a quick look, realizing that another unconditional truth was just told. Without speaking about it at that moment, the two women realized no matter how epic Joshua's nighttime battle with the eels was to them, the skirmish was not anything special to him. If being wounded and outnumbered by hundreds of hungry eels wasn't intense to Joshua maybe the Gham will be in trouble. Sophee and Mere decided to leave this subject alone for Joshua told them far more by what he didn't say than in conversations.

Seeing the two women nod at each other, I shook

my head. "I wish I could sense what you were thinking, because whenever women nod to each other they have made a discovery about something and it makes me nervous."

Sophee gave me a quick kiss. "Funny, but nervousness is not something we are sensing," she said. Sophee smiles at my comment; all she and most likely her mother can sense is that I am happy and calm.

Dinner was such a casual affair for the Sooul. They take a long time to eat because they have these profound conversations. I am a pretty intelligent person but the depth of their thoughts must be attuned with their empathic abilities, I see deep reason and it amazes me about how they can micro-analyze thoughts or actions.

"You're awfully quiet, Joshua," Mere said kindly trying to draw me into their discussion.

"I am merely enjoying your conversation. The amount of kindness you show each other is incredible. It is not just with your own family but everyone, me included" I grin at my hosts. "Not having your empathic skills puts me at a disadvantage, as I have to think about what you say rather than sense the emotional content."

"Joshua does not feel uncomfortable around us mother." Sophee points out. Mere lays a hand on my arm; "You would tell us if our ways disturb you?"

"Me get disturbed?" I grin at that. "I am more of a go-with-the-flow kind of person."

The conversation goes to New Harvest at what they can expect. We discussed life styles of the New Harvest people. I explained that we try to work together well but not having the Sooul's social ability makes it difficult sometimes. There are just some people who don't like social interaction. This is fine and those people find places to work or areas to live where they can reside in relative peace. Most ordinary people don't look for adventure anymore; they look for stability and family. New Harvest is a good place for someone who wants a decent family life.

"Why, then, did you leave to join the Peoples Free Force?" Hyun inquired.

My answer was not what he expected. "I wasn't very mature when I was eighteen. Working the farm and managing New Harvest was boring to me, especially when making a difference for mankind is what I really wanted to be doing. Who wants to be trapped in a relationship and tied to the farm? Where is the joy in that? That was my way of thinking for a long time. Heck, my decision to go hunting a few weeks ago before going home would also fall into the same category."

Hyun's expression was one of disbelief. In front of him is his only daughter's bonded one and he doesn't want a family. "And now?" He asked.

I reach over to Sophee, gently pull her on to my lap, and give her a kiss. "All my training and work experience was to make an effective leader. I no longer think of myself as being tied down to New Harvest. Trapped? I feel that Sophee has freed me. Meeting the Sooul has been good for me, and my life is forever changed."

I look at Hyun and Mere, and see Hyun smile as he reads my emotions. Mere never stopped smiling or was even worried a bit because her abilities allowed her to look deeper into my mental state.

"Thank you for everything you have given me," I say with the utmost of sincerity.

A few tears roll down the cheeks of both Sophee and Mere as they digest the truthful emotions in my statement.

"I wish you two would stop crying because you make me feel like I am playing with your emotions." By my smile Hyun could tell I was not serious, the girls on the other hand knew and I received a kiss from both of them.

"We wish that ship could take us away from Sooul before the Gham come back," Hyun states. "It would be a terrible tragedy if we couldn't see New Harvest after learning we are not alone in this galaxy." Mere nods in agreement to her mate; "We had always wondered if the Gham had killed the beings that supplied the DNA."

"Please remember my promise to you," I said in a firm and, I hoped, positive voice. "All of you are coming to my home, and I do not ever make promises lightly."

Mere looks at Joshua closely, his honesty and conviction is as plain as the smile on his face. There is something else, unfathomable resolve that moves like lightning around a spot of darkness that he is trying to hide. *Whatever he does will be for our betterment.* Mere gets up once more and steps back over to hug us both. She then sits back down beside her mate.

Sophee poured me another glass of wine, and asked me if I would like some more dinner. I shook my head with a smile and pulled her closer, not wanting to let Sophee go. Damn, Mere is very perceptive, I must not let the Gham into my thoughts or she might find out what I am willing to do.

I had to ask about the crawlers we had for dinner,

and was informed only the small ones were edible, as the shells on the big ones are like armor and are impossible to harvest. Sophee told me that she was tired of eating the small crawlers, which was one of the reasons she was fishing the day I saw first her.

"Do the larger ones taste better?" I asked.

"No, they are about the same," Mere responds, "but there is much more meat on them, so they are better to eat."

I had to enquire what parts they actually do eat, and realized they were nothing more than a land crab. Legs and claws were about all they eat which was similar to crabs I wonder if their food units could produce butter? I haven't had a good feed of crab for years. Just the thought of crab with butter makes my mouth water.

"Do you want one or two for dinner tomorrow? I'm sure I can take them down without blowing it apart like an eel," I offer.

Before Mere or Sophee can say anything Hyun jumps up excitedly and says; "Yes."

He then asks if he can join this hunt with a few other men. They have never seen a hunt done in their lifetime and had only read stories about it from way back.

Damn, I will have to go slow enough to allow them to keep up.

"Certainly, I would be honored."

Sophee looks at me and can read that bit of hesitation on my part, but doesn't comment on it. I suppose she will question me later as Sophee doesn't let anything go unsaid. Hyun is very excited about the prospect of our excursion, and leaves to organize the hunting party as well as a group of volunteers to do the cooking of whatever we manage to capture. I could hear him muttering plans to himself as he walked out the door.

I look to the women in confusion. "Why is it such a big deal? What is so special about crab hunting?"

Mere smiles and says, "You might have a difficult time fathoming all we have lost as a people since the Gham have came," Mere said with a sad smile. "Hunting the large crawlers were some of the only adventures the men had on this planet. Hyun never thought he would ever see the day when he would be able to hunt large crawlers, he is excited."

It is sad that the Sooul have lost so much. People need adventure, even if it is only a crab hunt with a Gunman as a guide.

"Vicky, please search the Sooul database and get me any information on how to kill and clean these creatures," I instruct out loud.

Within moments she has a reply for me. "Sir, the big ones the Sooul hunted were the size of a medium dog. They captured the creatures by netting them and then tying their legs up before using a drill of sorts to destroy the brain. Then the Sooul spent hours with knives cutting between the joints of the crawler to break up the legs and claws for cooking. They boil the segments for half a day before they are cooked enough to eat. Beware of the danger to the Sooul, though, as the large crawler are now the size of your cows and are a lot stronger. Their exoskeletons would be much thicker, and this will pose a challenge to the Sooul. An armor-piercing round above the mouth and slightly below the eyes should kill them easily."

I listen to Vicky with Sophee and Mere. I want them to

feel comfortable knowing I am going to ensure everything is done safely.

"Vicky can…" I start to ask a question when I am interrupted.

"I can program the processors to produce butter because of the all the raw meat held in stasis."

Sophee smiles and says; "we will help prepare for the cooking of the crawlers. You will watch my father?"

"Maybe a man of his age would be able to teach me something." I ask.

Mere slowly shakes her head. "He is not a warrior like you. We must rely on your skill and common sense to protect our mates."

Babysitting then, how much fun will that be?

Sophee looks at me and pats my arm. I smile at her and think that I will be forever unable to hide my sarcasm from now on.

The amount of food I ate was making me quite tired. Sophee noticing went inside and set up the sleeping cushions. When she came back out her mom had gone looking for Hyun and I was all alone. I took the time to carry the dishes inside to the prep area. Sophee motioned to the bed so I left her to load the plates into the cleaner. She briefly disappeared for a minute of two then walked back to where I was laying and removed her clothes. This time I didn't feel too bad about checking her out. Her petite slender body was almost elfin in appearance. Sophee met my eyes as I was watching her undress.

"You are beautiful." I said.

"Only to you, I think." was her humble reply.

Inwardly I chuckle; Sophee has no idea that she is so

breath taking. Of course with their gifts the heart and mind is the most important thing. I think back to time at home and what my Grandfather said about a very nice looking woman who worked as a clerk in the business office. I said she was hot, Grandfather agreed that she was easy on the eyes but to remember her heart was more important than the skin surrounding it. Sophee was the easiest thing on my eyes that I have seen, her heart is much larger than her skin.

Lying under the blanket with Sophee all naked and snuggled up with me is my new favorite thing to do. Dealing with the Gham is number one on my list, marrying her is number two. I find myself thinking about the wedding night and realize my life is going to be just splendid.

Sophee lifts her head and gives me a kiss before looking into my eyes very seriously. "I expect you to stop my father from endangering himself on your hunt."

"Of course I will, was there any doubt?" I ask.

"Why were you uncertain when he asked to go hunting with you?" Sophee asks

"I am not used to having to watch other men with no combat or hunting skill. I am used to going quite fast and I realize this trip will take longer than what I am accustomed to. I suppose this will be a learning experience for both your father and me."

"Keep them all safe, please. We don't need to lose anymore Sooul."

I quietly laugh and agree. Without her asking I would have been very careful with Hyun's and the others safety.

Of course the way she was lying with her leg over mine her body against me is causing me to react in a rather unfortunate manner, and I get a little more than uncomfortable. I slide out from her grasp and roll Sophee gently onto her stomach, so I can distance myself from her warm body.

I sit up and start giving Sophee a very gentle massage. Sophee lets out these little gasps as I find tight muscles and work them gently until they are soft again. I can only imagine that carrying the shield generator part way to the mouth of the cove and the long walk made her sore. After about an hour of stroking and gently kneading her back, Sophee had become very relaxed and fallen fast asleep.

She snored very softly, which I found cute as hell. This is all mine was all I could think. I cover her back up, pulling the blanket over her bare shoulders, and ease myself onto my side to watch her sleep. I lie there quietly with my arm over Sophee until I too fall asleep.

It seems like I had just shut my eyes when I hear a clunking noise and, upon waking, realize it is dawn. Hyun is moving around, getting dressed and picking out a knife from the prep area. I slip out of bed and pull on my battle suit. There is a plate of food on the counter in the prep area so I join Hyun and have a few pieces for breakfast. Hyun leaves first so I grab my rifle, pack and step outside the door.

Hyun looks up from putting his shoes on and examines me from head to toe before speaking. "It must be difficult to sleep with your bonded one without mating." Hyun says with a sly smile.

"Well, Sir," I said. "She, you, and everyone here will be safe before I have my pleasure or…" I stop, realizing I just called Sophee my pleasure and disrespected our relationship.

"I am sorry, Hyun, that didn't come out the way I mean it." I dropped my head in shame for my stupid statement.

With a dismissive wave of his hand, Hyun says, "Do you

not think I know the difference between what you said and what you are feeling? I may not be as sensitive to nuances as Mere, and I am nowhere near my daughter's level, but I don't have to be. I can read you like a book, so I know of your love and commitment to Sophee. Let's just hope the swelling goes down today, heh-heh."

Man, there are some things you can't hide in the morning.

Hyun and I walk to the meadow to meet up with the six other Sooul coming on our little hunting excursion. The other men are all wearing grins as large as Hyun's; Lian who is Shoran's dad introduces me to the other five guys.

"Girls don't hunt?" I ask.

"Women cook, hunting is for men." Hyun states in a very firm voice.

Lian laughs at Hyun and says; "Only because they say cleaning crawlers is messy." All the guys are chuckling when Roin says; "we should leave quickly before they find chores for us." Their laughter is a good thing to hear, as it means they are starting to relax a bit.

Mein says he had seen a very large crawler a few days before in the small ravine. I know where that is from my scouting when I found the Sooul but motion to him to lead the way.

I follow the group, but stay off the trail and to the right so I can cover them should something dangerous decides to attack. I don't pretend to know the wildlife here and I will not be surprised by any creature. I keep my rifle across my chest in a close combat carry, because I promised to watch over all the men and keep them safe. I don't pay much attention to their conversations as I am listening for footsteps or the sliding sound the eels make. The brush and forest we are walking through is fairly sparse and shooting would be easy in the openings. The sun is warm and I realize that the men are totally relaxed and are sure that nothing bad is in the area.

"Hyun, are there any dangerous creatures here on Sooule?" I ask.

"Just the eels near shore," he pauses to smile at me. "There is also a really big Gunman wandering around but Sophee has him tamed."

My mouth drops open in surprise at Hyun's slam as his friends break out laughing.

I hang my head; "Should I go back with the girls?"

"No, we will try and man you up." Says a very generous Lian.

I grin at the group as they try and regain some composure.

As we get closer to the ravine the brush and trees thinned out. Hyun points up and one of those green dragon things flew over us. All the men were looking at it intently and I wondered if they could be dangerous.

"Our ancestors used to trap the grull as well," Hyun said. "I read that they were very tasty when slow roasted."

The grull, as I have now learned the dragon-lizard-bird is called, was swooping around in the sky just ahead of us. I watch the avian for a moment as it searches for dinner among the small boulders and rocks for the smaller crawlers. I sling the rifle over my shoulder, pulled out my sig, and cut closer to the diving creature. The creature makes few more hits on rocks before it finally discovers a spider rock. The grull grabs the small crawler with its mouth, and turns to fly toward the ravine.

I judged the grull's flight path and estimated it would come almost directly overhead at about eighty feet above the ground. I thumbed off the safety on my handgun, and fired almost straight up. The hunters were watching the grull and missed me pulling out my weapon and shooting. I take a bit of satisfaction that they all jumped at the sound of the shot.

The bullet blew the crawler in half inside the gull's mouth and then continued its path upward until it punched out the top of creature's head. The grull just folded up like sack of wet laundry and fell right at us. It would have hit Lian and Hyun if I didn't take ten fast steps toward the Sooul in order to deflect its trajectory. Sure, the thing weighed only a couple hundred pounds or so, but at the speed it was falling, it would have severely injured or even crushed the smaller men.

Hyun and the other Sooul look at me in with wide eyes in silence. I can imagine that the shot and the speed of my movement to deflect the grull caught them off guard. *Not that tame now, eh boys?*

I just smiled and ignored the looks of awe on their faces. They knew I believed they would be too slow to get out of the way. I didn't want to have to reveal that Sophee and Mere asked me to babysit them, nor did I want to try explaining to the womenfolk why I let someone get hurt or killed.

Looking at the grull I asked if anyone knew how to clean it, but from the blank stares I received I took that as a no. Considering the creature, I figured I would just need to treat it like a small pig rather than lizard with wings. I removed my knife from its sheath and rolled the grull on its back. Using the tip of my knife I split the skin of the grull from the crotch to the neck and pulled out all the organs.

One of the men who, for the life of me, I could not remember his name grabbed a few of the organs I had piled beside the carcass. I think it was the heart and what may have been a liver that the man took, and he put them in a flexible container that he pulled out of his pocket.

He then spoke to Hyun and asked if he and another man should take the grull back so they could start roasting it? Hyun agreed that they should get it cooking. The two men together weighed about what the cleaned grull would and it was still too heavy for them to carry. I used my knife, cut down a small tree and used some cord to hang the animal from it so they could carry it on the pole. They left slowly and I wondered how far they would get before taking a break.

We continued on our way looking for the elusive giant spider-rock-crab-thingy. Sure, I could call it a crawler like the rest of the Sooul do, but the creature doesn't really crawl and I am stubborn at times—particularly when it comes to names. Actually the truth of the matter is I am lousy with names, if I had my way I would just call everything Bruce.

We walked up to the ravine's edge until we could look over the edge and right below us down about twelve feet is the elusive creature, okay it is not that elusive.

I pulled out my sig again, but this time I handed it to Hyun. The look on his face is priceless as he held the gun safely pointed in the air. I show him where the safety was and ask him if he would like to shoot the crawler. Hyun carefully aims and fires and drops the handgun on the recoil from the first shot. I reach down and pick the handgun up. I blow the dirt off my weapon and check the barrel for obstructions before handing it back to the surprised Hyun.

"I did exactly the same thing when I shot my first

handgun. Why don't you try again, but this time using two hands, sir," I said.

To Hyun's credit, he tried again with two hands. Some of the bullets bounced off the crawlers shell the others never hit it. I could tell that the thickness of the shell was defeating the forty caliber slugs. I let Hyun empty the weapon at the crawler anyway.

"It is quite possible that the handgun does not have enough power to penetrate the shell." I said as I pulled my rifle off my shoulder. Reaching into my pouch I grabbed a programmable warhead round and set it to armor piercing. Once the bullet was set, I reloaded the rifle. The bullet set this way would have enough power to penetrate a ship's hull; this crawler should not be much of a challenge.

I was too close to the animal to be able to target it with the scope, so I had to come up with another option. I took two fast steps and jumped onto the top of the crawlers shell. I figured I could just shoot down through the creature's head and then step off the collapsing bug.

The frigging shell on the crawler was so slick that my feet went out from under me on the landing. My feet slid along the back of the huge creature until I went over its head and fell six feet onto my ass right in front of it. The crawler did not seem impressed or unimpressed, it just decide to walk away.

The damned thing then stepped on my leg and would have kept on walking if I hadn't reached up with the barrel of my rifle to touch just under its mandibles and squeezed the trigger. On hindsight next time it would be much smarter if I don't fall off the crawler and I also should wait to shoot until I am not under it.

The reaction from the crawler was immediate. It died and fell on me. I lay there pinned by the crawler laughing at how things keep falling on me. First it was the eel, now the crawler. Maybe I need a different vocation. I push the crawler straight up off of me. I find Hyun and the other men looking down at me with worried expressions on their faces.

"Why do these creatures always have to fall on me?" I ask with a laugh.

Hyun, upon seeing me safe, made a suggestion. "Maybe it was this thing called gravity."

I am grinning at his humor as I fasten a cord around the carcass. I then climb back up the side of the ravine to join the men. Together we pulled the crawler up quite easily to inspect our kill. Lian and Hyun both said that they wished they could take it back in one piece as a trophy to show all their families. If the crawler were on New Harvest I would estimate by its density it would weigh around three hundred and fifty pounds.

The gravity is lighter here, so the mass would be easier for me. I unload the rifle and hand it to Hyun while Lian gets my pack. I then crouch down and pull the crawlers underside up on to my back and shoulders. With a grunt I straighten up. I had to ask a couple of the other men with empty hands if they would steady the load by grabbing the middle legs and slightly lifting up on them for the walk back to the village.

We had only trekked half a mile when we caught up to the other Sooul men who were sitting beside the grull. The several hundred pound animal was just too heavy for them to keep moving with.

I set the crawler down, and said, "Which animal will take longer to cook?"

"The grull will have to be slow roasted over a fire."

"I will carry the grull and run it back to the village and then come back for the crawler."

I picked the grull up on my shoulder and took off at seriously fast pace. No Sooul would be able to match my speed. Covering the last mile and a half took less than five minutes. How I love this lighter gravity.

As I rounded the bend approaching the camp, the Sooul that were out around their outside barbeque area went silent. I guess that they don't have a Gunman with a dragon across his shoulders running into the village every day. A roasting pit sat unused most likely because they didn't expect to get a grull. The men who were setting up the pots seemed really happy to see it. I mounted it on their spit and left them to prepare the animal for cooking.

There was a large jug of water sitting by Hyun's house so I decided to take enough time for a long drink. Sophee came out when she saw me drinking water through the open doorway.

"No crawlers?" she asked, looking surprised that I wasn't successful.

"Yes, we got a big one," I said trying to sound hurt. "I thought I would run the grull back first, so the gentlemen setting up the pots could start cooking it. I will be back in less than an hour with the crawler."

I turned to leave, but said *what-the-hell* and wrapped my arms around Sophee and pulled her up for a kiss.

"Everyone is okay," I told her.

Sophee smiled broadly; "Do you have to go?"

I laugh, "Yes, there is no way they can get the crawler back alone."

There was enough time for a few more kisses before setting her down. I sped up a little on the way back and made it to the hunting party in less time. Hyun and the rest of the men were being dummies and trying to drag the crawler back to camp. Now they were all out of breath and had only moved it a hundred and ten yards. I laughed and asked if they forgot they had an ox on contract?

After I had to explain what an ox was, they laughed and stepped out of my way. I picked up the crawler and began the journey to the village again. It was only a mile and a half, but by the time I got near Hyun's home I was starting to lose my breath. The truth of the matter is that the damned creature felt like it weighed a ton. Maybe next time I'll bring a cart or build a wheelbarrow. That would be the ticket.

I think everyone in the town saw us coming and walked out to see the large crawler I was struggling to carry. Hyun directed me to drop it into the cart so they could clean it. I thought about how I was holding it for a second and pressed it straight up to toss it into the cart, my tired arms dropped to absolute silence from all the watching Sooul.

"I can't read their minds, but that little show of strength will be forever burned in their minds," Vicky says sub-vocally.

I looked to Hyun; "I apologize for showing off but my arms were cramping up carrying that thing. It seemed to be the quickest way to put it down. I did not want the crawler to land on me again."

Sophee, who is standing beside Mere, asks, "Again?"

No way I am telling her about falling off the crawler; I imagine someone else will later. I smile and move over to

Hyun; I pull my combat knife off my belt and hand it to Hyun.

"This knife has a special edge and it will cut through anything organic," I said. "Use this to clean and section the crawler if you wish, but please be very careful as it will not be able to tell crawler from Hyun."

I take a few steps away from the group, as this is their show. With my size and strength, I could have the crawler done in a few minutes. Even with the Sooul using my knife it will take them a while to finish cleaning the crawler.

I take time to peel my bloody battle suit off as I walk toward the water. Between the grull and the crab I was covered in dried bloody slime. I rinse my suit out and lay it on a bench that someone had placed near the water to dry it out. I splash some water on myself to start cleaning the crawler blood off my head and neck. Sophee sees me cleaning myself and gets my new shirt and a towel.

The blood on my head and neck is almost as slippery as the terrestrial crustacean's shell, so I decide to go for a quick swim in attempt to wash away the slime. However, with all the Sooul hanging around and my preference for being discreet, keeping my shorts on was a must.

I dive into the cool water and splash around for a bit until most of the blood was off me, then duck back under the waves and swim to the shore. Sophee is standing at the water's edge keeping her eye on me, which makes me wonder if she can swim. When I get her home we will have to make sure she feels comfortable in the water.

It did not take the men as long as I thought it would to clean and section the crab. By using my combat knife with the edge that was sharpened to a single molecule, the cleaning went easily for them. The piles of outer shell and crab offal filled several carts. The legs had been cut apart at each joint and the sections of knuckles that joined the legs to the body were cut into four large quarters.

As I walked out of the water, Hyun called out to me that my combat knife had the sharpest blade he has ever seen. I smiled and told him I would get him one as soon as we got home to New Harvest. He then asked if I might lift the quarter segments into the huge pots they had brought down to the beach.

The two pots look about six feet tall and around three in diameter; they sit on large carts that have small element coils hooked to batteries. I lift the first quarter up and it drips blood all over me again. Shoran, Sophee, and most of the other people standing around get a good laugh at the look of annoyance on my face. Heaving a sigh of resignation, I put the second quarter in the same pot, and the other two into the other pot.

"Are you going to bathe again?" Sophee asks, looking at my crab-blood-covered upper body.

Without a second thought I grab her up against my chest. Sophee squeals in surprise as I run down to the water and jump into the cove. I made sure Sophee's head did not go underwater in case she really has she never swam before. Of course she has bathed and would be smart enough to hold her breath, but I was not going to endanger her.

I could feel her arms snake around to lock about my neck like a vise, and her legs wrap themselves around my waist, squeezing tight. The look of shock on her face was priceless. From the way she was latched on to me I figure she was unsure about the water but totally sure she would be safe with me.

"Are you going to bathe again?" I tease, hugging her close.

Sophee gave a small laugh. "I did not expect this."

"Are you afraid of the water?"

"Terrified of what is in it." She coyly whispers.

I pout. "Oh, that hurts."

"I could be afraid that some big, bad monster might eat me up," Sophee said, leaning back in my arms to lock eyes with me.

I pretend to ponder this before giving my reply. "Although I have seriously thought about it, my appetite today is reserved for the crawler."

I carry her out of the water. Everyone at the beach is watching our playful moment with wide eyes. I carry Sophee up the beach and set her down. It then comes to my attention that the thin cloth she is wearing is rather translucent when wet. I worry about her walking through the crowd of people embarrassing her, so I pick her back up and carry her to where my shirt and towel lay on the sand. I reach down with one hand and grab the items to pass them to Sophee.

From the look on Sophee's face I can tell she just realized I was trying to protect her modesty. Smiling softly, she put a gentle hand on the side of my face before we went to her parent's house to change our clothing. I finally comprehend that it is my modesty and not hers that caused me to react as I did, something she is able to convey to me with a single touch. Even though her modesty doesn't demand my actions she allows me to act like myself and do what I need to do if it makes me happy.

When I entered the house Sophee made me set my stuff down, and then leads me over to the small door to their sanitary room. The room is oval and maybe fifteen feet long. She pushes a switch, and a section of the flexible floor was pulled down to form a rather comfortably sized tub. Sophee then operated a small keypad on the wall to fill the basin with warm water.

"Are you staying, or is that…?"

Before I can finish speaking, Sophee is naked and stepping into the tub. I remove my shorts and join her. Sophee was far more interested in washing me than herself and was not self-conscious at all. As she used some spongy thing to remove all the leftover blood she made sure her body was against me. I really wanted to take the bait but I had given Sophee my thoughts and believed my stance, however uncomfortable, was correct. I sat very still and decided to close my eyes as she circled around me trying to entice me into action. My inaction was an invisible wall between us.

Climbing out of the tub, Sophee told me to stay seated and relax before leaving the room. I didn't have any idea about what she was up to but the warm water felt good. A few minutes later Sophee came back dressed. She silently keyed the drain to empty the tub. "Thank you." I said when she passed me a towel." I started to dry my head but when I looked over at Sophee I could see that her eyes were watery and about to start running down her face. I wrapped the towel around my waist and waited for her to speak. I know she was feeling some anguish as her hands were clenched as she looked downward avoiding my eyes. It was then very easy to figure out her problem, either I am a bad person for not mating or she is upset because she tried against my wishes.

"I am sorry that..." she starts.

I interrupted her firmly. "That what, you tried to get your bonded one to mate? Sophee, please look at me."

It took her a few seconds to raise her gaze because she was so uncertain. When she did the tears that were filling her eyes ran down her cheeks. I never want to see anyone let alone the love of my life so sad. When she finally meets my eye, I smile.

"I will most likely have to fight these Gham and, while our relationship is the best thing in my life, I can't have any more on my mind than I already do if I want to be at my best." I drop to my knees in front of her and take both her hand in mine. "But you need to remember one thing if you want to be with me."

Sophee looks quite surprised and a little nervous. I can imagine the turmoil she was feeling. Trying to seduce her bonded one into mating? If there were no Gham she would not have had to try, waiting is the hardest darned thing I have ever had to do.

"There are far worse things than desiring your loved one." I move her hand up and gently kiss it. "Please don't apologize for trying to love me." Her hands reach out to gently cup my face as I look into her eyes.

"I am forgiven?" She says softly.

"No, as you would have done something that would require forgiving." I say. I finish my statement by giving her the most gently slow kiss I could.

My honest words helped to buoy her spirit. The fact

she could read the truth with no anger or even annoyance helped a lot. The fact I was kissing made her much happier as well.

"One of the reasons I am not ready to mate is because I have to be ready for combat if the Gham do not leave, but if I am worried about you getting hurt I could not fight to the level that I should. I don't plan on this happening. Do you see my problem?"

She hugs me tightly then leans back to give me a firm look. "Don't die, then we will worry about the rest later."

I put my wet shorts on, pulled my shirt over my head, and meekly followed her outside. We walked holding hands over to check out the cooking area. Shoran was standing beside Mere at the tables where I imagine the food will be placed. Shoran sees us and smiles, she gestures at a jug and Sophee nods. The two of them poured cups of wine. I was grateful to receive a big one, as I was rather parched. Sophee joined me and we stood beside Shoran watching the men check the meat. The grull smelled like pork and was being basted with wine and some herbs. You could not see anything of the crawlers because they were in the big pots.

I then remembered to ask Vicky if she was able to make garlic butter. "Vicky, what is the status of garlic butter?" I ask.

She was quick to answer. "There are four gallons currently being heated over at the house. When I explained to Sophee's mother that it's your favorite way to eat crab, they decided they would all like to try it as you would not lead them astray."

I twist my neck to the side and stretch my shoulder out, the longer I stand around the more they are tightening up.

The 1st Gunman

Sophee notices my stiffness and pulls me over to the shade under a tree.

"You will sit here." Sophee instructs me to sit on the bench. She then stands behind me and massages my sore shoulders and neck. The crawler was damned heavy and it took a bit of a toll on me. Shoran joined us and offered to do one side of my neck. I don't know what any other man anywhere in the galaxy would feel, but having two absolutely beautiful women rubbing your neck and shoulders make me feel like a king.

After a massaging my shoulder and neck for awhile Shoran decides to talk about what the men were saying over by the cooking area.

"Dad said he shot a dragon out of the sky, and then had to block it when it fell."

Sophee didn't say anything, just leaned around and looked at me with the "Now what" expression.

I shrug. "It was going to hit your fathers."

"They found the crawler in a valley and he let your dad shoot at it," the other girl continued. "The gun things bounced off the crawler, making it mad, and a certain man jumped off the cliff to attack the crawler. After landing in front of the creature, he had to kill it from underneath because it tried to crush him." Shoran's eyes are wide as she continues to tell on me.

"And then, after it collapsed on him in its death throes, he lifted the crawler off himself like it weighed nothing. All the men tried to pull it home, but could only move it a short distance before that same certain man returned to carry it all by himself. It is no small wonder that all these muscles are so stiff." She finished poking at my shoulder.

I start laughing at the way she heard the story. "Your

fathers and his friends have been drinking wine the better part of the afternoon, and you girls should be able to read that they are exaggerating."

Sophee looks at me and raises an eyebrow. "You jumped off a cliff Joshua Garvie?"

Both names? I must be in trouble.

"No, dear, I only jumped down about twelve feet on to the top of the crawler. The damn shell was slippery so I fell off, landed on my butt, and then it stepped on me. I was not very graceful."

Vicky goes active sub-vocally. "Remember the Hercules thing? It took three of the Sooul to roll a quarter of the crawler over to clean it; you carried the whole thing two miles after lugging a two hundred pound grull the same distance at a run. This is why the men are making the story more; they are a bit embarrassed with themselves being inadequate physically when compared to you."

"Thanks, Vicky, I will work with it."

Sophee considers my moment of silent and guesses the reason for it. "Talking with Vicky?"

I nod. "Thank you for the shoulder massage, ladies, it feels much better. Please remember this skill, as I will most likely need you again. Now, I am going to learn how to cook crawlers."

I stand up and give Sophee a quick kiss. I give Shoran a peck on the top of her head and walk over the tables to find more wine. The Sooul really like their wine and one table has a dozen jugs. I pick one out and head toward the group of men cooking and laughing.

* * *

Shoran shakes her head. "Dad said the grull would have killed them if it had hit them. Do you notice that all of today was no big deal to him…again?"

"Yes," Sophee answers with a nod. "When I asked him to take care of the hunting party his emotions were of total amusement, both when we were talking about it and when he left. My Joshua doesn't get excited over what he thinks are the little things."

"I would be curious to see what a big thing is," Shoran said.

They both trade a look as they think about the Gham at the same time.

Sophee watches Joshua get a pitcher of wine from the table. "Shoran, watch the way he moves when he walks, notice how he checks the shield, then the water?"

"He is always on guard, isn't he?" Shoran asks.

"Joshua says we are not mating because he wants to focus on the Gham." Sophee shakes her head at the thought of Joshua fighting them.

"My dad said Joshua was so fast that when he blinked at the sound of the gun Joshua had already moved over twenty feet to block the falling grull." Shoran said.

Sophee laughed; "it was much the same when the eels broke the gate, one second I was eating and the next he had picked me up and ran so fast up the hill I got dizzy."

Shoran gets a mischievous little grin; "I hope for your sake he is slower at other things."

A red blush at the thought appeared on Sophee's face. "My Joshua is the kindest and gentlest man ever." She looked around until she realized they could speak without being heard by anyone else.

"I have been trying to get him to mate until just a short while ago; he needs to take care of the Gham." She leans over toward Shoran; "then he promises to take care of me….a lot."

The girls giggle at the thought.

* * *

I slowly make my way around the groups of families. It would appear all the Sooul are going to attend the feast. Thank god they are small people or there might not be enough meat to feed everyone. I look over at the shield for no good reason if there was a problem with it Vicky would warn me. Some of the children are down by the water but not going in. Most of the men I hunted with are in the area between the grull and the cooking pots. By the sound of their laughter the wine has been flowing for some bit. Hyun sees me approaching and motions for me to join the group.

"Gentlemen, we have wine. Please attend your cups." I say. I fill all their cups making sure everyone is taken care of. "Hyun may I make a toast?" I ask. At his nod I realized I don't have a cup. Oh well; "A toast to you men! I am in awe of how you have survived this long with the eels and these Gham assholes. Cheers!"

That got to them; they could sense that I was being honest about my awe. To a one they all raised their cups and drank.

"Now," I said, "would somebody explain how you cook something this big and know when it is done cooking?"

They all started talking about the methods, so I kept their glasses full and listened to their expertise. For people who had never cooked a grull and crawler this size before they had more than enough recipes passed down through the generations. Or maybe they just took the small recipes and made them bigger, hell I don't know. What I did know was the grull smelled like a roasted pig and the crawlers smell like fish.

The way the Sooul men were carrying on and laughing drew in their mates from preparing the extra food to go with the meat. The group around the pots grew to be quite large, and I was amazed again how much love and compassion they had for each other.

Quite a bit later Hyun asked me if my questioning was a ruse to make them forget how small and weak the Sooul men were. "Surely a man such as you would not be interested in something as plain and as boring as cooking crawlers?" Hyun plainly asked. Mere put a hand out to Hyun uncertain if he needed comforting.

I looked at him with all honesty and raised an eyebrow. "Sir, you are smaller than I am, you are not trained in weapons as I am. For what you have been through, the fact you're still able to smile and be kind to each other despite it all, you are a much bigger man than I will ever live to be. I wish you would not judge me by how much I can lift, but judge me for my heart, because that is how I judge the Sooul." I let him dwell on that for a few seconds while I maintain eye contact with him.

"Is it a ruse you ask? No, it is an opportunity for me to learn something. On New Harvest, we have creatures called crabs that are similar to your crawlers. They live in salt water and look much the same. I would love to catch some big crabs and have this kind of party for the people of New Harvest as well as the Sooul."

Mere, who had been standing a little ways back listening

and reading my emotions, now spoke up. "Truth…. and sadness?"

Sophee quickly came to my side to hold my hand as she searches my face; "Sadness Joshua?"

"Yes, I am sad we are out of wine," I said, as I shook the jug. When Mere gave me a look I sighed, knowing she wasn't going to let me avoid answering with the entire truth.

"These guys don't realize who they are, what they are, and how much I respect them. It saddens me to my core, I'm sorry! Rather than being sad I am now going for a walk with my Sophee."

Sub-vocally I ask Vicky to monitor the men of the Sooul. The Sooul men have more than enough on their minds with the Gham coming back. I am here to help them, not be someone they feel inferior too. If they need more help I can always ask Mere how to handle them better.

Sophee smiles happily at me because she can sense no annoyance and zero sadness now. She knows I have just made a point for the men to consider. Pointing out the strengths of the Sooul should let them recognize the fact that I think they are a pretty special bunch. I slowly stroll around the village holding Sophee's hand. We had to stop from time to time and kiss. We find a nice spot and sit holding hands.

It is when we figure it is late enough the crawlers would be ready soon that we start walking back to the beach when Vicky says, "Success, Sir. The men were given trouble by their mates and told not to be jealous of your muscles because it is unkind. The men are now laughing at how you fell off the crawler and are glad they didn't get blood all over themselves like you."

People smiled and nodded at us as we rejoined the

group. I managed to acquire a nice spot for Sophee and myself near Mere.

"Hyun and I would like to help cook those crawler-like-creatures on New Harvest; I would imagine actually that all of us would help." Lian said as he was passing by with a full jug of wine.

"We will have to try and catch big ones, as the small ones are the only sizes I am used to. I have no idea yet if the big ones taste like your crawlers but I am eager to try them." I said with a grin.

Sophee and I sit together in the shade until her dad comes back over. Hyun looks like he standing a bit taller. The talk we had and the fact he is actually starting to believe he might get off this rock is showing.

"We feel bad for using you like this," Hyun said, "but we could use your help to drain the hot tanks and move the crawlers to the serving area."

Shoran's dad added, "We also need someone to hit the shells with a club to crack them before we pull the meat out to cool."

"I have my price for these jobs," I say. Lian was quick to hand me another cup of wine so I reply, "Paid in full."

I jog back to the house and go inside to my pack retrieving a pair of gloves that have good heat shields. I jog back to the cooking area and slide the gloves on. A few turns of the handle opens the drains. Hyun shut off the heat source by toggling a switch on the batteries. As soon as the pots were empty I tipped the pot to one side and reached in to grab a leg to pull out the first quarter. Once the hot crab sections were in the tray I grabbed a chunk of gate wood and started banging the shells at the seams. Hyun and others pointed to what they wanted cracked so I worked in silence.

It took quite a bit of effort and time to get all the main quarter sections of crawler cracked in order to get the meat out, and I was not very surprised to see that it looked just like crab meat. The roasted grull was placed on a table as well; it looked kind of like a funky roasted pig with turkey wings. Golden brown and smelling so great it made my mouth water.

Once the tables were ready everyone looked at me; *sure I thought*. I filled a plate with meat from the two animals and got a small bowl with hot butter. I took the food over to Hyun. I ask him to sit, handed him the food and then got him a fresh glass of wine. Showing respect to Hyun and deferring to him is something that the Sooul will remember. His position is strong among the Sooul and if anything stronger because his daughter's future mate recognizes it as well, I know my place and here he is the boss.

Sub-vocally Vicky says, "Well played, Sir."

I sit beside Hyun with a glass of wine. "You lead the Sooul and organized the hunting party, so you should be the first to try it."

Mere takes a piece of crab dips it in the butter and gives Hyun a bite. The new flavor must have been overwhelming because he stopped chewing. Mere tried one as well. She sat down and started sharing Hyun's plate.

Hyun had a huge smile as he piled into his food.

The line at the tables was huge so I thought I would just wait a bit until Sophee came over holding one plate for me. "Please sit and try this." When she sat down I steered a small piece dipped in butter toward her mouth. She looked down at her plate sadly.

"I don't think I took enough," she says with a laugh.

If she knows about why I sat her down with the food instead of eating myself I don't know. Sophee is very intuitive and can understand the respect I am trying to convey to the people of Sooul. I do not care if it is pretense or show; I will wait until every Sooul has got food before eating myself. The Sooul will understand the respect I have for all of them. I sit back and sip on my wine as I wait for room at the tables.

Watching the Sooul, I am again impressed at how they treat each other. No one tries to jump past anyone but, like at most family gatherings, women and kids go first. Some of the Sooul men help serve. Even the kids are calm and wait their turns.

Everyone takes a fair bit of the meat and dips a piece in the butter to try it before they take a bowl. I don't think I saw a single person walk away without any butter. Seeing the joy on their faces as they eat is fun: they certainly like the big crawler and grull. They are happy and content, which makes me wonder how they can hide their terror over what has happened and the apprehension of what might again happen if I do not come through on my promises.

"Joshua, please give your attention to Sophee!" Vicky demands sub-vocally.

I blink once and look at Sophee. "Sorry, I was enjoying everyone's reaction to the butter. Like the chocolate, something so simple makes everyone so happy. Our people deserve so much better."

Sophee nods towards the tables. The line had gone down so I walk over behind a couple of small children and wait.

I see the grull has taken a beating and there is not much meat left on the bones. There is a lot of crawler still left on the tables.

* * *

"Did you hear what he said, Dad?" Sophee asks. "*Our people*...his love for us is in his words and thoughts."

"Your bonding has made this happen," Mere pointed out. "It made our Joshua the compassionate man he is."

"No mother, he was kind and good already, he would have loved the Sooul without me," Sophee said thoughtfully. "Look at him over there smiling as he waits. Joshua is a warrior when he needs to be, he will be an excellent mate. We have seen how protective he gets when something is wrong or uncertain."

"If you had seen Joshua while we hunted, Sophee, you would have been very proud of him."

"Why?" she asks.

"On our way to the ravine where we found the crawler Joshua stayed off the trail. He carried that big weapon of his like we were about to have an attack against us any second. He was keeping more than an eye on all of us; it was as if he was our guard. When he shot the grull it would have really hurt or killed Lian and me when it fell. He didn't allow that, Joshua moved to intercept the falling grull before we even realized we were in danger."

Sophee smiled at her father and doesn't say anything about her conversation with Joshua before the hunt. Mere was less secretive. "Maybe we asked him to take care of you guys."

"Obviously," Hyun states, with a small wave of his hand to quiet them down a bit. "But even if you didn't, I could

The 1st Gunman

sense his love for our people anyway, and he would have done exactly the same thing. Since both of you asked him to be careful, should we be annoyed to be treated like children? None of the hunting party was. We can sense that Joshua believes in his heart believes that we are his people." Hyun paused for a moment and points over to the table where Joshua was talking with a child. "Look at the children. They love him, and not just because he is different, but because he listens to them. Lucky for you my daughter you found him first because Joshua might have a line of women to capture his affections."

"It would be rather amusing to find out how many females would have pursued him." Mere agreed with Hyun. Sophee didn't care about their question, because she knew him better than they ever would.

"If you had the knowledge I do, you would be awestruck. In some respects, Joshua loves deeper than the Sooul." Sophee said.

"It shows when he supplied the meat and wants everyone to be fed before he looks after himself." Mere said as she was watching Joshua. "He does these things without any care."

* * *

I stand behind the last kid in line who was trying to reach up for some smaller leg meat, so I picked the child up with one arm, and pass him a bowl of butter to him with the other. In it and whisper, I say, "Sometimes I like to drop all my meat into the butter."

The child smiles at me. "My name is Ankh."

"Pleased to meet you Ankh, I am Joshua." I say seriously. He chuckles, "Everyone knows that."

He starts start picking pieces of meat out off some of the leg sections. The meat is white and looks absolutely delicious. I continue to hold the little guy as he reaches for some that is slightly past his arm length. I pull another bunch closer for him and he is absolutely happy as he works. I have to admit it was nice that kids don't think I am too big and scary.

"Let me take the bowl, Ankh, and I'll hold it up for you to fill with meat." I offer.

By the time Ankh finishes filling the bowl my mouth is watering, I think there is no way he is going to eat it all himself. Ankh pats my arm and points about ten yards away to a young couple sitting by the house next to Sophee's place. Maybe I am becoming acclimatized to the Sooul as I instantly recognize their facial features as Ankh's parents.

I carry the little boy over to his family, and set him down. Then I place the bowl of meat and butter down on the table next to him. His parents nod to me and start serving the meat on to their plates. I guess it was his job to get some food for the family. Sooul or New Harvest, children are the same: young kids always want to do things to show they are growing up.

I walk back to the serving tables and try a piece of the crawler. It tastes like crab but without the salt flavor. Fresh water land crabs, how weird is that? I select a section of the crawlers body knuckle with the leg joint attached and a bowl of butter.

I return to my new family and sit on the ground beside them. I look at them to see if they are enjoying the meal as I start picking the meat out of the joint. I feel their scrutiny but smile and go to work on the crawler.

It is nice to be with such social people, and the more I see the Sooul in communal environments the angrier it makes me with the Gham. These are families are full of love, full of life, and are truly decent people. The P.F.F. mandate was created specifically to protect people like this. I am not a good enough of an actor to sit back and be all stoic about the Gham's genocide against the Sooul. The best thing I can do at this minute is concentrate on the food and Sophee to hide the rage I am feeling toward the Gham now.

"Joshua, you do mask emotions that well. I can sense your love but the dark place and your resolve seems to be almost at the same level." Mere says as she looks kindly at me. I try to politely change the subject by looking blandly at her with a smile. I start dipping my crab into the butter and eating it.

"It is official your crawlers taste almost exactly like New Harvest crabs." I say as if she hadn't been trying to read my emotions.

"Do you wish to talk about it?" Mere asks me.

"That's not the way I roll Mere." I reply honestly.

A confused look briefly crosses Mere face which makes me smile. *Still can't figure me out huh?*

It must have been the humor because Mere tried once more to illicit a conversation about my emotions.

"You can talk to us about your feelings Joshua; we don't want you to feel alone."

Due to the fact I tend to try not to wear my heart on my sleeve, I can only reply with, "Can't talk; eating!" I say as I fill my mouth with butter covered crawler.

Sophee smiles gently as she puts her hand on the back of my neck. "Joshua is not ready to talk about all things yet."

I nod and look away as I eat. Talk about all things? Not likely. The way I solve problems is generally without support. The Gham are mine to deal with in my own manner. The solutions that come forth from me tend to be extreme, and there is no waffling in my mind in regards to severity. They say life can be a hard road to travel, but I generally travel a road only once, metaphorically speaking.

Most people went back to the buffet table for seconds, and Hyun for a third helping. I think I showed remarkable restraint only having one chunk of meat—even if it was size of a small child. I tried the left over grull from Sophee's plate; it reminded me of emu in flavor and texture. Quite a bit of crawler meat was still left, so everyone started filling up some platters to take home. All the leftover shells were taken past the fields and dumped for the smaller crawlers to feed on. By the time I crawled to my sleeping pillows I was just about done in.

* * *

Sophee was in bed with me before I could close my eyes. The day must have been as long for her as it was for me as she looked about as tired as I felt. I think she was a bit surprised that I kept my shorts on but with the ten day approaching I will not risk channeling my energy elsewhere. With her sleeping more on me than off, I can feel relaxation pouring into my body. Funny how, instead of frustration, contentment was the feeling our sleeping arrangement inspired. That comfort, and because she knew I did not want to talk, allowed sleep to come fairly quickly.

I was still half-asleep in the morning when Vicky's quiet voice woke me. "Joshua, the men of Sooul seem much better this morning. I think your statements about them were taken to heart."

"Really Vicky, you had to wake me up for that report?" I ask sub-vocally.

"Your breathing pattern and heart rate changed." Vicky said. "If it was important enough for you to have me monitoring the Sooul I figured you would want updates."

"Monitoring is no longer required, thank you." I said with a smile. I could tell the men felt better yesterday and am glad it has continued.

I decide then to get up, and begin my day. I open my pack and start searching towards the bottom, looking for a small pouch. When I finally found it, the bag had shifted off to one side under some ammo. Pulling it out, I sniff the pouch, *ah the smell of coffee beans.*

"Vicky, can you program the food processor to make me hot coffee with this?" I needlessly ask. After all if my A.I. can program and alien replicator to build shield generators, coffee should not be all that impossible.

"Yes, pour half a dozen of the beans on the pad and give me a few minutes."

I am standing there waiting in front of the processor until the little light flickers and a cup appears on the platform filled with coffee. It was mountain grown and its rich aroma was intoxicating to me. I take it and sit down happily only to burn my lip on the first sip. Sophee must sense I am out of bed because I see her reach for me, and then open her eyes. She sits up looking around the room for me. I wave to her and then ask myself if I should have asked her first if she wanted to try coffee.

"What is that horrible smell?" she asks, wrinkling up cute her nose.

"Coffee, for a very long time this has been the wake-up beverage of choice for mankind." I answer.

Sophee gets out of bed and stretches like a cat. She doesn't bother to dress and walks naked over to me. I don't avert my eyes because she is mine and I really like the view. I get a kiss on the forehead as she takes the cup. "Careful," I warn her. Sophee smells it from close up and scrunches up her nose again before trying a tiny sip. She looks over the cup at me to see if the foul tasting liquid is a joke I am playing on her. Getting no reaction she makes her call.

"Hot and awful," she simply states.

Her mom sticks her head up from the wall bunk after hearing Sophee's comment.

"What is hot and awful?" Mere asks Sophee with raised eyebrows.

"Coffee," Sophee answered. "Joshua says mankind lives on it."

Mere hops out of bed and walks over without clothes. I try not to look at anything but her eyes. She takes the cup from her daughter and tries a tiny sip before looking intently into my eyes. I guess she was trying to figure out the joke as well. Hyun wouldn't be left out so he gets up and joins us. Mere passes him the cup.

Hyun takes a sip and looks at his mate, "I sense unease," he says; "This must be a joke."

"No, you're all naked and I have no desire to see my future mother or father-in-law naked," I answer as I get to my feet. "Sophee, yes but we have not mated and I don't want to treat her like a sex toy." I keep my gaze above their heads as I stroll out of the house. Nudity does not bother me, but her parents should have privacy, this openness is a bit disconcerting. As for Sophee, I could look at her all day long…just not in front of her parents. I worship Sophee and love to look at her, but adding her naked parents into the mix makes for an awkward situation.

I sit outside for a few minutes trying to figure out how to explain myself to my new family. Sophee steps out of the home dressed with another fresh cup of coffee. "Vicky sent this out for you." Sophee says with a serious expression. I take the cup and have a sip before starting my apology. Sophee beats me to the punch.

"Mother and Father are sorry if they have crossed your line."

"It's not that," I said. "I love and respect them, but I am kind of old fashioned. I don't know why I feel this way but I think that nudity is great between bonded ones but not in public. Please don't ever walk naked around my friends, because your mine and I don't share well." I realize I am blowing my explanation and continue anyway. "The only reason we are not mating is because, should something unforeseen happen to me and I die, you will still be alive." I look into her eyes before continuing; "That would be the main reason."

She sits on my lap and put her arms around me. "Do you think it would be better to let me live if you were dead and die eventually from the Gham anyway?"

"It will not happen, the Gham are…" I stopped because the decision I have made about the Gham should not be spoken about and I am letting too much out of the bag. Damn it she really makes me to want to talk about stuff. I feel like a tortured soul, because never in my life have I felt as awkward as I do around the Sooul. Knowing what needs to be done and being willing to do it may change how they feel about me. The Sooul may have a hard time accepting what I am going to do.

Instead of talking about my battle plans I stand up, take Sophee's hand. We walk into the house so I can apologize to Mere and Hyun. The last thing I want to do is make them feel that they have to change for me or that they owe me an apology.

I find her parents in the prep area making breakfast. Mere seeing me standing and waiting nods to me. I look them both in the eyes. "You haven't crossed my line at all. I am just so focused on what is coming that I need a good whack upside of the head." Difficult as that was they were still giving me their attention. "Please realize that the boundaries I have are all self-imposed, and I am not offended by our cultural differences. My society is a bit more modest, because people are able to mate without bonding and therefore we meaning me specifically, can be more uptight. I do not want you to think I lack respect for your way of life."

Mere moved around her husband to reach up and pull me down to her level to give me a kiss on the cheek. "We know, dear. What's a sex toy? It sounds interesting." She asks.

"How can you be so decent at one time and then so unkind the next?" Hyun asks me with a smile.

I decide to answer Hyun, and leave Mere's question alone. He is very easy to figure out now. "Maybe coffee is an acquired taste, more for me." I said

We had some more rolls made with vegetables and crawler meat for breakfast. Since there was no real work to be done Sophee and I wandered around to see if anyone needed help or had questions. I was not used to having so much downtime. We had a wonderful three days. I spent quite a bit of time fishing at the gates of the shield and always had sillfish to share with whoever wanted some. I did not realize how much I missed fishing while in the Element. Sophee just leaned against me or sat with me, I figured we looked like disproportionate Siamese twins because we were always so close to each other. I was the object of scrutiny everywhere we went. Sophee fielded many a question about her mate-to-be. Sooul girls and single women were curious about New Harvest men. Whenever females gathered in groups I beat a hasty retreat. The kids were fun and always trailing us, I wondered if they were expecting some superhuman feats of strength, or waiting to see if I did something funny. It was amusing that they would walk beside us and one would always take my free hand. Ankh came looking for his big buddy every day. He would sometimes ask so many questions about New Harvest kids and families that I swore he had to be writing a book.

I thought about going out to capture a live crawler and trying to harness it to use for plowing, or use it as a stump puller, or maybe just ride it around, but realized it probably wasn't worth the effort. Maybe after the Gham are gone while we wait for pick up we can get the men and kids involved in some kind of group adventure or game. I kept my eyes open during our walks but didn't see a large enough crawler for anything that would be amazing.

* * *

Shoran tried to pin me down on which of my single friends would make a better mate and why. I tried to explain that there would be lots of single men available on New

Harvest and that she shouldn't feel that my single friends were there only men she should be looking at.

"But why can't I have a Gunman too?" Shoran asked honestly. I grinned at that and decided to have some fun with her.

"Is it your opinion that all Gunmen are simply a piece of meat to be claimed?" I made sure my voice was neutral when I asked her. "That hurts a bit because I didn't think the Sooul were so shallow." I finished.

"Stop it, Joshua! You know as well as I do that is not the case." Shoran scolds me. "I think I am going to like men who are sure of themselves and honest. Your friends are Gunmen which mean they are brave and are warriors. Because they are your friends I know they are decent honest people." She smiles at Sophee. "My best friend also picked from that group and she is not totally miserable."

"Ouch, I am glad your best friend is not totally miserable." I said laughing.

When I met the Sooul I found them to be quiet and emotional. Their empathic gift made them seem very similar personality wise. Now that I have bonded with Sophee I can see the differences between their personalities. Shoran is very outspoken, nice and kind but forward. Sophee on the other hand can be fiery when she is annoyed but generally she is very calm and soft spoken. When you put these two together the differences between them is night and day.

Hyun was pretty interested in finding out about planters and harvesters. The Sooul had these large communal gardens and were absolute enthralled with the idea of having machines do the manual labor. I spent hours explaining what crops we planted, some of the information they wanted would take a biologist to know. After speaking for hours about New Harvest I realized that the Sooul have far more knowledge about plants than me. They will most like be put into development of new crops and seeds, but that will be their choice to do that or something else.

One of the other things that made them excited was red meat. Beef was something they had never heard of and my description of steaks and prime rib raised their curiosity.

Hyun did ask me; "This is not like your coffee is it?"

"Once you can try coffee with cream and sugar you might feel differently" I replied back. "Prime rib is one of my favorite meats."

During the conversations or the continual briefing as I like to call it, one point had the Sooul a bit concerned. Marauders, I explained that they were the reason for the mesh shields. Some of my stories about the marauders who continually probed for openings made them worried. The Sooul did not have any experience with large vicious pigs. I purposely tried to downplay some of the tales but, with the Sooul reading my emotions, they knew I was leaving out the more horrible parts of the story. I did tell them that they were now under control, handled by the shields. I also mentioned that New Harvest hired two more retired Gunmen for security, this made Hyun and Lian comfortable. Not to mention the fact it made Shoran smile.

Even with the relaxation and good cheer I found it difficult to avoid thinking about what was coming. From my viewpoint, I had still had concerns with how the Sooul will react to my fighting the Gham. Will violence used against a sentient being cause them to fear or loathe me? Never before in my life have I had so much to lose. I realize that I could be looking at this the wrong way. *Maybe if I politely explain that the Sooul are sad when they get murdered and it would be nice if the kind Gham would just fly away forever. Then we could all sit in a circle and sing campfire songs. Right, I will load my guns.*

A couple of evenings before the Gham would be here I decided to sit and play the guitar for Sophee. I did not want to disturb Mere who was cooking so I picked up the guitar and walked out to their porch. Sophee's eyes lit up with anticipation when she saw it in my hand. I sat down and struck a few cords. For being a fabricated metal guitar I was very surprised to hear it sound like an acoustic wooden guitar. Sophee was sitting on the edge of her seat watching with great interest.

"Vicky?" I asked, to activate her.

"Yes sir?" She responds aloud.

"Thank you for the guitar, it sounds amazing." I said honestly.

"You're welcome sir," was Vicky's quick reply.

"Sophee, you need to have your Joshua sing a few songs as his voice is acceptable." Vicky states.

"Vicky understands true artistry." I said with a laugh. "Sure hope you do."

I start playing an old song called More Than Words; Sophee listened to the melody and with a smile asked if there were words for this song. I smiled and restarted the song and tried my best to mimic the dead singer's voice.

Sophee's eyes started getting watery and she stood up. "Please stop Joshua." She asked very softly. "You can't do this for me alone."

"Music and your words should be shared." She walks

over to the door of their home and addresses her mother who was listening from inside the door.

"Mom, please let everyone know that my Joshua is playing his guitar and if they want to hear something very beautiful to come over. It would be very selfish of us not to let the others experience this."

I can feel my face getting warm as I was turning red. "Sophee, I play for fun and I am not a musician."

Sophee reads my honest emotions and says; "You bring joy and happiness to me, share a bit of this with our people please. I will get you another glass of wine."

With that she gives me a kiss and heads inside.

Better be a big one. I grumble to myself as I hadn't thought that I would be putting on an impromptu concert. I can play quite a few songs and know the words to at least several dozen. Playing guitar was always relaxing and I had always thought that maybe someday I would be able to play for a woman that I was in love with. Never had I thought I would be bringing music back to a group of people who did not have the time in their lives to experience it. Since the Sooul accept me I hope they are not too disappointed with my talent.

I start warming myself up by playing some ballads as groups of them arrive and start sitting on the ground in front of me. I couldn't guess at the amount that came but I would say only the babies and a few mothers were missing.

Sophee knows how I really don't like to be the center of attention so she brought out a huge glass and a wine jug to refill it.

When everyone is settled I addressed my extended family.

"Uh, this is a replica of an acoustic guitar. I started playing quite a few years ago to fill in time between jobs. My thoughts were maybe someday I would meet someone and be able to sing a romantic song to them. I guess that day is here." I explain.

"Just so you all know I did not plan on singing this romantic song in front of a crowd." I smile as I feel my face get warm again. Playing music does not embarrass me because people can simply like it or not, it's their choice. Singing a romantic song for someone I love embarrasses a little because I am not the guy to be wildly broadcasting my feelings. I would only do this for Sophee.

"Sophee, please come over here because this is for you."

I wait for a minute until she moves past the crowd and sits beside me. She looks relaxed and happy but a little curious wondering about what is coming.

I stand up and move a few feet to the side and start my lead in to the song. A look of surprised wonder comes over most of the Sooul's faces as they hear the guitar for the first time.

"I guess my nefarious plan of having a woman fall for me through song is working." I said with a grin. The Sooul look at me without expression and I realize they probably don't know what nefarious is. "Anyway this is one of my favorite songs and it is over two hundred years old. The song is called Thinking Out Loud, by Ed Sheeran." The song is somewhat poetic for our relationship because it was the touch of her hand that started our bond.

As I start the song and start singing I can see the people closest to us sitting with their mouths open in shock. Sophee's smile changes into a total look of surprise. I focus on her eyes alone and try to imagine that we are alone. By the time I hit the fifth line of the song I am in a groove. The guitar's sounds blend with my voice at a perfect level. My foot taps to give the beat as I work through the harmony.

Tears pour down Sophee's face and from the corner of my eye I see every female watching me sing doing the same. My belief in what I am singing and the emotions I feel flow. My voice has never sounded better and the music which should always be played with passion fit this moment better than I could have hoped for. As I end the song Sophee flies into my arms. I kiss her happily and then look at the still crying women sitting before me.

"I am sorry to make you cry, but I have waited my whole life to have that moment with someone I loved. Thank you for sharing that with me." The amount of joy and happiness I saw made my eyes feel watery so I decided to explain how I feel about music.

"Not being empathic like you I believe that music should invoke an emotion response. Joy, happiness, love can all be found in music, when I am alone and need a mental pick me up I have a list of songs I play. Or if I am in a serious mood I have other songs that motivate me."

"This song has been running through my head for the last day or two. I know that most of you sense what you call the darkness in my heart. Well, I think the Gham going away will get rid of that darkness. Since they generally show up late in the day I will dedicate this next song to them. 'It ends tonight', is by another old band called The All American Rejects."

As I play the song and sing with very positive emotions I watch Sophee mostly. As she digests the works to the song with how I am feeling I can see her understand that the Gham will be no longer an issue in my mind.

I played and sang some more songs, 'Rain Delays,' by Crash Parallel and the 'Give you Hell,' from the All American Rejects showed the Sooul that not all songs were about love but suffering sometimes and regret. The Sooul ate the music like they were starving. I played to the crowd as they all were my family.

"Hey Joshua, can you please sing another romantic song?" Shoran asks me with a huge smile. I can see several girls nodding at her request so I laugh and look into Sophee's still wet eyes. "Ready?" I ask with a grin.

At the end of 'Lay me down,' by Sam Smith, Sophee and most of the female present are bawling. Hyun crosses his small porch and gives me a hug.

"Maybe our people needed this, but I hope you realize that our un-bonded females are going to be expecting all men from New Harvest to play guitars and sing," He shakes his head at the thought; "We hope you are not setting their expectations too high."

Thinking about what he said I decide to tone down the love or romantic songs and just play the guitar for awhile.

"Not everyone has the time to learn to play the music like I do. I used to spend days and weeks in transit." I explain. Even if I said it aloud I could tell that it had the effect on Sophee I desired. Later when my fingers were tired and starting to bleed I put the instrument away and realized I had not finished my wine. Sophee, Mere and Shoran brought me some food they looked at me like they had seen a totally different person.

* * *

Joshua is so much more than a warrior, was all Sophee

could think. As he started his favorite song she realized that he was putting all of his passion into this song. Not until the four or fifth line did the words actually make sense, when he sang about the ways and touching hands her heart felt like it would burst. She could feel the tears pouring down her face as she realizes his bond is as strong as hers. *This man with all his passions is mine.* I can't even see his face because of these tears. No way is he doing this for me without him knowing how much I love him. I get to my feet and jump into his strong arms for a kiss. My Joshua's amusement was plain on his face; a sense of accomplishment is also there beside the love and adoration he is feeling. I look up at my soon to be mate and instantly know that he wanted me to feel the love and emotions that the music also made him feel.

The rest of the songs were very sad and about people that either felt pain or did not bond. Sophee looked and Shoran when she asked Joshua to play another song and nodded in agreement. Anytime Joshua wants to sing about their love he will always have her attention. He is very romantic and again she wonders if her Joshua is the norm for humanity or it is just her luck to get him. Feeling very dry and parched from the amount of water she lost from crying Sophee heads into the house with her mom and Shoran. As they warm up the meal and drink more water, Shoran and Mere talk about Joshua.

"If we live through the next ten day could you imagine the lives we will have?" Shoran asks her mom. Mere smiles and addresses the room softly. "Vicky, are you listening?"

"On line Mere, Joshua asked me to monitor here and ensure that any questions or concerns get to him as soon as possible. He is not invading your privacy and does not ever ask any questions that could be private in nature." Vicky informs the listening females.

"Is Joshua a normal man as you understand it?" Mere asks.

"Define normal please." Vicky asks.

"Music, his sense of humor, behavior?" Mere defines.

"Most humans don't play the guitar, most only sing poorly. Joshua is talented in that regard. His sense of right and wrong with the responsibility he shows exceeds what I have seen from other Gunmen. As a person he was very quiet, not shy but reserved or private. His friends hold him in very high esteem. I am sorry that I can't share specific things about him but you would be more impressed if I could." Vicky said.

Mere shakes her head, "Wow." Shoran's eyes are open wide and she looks at Sophee's smile and echoes Mere's "Wow."

Trying not to explode with the overabundant feeling of love and pride Sophee picks up the meal and heads back outside to feed her Joshua. After awhile most of the awed Sooul are all gone and Joshua looks very relaxed. "Why don't you come to bed and hold me?" I ask. He is quick to jump up grabbing his plate and empty cup to head inside.

Under the sheet he wraps his arms around me so tight and whispers in my ear, "I am feeling the love."

"You were not feeling it before?" I had to ask.

"Of course but I got the chance to sing a romantic song for you and show my passionate side it was better received than I hope it would be." Joshua said with a smile.

I look up at his smile. "Please save some of your passion for me later after the Gham are gone." I state.

"Planning on it." he said.

CHAPTER 11

As we sit in the sun on Sophee's porch after lunch, I still have to ask myself about all that would or could happen in the day to come. Will Sophee still feel the same? Will the people of Sooul all be afraid of me and other humans since they are a timid bunch?

Sophee's hand squeezes mine as she feels my emotional content; her warm hand brings me back to the present. I blink my dry eyes and realize I was staring far into the distance as I was thinking about tomorrow. Hyun and Mere were sitting across from us and they were silent and they tried to read me like their daughter.

"We should check on your shield," Sophee said. "Mother and Father, we are going for a walk and will be home around dark."

Mere smiles at her daughter, Sophee's smile gives her parents a blessed relief from the reality that consumes all their thoughts. I grab my pack from inside the house, fill the water pouch, and ensure all my toys are inside it.

"I am walking, not being carried like a child." Sophee said as I reach for her. Sophee walks away toward the hills so I fall in behind her for that wonderful view of her cute behind.

I let her set the pace. We are in no hurry and have no place to be other than with each other until tomorrow afternoon. We walk easily until we can over look the mouth of the cove. It is my guess that the extra meat and vitamins in their diet is helping with her energy level, as Sophee doesn't seem as tired as a few days ago. It is a sad thought that all it takes is a few vitamins and some meat to make them healthier. I do take a small bit of satisfaction at being the one who has provided it.

No eels are present yet at the shields entrance since it is only midday but that is to be expected at this time of day. The eels avoid bright sunlight most likely due to sensitivity to ultraviolet light. There are a lot more small fish than usual in cove now drawn either by the bits of eels or smell of the blood. This is a very good thing for the Sooul, as the fish will feed them well while we wait for pickup after tomorrow.

Sophee motions for me for me to sit. I remove my pack and put it across from me for her to sit on. *Here it comes*, I thought while wondering what she wanted to talk about away from her parents. Sophee sits down and waits until I make myself comfortable.

She says; "thank you for the seat."

Her green eyes search mine imploring me to speak. My throat felt dry and I do not know where to start.

"Out with it Joshua." Sophee says with infinite gentleness in her voice.

I know she has been sensing my dark side and that I have been hatching something as a plan. She doesn't know what I am going to do or how, and for this I am grateful. If she knew the amount of violence that I was capable of unleashing she may think differently of me.

"You are not concerned with the Gham, but I sense hesitation and worry about the Sooul. Why?" she asks.

I realize that my hands are clenched tight so I relax them and look into her eyes. My voice is flat as I explain myself.

"You open your eyes and can see the man I that want to be. I can't hide the man that I am going to be tomorrow." My voice hardens, "The Gham enrages me for how the Sooul have suffered. Even though they are sentient, I will either make them go away or end their existence."

"Your mom and you both mention the dark place in my thoughts and emotions which can rear its ugly head at times. I struggle with those feelings, trying to be fair and just. Might doesn't always make right in most cases, even though I believe here and now it is required. I am concerned how you will react when I actually do my job because you are the single most important thing in my life."

I can hear the anguish in my voice and it bothers me. My entire focus should be on the Sooul's need and not my need to be understood. Sophee's life and that of every Sooul must be protected. I want to shut up but am unable to stop. This bond with Sophee makes me want to express my thoughts, even the ones I am trying to hide.

I gently take her hands while imploring her with my eyes. "Your entire people were going to die, because you cannot kill. I can kill and will if it is for the correct reason. Protecting innocents or specifically protecting you and the Sooul is what I am about. I also understand that the way to defeat them is to do it fast and violently. Will your people be able to understand the depth of my resolve to keep them safe? Being a nice guy or showing kindness will not accomplish anything but our destruction."

I stop speaking because I am out of words.

"We don't like to see anyone killed," Sophee says slowly as her right hand is pulled away from mine and placed over my heart, "Sooul or even the Gham, but you know better how to deal with situation."

"What about when your bonded one turns into a killing machine? From what I have seen, the Gham will not leave and that will force me to become the absolute worst violent thing you have ever dreamed of." I ask plainly as her hand has a calming effect on my despair.

Sophee lets go of me and stands to say in a very firm voice. "Stop it! I dream of a world where the Gham will not murder my friends and family. The worst thing I could ever see you say? From my viewpoint it will be scary, but maybe the best thing I could ever see."

Sophee continues to look into my eyes as she moves closer to me and puts her hands on my neck. "Seeing you in danger has me very worried, but I know in my heart if you tell me not to worry I shouldn't."

This lifts me up emotionally as I feel the burden has been lifted off my shoulders. Sophee can sense the easing of my tension and worry. Her few statements about the battle also being the best thing she could see went straight to my core. The Sooul may not like my actions but Sophee accepts what they will be. Sophee uses the moment to climb onto my lap, wrap her arms around my neck, and kiss me. I almost feel like a new man, as I pulled her closer and get some serious face time. When we finally part Sophee's face is flushed and her heart is beating quickly enough I can feel the pulses with my hand on her back.

"Can I ask some personal questions to my soon-to-be-mate?" Sophee softly asks.

"Anything." I reply.

"How tall are you?"

"I am six feet, two inches tall." I answer.

"Are you really taking me to New Harvest?"

"When I can speak to my Grandfather I will talk to him about you and if he wishes me home then my entire family has to come as well. Either that or I will get all of us a new place to live. Knowing my Granddad he will welcome you and our people to New Harvest." I answer truthfully.

"I have one more question," Sophee said with a hesitant voice. I paused for a second because this was the first time Sophee actually seemed nervous.

"Ask away." I said lightheartedly.

"Do you think it fair that I have to wait to mate until you are on your home planet? I will wait, but I don't want to." Sophee looks intently into my eyes when she finishes.

I feel like laughing but don't want her to feel I am not taking her seriously; "In my culture, it is usually the girl who is holding back. When the Gham are dealt with, we can have the discussion again." I promise her.

Hyun and Mere were told we were not mating because of the situation and this makes me wonder if they have a ceremony or go through any rituals after they bond before mating. I would hate to take anything away from her culture.

"How is it done?" I ask her.

Sophee smiles as she tucks her head into the side of my neck and then giggles. "The male puts his..."

"Stop, I know that, Sophee!" I say with embarrassment for some reason.

"Usually the male who has bonded will tell the girl's mother that they have bonded and to drop her off tonight," Sophee says.

"That's it?" I ask.

"What else is there?" Sophee wonders out loud with a very puzzled look on her face.

"In my culture the male goes to the father and, as a sign of respect, he asks for permission to marry his daughter. Then the suitor explains to the father how he will provide for the daughter. It is the way I will do it, but don't tell your parents because I like the look on their face when I do the unexpected."

Sophee laughs at the thought. "Just as my mom starts to think she has you figured out, you do something that makes her realize she hasn't. It drives her a bit crazy, I think. As for myself, I accept what you do and enjoy the surprises. I know your heart, and for me that is enough."

I carefully lift Sophee off my lap and stand up. By the lower position of the sun the time has to be fairly late in the afternoon. To be home for supper we will have to head back now. I put my pack on and then sweep her up into my arms. Before she can say anything I touch her lips with my finger to silence her.

"I want you close to keep my heart happy." I said with a smile as I start down the trail. Sophee didn't fuss about being carried and smiled. Without her shorter legs setting the pace we made rather good time and to me it seemed like a very short stroll.

When we got to the beach I set her on her feet. We both have to smile because a lot of the town was fishing. Mostly the men fish while groups of women talked. Kids were running around playing tag and some other game I have never seen. This surprised me because of what could happen tomorrow; most humans would be basket cases knowing they might die.

"I find it very odd that everyone seems so happy Sophee, most people I know would have a very hard time and be unable to enjoy themselves this close to a rendering." I casually state.

"Our people have decided to have good family lives, even if they are cut short," Sophee answers. "After a rendering, it takes a day of holding your loved ones to regain our composure. For the next nine days, we try to spend our all of our time with our families. We ensure that happiness, not bitterness drives us. With no hope for the future, we can only give each other the best of ourselves."

I think it is wonderful but sad sentiment, but don't subscribe to their theory. A lot of violence applied in the correct manner would stop the issues they are having. I do not say this to her because I am planning on being the applicator of said violence. The loathing I feel for the Gham makes me tremble with anger when I think about the video I saw.

Sophee waves to a few people as we walk toward her parent's house. Shoran sees us returning and yells out; "Glad you're not too tired Joshua, Sophee can Joshua carry me to my parent's house?" Sophee giggles and looks into my eyes; "See what you have started?" I laugh as well.

"In my culture the parents live close by, but not under the same roof," I say, fishing for information on the Sooul's living arrangements.

"Is it because you don't want them to see you naked?"

"No, I would not want to scare your mother," I quip back.

To this Sophee laughs and says; "I will have to tell her about Vicky's compatibility scan, after she was so concerned."

"Please don't do it when I am around, because you will really make my face turn red." I said.

She doesn't even look at me. "Honesty and openness is good for your soul. You should not worry or be concerned with what my mom thinks."

A gentle pull on her hand stops Sophee. I drop to my knees in front of her and give a softly spoken. "You are good for my soul little Sooul." I say as I turn my head slightly sideways to give her a soft kiss. Sophee's arms automatically pull me closer and we kiss for a few minutes before continuing to her parent's home.

* * *

Supper before the rendering was another long casual affair. The conversation was more about New Harvest than anything else. Mere keps asking about chocolate dishes and I pulled her leg a bit about chocolate steak and coffee soup. I did tell them that, when we get to our ship, I would be happy to teach them about my favorites, like hot chocolate with marshmallows and hot fudge Sundays. After trying milk chocolate, deserts were a something they all wanted to try.

During dinner Hyun got out more wine, which I hated to decline, but tomorrow is not a day I can afford to be off my A-game. I don't ever go to war or battle with a hangover or feeling the effects of alcohol. Fighting is serious business and it either needs to be avoided or won. Having a few glasses of alcohol could result in reaction times that could get me killed or injured. Not just me but the fate of Sophee and the Sooul rests on every decision I would make. *Not a hard choice is what I am thinking as I sip my water.*

"What is a sex toy?" Mere asks again.

Damn I thought she forgot.

By the shades of red in my checks as I stammered out a bland answer, I could tell she thought I am repressed or something. Not being empathic and able to sense emotions I relied on her laughter to point her thoughts out. I would not let that ride; because I felt that I was far from being repressed. I just had dedicated my life to the Gunman's Element and did not take time for myself. Just wait until I get her daughter married then look out.

"Let me try again," I said when Mere stopped laughing. "Human's can mate without bonding and take sexual gratification from a partner they are not in a close relationship with if they choose. A lot of people form long term relationships and want to spice up or make their love life more exciting."

Loving isn't enough?" Sophee asks.

"What kind of devices?" Mere asks. "I want juicy details."

I turn bright red again. I also realize I am totally losing this battle. "When you get to New Harvest you can research it, but I think I am done talking about it." I stammer.

Mere is laughing harder than Sophee or Hyun. I start laughing at them as well because their laughter is not unkind. The night before a rendering they are relaxed and laughing. *Good job Joshua.* "I am sorry Joshua," Mere finally says as she tries to dry her eyes. "Your bashfulness is so cute."

"Cute? Come on Mere… I am a Gunman who puts fear into the hearts of evil creatures." I say with a wiry grin. "I could have a different theory on the Sooul…"

Now I had their attention. Mere reaches across the table to take my left hand because Sophee has the right. "Joshua, we would love to hear anything you think about."

"The Sooul have their bond which is much deeper level of commitment than most humans have. I imagine when you do make love it would be with your mind and body." *Damn I hope this is the correct way of explaining it.* "For non Sooul it is more of a physical act. Not that they don't love deeply but thoughts and emotions are generally private." I take a breath, "without the bond some humans can sometimes need the extra bit to keep the love life new and fresh. Maybe I am wrong but that's how I see it."

Sophee looks down for a minute; "Do you see our love life needing extra bits?" She asks openly.

I give Mere's hand a gentle squeeze before letting it go. I turn to my bonded love and gently hug her. "You are the center of my existence; I have bonded like your people do. Our love life will be whatever we make of it; I do not feel the need to think about of these things." I explained.

Mere takes a sip of her wine and looks at Sophee and I. "You are a fascinating man Joshua, I still think you are too shy."

To hell with that…..

"An example of a sex toy would be a personal vibrator which is shaped like a human penis, operated by batteries and is used to bring the woman to orgasm. The male can use it on the female or the female can use it when she is by herself and wants sexual relief."

Mere and Sophee's eyes are wide at my explanation, "there are many other such toys and aids for people." I finish and realize it was much easier to say than I thought it would be.

"I sense truth, but this is a very different type of life style we are going to." Mere said with a look of incredulity.

"I would not know the percentage of people that use sex toys Mere" I say. "I think it would be a much smaller percentage than the amount that do not."

I hope that fills her curiosity, trying to give her information without embassing myself is very difficult so I think about where I am and how much I love these people for a minute or two.

"Before tomorrow happens I would like to express my gratitude for the way you have welcomed me into your family. I have never thought I would love as much as I do." I said.

Sophee's eyes go wide as I thank her parents. Mere and Hyun get watery eyes as they likely wonder if I am thinking I will not survive.

I get up and excuse myself before heading to the sanitary room.

* * *

Sophee waits until Joshua has left the room before speaking. "My Joshua's emotions are odd."

"Was Joshua saying goodbye if he doesn't make it?" Hyun asks bewilderedly.

With a shake of her head Mere put her arm around Hyun. "Sophee, please tell what you told me to your dad." Mere asks.

"My Joshua is afraid of what we think about him afterward." Sophee says. "As a warrior he believes there will be a fight. Joshua is going to protect us by destroying the Gham quickly and violently." Sophee said. "Remember when he said the eels were not a fight? I suspect knowing how my Joshua's manner is to understate such things that he will be a totally different man tomorrow." She finishes and stands to go make up the bed.

"Should we talk to him about our love and respect?" Mere asks.

"No mom, he knows our love. I feel he believes his actions will be so severe against the Gham we could change our minds about him." She looks at her mom, "I will prove him wrong later tomorrow."

Sophee smiles when she hears Joshua returning; "For now let him be."

* * *

Fairly early in the evening Mere opens their bed and pulls a curtain around the sleeping area. With tomorrow being the ten day I imagine they want to spend their possible last evening with their loved one. Mere and Hyun both undress in the open then climb into their bed behind the curtain. At least some things are the same, I laugh inside. The curtain tells me they are going to mate and don't want me freaked out. *Silly Sooul; tonight is not your last night!!!!* I undress and lay down on my pillows to wait for Sophee. Sophee gives me a kiss and slowly undresses as she is looking at me.

I lay there, thinking she is going so slowly on purpose, she knows I do not have any restraints and wants to play it.

The 1st Gunman

Sophee finishes undressing then decides to brush her hair. The view is terrific; I am blessed to have such a beautiful woman as my bonded one. When she finishes her hair she then slides in bed beside me. Even without being able to sense emotions like the Sooul, I can easily figure out what is going through her mind.

What if tomorrow is our last day?

"Come here, vixen!" I say with a laugh, and give her the best kiss she ever had.

Her heart is hammering against my side when I break the kiss. She is warm and smells like flowers. My head is pulled down so she can look into my eyes, "I love you." I say softly.

"I love you too," is Sophee's husky reply as her leg moves over mine. I give her a kiss on the forehead and a pat on her cute rump. I lean back before closing my eyes.

About five minutes pass with Sophee's leg over mine before she meekly says; "Really, it could be my last night?"

"No, this is not your last night," I sigh. "Let me deal with Gham tomorrow then we can have the rest of our life together. And yes my dear we will make love, but if it really bothers you tonight I will sleep outside."

"Don't battle them all day because I am going to love you sooner than you think Joshua." Sophee says. She then proceeds to snuggle tightly against me.

When I woke up early in the morning Sophee was lying across my chest with her arms around my neck. I don't remember when that happened, but I could not be happier. Her breast was pressed into mine and my hand rested on the small of her back.

Prior to meeting her I would have thought that sleeping

with someone on or near you would be annoying. I find this is not the case as it is calming. I hear Sophee murmur my name and I smile. I open my eyes realizing that she must have been warm when she was sleeping. The blanket was entirely kicked off us. Who needs a blanket when you are lying on a heat source? I looked at her body with wonder.

My good god, she is beautiful.

I notice her ribs are showing, and her slimness borders on a lack of nourishment. I feel like a piece of crap because this woman needs more food, more protection and love. Here I am looking at her like she is my play toy. I know that I can make life better for her. The Gham will not be an issue; the Sooul will have a stable well fed existence. I pull the blanket up to cover her and wrap my arms protectively around her. Later today I will begin their journey to a better life by taking away their enemies, for now I will close my eyes and enjoy a few more hours of sleep.

* * *

"You will be careful?" Sophee looked up into my eyes as she asked, seeking some reassurance.

"My love, I will be violent and nasty, and at the end of the day all the Sooul will be alive." I said this because I would rather tell her a great truth than lie to her by promising that I would be cautious.

Sophee gave me a quick kiss and left to wait outside with her parents while I got ready. It was not too hard for any of them to sense my frame of mind. The darkness that the Sooul can sense is actually the promise of violence and great vicious unyielding brutality.

I don't have to psyche myself up for the pending battle; I

start visualizing the pending engagement close my eyes and take some deep slow breaths to focus. I can feel my pulse slow, but my nerves still tingle. It must be that I am eager to deal with the Gham and want to make the Sooul's problems vanish, or maybe it is the fact I like to battle when it is for the right reason.

When I decided it was go time, I stood up and pulled my battle suit on. With one touch on a cuff key, I feel it shrink to my body and tighten around waist. I strap on my knife and sig; I cannot risk damaging the ship with the railgun, and my rifle has too slow a rate of fire. Slipping into my boots, they automatically tighten and mold themselves to my feet. With one more tap on the sleeve, fingerless gloves slide onto my hand and tighten up as well. The backs and palms are reinforced with flexible carbon fibers that will help protect my fists should I need to hit something.

I touch the sleeve again and green tiger stripe camouflage appears on my battle suit. I realize a camouflage pattern is not a necessity, but feel the Sooul need to see their 1st Gunman in ultimate warrior mode in order to give them some reassurance. The suit feels good, because, other than the few weeks of being inside a rejuvenation tank while I was being fixed up for one kind of damage or another and the previous few days, I think I have not had it off for longer than a day or two in six years.

Sophee, her parents, and the rest of the Sooul are still waiting outside for me. I take a quick look at my reflection and wonder how I will look tomorrow to everyone else.

I then shake my head clear of these thoughts, no longer am I a potential mate to a kind young woman. Today I am the 1st Gunman only, for today the Gham will know the

Sooul have a protector. *Be brutal, be a killer, save these people* rolls repeatedly in my mind as I walk out to the silent crowd.

* * *

Sophee and the rest of the Sooul are standing outside of her home waiting for their Joshua to come outside. Mere and Hyun are holding hands, as every family in the crowd is doing. The people of Sooul had tried hard to put the rendering day out of their minds because of the wonderful week they just had. A huge group barbeque, new tastes treats and a Gunman to take them away had relaxed them until today. Now that the time was here, the adults were comforting their kids and trying to appear strong for each other.

Sophee tries to calm her parents who are quietly holding hands as they watch the rest of the Sooul. Her father's apprehension and despair may not be evident to anyone else but Sophee with her skill saw it clearly; "Our Joshua will handle the Gham like he does everything else."

Shoran is standing close by with her arms wrapped around her parents and takes the time to nod at Sophee. There was more hope than fear when Shoran looked at Sophee. She then pulls her parents closer, just in case Joshua is not able to defeat the Gham, and this is the last time she ever gets to hold them.

"Joshua has not been in a battle here—by his standards—and the side of him which he tries to suppress is not hidden now." Sophee reminds her parents. "I can sense his love for the Sooul as well as the darkness, or maybe the fight in his heart, from out here."

Hyun looks down and then at his wife knowing he should have more faith in Sophee's opinion of her mate-to-be.

She is the strongest empath and would know him so much better then he could. The gham are relentless, always coming here, always taking his people, and always killing families. Mere doesn't seem anywhere near worried as him.

The door dilates open and they all watch as Joshua steps out. It is apparent to everyone present this is not the smiling, happy man that bonded to their Sophee. The firm expression on his face and the posture of his body screams "*DANGEROUS*". The dark green and black pattern on his clothes and boots are frightening enough without the handgun and knife that hang at his waist. He walks slowly toward the crowd of Sooul and takes a minute to meet everyone's eyes.

* * *

Everyone is dressed in plain garments that would not make them stand out from one another. As I meet their eyes a few interesting things happen. The men and women seem to draw from my strength and stand taller. The young people look a little less stressed as well. Color starts to appear on their faces as the fear goes away.

It is now about the show. It's about looking dangerous, far more dangerous than the Gham. The Sooul need to see that a warrior is on their side, someone who would defy the odds and beat their enemies. Normally I would just do what needs to be done without any fanfare, but these people, these kind decent people, need hope. I look across the crowd and, in a calm voice, I address the Sooul. I do not use the softer voice the people are used to, but my command voice, which is now filled with absolute conviction.

"I am 1st Gunman Joshua Garvie from the Gunmen's Element of the People's Free Force and I protect my people."

Slowly we walk as a group toward the landing site, the Gham being creatures of habit land at the same place every time. When we get to the meadow I tell the adults to put the children in the very back of the group so they won't have to see what happens. The Gham give them enough nightmares and I would hate to scare the children or scar them for life when I pay them back for the genocide.

I do not take Sophee's hand as we continue to walk across the meadow with the group of Sooul. It kills me not to do it, but I have my game face on. I hope she understands that the 1st Gunman is here and her Joshua is not.

I know where the ship is going to land since that area crushed from repeat landings. The ground has a semi baked appearance and no foliage grows from the sunken foot print made by the Gham's vessel. The video I saw on the first day with the Sooul shows this to be the same spot.

I look at Hyun and Mere. "Please take the group over to this side." I point near a slight knoll; "and keep hold of Sophee. Do not let her leave the group. Also, tell our people they can turn away if they wish. I don't want anyone to have to watch what I think I am going to have to do." Once they nodded their agreement, I turn and walk away without saying goodbye.

Just focus on the future.

I continue to separate from the group until I am standing in the opening maybe a hundred feet from the landing site between my people and where the Gham will land.

"Sir, there is an incoming holographic message from your grandfather," Vicky said.

"How much time do I have?"

"Twenty minutes until the Gham land."

"Go ahead and play it," I command.

A holographic figure of Granddad and my mother appears in front of me. By the gasps I hear from behind me, quite a few Sooul have decided to continue to watch whatever is going on.

"The Boy Named Joshua is in route and will be there in six days or four from when you receive this, Granddad says. "We were outside Tertian when you disappeared. Those two friends of yours we agreed to hire are on board with us and ready to deploy the second we are in range."

Granddad takes a breath before continuing. "Your AI has also updated us about the Sooul, and they will be welcome on New Harvest. We will be lucky to have them. Please be careful, Josh. These Gham creatures sound dangerous. Here's your mother." By the time he was done speaking, I could tell he was getting a bit emotional by the way his eyes watered and the slightly shaky tone of his normally robust voice.

My mom appears briefly, "I can't wait until I meet Sophee! Now, we have done a bit of research on these Gham. What little data we were able to find told us they are from a hive-type collective; they don't respect any life but their queen." Mom looks upset, like she is on the verge of crying as well. "Fight carefully. I love you."

The holograph fades away to nothing. I am going to see them soon. Had I known they were so close I could have just blasted the Gham ship when they come down, it would have meant leaving before another Gham ship could make it here but that would just leave the rest of the collective to kill others like the Sooul.

"Scans show the Gham are entering the atmosphere." Vicky says to refocus my thoughts.

I look up to see a different ship than the one on the original video. This looks at least two or three times the size of the ship I saw in the video. The ship is flat black and seems to absorb light making it hard to see any of the features or edges of the ship.

As I stand unmoving, except of the slight flexing of my right hand, a thunderclap sounds from the spacecraft's deceleration when they cross the sound barrier. I touch my sleeve keys to activate the fighting mode of my suit so my neck and head covering forms leaving only my face open. I was not sure if it would help because of my general lack of nanites but it would help protect me from light wounds or shrapnel.

I focus on clearing my thoughts until calmness washes over me like a wave. Within a few minutes, I can feel the drive's vibration as the ship settles on to its landing pads. I can also hear whimpers of fear and crying from some of the crowd behind me and wish I could comfort Sophee.

The ship's quiet drive stops humming when they shut down.

I hear Hyun tell his people; "The bad ones are coming."

I am already here; passes through my thoughts as coldness creeps up my spine. I start walking to where I presume the ramp will come down and I am not disappointed.

Sub-vocally I say; "by the size of this ship do you think there will be more than four Gham?"

"Yes, between twelve and twenty-four based on ship size alone," Vicky replies.

"When the hatch opens, give me a life form count please."

The ramp slides out of the bottom part of the ship about twenty feet straight out and then hinges down. It's an ugly ship with no esthetic value. The color is dull black and there are no external features like hatches or view ports.

What a piece of crap, I think. Take a brick and stick it on its side, it was not designed by anyone or thing with style that's for sure.

The previously invisible hatch starts to slide upward and a warm mist rolls out for a few seconds before dissipating. As the hatch fully opens, the smell that accompanies the mist is like marsh mud, slightly acidic and rotting. Inside the ship it is darker and my eyes are not able to discern any features.

Vicky chirps; "Twenty eight life forms and they all are moving toward the hatch."

I stand in the open field about forty feet from the end of the ramp and don't move. My soul is locked into a very black place; something ugly feels like it is just buried below my skin. I have never felt as willing to fight as I do now. It surprises me on a different level because my mind has taken the leap to fully commit to destroying them all and not just to be fighting to win. My handgun carries enough ammo in two magazines to deal with this threat. Then I have a ship as a weapon. The number doesn't concern me a bit. If I keep moving and stop the Gham from making it to the Sooul or back to the ship everything will be just perfect.

As the Gham come slowly down the walkway they notice me. It would be very hard to miss someone my size between them and their prey.

"Vicky, you're recording this?" I ask.

"Yes, from several buildings, now get your head in the fight!"

Sure wish I could tell Sophee I love her again, I think. *Focus, Josh, focus. Twenty-eight against one seems a tad unfair; I sense a melee in the making.* I may try to hide the emotions that come over me but twenty-eight is so much better than four. And having more opponents allows for using so much more violence and general nastiness.

The Gham continue to come down the ramp, and every other Gham is carrying the six foot wooden staff with the dull stone on the top that absorbs the dying people's energy. It will not be used today I hope.

Darn, they are bigger looking in real life. It looks like their arms are double-jointed and the three talons on the end of their arms appear to be sharpened. *I wonder what the costs would be at a local nail parlor.* Their legs are bare and almost seem too skinny to support their weight. By the slow mode in which they walk they think nothing could stop them, being slightly insectiod I am betting they can move much quicker when they need to.

Hello ugly. The Gham's faces are no prizes with large mandibles on either side of their jaws crossing in front the mouth and covering their noses—if they have one. They have very small black eyes that are busy scanning the whole area in little jerky movements.

I continue my live assessment of them as the Sooul are audibly getting upset and thinking like me. Seven teams of four or fourteen teams of two make me guess that this was the last time they were going to stop here. With the depleted population on this planet there were more than enough Gham to finish them off.

None of Gham are wearing anything more than an upper body harness. Due to their being from a hive means these have to be drones. Single sex warriors, the Queen either controls them or they work to support her.

Guess I can't kick them in the nuts to get their attention, I think inwardly, smiling. Not that I'd need to as the Gham are already moving toward me. I hear noise from them as if they do talk, one chirpy tone, which is answered by another Gham.

Sub-Vocally I ask Vicky if she can translate what I am hearing.

"Online" she says.

I take a step forward towards my foe and raise my voice. "The people of Sooul are under protection by the Gunmen's Element of the People's Free Force and you will leave this planet or bear the consequences."

* * *

Sophee and her parents were all holding each other when the ship opened up. The family groups had not split up this time. Her arms were around both of her parent's waists as they held each other. Most of the Sooul were fairly close and were able to reach out to touch other families. Sophee leaned further towards Joshua but her parent's arms stopped her from moving from the group. The rest of the Sooul waited close behind them.

As the Gham started filing down the ramp, Sophee started panicking. Never before had they seen so many Gham. Tears roll down her face as she looked to her father and mother.

"Will my Joshua be able to live through this, against so many Gham? Mom, please tell me?" Sophee begs for hope.

A black fog of something feral and violent emanates from the lone Gunman. It is so strong even Hyun can sense it. He was worrying for his people, now it seemed like a smaller thing as for the first time in Hyun's life something else overrode his fear. The total lack of any kind of fear or uncertainty that Joshua emanated stopped most of the Sooul from shaking.

"I would not want to be in the Gham's sandals right now!" Hyun states. Mere's hand goes to her mouth; "He not our Joshua anymore, this must be what his Vicky said about him being the 1st Gunman. I hope our people with weaker stomachs have faced away because when he fights it is going to be awfully violent."

There is nothing the Sooul can do to help in the fight without going insane, so they can only watch as Gham move off their ship and wait to discover if Joshua's stand against the Gham will be successful, if they will be free of the threat they had been living under for the hundreds of years.

Sophee stops feeling so scared for Joshua she becomes more aware of Joshua's state of mind. She nearly collapses under the horrible weight of it. Her knees shake as they strain to keep upright even as the ferocious darkness in his mind threatens to drive her to the ground.

This was the one thing that concerned Joshua, the violent side of his personality. Sophee had caught a glimmer of it when he viewed the video from the last rendering, but since she had bonded with Joshua the love and respect overshadowed the darkness. Now with it in the open, everyone can see what he is becoming. What Joshua is like when he is on the job, protecting the Federation is not what he is like generally. The contrast between the man that sings love songs and this man standing between them and the Gham makes Sophee realize that he truly is a warrior.

Contrary to Joshua's worry about how the people of the Sooul may end up fearing him, the opposite was happening. The Sooul could sense his decency, his absolute commitment to keep them safe. Instead of horror, they feel saddened that Joshua has to be this way on their behalf.

* * *

The warrior drones of the Gham sensed that something different is in the air as they departed their ship, and it does cause them some minor concern. They could see one bigger life form, has placed itself in front of all the rest as though it will stop the harvest. Pre-landing scans showed no advanced weapons active. This brings a very quick decision to claim its life first before finishing the entire source.

* * *

The Gham start to circle around me, they move smoothly, flowing around me like animals in a herd. *Come on, move away from the ship.* I mentally beg the creatures. I will need to finish all of them if I want to keep their ship. The first Gham stops directly in front of me. It appears similar to the others in size and shape. The harness is almost exactly the same with the exception of a round disc that sits high on its chest just under the throat.

"We have claimed this source," it said in a very raspy voice, "and will leave after we have their energy. You, too, will be claimed and your energy will feed our queen."

Really? It calls Sophee and her people a source? The second of blind rage I feel needs to be channeled into something else. The Gham's arrogance pisses me off to an extent that is unreal. Nothing short of surgical precision is required with how I battle. It takes me a bare second to calm myself. Sure they are a foot taller and a hundred pounds heavier, but it is time for them to get a clue. I feel slight warmth rising from within my heart as I realize there will be no other avenue to take other than their complete and utter destruction. I knew when I saw the video of the last visit I prayed it would come to this, but didn't realize how badly I wanted it. *You're making this easy not heeding my warning.*

I smile. "Leave now. You don't have to die!"

From the corner of my eye, as I finish speaking, I see a Gham start to swing his staff at my head. To the people of Sooul, all was lost. The Gham explained their purpose and brought enough soldiers to finish off everyone on the planet. Shock rolls through the crowd when they come to the realization that they all could die. The Gham took a family group and went away never before had they brought so many drones. Even when Joshua told them they did not have to watch most Sooul could not tear their eyes of the scene before them.

* * *

Joshua's body is directly between the ship and Sooul and that made a statement to everyone. If you want a Sooul you have to come through me. He is not saying it aloud but his posture and emotions convey this clearly to the Gham. The sound of the Gham's raspy voice was plain and blunt when it explained the purpose and what they were going to do.

Then the Sooul hear Joshua's final cryptic warning.

Surrounded and outnumbered their Joshua is just as blunt when he tells them, "Leave now, you don't have to die." Eyes widened and mouths gasped in the watching crowd of Sooul.

The talking Gham tilted its head as if questioning the sanity of the being in front of it. One of the Gham to the right beside the leader swings his staff at the Gunman's head, possibly under instruction from the leader. Joshua blurs into action…

* * *

My battle reflex kicks in. I step inside the staff's arc to deflect it sideways and grab hold of it with my left hand as I draw my pistol with my right and fire into the Gham's face. The creature's head explodes in a puff of grey and pink mist so I continue rotating and shoot the next three Gham standing to the right of the first one, leaving twenty-four standing.

A set of talons misses the back of my neck by an inch or two and, with a backwards sweep with the staff still in my left hand; I slash at the Gham's knees to take its legs out. The Gham hits the ground, on its back, momentarily stunned so I stab downward, driving the sharpened wooden staff's tip through the creature's face. The staff goes all the way through the Gham's head to lodge in the ground. Instead of wasting time trying to yank it free again, I use the wooden post as a pivot point to spin in a fast rotation to the further to my right to continue my attack.

Three more shots snap out of my Sig, dropping the next trio of Gham. As I move until behind the spot where the last body fell, I drop into a crouch using the dead Gham as a shield. I use a combat weaver grip for complete control of my weapon and address my enemies.

Ten more fast rounds slam into the scrambling Gham's heads. My handgun sounds like one long boom as it cycles rapidly thru the ammunition in the clip. The Gham drop headless, leaving more pinkish-grey haze floating in the air over their inert bodies. I take a step back to clear my immediate zone to give me enough time to reload. I pull a new clip out of my speed loader and slam it into the butt of my gun.

Two more Gham rush at me, around the pile of dead Gham, one is about to throw his staff at me like a spear. There is barely enough time to raise my pistol and shoot it in the center of the chest. The staff flies like a spear harmlessly by my head missing me by all of a foot as I shoot the falling creature again. Its partner receives a double tap to the head as it brings its arm back to slash at me.

Four of the Gham are moving toward the crowd of Sooul. I don't know if killing their leader changed their tactics or if they were going to try and circle wide behind me. Either way I pause for half a second to find them behind my gun sight and then head-shoot them being careful not to miss and send bullets flying toward the Sooul.

Unfortunately, the distraction gave one of the surviving Gham circling me an opening to attack. The creature smashed his staff down on my arm, breaking my wrist with a very loud snap and knocking the pistol out of my now useless hand.

The pain is intense, radiating up through my arm and leaving my hand flopping around without control. Not about to be defeated, I use my left hand to draw out my knife from its sheath strapped to my left leg. Taking aim, I throw the knife into the nearest charging Gham's chest. It appears to stagger a bit at the impact but it was so close to me that it could still attack before succumbing to the knife wound.

I duck the wounded Gham's slash and drive my foot into its stomach causing the creature to bend forward upon impact. I throw an upward elbow to the base of its chin resulting in a nice snapping noise from the Gham's neck as it reels over backwards. I scan quickly to see if I can retrieve my sig or knife and decide it was not something I have time for.

There are only three Gham left standing.

I turn, weaponless, to find one of the Gham had crept up closer behind me than anticipated. Too late to evade the blow, a staff slashes down the side of my face and its momentum continues down to hit my right shoulder. The wound on my face burns like hell and bleeds instantly like most head wounds leaking in a steady stream. And, from the feeling in my shoulder, something may be broken there too.

I am able to grab hold of the now broken staff that flops over on to my chest. Stepping to the side, I stab the jagged end of the pole though the offending Gham's neck. A loud gurgling noise bubbles from around the wound as the Gham sinks to his knees before falling face down in the grass to bleed out.

The damage I'd taken from various blows, the broken bones, is beginning to affect me and I am starting to move slightly slower. The second last Gham is able to slash at my back with its sharpened talons, opening a horrendous burning wound from my right shoulder to hip. The pain is immediate, but pausing will get me killed.

I throw a backward kick into the Gham's abdomen before it can strike again. The blow causes the creature to stop in place and lean closer towards me, while I spin left to grab around his neck with my good arm and arch myself backwards. A loud crack sounds as the neck snaps and the Gham goes limp. I drop it and turn to face the only threat left alive.

The last Gham, seeing me badly wounded charges. I have no ability to evade in the second it took as my battle reflex is slowing due to blood loss. The creature reaches me in that second and launches its attack. Both of its hands streak forward to impale or eviscerate me with those razor sharp talons.

I semi-block a pair of stabbing talons as I grab onto the Gham's harness before allowing myself to fall backwards to the ground. Throwing my foot into its abdomen as I pull it on to me, I extend my foot out to flip the creature over. I use the momentum and weight of the falling alien to pull me on top of it.

With no weapon to finish the creature off, I continually rain my left elbow down on its face as hard as I can. Aiming, I visualize driving my elbow through the alien's skull into the ground. Eight or nine hits later, its head is crushed and I am almost done in.

The agonizing pain from the slashes and my damaged shoulder make me almost scream, but with the blood I'm losing and the fact I can barely move made it not worth the energy. I give a slight cough and am very surprised to see bright red foamy blood hit the ground. *What the ......?* Maybe I am hurt worse than I thought. I look down at my chest and see a talon protruding out from the rib cage.

Crap. That's not good.

I look up towards the alien spacecraft, wondering if there could be more Gham on board. Vicky did say they all approached the hatch. I have to finish what I started... I hope that I can finish what I started.

Slowly I rose to my feet and moved with great difficulty toward the Gham ship.

"Lay down before your bleed out," Vicky quickly says.

"No." I stagger toward the ship, but don't make it. I fall to my knees, blood loss and shock is quickly taking its toll, weakness is not something Gunmen ever acknowledge. I struggle to get up, but I have to protect the people of Sooul from whatever may be onboard.

* * *

Sophee and her parents, along with everyone else, watched with utter shock as Joshua turned into a Gunman and then blurred into action. His appearance as a brave warrior standing before their enemies changed as he moved. Joshua became a weapon destruction that moved so fast that he was hard to follow.

The Gham were swinging their staffs and slashing at him; the speed of his reciprocal attack was astounding as the weapon in his hand roared. He had already killed twenty of the creatures when four Gham broke away from the fight and charged the crowd of Sooul. Not knowing if Joshua would be able to help them right away Sooul men started to pull their families behind them. Not that they would be able to fight but they could shield them with their bodies.

All four of the monsters came to the end of their existence with a cloud of brain matter before dropping to the ground in a crumpled heap a few feet from the Sooul. The men who bravely stood as shields in front of their loved one recoiled when blood and brain matter from the attacker's heads settled on them.

Sophee was distracted from trying to watch Joshua as he fought when her father and other men moved between her, her mom and the fight until she saw the four Gham charging the crowd. She could only see the Gham falling, a fog of brain matter and then she gasped at the surge of pain that emanated from her mate-to-be as he was wounded. Sophee's heart was almost in her throat as the blackness or intent that Joshua had at the beginning of the fight was replaced with desperate need.

The dead Gham were laying all around the meadow, some on top of each other and others spread out in the circle where they died when they surrounded Joshua. The apocalyptic scene before her did not even get a second glance as she sought out her bonded one.

The gravely wounded Gunman pushed up off the last Gham and was staggering toward the ship. The wound on his back was plainly evident and Sophee's mouth took a hard line and her eyes narrowed as she accessed his damage. Sophee let go of her parents and yelled for her dad to follow her as she ran toward Joshua jumping over the dead aliens.

* * *

As I finally make it to my feet, Sophee and her father run up and put their shoulders under my arms. Grateful for the aid but unwavering I continue to move toward the ship. Neither Sophee nor Hyun said a word as my bloody and gore covered arms and torso ruined their clothing.

"Please help me to the ship." Blood sprays as I speak because the talon in my chest must have hit a lung. My helpers remain silent as they help instinctively knowing whatever I am doing must be critical. My vision is slightly blurry and I hope that I can get Vicky into the ship before I die or pass out from blood loss. As we stagger into the ship Vicky says "Clear of all life forms." Once we pass through the airlock we find ourselves on the Gham Bridge. I sub-vocally speak, because I don't want Sophee to know my intentions. "Can you plot a course to their home world, Vicky?"

Scanning the Gham's systems for the few seconds it took her seemed like an eternity to me as I get weaker. Sophee trades a look with her father; "Joshua you need to lay down." I shake my head slinging blood on them. *Oops that wasn't nice.*

"Yes," Vicky finally replies after a very long ten second pause.

"Can you plot this ship through the planet at full power from the Faster than Light drive?" I elaborate.

"Done, safety protocols have been reprogrammed and the course plotted. You have thirty seconds to leave the ship." Vicky says out loud to motivate Sophee and Hyun to help me leave the ship.

"Quickly! We need to leave," Sophee said. She lifts me with more strength because as my face is going pale as I am getting weaker and leaning heavily on them. Hyun realizing that Joshua cannot support himself takes a deep breath and lifted with all his might. We make it to the hatch with seconds to spare. When we stumble down the ramp everything starts getting hazy, like my eyes are trying to look through fog. My legs are not working all that well either, so I try to lower myself to sit on the ground and fail, falling forward and rolling to my back. Sophee and Hyun had no chance to stop my sudden collapse. As I look up from my back I can see the sun but it doesn't feel warm. Instead there is a creeping chill that invades my body, taking with it my pain from my wounds. The cold seems so real, I feel myself sliding towards a void. *Is this what dying feels like?* I thought there would be soft music and cold beer delivered by angels. This was not the plan. Sounds of crying make me refocus briefly on the present.

Sophee's tear-streaked face is the last thing in view, and I can't tell her that she is now safe, the rest the Gham will not be coming back. There is no energy left for words, I wish I could say I love you one more time and hear her soft kind voice….. *God, I am going to miss her.*

I smile as the darkness takes me.

* * *

Sophee cries out as Joshua gives her a bloody smile then goes limp. The entire crowd of Sooul gathers around the fallen Gunman as the Gham ship raises and quickly moves out of the atmosphere.

"Vicky, can you help him?" Sophee asks holding direct pressure on the face would which seemed to be bleeding the most.

"I am putting him into a coma," Vicky replied. "That way he will not move or feel pain so the remaining nanites can treat the worst damage. There are not enough nanites left in his body to fix his wounds, so you will need to get him to shelter—*carefully*—and I will talk you through advanced medical aid. Hurry!"

It took a dozen Sooul to carry Joshua to Hyun's family's home. They moved cushions away from the seating area and laid him on a clean sheet on the floor. Sophee gets Mere's help roll him to his side and then asks for a knife. Leaving Joshua for a minute Mere finds a sharp knife in the prep area and passes it to Shoran to take to Sophee. Sophee takes the knife without saying anything because her attention is on Joshua while she cuts the suit off. Shoran is quick to pull the damaged battle suit away to give Sophee room to work.

"Vicky, what more should I do?"

Vicky quickly instructs Sophee from the pack's speakers sitting on the floor by the door. "Go to your processor's output pad. Retrieve the bowl of fluid and pour it in the length of the back wound quickly. Sew the wound up as fast as you can, and don't worry about being neat."

Sophee is throwing commands at her family and starts to hold the wound closed with her hands, until her father brings her the bowl of medicine from the output pad. She quickly pours it into the deep, two-foot long slash.

"Father, bring the pack closer so we can hear Vicky better." Hyun is quick to bring it within arm's length.

"Mom, help! Hold the wound closed please!" Mere also took the order and dropped to her knees to comply.

Her best friend, Shoran, had been preparing a curved needle with thread. She then hands it to Sophie before helping to hold the gaping wound closed. Even as the bleeding slows down from medicine the skin was wet and slippery as Mere and Shoran continue to push the sides of the gash together while Sophee quickly begins sewing it shut.

After about thirty minutes it was done. There was not enough time to relax as Shoran quickly prepared another thread and needle.

Shoran and Sophee carefully grab Joshua's shoulder and hip respectively to roll him off the last of his ruined clothes and onto his back. Sophee takes a quick look for other wounds. There is a broken talon sticking out of his ribs just below his nipple and another one in his thigh.

Sophee nods to herself as accepts the sight. More tears cloud her vision at the damage and she paused for a minute not knowing what to do. The uncertainty she was feeling about treating Joshua must have been evident in her voice. "He has also been stabbed Vicky."

"Deal the wound on his face first," Vicky instructs. She picks the bowl of remaining medicine off the floor while Mere gets ready hold the wound open for the medicine.

Joshua's injuries are severe enough that he could die. The wound that damaged his face was a fairly even cut went from his cheekbone across to where his jaw hinged. It was deep and the bleeding stopped when the coagulating medicine was added. The impact started to affect Sophee's emotions enough that she cried as she worked.

Mere holds the wound closed as Sophee continued to cry over the seriousness of the wounds. Shoran offered to take over and finish sewing but Sophee shook her head to either disagree or to clear her thoughts. When the face wound was sealed Vicky instructs Sophee to remove the claw impaling Josh's ribs.

"Just pull it out." Vicky instructed.

"Will that not cause more internal bleeding?" Sophee asked.

"The lung damage is the most important thing at this time to fix; the majority of his remaining nanites will be working on it." Vicky said.

The broken talon came out easily enough when Sophee grasped it and pulled hard. There wass no bleeding, so more green fluid was added before stitching. Then, barely pausing for breath, Sophee began to cut Josh's shorts off. There was no help for it, as she needed access to the injury on the front of his hip. When Sophee completed her task and removed the shorts, Shoran turned bright red.

"I had no idea…" She stammers at a loss for words.

Sophee sensing Shoran's surprise gave her a quick grin, her first that day, and yanked the talon out of the wound. It was too was barely bleeding, but she gave it the same treatment as the other wounds. Mere picked up the bloody shorts and took them over to Joshua's cut up battle suit. They would need to soak to get rid of the blood before she could try and repair them.

Now that the wounds were closed, Sophee looked up to the visitors who were standing around feeling that they need to help but unwilling to force themselves on the situation.

"Everyone out please, Joshua needs rest and time to heal!" Sophee orders firmly.

Knowing that things were under control as much as possible everyone leaft fairly quickly including the red faced Shoran.

"I will come back later," Shoran promises before walking calmly for the door.

"Thank you Shoran." Sophee looks down at Joshua and notices his breathing is quite shallow.

"Vicky, is there anything else we can do? Is it possible to give him back his nanites?"

"The nanites he gave to the Sooul were base units; once they were set for your language centers their programming was locked." Vicky replied. "All remaining programmable nanites are either repairing his lung or fighting infection. He will need fluids to keep him alive until the others get here."

"The others?" Sophee asks.

"Yes, his grandfather and mother are on their way and should be here in no more than four days as their ship is at full power. They have full medical staff so we just need to keep him alive until then." Vicky paused to give Sophee a second to realize that support was coming.

"You have done a good job on the wounds, don't worry. As soon as we get more nanites Josh's wounds can be repaired so you will not be able to even see the scars."

"Okay, Vicky." Sophee gave a sigh of exhaustion, but there was more work to be done. "Mother, could you please get me a basin of warm water and a cloth so I can clean my Joshua up?"

Sophee cleaned up the thread and curved needles that she used.

Mere brought a basin of warm water and Sophee proceeded to gently wash blood off Joshua's damaged face taking special care not to disturb the stitches when she removed the drying blood. His face and head were pretty well covered in blood but the short hair was easy to wipe down. Anything she missed would be caught tomorrow when she wiped him down then. When she got his face and head clean Sophee gave him a gentle kiss on the lips and then continued to cleanse the rest of him.

Mere fetched a blanket and waited patiently until Sophee wiped all of the blood off the unconscious Joshua, before throwing the sheet over him.

"It's a shame to cover that up," Mere says lightheartedly trying to make Sophee smile.

Sophee blushed before taking the clean-up material over to soak as well with Joshua's clothes. When she finished washing up and changed out of her blood soaked clothes she was back at Joshua's side. Sitting on the floor she carefully lifts Joshua's head onto her lap. Her armed wrapped around Joshua's head almost in a desperate attempt to protect him from dangers while he healed. She bent over until she could feel his breaths and for the first time in hours felt maybe a small bit of relief.

"Sophee, you need to get a cloth, dip it in water and slowly trickle water it into his mouth a few drops at a time," Vicky orders. Mere on hearing the order jumped up to get some water and a clean cloth grateful to have a task because watching Sophee care for Joshua was difficult. Not just because Joshua was wounded but Sophee was so focused and if it ended badly for Joshua she thought Sophee might not recover.

Mere set the bowl of water beside Sophee and handed her a clean cloth. After trying a couple of dunks Sophee was able to ensure no more three or four drops would be given to Joshua at a time. The raised position of his head allowed the water to pass to his stomach.

After an hour of this Vicky ran another scan to check on Josh's status. Once the fluid level was up she sent a signal to quick start more blood production from the bone marrow.

"Good job, we can start to replace some of the lost blood. Keep it up."

Sophee stayed at it until well into the evening. At one point Vicky said, "You need to eat and rest as well," but Sophee would not leave until Mere sat with Joshua. There was no way that he was being left alone for a second in Sophee's mind. When Mere was watching Joshua, Sophee was able to use the sanitary room and head over to the prep area for some food that Mere had been making. Her father gave a smile when she stood at the counter with him for a few bites of food.

Hyun was having a difficult time with Joshua being wounded. He felt rather useless since Sophee and Mere were handling everything without his help. He went outside to talk with the crowd camped out in front of his home waiting for any information or new updates on their critically wounded Gunman—after all, Joshua was one of their own now. Hyun felt touched by their silent support.

After quick bite to eat and hygiene break, Sophee returned to where her mother sat with Joshua. "Thank you mom, I will stay with him now." She took a second to retrieve some cushions and lay them out beside Joshua.

"Does he need more water yet, Vicky?" Sophee asks.

"No, you can rest. I will wake you when he needs more."

Sophee stood up and undresses in front of her mother. She then raises the sheet and slide under the cover beside him on his non-wounded side. Carefully she put her arm around his neck and pressed her body against him. Even in a coma Joshua's weak pulse started to beat a little stronger. After a second, his breathing seemed smoother and Vicky was very quick to understand what was making the changes.

"Sophee, you need to physically stay in contact with him as much as you can. His pulse is stronger; your presence is calming his injured body," Vicky states. Being glad that she could have a positive effect on Joshua made Sophee smile a little bit.

The 1st Gunman

* * *

Mere, seeing that Joshua was stable and Sophee was resting, went outside with the update to be surprised by the size of the crowd. Every Sooul was there, most standing quietly in groups, though a few of the girls were still crying over the day's events while some of the men remained rather shook up. It wasn't the fact they saw violence; it was that one of their own was so critically injured.

Mere found Hyun to give him the update to share. "Our Joshua is unconscious. His A.I. is keeping him in this state because of the nerve damage. This way he will stay in a stable state until the starship with his mother and grandfather get here later this week. The ship has full medical support and they will be able to heal Joshua if we can keep him hydrated and alive.

Mere looks over at Shoran as she moved to the front of the crowd to hear the report. "Sophee is staying in physical contact with Joshua as the bond is making his heart beat stronger. I could also tell that his breathing seemed better too"

As Mere discussed Joshua's status with her husband, all of the Sooul women had also moved to the front of the crowd to ask what they could do for Sophee and Joshua. While the women talked quietly with Mere and Shoran, Hyun gestured to the men and they gathered a few feet away to discuss the battle they had seen. The women had Joshua's health as their primary concern which left them to discuss the status of the Gham and the battle they had seen.

Those who hunted with Joshua had seen how quick he moved to deflect the falling grull before it hit them, but they were almost speechless at the speed in which

Joshua attacked the Gham. Knowing how he shot his more powerful weapons most tried to figure out why he did not use them. They replayed him standing alone against the Gham over and over again in their minds and talked about his emotional state.

Shoran's father Lian, made one point that all the men found to be interesting when they thought about Joshua's battle. "Did anyone notice that he smiled before they attacked him? It seemed like he knew there would be a battle and was almost happy with it."

Most of the men were concerned how the Sooul would be able to repay Joshua's sacrifice. "I think our Joshua would be embarrassed if we spent too much time trying to reward him." Hyun said with a grin. Mere noticing that several people were still upset with the day's events had Hyun had get out some wine and proceeded to ensure that the Sooul who were stressed out from seeing such violence had a drink or two to help calm them.

No one left the area in front of Sophee's parent's house because they did not need to hold each other and cry for their dead. It to all the Sooul seemed that this was where they needed to be. The weather was warm and dry so the kids curled up in blankets and slept while the adults talked softly during the vigil. It was more of a quiet celebration. After deciding what needed to be done the women joined their mates for the discussions.

Shoran was one of the vocal females wondering how lucky they were that such a man was brought to them and that maybe finally a God has seen their need. Hyun and most others stayed silent but agreed with her sentiment. The other men who had minor leadership roles—like the garden leader, maintenance leader, and gate minder—all talked about the ship that was coming and if it would be able to take them away fast enough to prevent the Gham from finding them. A few leaders hoped Joshua would be able to heal quickly, so he could be awake to talk with them when they came. Hyun knowing Joshua shook his head, "Whatever type of man Joshua has become is strictly due to his upbringing and influences. His Grandfather will be a good man like Joshua and will treat us well." He smiles kindly at the others; "Remember, Sophee can read a person better than anyone else and she thinks very highly of her mate-to-be."

The children slept on and, with the exception of three people who were so emotionally disturbed by the events of the day that drank too much, the rest of the Sooul stayed up all night. At dawn Hyun addressed the crowd. "Please go home and get some sleep, spend time with your families, for the first time in our history we have not lost anyone to the Gham. If a few women wish to stay around, I'm sure Sophee could use some assistance."

Vicky woke Sophee several hours before dawn and had her give Joshua more water. She didn't even take time to get dressed so, when her parents came in after sending the rest of the Sooul home they saw Joshua's head in their naked daughter's lap giving him water. Unconcerned that she was naked but knowing more people would be coming by Hyun got a long shirt out and pulled it over Sophee's head. With a kiss to her forehead her father then went over to help Mere get Sophee some breakfast.

Mere ended not having to cook anything after mid morning as the other Sooul women started bringing food to keep the family strong. Vicky suggested some weak broth for Sophee to drip into Joshua's mouth and there was always a fresh supply of that as well. Different Sooul women were in the prep area all of time taking turns to either warm broth or provide water for Joshua.

Shoran and Mere made sure they were both present at all times to give Sophee bathroom breaks. They would place their hands on Joshua's face and over his heart to try and keep his heart strong; it helped Sophee to know loving people were watching Joshua. The two of them together would not make his heart beat as strong as it did when he was in physical contact with Sophee. Whenever Sophee had to roll Joshua over on his side to clean the slowly healing wound there always someone present to help. Mere, Shoran and whoever was in the prep area were aggressive in their support of Joshua. Hyun stayed mostly outside helping people to get ready to leave.

Nothing changed for the next three days. All of Sophee's time was spent providing water, and touching or laying with her Joshua. Even in a coma the bond's strength between Sophee and Joshua continued to increase. As he stabilized his pulse got stronger and his color came back. The realization that he was feeling their connection and the way his unconscious body reacted so positively to her made Sophee feel happy but determined to maintain contact. Her mom and friend could see the difference in Joshua and encouraged Sophee to stay as close as she could.

CHAPTER 12

"Shuttle coming in," Vicky announces loudly. Vicky could have let Sophee, Mere, and Hyun know a day earlier when the ship would arrive since she was sending them medical scans but decided to wait. Sophee and her family had enough on their minds without being nervous about Joshua's mother and grandfather showing up.

Hyun looks at Mere with a smile feeling relieved that they made it and the Gham had not came back. Shoran and her mother left to be with Lian when the ship landed. Mere looked around quickly to ensure the home was neat enough to make a good impression.

"Father, please go greet our new family." Sophee was not willing to let go of Joshua for the few minutes it would take to greet her soon-to-be-relatives.

The sound of the shuttle was different than the humming sound associated with the Gham's ship. This was a constant roaring noise as the assault shuttle came in fast banked around the town looking at landing sites. The shuttle quickly approached Hyun's house as if drawn to it. Several jets of braking fire helped to lower the shuttle onto its landing pads less than thirty yards away from Hyun's home.

The nearby landing surprised Hyun, but he didn't

know Vicky was acting like a homing beacon for Joshua's family. Within seconds two heavily armed Gunmen cleared the open doors of the shuttle and they took up defensive positions. They were dressed like Joshua when he battled the Gham but did not look as menacing because of the pattern on their clothes was sandy colored. Both of the Gunmen were carrying big weapons that appeared different from the one he had seen Joshua use. All Hyun could think was that these people are like Joshua and we should trust them.

Hyun took a few steps closer to the shuttle and waved to the Gunmen. "Your medic needs to come this way," he yelled as he pointed unnecessarily at his home. "Our Joshua is in need of medical aid!"

One of the Gunmen moved away from the hatch on the ship to be joined with an unarmed medic and then ran down the ramp toward the house. He was faster than the medic who followed him but not as fast as Joshua.

* * *

The Gunman led the medic toward the building being pointed at and did a fast entry through the open doorway not knowing if he was going to take fire or be attacked. An active scan for weapons showed none, so he called "Clear!" Mere jumped when he entered at the suddenness of his appearance. The Gunman looked down to find his wounded friend lying with his head on a young girl's naked lap; she was wearing a shirt but nothing else. Inwardly the Gunman grinned when the other young woman jumped at his entrance and then again when he barked, "Clear" into his headset.

Hearing the clear signal over the link, the second Gunman guarding the ship flipped his weapon to safe and walked back up the ramp. The only person who witnessed this Gunman's movements was Hyun, still patiently waiting at the bottom of the ramp. He wasn't aware of the happenings within the house, but did not worry about the armed man as these were relatives of Joshua and thus safe.

The medic entered a second after the Gunman and quickly opened a scanner to confirm Vicky's assessment. He opened his medic bag, pulled out a large needle that was filled with dark red fluid and injected it directly into Joshua's carotid artery. "Jumpstart nanites." He said before starting an I.V. with whole blood, also infused with nanites.

"Miss, we can take it from here," the medic said to the young girl, hoping to move her out of the way. Nice that she wants to babysit the wounded man but adults can handle the situation now.

"I'll bet you could try," Sophee said with a tired voice. Even if they have the medicine and the knowledge to heal Joshua, he was her responsibility.

The medic looked at the firm expression on the girl's face and then over at the other young woman who had her arms crossed and the same expression. He could tell right then that he would have a fight on his hands and decided that he should let somebody with a higher pay scale make the decisions about these people. His main concern was the wounded man, and not moving the girls away from him

"Did you provide the medical aid to him?" he asked Sophee quietly.

"Several of us did under his A.I.'s direction."

"You saved his life. He will be stable enough by tomorrow morning to move onto the ship, and then we can put him in a regeneration tank to speed up his healing. You did a great job Miss."

The medic turns to the Gunman. "Joshua is out of immediate danger."

The Gunman hearing the conversation had already figured that Joshua was in a safe area and decided to leave the medical stuff to the medics. With a curt nod in agreement he turned away and walked out the door. He nodded to the Chandler and Caroline Garvie as they reached the house. Caroline knocked on the open frame eagerly looking for permission to enter and see her son.

"Come in please," Mere says, turning away from Joshua and Sophee to greet the visitors.

Caroline strode quickly to Joshua's side. "Status?" she asks standing beside her son.

"His AI put him into a coma, and he is stabilizing now. This young lady was able to keep enough fluids in him to keep him alive," reports the medic. "It will take less than a day to reconnect the damaged nerves, and then he can be transferred to the tank in the ship."

Caroline looked down at Sophee. "We will watch him now if you would like a break."

Sophee shakes her head negatively. "I am fine with my Joshua."

Caroline lowered herself to her knees beside them and gently touched the side of Joshua's damaged face. She looked at Sophee and put her other hand softly on Sophee's shoulder.

"I'm Caroline, his mother. Thank you for saving my son."

Sophee was reading Caroline's emotions as the woman spoke. There was utter and profound joy at the fact Joshua was alive, and then pleasure when Caroline looked at her. Sophee liked her immediately because she was kind and accepting. She was also filled with a pleasant curiosity but refrained from any questions.

"He saved us several times." Sophee answered back honestly. "Vicky, can you send videos to Joshua's family of the Gham attacking that Joshua watched, the eel attack, as well as Joshua's battle with the Gham? Maybe seen the update about the Sooul without breaking Joshua's privacy rules?"

"I have updated the Chandler about the Sooul. The rest I can't do unless Joshua agrees," Vicky replied. After a pause Vicky then said; "Sir, I have been requested to update the Chandler and your mother on the eel attack and battle. If you don't wish me to do that, please let me know."

Sophee and Caroline both look at the unconscious Joshua to see if he would wake to answer the question. There is only about a two-second delay before Vicky says, "The files have been transferred."

Caroline smiled, "Sneaky...but I like it."

The Chandler, standing close yet not saying a word as he looked down at his wounded grandson, now spoke. "We are grateful for the way you have treated Josh. Tomorrow, when we can move him, we will take him the ship and get him tanked for faster healing." Turning to the medic, he asked, "How long will Josh need to be tanked?"

The medic looked up from the scan he was running. "Five days. The help he got here made it possible to stabilize him quickly and, with full nanites, recovery will be very fast." The Chandler turned to see Hyun walk in over to Mere and take her hand.

"New Harvest will accept all your people and provide a safe place to live in peace should you decide that you want to stay with us." The Chandler said looking in Hyun eyes;

The Boy Named Joshua is in orbit, and has enough room to bring all of you home with us."

Hyun did not need his mates or daughter's skill to be able to read the older man. "Truth, and I accept for our people." Hyun replied with tears running down his face.

Chandler looked away because he's is not empathic and didn't want anyone to see his watery eyes. The happiness and relief that caused Hyun to tear up affected Chandler more than he ever thought. The Chandler knew about the cruelty and history but this was the first time he had seen it on such a scale.

"My Joshua has a ship named after him?" Sophee asked amazed at the thought of such a thing.

Chandler looked down at the beautiful girl holding Josh's head before answering back. "The flag ship of our fleet and several bulk carriers are named after him." Having appeased the girl's curiosity, Chandler walked out of the house with Hyun to see a huge crowd of people all standing staring at the house and the shuttle.

Hyun addressed the crowd. "Joshua's grandfather, the Chandler, will take all of us to New Harvest. We need to finish packing and be ready to go quickly before the Gham come back in force."

The uncertainty that had been felt by the crowd disappeared in a flash and was replaced by smiles and tears of relief. Everyone started to leave talking excitedly as they moved toward their homes.

"Our Joshua told us you would be open to the Sooul moving to New Harvest, I thank you for my people, and we will be ready very quickly." Hyun gratefully addresses the older Garvie. The Chandler wasn't too worried about the

Gham due to the ship being heavily armed, but agreed it would be safer for the Sooul to leave as quickly as possible. Let the Gunman's Element deal with the Gham if they come back. The sooner they get his grandson into a med tank the faster they could go home.

"Sir, orders?" Gunman one asked. The Chandler looked at the two Gunmen who were watching the large dissipating crowd with a detached eye. They didn't seem to feel the people would be a danger, but their job required a constant vigilance.

A bit surprised as he thought they would only report to Josh, the Chandler answered, "Let's go check the battlefield and these dead Gham."

* * *

The Chandler and the Gunmen head through the village with Steve leading and Mike following. It was a slower walk then either would have liked, but even in the light gravity the Chandler was getting older. As they walked, Steve used his helmet scanner and reported to the Chandler and Mike. "Clear of large life forms, lots of smaller ones." Mike answered; "Roger," as he performed his secondary scans while following behind the Chandler.

Entering the meadow, all three men saw the battle ground. There had to be thousands of small crab like creatures swarming over the dead aliens like a moving mass or live shifting carpet of brown shells. Clicking noises from their feeding was clearly audible without the helmet sensors the Gunmen wore.

Steve's scanner chirped once, as he reported, "Scavengers, not dangerous." He pulls a variable concussion grenade from his belt, adjusts it to the lowest setting, and tosses it twenty yards toward the crab-covered cadavers. Wanting to see the dead Gham clearly Steve knew that a very loud bang would scare the small creatures because of their sensitive hearing. It worked on other planet's battlefields.

The grenade went off precisely at fifty feet in the air. The results from the vertically focused shock wave were terrific: some of the creatures were killed and a lot were blown away from their food source. The scavengers scampered away in mass. They were not very fast but moved at a steady pace heading for the hills and safety. Chandler removed his hands from covering his ears since he did not have a helmet. "Nice!" he said with a grin. Mike didn't react as he was looking at the dead, partly devoured aliens Josh had killed.

Steve led the group slowly into the mass of bodies, the stench was overbearing but neither of the Gunmen took notice. Chandler just followed Steve into the area looking at the carnage. Most of these Gham's were totally missing their heads; the few that had heads were missing parts from the scavengers feeding. The smell was bad enough that the Chandler pulled out a cloth from his pocket and held it over his nose. When he turned to look back at the Gunman behind him, he saw Mike looking at the dead Gham dispassionately. No reaction to the smell or carnage.

Steve looked at the dead sadly. "This would have been a great fight, what do you think, two dozen?"

"Plus the four over there," Mike agreed and pointed off toward the slight hill. Mike looked at a knife sticking out of a chest on a Gham a few feet away. "Gunman knife," he says to get Steve's attention and walks over to remove it. "You think he will want this back?"

Steve nodded as he spies another weapon twenty feet away by another dead Gham. He casually strolled over and picked up Josh's Sig Sauer. "Yes, I imagine that he will want both of his toys back." Steve dropped the clip out of the handgrip and racked the slide to remove the live ammunition. He then slid the safe weapon into a cargo pocket on his battle suit.

"Wonder why he didn't just railgun them?" Mike murmured, thinking aloud as he strapped Josh's knife on the outside of his knife case.

The two Gunmen walk back over to the Chandler who decided he had enough of the smell and had moved outside the group of dead aliens to listen to the two Gunmen.

"Great fight?" The Chandler looks clearly aggravated at them. "Josh was outnumbered and badly wounded fighting these monsters to save the Sooul! Maybe you should show respect to a true warrior. Could either of you have done better?"

"Sir, no disrespect is intended; if Josh would have used a railgun or his rifle he would not have been wounded." Steve explained. "Of course he would have damaged the ship, which, for some reason, he decided not to do."

Mike looks at Steve's and nodded at the assessment. A wiry grin at the Chandler lets him know that they were not showing disrespect but rather sorry that they were not involved in this fight. The expression on the Chandlers face softened a bit with the realization.

"If we had been here together the outcome would have been the same for the Gham, while Joshua's current physical condition would have been better. But no sir, neither of us alone could have done this as well as he did."

The Chandler gestured to the dead alien after making his decision on what to do. Humans don't generally leave dead bodies for scavengers even if they are killers.

"Boys, we are not leaving these creatures like this, can you erase their existence?"

"So that no trace of so vile wretch may ever be found?" Mike asks with a wiry grin.

Chandler nodded before turning toward the town. He doesn't know what the Gunmen would do to destroy the bodies and didn't want to see anymore carnage. Joshua's battle wounds were horrific, but seeing twenty-eight dead aliens was just about enough for this day. He wondered where the ship went but would have to ask Josh about it when he woke up.

Steve and Mike walked backwards until they were a safe distance from the site. Standing on the crushed area where the ship landed, they could see all the dead and the only thing in front of them was the small rise. The town was at their back and safely away from their firing direction. Without a word, both Gunman switch from rail-mode on their assault rifles to the laser option and set it to wide beam. Pausing a moment, they looked at each other and grinned.

"Crispy critter time," Steve said as they turned back to their task. Both Gunmen pulled their triggers and walked the beams of coherent light across the dead bodies burning the entire area.

The heat was so intense there was almost no smoke, just shimmering heat waves with sudden flare-ups then ash on the ground. The Gunmen continued to move their beams until nothing flared then shut down the lasers by releasing the triggers. Mike looked over at Steve and blew some ash off his shoulder; "Josh owes us a beer for cleaning up his mess." Steve wiped the sweat off his forehead with the back of his head before answering. "Josh will probably tell us it was our duty, and then give us beer anyways." They both turned and jogged to quickly catch up to the Chandler.

The Chandler hearing their footsteps did not stop but just continued toward the shuttle sitting in front of Hyun's home. Steve took a few quick steps to move beside the Chandler to give him an update. "Nothing left but ash sir, orders?" Chandler rubbed his eyes as if tired.

"My grandson's AI has sent the videos of the attacks to our ship," the Chandler said. Steve looked over his shoulder at Mike and raised and eyebrow; "It would be a hell of a fight to see sir." Mike nodded because not very often are high-level battles ever seen by anyone other than the combatants. The Chandler continued; "Since Caroline is at Josh's side with his girlfriend and the medic, he is in good hands for the time being. We, on the other hand, need to watch the videos and decide if these Gham are coming back."

The Chandler wiped some sweat from his brow. "I don't know about you, but I could also use a beer. It would also be beneficial for the Captain of the B.N.J. and senior officers to see these creatures in case they need to fight off a Gham ship."

When they reached their shuttle, the two Gunmen look to the Chandler and Mike asks: "Should one of us stay with Josh?"

The Chandler snorts. "No, I will need you both for your input on the dangers these Gham pose."

Steve removed his helmet and scratched his itchy head. Thinking about what the Chandler was saying made him smile. "What's this about a girlfriend? Not that little semi-naked girl holding his head?" Mike laughed out loud. "Yes sir; come clean, the Josh we know is far too serious to date children." Steve starts laughing as well at Mike's comment.

Chandler's amusement was evident in his next words. "She is twenty years old. From his AI's update, the Sooul appear younger than they actually are. If I was you two clowns I would only tease him about it while he is sick—" his mouth twitched, fighting a smile "—because from what I have seen he will kick your asses otherwise."

The Chandler walked away from the chuckling Gunmen and headed into the shuttle. Mike and Steve both followed Chandler up the ramp and into the ship with silly grins on their faces.

"Wonder if he'll hire a nanny for her when he's at work?" Steve says quietly even though he knew Josh's grandfather would hear.

Mike is still chuckling when answers. "That's cruel, maybe he is just picking out a woman that he can actually satisfy in bed."

Steve put his hand over his heart as if he couldn't catch his breath as he almost falls. Both Gunmen actually had to pause to wipe the tears out of their eyes and even the Chandler had to smile. With Josh out of danger things were a lot less stressful. Josh's friends had a good attitude and their laughter made the Chandler feel better.

The Gunmen put their assault rifles into the racks by the shuttle door and strap themselves into their seats. Chandler who had already found his seat hits the comm. and told the pilot, "Signal the B.N.J. that we are returning to collect more provisions and a gravity gurney. We will also need to watch the Sooul videos before our return to the surface."

The shuttle rose from the surface with a roaring sound on small pillars of fire and disappeared quickly into the sky. The acceleration pressed the passengers into their seats. The G-forces dropped off once the shuttle left the atmosphere and the flight smoothed out. The flight was not long as the B.N.J. was directly overhead providing additional security for the assault shuttle. As the shuttle approaches the star carrier, the landing bay lit up as the force field protecting the bay door dropped. As soon as the ship's AI received the signal the door opens and a tractor beam engaged with a pale blue beam to envelope the shuttle. The force applied by the beam is smooth and powerful enough to drag much heavier objects than the shuttle. As soon as it passed through the outer hull into the landing bay, the bay door closed once more to protect the ship. The bay pressurized with a breeze of pre-warmed air as the shuttle settles on the landing pad.

"Let's go to the main mess and view what Josh has been up to," Chandler said to the Gunmen as he rose to leave the shuttle. Steve quickly unclipped his seat belt and moved in front of the Chandler. "Sir, please wait a minute until the skin of the hull warms up." Steve said as he blocked the Chandler's path. It would not be a good thing if Josh's grandfather froze his hand while leaving the shuttle. Mike followed behind the two men silently playing rear guard. Captain Grey was waiting for them inside the airlock. "How is your grandson, sir?"

"He is stable, but will need to be tanked for several days at least."

The Captain remembering his last stressful flight with Josh commented, "On his last trip he was tanked too."

Steve and Mike trade a look, each of them wondering what happened but don't pursue the subject.

"I need you and your department chiefs in the main mess in five minutes," the Chandler said before heading off in that direction himself. The Gunmen followed quietly to the galley, which was a bright and open space. On entering the galley they notice over a dozen crewmembers sitting in pairs eating their mid shift meals. The cafeteria style serving line was staffed as well. By the amount of food being presented on the warming stands it was the beginning of the meal service.

Steve looked blankly at the crew and asks, "Sir; would you like this room cleared?"

"No secrets, they are fine to see this." And then in a whisper, Chandler adds "It should give them some respect for their future leader."

Mike snorted. "If they don't already have respect, we will give it to them."

The Chandler hearing the mild threat shakes his head slowly at Mike. "These are our people and you will do well to remember that."

Mike being concerned about the reprimand rubbed his eyes for a second thinking about how he will retract his statement when Steve put his hand on his shoulder. "It is nice to be with well thought of people; I for one will enjoy this change from what we have dealt with in our past."

The Chandler took in the comment for what it was worth. Josh said they were honest and honorable.

The 1st Gunman

A steward seeing the Chandler walked quickly over to the small group. "Mr. Garvie, how can I be of support?

"Clear out the area in front of the projection bulkhead and put a bunch of chairs over here," the Chandler ordered as he pointed to the best viewing zone. "And bring us a pitcher of Church Key please."

Steve and Mike stood with the Chandler as the steward got some help and quickly slides tables out of the way. Some of the crew who were finishing their meals jumped up and carried some the bigger comfortable reading chairs from the lounge area over.

Within a few minutes the area was arranged to make a theater, while the captain and the department chiefs were starting to arrive. Quite a few of the crew stayed to see the show as well since the Chandler had not made them leave and they all knew that his grandson was down on the surface hurt.

"Vicky, are you linked in?"

"Yes."

"Play back the message from my grandson after everyone gets a drink and sits down." The officers did not get a drink but Steve poured three, he handed one to the Chandler and one to Mike then sat down.

"Ready." At his words, the galley lights dimmed and Josh's holograph appears.

"Grandfather, Mother, I am sorry that I was so selfish…"

The message continued on, and near the end of the holograph Joshua declared his intentions for the Sooul. Upon hearing that Joshua was going to bring them all to the safety of New Harvest the Chandler just nodded; there was a data file about the Sooul and a breakdown of the people that he had already reviewed. The video ended with Joshua saying "thank you, I love you and hope to see you soon."

"The next video is of his second night and shows an eel attack. It is a bit grainy, but enhanced enough so you can see." Vicky's voice informs them through the sound system.

They all watched as Sophee brought food to Josh who was watching the gate when the first eel smashed through it. When the last big eel hit the ground the ship's crew cheered, which surprised Chandler, as this was serious in his mind and not an entertainment video. Josh's seemly casual attitude when he was dealing with the two hundred and forty-seven smaller eels at the water's edge was a point that Mike found amusing. Gunmen don't normally hold low key conversations with potential father-in-laws in the middle of a clearing operation.

"Look eel, take a bite of dinner, shot to the head, talk a bit, shoot some more, take another bite, shoot…" Mike keeps going on with his comedic narrative as Steve laughed thened turns his head to address the Chandler.

"Your grandson is so cool under pressure I would not be surprised if the Sooul didn't think he was a robot," Steve said with a smile. The Chandler did realize that he was seeing a very different side of his grandson.

"He never showed fear at home but his jumping into the eel's mouth seems reckless to me…." The Chandler mused.

"No Sir! As Gunmen we protect people. He blocked the eel from getting that girl and I bet he would do the same thing again." Steve explained.

"Did you see the look on that guy's face when Josh

walked over to stomp the heads on those two eels by the wall?" Mike asked Steve.

Steve opened his eyes wide and dropped his jaw. "Like that?"

Vicky's next clip was introduced simply. "This is what the Gham do to the Sooul."

Chandler watched briefly until he felt nauseated, and had to turn his head away from the horrific sight. Upon doing so, he noticed the two Gunmen were watching with clenched jaws trying not to react. It was easy to surmise that they wished they were present to save the girl from being murdered. Mike almost came out of his seat looking like he wanted to jump into the video. Steve's eyes were hard as he watched the death of the Sooul female. When the video ended the two Gunmen traded a glance and although nothing was said aloud, the Chandler could tell that the Gham had two new mortal enemies. A couple of the crewmembers lost their recently eaten lunches on seeing the gory video. It was so shocking that anyone or anything would act in this manner to sentient being. The Gunmen knew that a lot of bad things happened, and that they were the keepers of civilization, but the ship's crew who were sheltered from these types of abuses were shocked and dismayed. Not to mention ill from the gory spectacle.

There was a couple of minutes of a pause between videos, Vicky made them wait because she understood how human minds worked and that they needed time to process what was seen.

Vicky then announced, "And the final battle."

The camera had recorded Joshua standing alone, unmoving, in front of the ship with absolutely no expression upon his face. Steve looked over at Mike to whisper "After all the shit we been through with him, I have never seen him so keyed up."

"Stop playback, Vicky!" Chandler turns to the Gunmen. "Why did you say that?"

Mike calls out, "Restart it from the beginning please, Vicky."

"Pause!" Steve gestured to the screen. "There, did you see it? His fingers twitched." Lowering his voice to address his next words towards the Chandler only, he adds, "I have served six years between training and in various combat areas, and I have never seen him so much as twitch before. He must be fucking mad…sir."

Chandler didn't know if they were telling him that for show or if it was the truth, but he suspected is was the later. The video was restarted and, at the end of it, the Sooul were seen carrying Josh away from the carnage so that he might receive necessary medical aid.

The Chandler took a minute to dry his eyes before standing up to address the Captain and crew. Seeing his grandson fight and win filled him with pride but getting so badly hurt made the tears flow.

"The man who stood alone displaying true valor will be your leader in a few weeks. One hundred and ninety colonists from this planet are coming back with us to New Harvest and, as my grandson said to the Gham, they are under his protection."

"AND MINE!" Steve said, standing.

"AND MINE!" Mike's voice overlaps with Steve's as he too stood.

The two Gunmen continued to stand by Chandler as he

continues speaking. "My grandson will be well enough to travel as of tomorrow, and then he will need to be tanked. As this happens we will start bringing up the Sooul and, I will say this only once, every courtesy and every kindness will be afforded to them!"

Steve smiled pleasantly. "And Mike and I will be the judges."

"Captain," the Chandler continued, "I am going back down to be with my grandson. Send the gravity gurney with another medic, as well as a couple of cooks, some Church Key and foodstuffs to feed the Sooul on their last night here."

"I will accompany you, sir, and Mike will stay behind to help ensure your directions are being met," Steve said.

Wondering if his grandson's AI was still online with them, the Chandler spoke. "Vicky?"

"Yes, sir?"

"How long before these Gham will be back?"

"Joshua will be awake tomorrow. Ask him," Vicky bluntly states.

"Damn, you stubborn machine, give me an estimate!" Chandler says, only to be interrupted by, "Going off line, Sir."

* * *

Caroline was amazed at Sophee's maturity and bearing, and that she seemed wise beyond her years. Sophee's primary focus is on Josh and while holding his head she was able to direct whatever needed to be done for Joshua easily. Once Caroline got about six seconds past Sophee's younger appearance, she could easily understand how Joshua could be attracted to such a beautiful young woman. As they talk quietly, Caroline's curiosity about how strong their relationship was got the better of her and she has to ask the question.

"I guess you are his fiancé?" Caroline asked softly.

Sophee stammered for a minute before answering; "I don't know."

This surprised Caroline and made her speechless. Mere easily sensed Caroline's confusion and smiled. "Our ways are not the same as your ways, and we do not take time for ceremonies or celebrations since the Gham have been coming. Would you like to sit outside with me and have a glass of our wine while we talk about it?"

Mere's openness and warm friendly attitude won Caroline over instantly. Caroline had found it hard to talk with strangers until now and was mildly surprised that these Sooul were so open and nice. She stood up and followed Mere over to the prep area. "Your daughter seems to have everything under control; I would love a glass of wine." Mere read Caroline's complete acceptance and pleasure of seeing someone care for Joshua as much as she did. Mere got out a couple of cups and put wine in them. "These are not wine glasses as our Joshua explains it, but they work well anyways."

Caroline picked up a cup and took a small sip of dark red wine. "Oh, that's really good!" A smile appeared on Mere's face as she led her guest outside to talk.

"Our Joshua has been telling us about life on New Harvest." Mere sat and motioned to the other seat. "It seems like a very wonderful place to live."

The way the Sooul use Josh's full name and refer to him like he belongs to them made Caroline happy. Sophee also cared more than a little bit which makes his mother thrilled that Joshua had found someone that obviously loved him.

Sophee didn't even look up when they left. Hearing the mother's converse quietly and being able to sense that Caroline was a bit confused but happy for some reason was enough. Even if Vicky and the ships medic said Joshua was safe there was no way she was leaving his side.

* * *

Three glasses of wine later all doubt had been erased from Caroline's mind about Josh and Sophee. Mere explained the bond very well to Caroline. Even though the bond was a different phenomenon than anyone from New Harvest had ever experienced Caroline could tell from the way they loved Joshua that he would love them back. Caroline took another sip of her wine, which helped to loosen her inhibitions a bit.

"So they will not get married?" Caroline asks.

"We don't know, all we do know is that he will surprise us one way or another because he is not an easy man to figure out." Mere says with a smile. Then she leaned forward and whispered; "I hope they mate soon though, because we're all afraid that eel might burst out of his pants and eat the town."

Caroline laughed so hard that she cried.

* * *

Chandler and Hyun sat on the other side of the door having a couple mugs of cold beer while the girl's laughed. The sound of the laughter from the other side of the door was a pleasant sound to the Chandler's ears. After all the violence the Sooul have endured it did seem rather out of place here. Mind you, seeing Caroline enjoying herself and making friends with Mere was a good sign. Her son was going to be fine and is coming home. Maybe this woman will be able to draw Caroline further out of her shell and turn her back into the outgoing person she was before her husband died. It was also odd that he liked Hyun as much; talking with him was interesting because there were no hidden emotions or attitudes. What you see is what you got with the Sooul.

Chandler smiled as Hyun finished his beer.

"Thank you Mr. Garvie, I really enjoyed that." Hyun said openly. The Chandler picked up the empty mug and refilled it.

"My friends and relatives call me Chance. I am not sure if we will be related by marriage or friends but either way, please call me Chance." Hyun nodded in acceptance "Chance." Hearing the two women laugh and chat the Chandler nodded in their direction; "I think they are getting along very well."

"Mere likes people; in this short time we can see where Joshua gets his personality and compassion from." Hyun picked up his mug and took another sip. "The compassion and decency is a trait you both have passed on genetically, the focus or depth of resolve comes more from your side." The Chandler smiled at Hyun's opinion.

"We don't know where he got the toughness." Chandler says. The two men sit in silence for a few minutes enjoying the beer.

Hyun looked at his mug. "This is the second best thing I have ever experienced." Hyun says holding up the mug to look at it.

"And the first is?" Chandler asks.

"Our Joshua; how one man can make such a difference in so many people's lives."

Chandler smiled; "From what reports I have gotten from his former trainer, Josh has made a rather large impact everywhere he has gone. He holds a deeply rooted belief in fairness and the utter conviction that his actions and how he deals with people will make a difference."

"His actions have made all the difference for my people, and especially for my daughter." Hyun takes another sip of his beer. "One of the nicer things about that young man is the respect he shows for everyone. He calls everyone older than him sir or ma'am. He listens to everybody including the children and treats them like they matter to him personally."

The two men sat in silence for a few minutes. Hyun said nothing else because he thought that his new friend Chance should know how the Sooul feel about Joshua. Chandler said nothing in return because he was thinking about his wounded grandson and how good of a man he had turned out to be. When Josh sent the message about him being where he was needed, the Chandler just now realized how important it was that these people were saved and brought to New Harvest.

At the ruined gate a lone Gunman was keeping vigil. Both Hyun and Chandler could see him watching the water for any sign of eels. From time to time he would look over toward the house like he was checking up on them. Hyun looked toward the Gunman.

"Is that man like our Joshua?" He asked with a nod in his direction.

"Similar, but if you ask Steve or Mike they will tell you Josh is the most dangerous person they have ever known," The Chandler says before he took another sip of his beer.

"He is only dangerous to the bad things. In the short time Joshua has been here, our people could read him. His attitude and kindness made us respect him. It was not just the fact he repeatedly saved us, it was more that he felt it was his duty to protect everyone. My daughter thinks the sun rises with him or for him. He is truly a good heart."

"Josh is not his father. My son had a wild reckless streak and only thought of having fun. Josh seems more interested in helping people and contributing to society. Maybe with your daughter for a wife he will slow down a bit and enjoy life more."

* * *

A second shuttle came in slowly and landed near the assault shuttle. Once the cooks had gotten set up Hyun announced the meal that evening was compliments of Joshua's grandfather. Since all the Sooul had tried Joshua's chocolate and butter, it did not take very long for them to stop packing for their departure and wander over. The cooks from the ship were busy making burgers and hot dogs for the Sooul who now were eager to try anything. One of the cooks, knowing there were children on the planet, was quick to make sure ice cream made it down from the ship's stores as well. Children were delighted with the ice cream and their parents enjoyed the new taste as well.

After eating, someone from every family was quick to approach and thank the Chandler before they went home to continue packing their meager possessions. Since none of the Sooul had ever traveled anywhere all of their clothing and keepsakes were in simple bags or wrapped in blankets. Each family took their items to a common area ready to be loaded into the spacecraft. The people of the Sooul were happy that they going to a new planet and hoped the Gham would not be able to find them this time.

* * *

It is still dark, quiet and I don't hurt as bad as when I collapsed. *Shit; I hope I'm not dead.* Focusing on the quietness my awareness increases. There is some someone softly talking close by. My mom's voice is there with Mere's. A clink or metallic noise is there too. I struggle mentally to regain control of my body as I pull myself out of the darkness.

Vicky's voice softly tells me; "Stop trying to move. You're still hurt, sir."

I start to open my eyes, yes it is too bright. The darkness is gone and it feels like I am under a spotlight. I try to squint, but my face doesn't move right. One side feels frozen in place and I remember getting slashed there.

Ah, there's the pain. Something tangible to focus on as the dull ache forms and then sharpens into a riot of stabbing grief from the slowly healing slashes. I try to ask for Sophee, but all I can do is give a slight croak from my dry throat. I then realize that a small hand is resting on my forehead and an arm comes into focus. A straw is put between my lips and a drink of water lends me my voice.

"Sophee?" I hoarsely ask.

"I am here with your mother and grandfather." Her voice instantly makes me feel better as the blurriness continues to fade and features come into focus. She looks tired but her smile is absolutely everything I need to feel better. That smile alone tells me that everything is going to be okay.

"Please get my Granddad!"

Her face slides out of my view as she leans back, and

I realize my head is resting on her lap. I worry briefly that Sophee had not been taking care of herself but realize if Mere and my mom were around they would take care of her. Granddad's worn and tired face appears looking down at me.

"I am not leaving here without the Sooul," I say, my voice getting stronger with each word.

Granddad smiles and laughs loudly at my stubbornness. "When the ship seems crowded do not complain; your new friends are going to be coming with us. Shuttles have taken about half of them onboard already and the rest will follow. What we need to do is move you to a gravity gurney and then get you tanked. After that we will discuss the Gham and what you are going to do about their crimes."

The pain from my wounds makes me grit my teeth tightly. I can't even nod because of the pain. Granddad's face gets a look of concern as he notices my discomfort.

"Moving you will cause even more pain you are feeling now. We can't dial your pain down yet, not until the damaged nerves are completely rebuilt, so the medic will put you out for the trip to the ship's tank," Granddad told me even as he motioned to the medic.

"Just a minute," I say. "I need to see one of my men."

Steve must have been standing by close because his head leans over to where I can see him. "Hey pal, what's up?"

My eyes look up over and focus on Sophee. "She stays with me," I order.

Then as I start to fade out I hear Steve answer, "On my life!"

* * *

The medic seeing Joshua go unconscious on his med scanner speaks to the Chandler. "His AI put him out because the pain from the nerve damage was causing his blood pressure to drop. His behavior is odd; anyone else would have been screaming from that much damage." The medic shakes his head in disbelief; "I know he is a Gunman but he must be a particularly tough guy," the medic muses aloud.

That statement from the medic causes Sophee to chuckle. "You have no idea."

Steve has not moved an inch away; "I think that I have an idea." And then with a laugh he introduces himself to Sophee.

"You and I are going to be good friends, Sophee. Hopefully between the three of us, after you meet Mike, we can get Josh to be a little less of a madman." Steve says with an honest openness. Sophee could read him almost as well as Joshua but did not know what to say.

The medic decided to get the ball rolling and move Josh to the shuttle for the trip to the ship. The faster the patient got into the Medical Bay, the faster he would heal.

"Excuse me, Miss," the medic interrupts, "you will have to let him go."

Steve clamped a firm hand on the back of the medic's neck and with a gentle squeeze to get his attention. "Why don't you sit here Sophee?" Steve said as he points at the gurney. "We will lift Josh up and put his head in your lap."

Sophee scampered to the gurney as the two medics and Steve positioned themselves to move Joshua. The smaller of the two medics lifted at Josh's feet. Steve and the larger medic put their hands under his waist and shoulder. For

Sophee's sake Steve did not wince when he felt the broken bones in Josh's shoulder grate against each other. They placed his head on Sophee's still-naked lap. She looked over at Steve while cradling Joshua's head, as the gurney was raised to operating height.

"I like you already."

Steve grinned at Sophee's simple statement and turns to address the Chandler; "I have to leave now sir, I have my orders." He then turns to follow the gurney out to the waiting shuttle. Hyun looked at the Chandler with amazement after seeing Steve align the medic.

"Our Joshua works with men like that?"

"He commands men like that," the Chandler simply states.

* * *

Five more days passed with Joshua being immersed in the rejuvenation tank. Huge amounts of nanites were required to rebuild his broken shoulder and to fully reattach the nerves that were destroyed by the talons of his enemies. His lung that had been punctured was the easiest to fix and almost a hundred percent before he left the surface. Neither the Captain nor the Chandler of New Harvest could get any more information out of Vicky about the home planet of the Gham or even where the ship went.

When you walk through the doors and enter the sickbay, doctors seem to believe you lose all rights. Taking care of a patient takes precedent over how a family feels and the doctor aboard the B.N.J. had no different attitude. While prepping Joshua for the tank, the doctor thanked Sophee and told her to leave. She stood by her Joshua's side, unmoving, and the doctor was about to take her arm to lead her away when the Gunman on guard duty spoke up.

"If you so much as touch her I will tear that arm off you and beat you to death with it," Steve said very softly. The feelings that Steve broadcasted were very similar to Joshua's. Protection, absolute loyalty and fondness emotions emanated from the big Gunman. The mix of seriousness and humour he had was contrast against each other but Sophee could tell he was would do what he said.

The doctor was smart enough to realize the heavily armed Gunman was dead serious. He politely asked Sophee to allow him to put Josh in the med tank and then went and got her a tall chair. Sophee thanked the doctor then sat in a chair beside the tank with her hand on the patient for the next five days that Joshua was being healed. A few times one of the Gunmen bodyguards would have to restrain Sophee with a gentle hand to keep her from falling out of the chair to the floor when she fell asleep. Steve and Mike were impressed that Sophee would not leave Josh even if they thought it was silly.

Mere or Caroline would sit with Joshua whenever Sophee needed a trip to the facilities. At least she could put pants back on now that Joshua's head was not in her lap. Mere brought clean clothing to Sophee and asked her to dress in case the rest of the people on this ship got as uptight as their Joshua.

Mere laughed when Caroline explained that many humans don't mate for life and the sight of a semi-naked young lady would put her in danger in a lesser environment.

Mere shook her head at the thought of this wonderful

ship being dangerous. "This is not such an environment, but we will try to fit in."

Sophee on hearing her mother's statement was still concerned that Caroline would want her in the family but could not find any negative emotions or thoughts when they spoke. She decided to explain about her previous nudity in the hope of making Caroline understand why she was not fully clothed.

"Mrs. Garvie?" she started.

Caroline looked at her and held one hand up to stop her. "So you know now, young lady, I am Caroline or mom number two. With your relationship to my son nothing else will get a response."

Sophee looked down at her hand on Joshua's shoulder in the tank thinking about the physical contact she had with him. "Do you know of our bond yet?" Sophee hesitantly asked.

Caroline and put her hand gently on Sophee's arm and looked her in the eyes. "Yes, I do. Your mom has told me," Caroline paused just a moment for emphasis, "and I am *very happy* about it."

Sophee's heart jumped a bit at the truth in Caroline's words but had to continue her explanation anyway.

"Joshua's Vicky told me, because the strength of our bond was so strong, that even in the coma he could sense me. That I should have direct skin-on-skin contact to help him cope with the pain and ensure his heart was beating stronger. When his head was on my bare lap even if I fell asleep he would have skin contact. I was more worried about this than anything else and did not mean to cross boundaries with your culture. I am so very sorry for not wearing full clothing until now." Sophee had struggled to meet Caroline's eyes, and when she finished speaking Sophee lowered her head in shame.

Caroline mouth dropped open in surprise. "Are you kidding me? Your entire people could have burned all their clothes and have decided to live naked on New Harvest if that is what my son needed! My son is healing because of you; my son is *alive* because of you. When Josh wakes up I am certain he will be happy because of you. So when you ask for forgiveness you are wasting your time. I should be kneeling at your feet in gratitude." Caroline reached out and put one hand on Joshua with Sophee while her other arm wrapped tightly around Sophee. "Whatever the future holds I am absolutely certain you will be my daughter-in-law."

Sophee took enough time to wrap both of her arms around Caroline to give her a hug before returning one of her hands back on Joshua. Caroline moved back to give Sophee some space, because she didn't want Sophee to think she was trying to take over her vigil. Sophee could sense the sincerity of Joshua's mother and that Caroline was talking about her feelings with the utmost honesty. At this, Sophee felt quite relieved. "Our Joshua is a little more uptight than the Sooul are around their families. Whenever my parents were not dressed he got edgy, but it didn't bother him when I was naked at night."

Caroline thought about it for a minute, and then just had to ask. "I think your mother believes you two have not mated yet?"

"What does that have to do with sleeping without clothes?" Sophee asks with an honestly confused expression on her face.

A quick laugh from Caroline about the nativity of this young woman escapes her lips before she regains control. "I think for most of humanity being naked in bed would only be the beginning of what happens."

Sophee blushed at the pleasant thought. "Joshua told me this and oh how I tried, but he told me….." Sophee lowered her voice to a fair impersonation of Joshua—"Gham first, then you when you are in my home."

Caroline laughed out loud at Josh's stubbornness. Sophee reading the amusement Caroline was feeling, laughed with her as well. Mere walked into the medical bay and smiled at Joshua's two favorite women. "Our Joshua would be very happy to see the both of you getting along so well. I feel that our extended family will blend together seamlessly." Caroline nodded in agreement then looked at Sophee to explain how Josh was different than most other men.

"A lot of our human males would say anything to get someone as pretty as you in bed, and not for sleeping." Caroline tells her this as she wonders if the Sooul will would need some advice on what to expect from humans, and decides to wait to see if the Sooul will want acclimation classes.

"The bond allows us to know when it is time to mate, and our ability to read emotions makes it rather easy to know if the bond is happening or not," Mere said in response. She paused a moment before continuing, "Maybe some training about life styles and human behavior would allow the Sooul to blend in easier."

Sophee's silence let Caroline know that she understood Josh very well. The "Oh how I tried," comment almost put Caroline into another laughing fit every time she thought of it. Since Sophee had bonded with her son, it would be Josh's responsibility to educate her. The Sooul's innocence and decency was so refreshing.

Every single person from Sooul stopped by during the time Joshua was in the tank. Some stayed for a minute and others hours; it was like they had to visit, drawn by Sophee's caring and a need to ensure her Joshua/their Joshua was okay. The sight of an armed Gunman standing with her didn't scare them away—after all, they had seen the truly scary actions of Joshua. It did seem funny to them to think a Gunman was on duty to guard their wounded Joshua; no one realized they were really there to guard and protect Sophee.

The guards were working split eighteen-hour days ensuring that Sophee always had a protector and the Sooul were being well taken care of. Even though the Chandler's instructions of every courtesy and kindness were being followed to the letter of the law by the crew, a Gunman checked on them constantly. Since the Gunmen's leader also told them that "she stays with me," Steve decided that her security and well being was paramount. It was a silly thing to think they would need that kind of supervision or even that Sophee would need protection but Gunmen being Gunmen take orders very seriously.

Sophee grinned at more than a few Sooul females when they had to look at her healing mate-to-be. She knew some of the girls just wanted to check out the naked Gunman, because ever-talkative Shoran must have said something. It just didn't matter because Joshua was *her* property.

The people of Sooul settled into a safe routine while Joshua healed, and the days passed quickly for everyone but

Sophee. She read up on New Harvest on a data pad that the Chandler brought her but the majority of her time was just waiting for her mate to waken.

Caroline and Mere both knew that Joshua was almost done in the tank from the doctor's morning report, so they decided to leave Joshua to Sophee's care because they had no privacy before now.

A few hours after the mothers had left Vicky and the medical AI both concluded that the healing process was complete at the end of their thousandth scan. Each scan took precisely 7.2 minutes and was performed back to back with continual reprogramming of fresh nanites for specific tasks. The five days of prescribed tanking had finally elapsed and Vicky announced to the Doctor on duty that Joshua was ready to be let out. He looked at the Gunman for some direction as it was very apparent who was in charge.

"How do you want this handled, Sophee, with everyone present or just you?" Mike asked.

Sophee wanted Joshua to herself but was concerned she was being selfish so she asked Mike to call Steve in. She knew between the two Gunmen they would know what is proper. Steve made it to the Medical Bay within a few minutes. His AI had been told that Josh`s damage was repaired and he was already close by. Mike raised an eyebrow at his friend and reiterated the question.

On hearing the question Steve thought about it for only a second. "Okay, I'll make the decision: just you. That okay Doc?" The doctor nodded and checked the readout one last time.

Steve turned away from the tank and then, with Mike and the doctor in tow they all walk out. Knowing Josh and the way he felt about crowds, the less-is-more approach would be what he'd want.

The gel level in the tank slowly dropped when Vicky activated the drain and initiated the awaken function. Joshua's eyes open and then, after spitting out the mouthpiece, he looks to his bonded one and smiles.

The wounds have completely healed and only very faint lines across the skin show where the horrible slashes were. Sophee was unable to hug Joshua, as the rinse was still pouring down to wash the dead nanites and gel off him. She was so happy to see him stand in the vertical tank and smiled at her that tears ran down her face.

Finally the front of the tank popped open and a nude Joshua walked out. Joshua lowered himself until he could look in Sophee's eyes and threw his wet arms around her. Standing, Joshua picked Sophee up in tight hug. They didn't move for a long time, the relief Joshua was feeling at seeing Sophee was almost overpowering. Sophee did not say anything but just decided to kiss Joshua and go with the moment.

* * *

"Steve now has clothes for you outside the door." Vicky announces, interrupting their embrace after ten or so minutes. Sophee giggled at the interruption. "Oh good, it would be terrible if you shocked someone on this ship." She waited a minute while Joshua rolled his eyes at her humor. "Besides it's not like all the Sooul haven't already seen you naked."

Joshua's face did not turn even a little red. Sophee found that his emotions were tranquil and his embarrassment almost non-existent. It was almost like he had other things on his mind.

* * *

"Send him in Vicky," I instruct as I gently set Sophee back on her feet.

Steve strolled in fully armed and in battle dress. "Hey pal," he said as he threw me a towel and my clothes. Steve stood beside Sophee as I dried myself and get dressed.

"Good morning again Sophee, how are you feeling now?" Steve asked pleasantly.

"Much better now, thank you for all your support." She replied.

"Now that he is out of the tank you need to get some rest. Mike and I will be more than happy to babysit Josh for you."

Sophee grinned at her new friend, "I would not wish that responsibility on anyone." They both chuckle and Sophee gave the big Gunman a hug. I shake my head; leave it to Steve to already have charmed Sophee into liking him.

"Thanks for being here for Sophee," I said.

Steve smiled wickedly. "We are becoming great friends, but I have a question," he says as he walks toward the door. "What was your pickup line that worked so well on Sophee? Hey little girl, want a piece of candy?" Steve smartly ducked out the hatch before I could find something heavy to throw at him.

Sophee laughed at the look on my face. "I get it."

"So will he," I grumble. "Where are your parents?"

"They are in the cabin beside the owner's suite. The captain and all of the crew are in the cargo holds as they insisted that the Sooul have comfort and privacy after their ordeal… My other friend Mike said the worst part of their ordeal was getting to know you; Steve said it was trying to keep you alive. Mom and I have finally figured out that your soldiers, you included, like to use humor when dealing with terrible things to lessen the impact." Sophee looked up and smiled at me because she was pleased with her understanding of our behaviors.

"Yeah, we are jerks," I say with a smile.

Sophee shakes her head. "No, my mom said it is because tough guys believe they must show compassion in a way that doesn't harm their tough guy image."

I found it funny that we have only known each other for such a short time and she already has us pegged. "I would like to see my mom and granddad, and then we can see your parents."

I grab Sophee's hand and we walk together out of the hatch and, the second we leave the sickbay, Steve and Mike join up to walk at either side and slightly behind us. My friends always cover my six, but judging from Mike's smirk I could tell Steve told him about his joke. *Payback is going to be a bitch, buddy.*

"Sophee, is Shoran still un-bonded?"

"Yes, why?"

As we walk along I say, "I am worried about her."

Sophee doesn't know where this is going and remains silent with a slightly quizzical look on her face. I glance back at the two Gunmen following us to make sure they are listening.

"There are no Sooul men who are near an appropriate age for her to bond with, am I correct?" Sophee merely nods in reply to my question, and I continue to ask another question. "Shoran is nice, but is more delicate than you?"

Now Sophee understands and looks at me with a grin. From her expression I can tell that she knows humor is coming at Steve's expense.

"You know your new friend Steve?" I ask nicely.

"Yes. I think he is a kind and decent man." Sophee says as she looks back at Steve.

"He is, and he has one trait that would make him a perfect mate."

Now Sophee is fighting not to break out laughing at what is coming. I hold up my hand with my fingers about three inches apart. "Small; like a baby."

"Oh good, I will have to introduce them!" Sophee says honestly, forgetting the prank in her excitement at a match for her friend.

Out of the corner of my eyes I see Steve's red face on one side and over on the other side Mike is walking quietly with tears rolling down his face as he tries not to laugh. I wonder if Sophee can sense Steve's embarrassment and Mike's struggle not to laugh. I know I am going to have to explain that it is just a joke before she tells Shoran.

I assumed my mom and granddad would be in the owner's suite, but it was empty when we arrived. I had to ask Vicky where they might be and she informed us that my family was in the Captain's cabin, so we change direction to go there.

Upon arriving I open the hatch without knocking and in an instant my mom runs over to hug me. "Glad your okay."

Granddad walked over and grumps; "About time," so I give him a hug, too.

"Thank you for coming for us," I say to discuss what was really important. "I am amazed you were able to get the Sooul packed and onboard so quickly."

"Well, they were tired of being harvested by these Gham. The losses they suffered made them lose all of the love they had for their homeland and they just wanted to leave to start anew," Granddad says. "You're damned AI will not tell us where the Gham live or what you did with their ship, though. Did you send it to New Harvest?"

"Not yet, Granddad, please." I reply shutting down his questions. "Are we on course for New Harvest?"

He nods. I can tell he wants to ask more question about the Gham and their ship but he holds back asking them.

"I need to see Sophee's parents and then we can have dinner together tonight. I may be able to talk about it then."

Granddad looks at me, and reluctantly agrees. "I will have the Captain join us, so bring Sophee's parents, heck, bring whoever you want, and if you feel like releasing your boys from guard duty they should be there too."

My mom gives me another hug and then she hugs Sophee as well. It doesn't surprise me that my mom likes her. I can only imagine what they talked about while I was in the tank healing. Knowing my mom she probably found out everything about us, the Sooul and how to prepare sillfish.

I nod to Granddad and we walk to the door. "We will talk at supper, love you both."

Once we are all out in the hallway I stop. Steve's face isn't as red anymore, but Mike still appears as though he is going to bust a gut. I put my hand out and shake Steve's hand; "Close call pal, next time call for backup sooner." He says shaking his head at me.

"I don't know, I had a really nice nine day nap." I said making light of my coma and tank time. Mike is next with a hand shake and doesn't say a thing.

"Effective now, you're both off guard duty until New Harvest. How are the rest of the Sooul?"

Mike answers. "Fine, the crew is treating them like family."

"Great," I nod. "Now get out of your combats and be back here in four hours for an open bar and then supper."

The boys throw me a quick salute and turn on a dime to wander back to wherever they are sleeping. I turn to Sophee and think, *to hell with it*. In a quick movement I sweep Sophee into my arms the way I carried her on the planet and begin to walk to her parent's cabin. Sophee didn't protest me carrying her because I stopped frequently to kiss her; I think she knew that I felt holding her hand was not good enough for me.

"You had better ring or knock," Sophee said. "They haven't had much privacy until now and, with your weakened state, I would not want to see you get a shock if they were naked."

She then giggles and tucks her face into my neck as I sub-vocally command Vicky to ring them. We had to wait twenty minutes until they opened the door, so I had sat on the floor with Sophee and snuggled a bit. Once the door opened I stood, and set Sophee on her feet before walking in holding her hand.

Mere gave me a huge hug, followed by one from Hyun.

"We thought you might not make it when you fell," Mere says.

"Nope," I answer with a grin, "a bad penny always shows up."

They look at me with bland stares. "It is an old earth saying," I inform them with a shrug.

Mere gives a very kind smile; "We think you're worth more than a penny."

Hyun motions to the cabin's sitting area and Sophee and I share the lounge and her parents sit on the small couch. We relax for a bit without talking. I was just glad to have Sophee close and near to me. I am not sure why her presence is such a big deal; it could be the side effects of the bond. After ten minutes of relative calm, I could feel their scrutiny and there was no way I wanted to discuss anything about the Gham as the bloody battle felt like it happened an hour ago. I know that I had issues to work through with my actions and decided to shelf them for awhile so I issued granddad's invitation.

"Grandddad wants you to attend a dinner party. Would you join us? Bring Shoran with her parents if you like," I say with an evil grin, "my friend Steve will be there." They won't understand the joke, but Sophee does. "I won't tell Shoran why he's good for her." Mere raised her eyebrows at the joke and Sophee explained it. When both of her parents stopped laughing we talked about the ship and how well the Sooul were taking the journey.

I sit with them for a while making small talk until Mere says; "Joshua, I will take Sophee to find Shoran will you be okay?"

"Oh, yeah," I said, deep in thought. *Me okay?* Darn

she is as sensitive as Sophee to emotions and feelings. Here I sit thinking I am fooling them with my pleasant cheery attitude and they see through me. The Gham are in my thoughts, I wonder about their fate as a species, at the same time now the Sooul are safe I have Sophee to think about and her wishes.

* * *

Mere stands and motions to Hyun to follow her outside the cabin. Hyun and Sophee stop in a passageway to talk with Mere after the door closes. Mere turns directly to face Sophee.

"What is wrong with our Joshua?" Mere asks Sophee. "He should be happy, but his emotions are in turmoil." Mere looks over at Hyun who even could sense something. "He is very uncertain and is trying to hide it, poorly I might add." Hyun is unable to sense as much as the girls but gives a small nod to his mate. "I don't know either, maybe warriors feel bad after killing their enemies?" Sophee shakes her head in disagreement at her father. "Dad he is glad he killed the Gham it is something else."

Sophee glances at the door still trying to read her bonded one and then shrugs.

"Mother, he is hurting. Not from his injury, from his thoughts, he is in conflict. With his self-control no one can see that he bleeds inside. He has not spoken about it, but we have not had much time to ourselves yet." Sophee gets a very determined look on her face. "We will have some time to talk soon but let's give him a little time to come to grips with whatever is bothering him."

"Maybe Joshua and I need some of his guy time," Hyun

said. "I will be more than happy to talk with him and see if I can provide any support."

Sophee reads her father's emotions as compassion and respect for Joshua which warms her heart. "Mom our Joshua is in good hands, let's find Shoran." They leave as Hyun goes in to talk with Joshua.

* * *

Hyun comes back into the cabin and takes his seat across from me.

"Joshua, what is bothering you?" Hyun asks. Great thing about Hyun is that he never leaves you wondering what he is thinking.

I look at Hyun in the eye and decide to tell him about my some of my conflicting issues. Burying my emotions and feelings about what I have done is not easy and I struggle a bit before answering him.

"Your daughter has given me a small problem." I muse aloud putting as much warmth into my emotions as possible. "I told her we would not complete our bond until we were on my planet and the Gham were dealt with. Now that the Sooul are safe and happy, I realize that I should make Sophee happy. I wish to complete our bond, but this not my way. I would like to propose marriage and then marry your daughter." Telling Hyun that Sophee wants to love me physically would be awkward. Sure I would love to explore that part of our relationship but only after we did the right thing and married. The thought of that makes me grin, I hold myself to a higher standard than other men that I know and nothing is wrong or improper about that. Granddad would likely be proud of me for having so much of his discipline and control, then laugh at me and tell me to do what I think is right.

Hyun doesn't look surprised by my declaration and I wonder who he has been talking to. "Chance and I have had some very informative discussions about your people. I have learned about this marriage thing you do. It seems to be a declaration of love for people who don't have something as deep as a bond."

Chance? I only know a few people that call Granddad that. They must be developing a solid friendship. Good for them, except they probably get together and discuss a grandson and future son-in-law.

As Hyun finishes speaking he got up and walked to a small cooler in the corner. He grabbed two Church Keys and handed one to me before returning to his couch. I took the cold beer and raise my eyebrow in question to him.

Hyun chuckles at my questioning look. "My new friend Chance gave me this cooler so I could have a cold beer here when I wanted one."

"I was so focused on asking if I could marry your daughter I never noticed the cooler."

I opened my beer and took a sip. "Thank you, sir."

"The Sooul don't need or require this marriage thing Joshua. However now that we are going to be New Harvest citizens we should get used to your ways. Joshua, I am absolutely convinced you are the man for my daughter," the older man said honestly.

"Then tonight, at dinner with my family, you will see how a proposal happens. Please don't tell Sophee or Mere my intentions. I would like the experience to be a complete surprise for my future mate."

I try to put these other thoughts of the Gham out of my mind and only focus on the positive. I am going home with a woman who loves me and will be my wife. The people from Sooul will be safe and happy. I know that granddad and my mom like Sophee and they are pleased with my choices. Proposing in front of my family and friends does make me a bit nervous but what the heck, they should enjoy a show.

Hyun sits across from me sipping on his beer and I know he is sensing that I am shielding or trying to tuck something away, but gives me room. I like the fact he is a lot like Sophee and doesn't push or try and force his help on me. If that was Mere she would playing the "Ask questions until we draw it out game", not that is a bad thing because she is only wanting to help.

Hyun and I have a very relaxed conversation about what marriage means to me and about why I think Sophee would actually like our ceremony. Sophee and Mere returned after an hour and said that Shoran and her folks decided to come with only a little arm-twisting. Dinner with the Chandler must be an intimidating thing. I had Vicky had let Granddad know who all was coming.

It was a good evening, all of our best friends and family sitting in the Captain's suite drinking a few different beverages and socializing. The prime rib was an amazing success; I think Grandddad enjoyed watching Sophee and the rest of the guests from Sooul experience good red meat as much as he did eating it.

I did not speak much, but managed to say that I thought the Gham would not be an issue anymore. Steve and Mike exchanged a knowing glance and both looked oddly at me, but didn't push the subject. I saw them give each other a small very subtle raised glass salute. They know me well and believe the Gham to be dealt with.

My nerves were quite on edge, not because I thought there was any question of Sophee accepting my proposal but I generally am a very private person with my thoughts and personal life. The only reason I would actually propose in front of a group is because of whom they are and how they live interconnected by their empathic abilities. After all the hardships they have endured my desire to make Sophee happy means I should include her family and best friend. To that end if I was including her family, my family deserved to be included as well. So I sat at this meal a bag of nerves and feeling awkward. Sophee and her mom could likely sense my uneasiness and they both managed to jam themselves tightly into my sides, possibly for moral support. Once I had a few drinks into me to raise my courage level I stood up and push my chair back.

"Can I have everyone's attention please?"

All talking stopped and everyone looked up at me. All eyes were questioning, except Hyun's. He has a smile a mile wide so I instantly know how the Sooul would feel. Granddad has a little smile as well and I wonder if Hyun let the cat out of the bag. This was so much harder than facing the Gham in battle.

Here goes nothing…

I took a deep breath to calm my thoughts, as this is what I want.

"Grandfather, thank you for having the people I love the most here for dinner." He nodded slightly as if this is no big deal. I took a second to meet everyone's gaze so they could realize how important they were to me. I then turn my body slightly to face Hyun who is sitting on the other side of Mere beside my Grandfather.

"Hyun, I love your daughter and I will do anything to keep her safe for the rest of my life." I pause for breath before continuing as I thought about how much I loved his daughter. Hoping that my thoughts and emotions would be read by the Sooul as I felt them as I asked; "May I have your permission to ask Sophee to marry me?"

My mother and grandfather both gasped in surprise at my asking in front of them, Steve and Mike were grinning at their best friend taking the plunge. Steve was ready to assist me and had my guitar sitting against the wall behind him.

Mere, Shoran and her parents were surprised that I would ask permission, as this was very different from their culture.

"Yes, my son!" Hyun answered throwing his arms wide in happiness.

I turned to face Sophee and backed up a few feet raising my hands the catch the guitar tossed by Steve. Sophee loves music and told me I could sing to her anytime. I start the lead in and began singing *Marry Me* by Train. Sophee had the biggest smile on her face I have ever seen. As usual all of the Sooul cried, mom cried and I was really certain I saw granddad wipe his eyes. I finished the song and tossed the instrument back to Steve before dropping to my knees. Sophee had tears in her eyes with a smile that outshone the sun. Her arms circled my neck as she virtually launched herself out of her chair. "Please marry me and make my life complete?"

Sophee didn't give me an answer right away since she

was being overwhelmed with emotion. I could tell by the tightness of her hug that the answer was yes. I stood up with Sophee kissing me and her arms still wrapped around my neck. My nervousness was gone now and I feel a slight easing of my stress.

My granddad laughed out loud. "What a great cruise." He walked got up to walk over and shake Hyun's hand as my mom was crying and hugging an equally weepy Mere.

Cruise? I didn't feel this was the appropriate time to remind him it was a rescue mission with urgent medical aid.

"We need two days before we can hold the ceremony; I want to have a stag party tomorrow night and then you two can marry," the Chandler said.

"I don't need a stag."

Granddad laughs. "It is for Hyun, the rest of the Sooul, and your friends." Smiling ear to ear he adds, "For me too."

How the hell can you argue that? Granddad, like me, wanted to include the Sooul in these new experiences. My granddad wants to celebrate too which is different from the way he used to be only focused on the farm. I could understand Granddad's happiness; he wanted me at home with a wife and all of a sudden it is happening.

My mom looked rather amused as well. As she was drying her eyes with a tissue; "Josh, Sophee and a bunch of us girls are going to have a little get-together as well." She looked over at Shoran and her mom; "Humans enjoy celebrating happy events, a bridal shower is usually what happens why the boys are at their stag. I would enjoy throwing one."

Sophee relaxes her grip around my neck a little and motions me to sit with her. I put her down on her chair and sit down with my arm around my fiancé. My stress level dropped considerably and I did not feel anywhere as uptight. My mom was talking intently with Mere; there were a lot of smiles and nodding back and forth between our mothers. It was not very hard to figure out some wedding preparations were being made. Granddad and Hyun talked with Shoran's dad. I bet he was telling them about stags. Mike and Steve caught my eyes when they were mimicking being hanged with their tongues out. Pretty much everyone seemed to be having a fine time.

Later in the evening I walked Sophee back to her parent's cabin. The dinner party had broken up on a high note with my mom crying again when she hugged Sophee. Mere and Hyun were weepy when they hugged me. Granddad had watery eyes until he saw Steve doing the hanged man impression again and he too laughed. When we left I saw the boys sitting back down to open another bulb of beer, Granddad decided to join them while the rest of us had enough and headed back towards our cabins. Hyun and Mere walked ahead of us to the cabin. I felt no need to rush as being with Sophee was all I needed. Shoran waved as she turning down a different passage with her parents.

"Because of your silly rules, you are going to leave me alone tonight?" Sophee asked sadly when we reach the door.

"No," I reply, nudging her inside. "I am going to sleep here with you."

Sophee looked a bit surprised at the mattress that was on the floor in the living area of her parent's cabin. The door to the bedroom was closed already signaling that her parents were either tired or wanted privacy. I dimmed the lights, strip down to my shorts and laid on the mattress that was delivered from my cabin by the cleaner bots. I could have taken Sophee back to my cabin which was empty but thought it was better for appearances that we were not alone sharing a cabin. I chuckled to myself because Sophee and any other Sooul would not think twice about such arrangements. Matter of fact my mom or Granddad would not care either. I wonder why I held myself to such standards and came up with no good or reasonable answer.

Sophee lost her clothing in about a second flat and joined me on the mattress. With a few blankets over us we could have had some fun—she was more than willing—yet I would not. It was just two more nights before we were man and wife, but when a lovely young thing is laying on you and wants to do more than just talk it takes everything in a man to be honorable.

Somehow we made it through the night without anything untoward taking place. I woke up later than my usual time in the still dark cabin and had to ask Vicky for the time. "08:30 sir, I might add that this is the first time you have ever slept so late. I will do a scan to make sure you are not coming down with an illness."

Sophee looks at me with mild concern; "Are you well?"

I give my fiancée a kiss, "Vicky is trying to be funny. Normally I am up much earlier."

"I am going to the gym for a workout."

Sophee was sitting up with the blanket draped over her crossed legs. How someone can wake up looking as fresh and happy as she does is a mystery. Her greens eyes watched me as I dressed. I gave her a quick kiss and the smile I got back was absolutely sweetest thing I had ever received. I wondered at the wisdom of leaving her to go workout in the gym but Sophee's loving smile changed a bit into a grin.

"In two days you may not have the energy," was Sophee teased playfully.

I stopped in my tracks for a second, surprised, and then smiled. There was no need for further discussion, as I fully expect she may be right. I head to my cabin for some workout clothes. Upon reaching the room I took a seat on the lounge, needing a minute to ponder the Gham, wondering if my attack on their home world was successful. All the Sooul saw me kill the Gham and seemed to accept the Gham's fate; would they feel the same way about the Gham's home planet? As a Gunman I leave absolutely nothing to chance and need to know if further plans needed to be made. Did the Gham have advanced AIs that could shut the navigation on an incoming ship down? Was my attack successful?

"Vicky, how hard would it be to tie into the ships scanners, without any of the ship's officers knowing, in order to scan for the Gham's home world?"

"Sir, the ship's navigation computer already scans all stars and registered an interesting anomaly before they picked you up. A new sun formed shortly after your battle. I didn't have to scan it, as it was on the same direct heading we sent the Gham ship. If a ship hits an extensively mined planet at close to the speed of light it would create such an event."

A feeling of sadness washed over me. It wasn't for the Gham; it was for the Sooul. If I had heard about them six years ago I could have done something. Could have brought my men to fight against the Gham, to find their home planet and stop them from attacking anyone ever again.

How many generations of the Sooul would have been saved if I had?

I shook my head to clear my thoughts at an act of such genocide. Gunmen are trained to protect humanity in a permanent and serious manner. The only emotion I felt was trepidation, a fear of how my actions would seem to my family, new and pending.

Standing up I decided it was time to go burn off my excess energy, so I changed into a pair of shorts and running shoes. I grabbed a quick drink of water and a breakfast bar before I leave. Maybe I should have had breakfast with Sophee before I left; she will likely eat with her parents or Shoran. As I head toward the gym and passed various members of the crew I was greeted as a hero. By now the entire ship has seen the videos from the planet, which should have been classified. Vicky was right to show them to granddad, but I wish they were not common knowledge. Knowing my grandfather he showed them publically for a reason.

I don't feel much like the hero and try to avoid as many of the crew as possible. Maybe the same people who shake my hand and say: "Hell of a battle." would be shocked if they knew about the genocide I was responsible for. What concerned me is not the fact I killed all the Gham, I would do it again to protect Sophee, but what granddad and the rest of the Sooul will think when all my actions came to light.

The gym had not changed much from my first visit seven years ago, with exception of a new running track around the perimeter. I needed to sweat and decided to start with a run. I warmed up with a jog for a couple of laps and when I felt ready I broke into a run. There were a couple of other joggers on the track who must not have like being passed several times because after a few laps I had the track to myself.

After running for an hour my body was good and warmed up. It was time for some weights, it felt good to push and stress my body. After going through a complete workout my body felt good but I knew I still had to work off a bit of the repressed stress I was feeling. I walked over to use the two hundred pound heavy bag stopping briefly to get a music player and a bandanna from my workout bag. I selected some old 20th century music from my playlist. My friends would have laughed at my titles on my unit, workout tunes, music to die to and stuff to learn. I could have had Vicky store the music and play it back to me but I like to control my play lists. Eminem's song *Cinderella Man* was at the top of my Workout Tunes play list. Music from that era has the kind of tempo that I like. With ear buds firmly placed I moved around the bag striking at the hard beats in the song.

I decided to practice one of the old Gunman drills, which involves blindfolding yourself and working a heavy bag. You can't reach out and touch the bag, only hit and kick. What makes this difficult is that you have to move around the bag and using your senses to gauge the bag's position to accurately target the bag and not break a wrist or foot.

I kicked the bag to get it moving and then reached up to my ear buds and hit max volume an selected repeat for the song before pulling the bandana down cover my eyes. As the music started, I began to move around the bag and, with every hard beat in the song I kick or struck the heavy bag. One beat; one kick, two beats; punch and knee, three beats; a combo. I move to the rhythm of the music and started striking with serious intent. I thought of the Gham and let my anger at them flow into my strikes.

With the song repeating many times I lost track of time. Hit, dance to right, forward kick, step back, roundhouse kick, back fist, jab, elbow, and it went on and on.

Because of the ear buds and my covered eyes I can't see the gym filling up with spectators as word travels to the Sooul about my impromptu show.

* * *

Steve and Mike had decided to meet and work out together before they left the dinner party the previous evening. Mike waited at Cargo Bay Two's entrance for Steve to gather up his workout gear. Steve walked out with a smirk seeing Mike waiting. "Ready to pump some iron little girl?" Mike raised a fist for a knuckle hit at the challenge. As they were walking to the gym, they discussed how much Josh had changed since he has been with Sophee.

"I think he is whipped," Mike said with a grin.

Steve looks over to Mike. "Be the last person to say that to his face or you will be the one who gets whipped."

"You think he is capable?" Mike asks.

"The beast in him is resting. Do not for a second believe it will not awaken when riled." Steve said.

Mike opened the door to the gym and let Steve go in first. Both Gunmen sense something was different immediately by the silence. There is no sound of weights clanking or treadmills just a muted thudding sound. When

The 1st Gunman

Steve turned the corner to see what was happening in the gym he was surprised to see a crowd of Sooul. Looking over their heads Steve and Mike both saw Josh working a heavy bag. Obviously he was not resting.

Mike's eyebrows rose. "No way is he doing that to music."

"Listen to the sound of his hits; there is a pattern," Steve said as he scaned the growing crowd. A few Sooul men walked past them to join the rest watching Josh.

"Word must be out that Josh is putting a show on." Mike gestured to more Sooul entering the room.

"It would seem so." Steve replied. "Do you think we should tell him he has an audience?"

Mike watched the fury in Josh's strikes. "Let him work it out. Whatever is bothering him must still have real significance."

The two men moved through the crowd closer to Josh and watched with the gathering crowd. As Josh went into his kill zone no one else can hear the music, just the hammer like thuds from his fists and feet, but they could feel the rhythm of the music from the cadence of Josh's punches and kicks.

Hyun, on hearing about Josh's workout, walked in to see his future son moving around and slaughtering the oversized heavy bag. Once Hyun scanned the crowd and found the other Gunmen he approached them directly. Quietly, he asks, "What is this?"

"A fighting drill we learned in training," Mike answered more than a little awed from the beat of the music.

"Is it difficult?" Hyun asked.

Steve laughs. "Most of us do this for fifteen minutes,

not an hour and certainly not to music." Mike nodded in agreement, "Josh has a habit of doing things to the extreme."

Joshua's bare hands are starting leave small red stains on the bag as his single beat strike became two strikes and the combos were up to six strikes. As the strikes started tp speed up, his arms and legs appeared to blur while the thuds started becoming one continuous noise. The heavy bag was getting wetter with bright red smears.

Hyun's eyes widen. "Does he have to hurt himself?"

The older man started to head over to stop Joshua, but a hand snaked out, gently grabbing Hyun's arm to intercept him. "Trying stop him when he is in the zone might get you killed if he reacts wrong, sir," Steve warned.

Just then Sophee walked in from a different door and went straight to Joshua. She had been talking with her mother when Shoran found her and said what Joshua was doing. When she got closer to the gym Joshua's emotional state concerned her, he should be happy not conflicted.

Before either of the off duty Gunman could so much as take a step, let alone get through the crowd filling the gym, Sophee stepped up to Joshua and grasped his bloody hand mid-swing. Steve and Mike gave up on decorum to rush through the bystanders, jostling them about in attempt to get into position to grab Josh before Sophee could become the bag's replacement.

Extremely honed reflexes and the touch of his bonded one met, the looping roundhouse punch stopped like it hit a wall when it encountered Sophee's hand. The impact on Sophee was no more than a gentle touch as his lightning fast reflexes kicked in. Joshua was breathing hard and as much sweat dripped from him as blood from his mashed hands.

Sophee stepped around the still extend punch and lifted the covering from Joshua's head. As he straightened up from the crouch, she took his right hand which was the one that was dripping blood the worst and wrapped with Joshua's blindfold in silence.

Mike finally made it through the crowd of Sooul and handed Sophee a small towel for her to administer to Joshua's other hand before he turned to address the silent crowd. "Thank you for coming to the show. Hope you enjoyed it."

"We'll be here all week!" Steve added with a grin.

Then Steve and Mike both started laughing at their own wittiness, hoping to dispel the seriousness of Josh's distress.

Hyun didn't know what to think at the laughing men or his daughter's future mate. One minute it is dangerous to go near Josh and he could get him killed. The next minute his daughter does the same thing and is safe. Joshua's friends found all this so funny; human's are so very confusing.

Sophee, holding the worst hand, started to lead Joshua to the door. Just before reaching the exit, she stopped for a second to look at the two laughing fools. "I expected you two to take better care of him."

"Really?" Steve said with tears of laughter in his eyes, "I thought we were off duty."

"If you want to do your stagy-thing tonight, boys, you are back on," she says with a smile. She continues out of the gym with Joshua silently in tow.

Steve looked at Mike and shook his head. "Man, was he in a zone! Whatever is bothering him, it *can't* be a little thing."

"That bond is affecting him weirdly, too. Could you imagine what could have happened to her otherwise?"

"I wonder if Josh's funk is about the Gham. I hope it is because it would be fun to get a crack at them." Mike said. Steve smiled but didn't say a thing. If Joshua is planning marriage and returning to New Harvest, it is not likely the Gham are still a threat. Being a Gunman, he knows that you never leave an enemy alive or a target standing. Knowing that Josh is the hardest, meanest son of a bitch when necessary, it stood to reason the Gham were not relevant anymore.

* * *

"Look at your hands, Joshua," Sophee gently scolded me as she led me slowly towards the medical bay. "Whatever is bothering you is not good for you and we will talk about it." I figure it is time to man up about the Gham; this gut wrenching feeling is not something that makes me happy.

I feel gross; my workout sweat is getting cooler and starting to feel sticky. I am wondering if I could get away with going for a shower but her firm grasp on my arm makes me know that she will have none of that. The Medical Bay is completely empty when we enter. An alarm must sound in the doctor's office because the door opens and the doctor casually strolls out. The doctor looks a bit surprised when he sees me back so soon.

Dr. Cliff was on duty, seeing the bloody cloth wrapped around my hands he shook his head. "What does the other guy looks like?" he asked. Pointing to a chair for me sit down he picked up a small handheld scanner before removing the temporary bandages. He quickly scanned the damage to my hands.

"Soft tissue damage, no broken bones." He states as

he looked into my eyes troubled by my silence. Dr. Cliff is a pretty good guy and my nod at his assessment didn't satisfy him.

He took a preloaded syringe from cabinet and gave me a shot of booster nanites. He then got a bowl of green medical sealant and set it down on the table beside me. Sophee looked at the bowl of fluid and nodded like she has seen it before.

"Dip your hands in this," the good doctor ordered while continuing to study my demeanor. Sophee picked the bowl up and held it on my lap. "This fluid seems heavier than the stuff we used to treat Joshua back at our old home." Sophee said to the doctor.

"I read the reports from Mr. Garvie's AI, there were no trauma nanites in that batch. This batch is fully infused and in few hours his skin will be re-grown." The doctor informed her.

"Doc, please call me Josh. Granddad is Mr. Garvie." I said without smiling. The green fluid stopped the bleeding immediately as it seals the smashed skin. A pleasant numb feeling replaces the stinging sensation. The doctor handed Sophee light gauze to be wrapped around my hands. I think it is funny that the doctor let Sophee administer to me, but then I see him smiling at Sophee and she must have won the doctors respect when I was in the tank.

The doctor, noticing my continued silence, looked at Sophee for an explanation. I saw shake her head almost imperceptibly. Dr. Cliff knows me well enough not to pry.

"Maybe take him somewhere quiet for the afternoon," he suggested.

Sophee smiled at the doctor. "Thank you again for fixing

up my Joshua." She tugged at my arm to get me standing. "Come with me Joshua."

We leave the medical bay and head to my cabin.

I still don't know how to tell her about the Gham. Her kindness and compassion make me feel like I am unworthy. Did all the Gham deserve to die? I think yes and I am a bit sorry that I could not have killed more of them with my bare hands. Here I have my fiancé and she is the kindest person I have ever met, her family and people are as gentle as the day is long. Can they be accepting of someone like me who can and did kill as many beings as I did?

When we get into the cabin Sophee notices the time on the wall chronograph. "Vicky?" she asks, "What is my Joshua's favorite quick meal?"

"Pizza with mushrooms." Vicky's voice answers through the cabins sound system. "The AutoChef will produce one in a few minutes, Sophee."

I still don't speak as I sit down at the table, so Sophee busies herself getting the pizza off the output pad. She serves me first and the puts a piece on a small plate across from me. I had to smile as she smells it enjoying the aroma before cutting a small piece and then using a fork to eat it.

She smiles again with surprised delight. "Wait until my dad tries this. Who ever thought you could use a cheese in such a manner? Are these things the mushrooms?" She asks as she points at a pepperoni.

I started laughing. "No, that is a pepperoni and it is a meat. The mushroom is the dark crescent shape thing beside it." Everything she does is adorable, simple things give her so much joy. I demonstrate how to hold and eat a slice of pizza without a knife and fork, but Sophee decides to stick with the utensils.

After we finished our lunch Sophee cleaned up our plates and dimmed the lights in the cabin. She pulled me into the washroom and then undressed. I was about to stop her and then decided to go with it. I undressed as well and followed her into the shower. Showering was nice. It did not seem if there was any urgency or reason to hurry. I dropped to my knees so she could wash my hair. I stepped out of the shower behind her and dried off while she wrapped a towel around herself and took my sweaty workout clothes into the main cabin. She put the cloth into the autowasher and met me at the door of the bathroom to pull me into the bed. I wondered if she was going to hassle me about waiting but she pulled a blanket over us. Wrapping her arms around me, Sophee snuggled into my chest. It was amazing just being with her but, after a while; she shifted position holding my face gently between her hands to looked into my eyes and softly says, "Please talk to me about what you are feeling."

I start with a slow breath. Even in the dim light of the cabin her eyes gaze into mine waiting. In her eyes I see love and understanding it empowers me to explain myself; *"Now I am become death, the destroyer of worlds."* I have to pause for a minute before continuing as the explanation is hard to vocalize. "I feel that… shit! Honey, I killed the Gham. All of them."

"We saw," she replies.

I shake my head at her; she thinks I just killed the twenty-eight Gham she saw.

"You don't know the scope of this action. When I sent the Gham ship away it was to destroy the Gham, I killed all of them; every single one, everywhere! Is one life of worth their whole race?"

"Is that life me?"

"Yeah," I answer. "While fighting the Gham, I somehow understood they would never stop coming for the Sooul. I don't know if they communicate like the way you read emotions, but I do know that the drone's lives were nothing to the queen. She leads all of the drones and was the center of their universe... It could only end with the death of the queen."

"All the Gham Joshua, really?"

"All of them."

She was silent for a minute while she processed the destruction.

"You have that much power?" Sophee asked while studying me.

"I believe in the endgame theory," I tell her honestly. "Never leave an enemy alive. Back before the fall of earth humanity fought and defeated each other and made statements about taking the ability to make war away from their enemies. The destruction of the planet from people that had been previously beaten taught us that in a time of war you do not leave your enemy to regroup and attack you again. The Gham murdered countless generations of Sooul, but in my mind I was ensuring you were safe first. Your people also, but you were my primary focus."

Sophee shook her head; "I think you made your decision based on the amount of murdered Sooul, *and* the knowledge that the Gham were never, ever going to stop killing. To end those parasites you had to make the hard decision." Sophee gave me a tight hug. "We feel sad for putting you into the position you were. Our people will accept the outcome, however severe it may be. Not because we are happy they are gone, but because our Joshua thought it needed to be done. No Sooul would second guess any decision you made."

We lay in silence for a few minutes.

"What was the death and world statement about?" Sophee asks.

I smile because everything I say she digests and thinks deeply about.

"Robert Oppenheimer was the head scientist on the Manhattan Project, which was during the Second World War on planet Earth. Right after the successful first atomic bomb test explosion he made that quote, which was from an old Hindu text. It had to do with the realization that he had just changed everything, and I know how he felt."

Sophee is looking into my eyes waiting for more of an explanation. She always does that, patiently waits while giving me her full attention. I find it refreshing that she wants to understand me so completely.

"His bomb changed the course of mankind and eventually led to earth's total destruction. My control of the Gham ship led to their total destruction."

Another tight hug and several very passionate kisses later she says, "Can I ask you what you were listening to in the gym?"

Smart girl, I thought. *Change the subject from one that causes me pain.*

"Old music from a long dead artist named Eminem; the song was called *Cinderella*." That particular song has a very fast beat that I enjoy working out to. Music as I said on Sooul is a very important part of life.

Sophee paused. "Your singing to my cousin's baby was

the first I had heard. When you played the guitar and sang I realized that there must be a lot of very good music. Do you know all of it?"

The honesty of her question stopped me from laughing aloud. "There are millions of songs in hundreds of languages. You will have to listen to some and figure out your favorites." I said.

"The songs you played are my favorites."

I felt like a rock star. "Vicky, play *A Thousand Years* by Christina Perri." I ordered.

As the slow music starts, I wrapped my arms around Sophee and pulled her as close as I could. "The ship's captain will do our wedding ceremony, we will be asked about being husband and wife. Your people say mate, mine say husband and wife. I will say a vow to you, but you do not have to."

She was silent for a few seconds and I could see her listening intently to the words of the song so I stay silent. By the look on her face she may never have heard a word I said.

"I love this song." She looks at me with an impish grin. "Who knew you could be so sensitive?"

"The song is okay," I said, "but compared to what I have with you it is nothing."

We spent the entire afternoon in bed without doing the one thing both of us had on our minds; after all, tomorrow we would be married. I sometimes felt like that some of the standards I set for myself were excessive but I only plan on marrying once and wanted do what I thought was right. I personally felt much better after explaining what I did to the Gham and getting Sophee's reaction. If she believed her people would not have issues with the severity of my actions then it was now time to come clean about the Gham to my grandfather, and hope he isn't too shocked.

We dressed just before suppertime and left the cabin to join our family for a meal.

The group in Granddad's cabin was everyone that had been there yesterday, which surprised me because I never remembered Granddad being so social. Mere and Shoran were talking with my mother and motioned to Sophee to join them. This led me to believe more female oriented plans were being made. I strolled over to my granddad as he sat with Hyun and my two friends. I found it surprising that Hyun, who is so gentle and quiet, enjoyed the company of such dissimilar people.

Deciding that now was better than later, I decided to come clean. "I set the Gham's ship on a collision course with their home planet at max acceleration with their faster-than-light drive. This will have killed the queen and turned their planet into a new sun when the ship hit the planets core. With her demise, all of her drones died. There should be no more problems with them, as the Gham have ceased to exist."

I look for their reactions, expecting shock or surprise.

"Good," Granddad simply says.

Hyun didn't look surprised at all, while Steve and Mike tap their glasses of scotch. My announcement doesn't shock them; if anything it is accepted by granddad and expected by the Gunmen present. The answer no longer matters to me because, as I said to Sophee, I would do it again.

"Where are we are going to put all the Sooul?" I ask my grandfather.

Hyun interrupts. "You mean *the New Harvest colonists* on this ship?"

Nothing like embracing your new home. I think they will blend in perfectly as the Sooul are such an easy group to get along with.

"Sorry, Hyun, I meant no slight."

"The hotel by the shore will have enough rooms until we can get more bunker homes built," Granddad answered, offering me a drink.

The scotch, on crushed ice, tasted perfect now that my tension levels had totally disappeared. I looked up to see Hyun smiling kindly at me and I assumed he sensed the lack of stress, so I nodded to him. I did not want to get into a discussion of my feelings with him. It was hard enough to explain how I felt earlier to Sophee. Steve and Mike moved close and took a turn shaking my hand. "Next time leave some for us." Steve said.

"What's up with the girls?" I give a nod in the direction of our womenfolk. They are all huddled in a group talking excitedly.

"Wedding stuff," Steve says, "so mind your own business."

"You obviously have intelligence you are not sharing, my friend, this concerns me."

Hyun laughs. "It was your idea to mix your traditions and ours."

"I was happy with yours alone," I say, "but for Granddad's and my mother's sake. They deserve a wedding."

"Damned right I do!" Granddad exclaims before he takes a sip of his own drink.

Hyun nods in agreement. "Maybe our people, not to mention their Joshua, need it as well."

I smiled at hearing *'their Joshua'*. Never before had I ever felt so much a part of something. From the second night I was on Sooul, Sophee referred to me that way when discussing me with her people. With the bond affecting me so deeply, with the changes I felt every time I heard it, I had to grin. Now that her parents and the rest of the Sooul referred to me as *'our Joshua'* I was going to have to be extra careful to ensure all of the Sooul were treated like family.

This does not put any extra stress on me; I would have done it anyways. But, my god, it is nice to be a part of something larger than your own self. If I had the maturity to act in a kinder and outgoing manner when I was younger maybe I could have had the same relationship with the people of New Harvest.

My mom announced that the food was ready when some of the chiefs rolled carts into the room. Supper was a rather casual buffet of various types of New Harvests foods. By the amount of different selections my new family was getting quite the culinary education. I helped Sophee pick out things I thought she would like. As we were sitting enjoying the excellent meal both Mere and my mom let me know that I would not see Sophee until tomorrow at the service. All I could think about was that it would be the first time I have been away from her at night since we met. I felt disappointed, I mean, if we hadn't had any physical relationship yet, do they believe we would on the eve of our wedding?

Hyun sensing my thoughts put his hand on my arm. "I will stay with you tonight".

My mouth dropped opened in disbelief as he laughed. It is good this to know that Hyun has sense of humor now that he is going to become my father-in-law. The thought of sharing a bed with Hyun was just plain weird, hopefully it is not some Sooul custom…. *God, I hope he is kidding.*

Sophee was getting ready to leave with the other girls, so I used that as an excuse to escape the conversation without replying. After I walked her to the door, Sophee reached up and gave me a brief kiss before exiting. I was stunned that she could just leave me so easily, but maybe she knew how difficult it is for me and decided to make her farewell quick.

"After you mate absences are easier. Until then, you will be rather uncomfortable emotionally," Hyun says explaining why I would feel so odd about Sophee leaving. It seemed odd that the bond had affected my emotions this way but since Hyun recognized my feelings I figured it must be a normal thing.

I was going to tell him how much I was looking forward to the mating, but the rest of the guys here wouldn't understand the emotional aspect of the bond. Steve and Mike would think I was just like them, needing sex.

"We are going to the main mess to allow the rest of New Harvest men and any off duty personal to join in," Granddad said to Hyun, Lian and my friends. "Come on Josh, we think your man enough now to join us." Granddad gave a laugh and walked out of the cabin. It may be a stag but I imagine they are going to ride me pretty hard. *Oh Joy!*

"Wonder what the girls will be doing?" Steve teases.

"Drinking wine, telling stories, and most likely congratulating Sophee on finding such a fine mate." I reply.

"Heck I don't know, as long as they are not teaching Sophee anything inappropriate."

Mike grins and says, "Inappropriate? This bond thing is really turning Josh into a bag of mush. I would be glad if someone taught my future wife inappropriate things."

Steve turned to Hyun with just as big a grin on his face. "I think he needs some fluid therapy."

I look at my buddies and shake my head; "Nobody will ever teach your future wife anything inappropriate Mike….. sheep can't learn." Mike stopped dead at the hack while Steve and I gave each other a fist bump. Our laughter could probably be heard all the way to the main mess.

"Steve, Mike, let's keep our eyes on the men of Sooul because I don't think they've had this type of party without their women. You never know how crazy they might get," I caution my friends as we get to the mess.

"Your mother and Mere had already discussed this with your grandfather and Captain Grey," Steve says. "There will be extra staff on duty to help them to their rooms and ensure they don't feel too overwhelmed."

"Excellent my friends, Once more into the fray…" I walk into the mess with my friends chanting, "To last good fight I will ever know."

Captain Grey and most of the ships officers were already partying and, by the sounds of things, they had been at it for a while.

Captain Grey saw us enter and came over join us from the position he had at the bar. I realized he was not in uniform. None of the crews were; all of the officers are wearing plain garments with no rank or insignias. Being off duty and at a social event must be rare to the crew. I imagine Captain Grey wanted the crew totally relaxed and without the hierarchy of rank. I remember when we served the crew drinks on our first trip together and the officers mingled with the regular crewmen. Captain Grey must have continued trying to promote a relaxed atmosphere between the officers and the enlisted. It seemed to be working.

Captain Grey was quite happy to be called Robert by everyone here. I saw one of his regular crew who was a maintenance tech pass him a shooter. "Robert, try this; it's called a brain hemorrhage." Robert took four drinks off his tray and handed out a round. The drink looked gross with what looked like a bloody brain floating in a clear pool of fluid.

"Cheers gentlemen." I said before quickly swallowing the drink which wasn't half bad.

Steve tossed his drink back and marched to the bar. After waiting a few seconds he received two drinks. Smiling he dropped a glass of single malt in my hand. "If you have your AI stop you from getting drunk I refuse to be one of your best men."

I smile at his lame threat; maybe he thinks I am still under a lot of stress. Now that everyone knows what I did to the Gham and they are not shocked or horrified by it my stress level is at zero. Maybe tomorrow I will be a bit nervous before the wedding, but right now a few drinks with my friends and family in this relaxed state sounds like a wonderful idea.

The Sooul men started partying slowly but eventually got a few drinks in and loosened up considerably. Many times through the evening I could see them talking with the other Gunmen and even my grandfather, who they found to be generous and warm. I always thought he was hard to talk to when I was younger; the Sooul men had no such problems. It was nice to see them feeling safe and opening up. I could tell that their comfort level around us was pretty darn high; they had learned to trust us.

We had lots of fun with Steve and Mike telling many stories from the Element, which I enjoyed as much as everyone else. I didn't tell any. When asked why I never shared stories I just said, "I never think any of the things that I have done are very funny."

"You do plenty of things funny Josh." Mike said. Of course that leads him into a new story of when I met the guys. "Josh cleared out a bar on Mars Colony because we were too drunk to fight. He then got beat up by a woman that he wouldn't hit back."

Steve explained with a grin; "Her boyfriend was one the spacers that tried to beat us up before Josh clobbered him. She was really mad and hit Josh until she broke her wrist. Josh would never hit a woman and he couldn't get away from her." While most of the group was having a laugh at my expense I decided to tell them about the time Mike, Steve, and I were training a ship's crew in hostile environment survival. It is a skill military crews might use if they crash landed.

When the laughter quieted down I spoke up. "I have a funny story." Steve and Mike looked at each other surprised that I would actually tell a story.

"We had set up the camp on a small planet. There was the required outer perimeter we had to guard. We were conducting watch drills and teaching the crewmen various Codes: Code Green was for all secure; Code Yellow was for dangerous life forms outside the perimeter, and Code Red for dangerous life forms outside the perimeter attacking. It was late in the afternoon about mealtime and everyone was supposed to be eating kcals. Mike had purchased some freeze-dried spicy tacos on Mars before we left to avoid the rations. The camp was in Code Yellow status when Mike sneaks his snack to avoid the Kcal rations." I shake my head at the memory and smile before taking a healthy pull of my drink. "You have to understand that kcals taste the way they look. When you squeeze it out of the tube it looks like gritty grey caulking, avoiding them is Mike's specialty." I see Mike and Steve both grinning as they remember the day.

"Whoever made the tacos that Mike brought put far too much spices into them and within an hour they gave Mike a case of the runs. Mike sprinted past us yelling; "Code Brown, Code Brown!" and everyone inside the camp panicked and started shooting outside the perimeter. Only one person other than Mike didn't shoot and that was me, I just sat and laughed at Mike running for the latrine. The training review officer there had to evaluate our performance wrote me up for not supporting defense of the camp. Even *he* didn't know what a Code Brown status was, and was shooting too… Good times."

Mike has tears rolling out of his eyes from laughing so hard and yells, "Josh got written up because he would not tell the training evaluator that Code Brown was a case of the shits!"

The whole crowd around the bar was laughing, I think it was because Steve and Mike roared and had tears running down their faces. I could see some of the Sooul men laughing and repeating "Code Brown" among themselves. I enjoyed sharing the story with them because it took the attention off me while they laughed at Mike. Granddad and Hyun seemed to be laughing the hardest. It must seem funny to them that me, Mr. Serious could chill out and have fun. I did not care but enjoyed the fact that Granddad and Hyun were having fun.

The Sooul men seemed totally at ease now and were enjoying themselves. Hyun said at some point that it really was the first time in their lives they had ever attended a male-only event. I bet the women were having a nice party too, I knew my mom would be working hard at making sure my future wife would never forget her stagette. The crew of this fine ship also ensured movies and popcorn was on, the kids were also not to be left out.

Another round of drinks and then some card games started at one of the tables. Steve introduced the Sooul to poker and they liked the game. Mike refused to play after a half of an hour when he suddenly realized he was losing his entire pile of chips. He stood up and claimed; "These Sooul men cheat." He passed the few remaining chips he had left over to Shoran's dad. None of the Sooul was mad at him for claiming they were cheaters; they could read his emotion as humor. As he walked away for the game he shook his head at me in disgust. "You cannot bluff a Sooul in cards, they know when it is a lie or not.

I laughed at the look on his face. "Guess they took away your game eh?" I asked. "Maybe you should have those guys open a casino on New Harvest, the house would always win." Mike suggested.

I sat down at one of the lounge areas and was talking with Granddad and Hyun. It was very pleasant talking about New Harvest and the changes Granddad made in my absence. They had enlarged the planted area that was shielded and got more harvesters. The Church Key was getting so popular off planet that they had to double the size of the brewery. It sounded like everything was stable and running well.

Before long, Mike and Steve started complaining that I greedily took out all the Gham without leaving any for them to fight. I smiled at their attitude, sober or tipsy always ready to fight. Granddad, Hyun and the others didn't seem to care. Granddad because he knew they are Gunmen and will be what they are, Hyun and the Sooul could sense their humor and respect for life. Steve then took the Captain aside at the bar and told him about the Gham. The Captain said he would send a message to all ships in the quadrant to watch for any derelict ships.

How someone Hyun's size can put away so much booze is a mystery. Unlike the strong wine he was used to at home our beer was weaker in alcohol content, but still he packed enough away to impress me. I sat down with Hyun much later in the evening; I had to slow my booze intake down so I didn't make an idiot of myself. During our conversation he told me about when I was wounded, what happened while I was in a coma and all that Sophee did to care for me. He also mentioned that he had some concerns for his daughter after having seen me naked. That comment that caused me to spit my drink all over myself and proceed to have a coughing fit from inhaling single malt.

Vicky, who monitors at all times opens sub vocally. "Sophee had me give the results of the compatibility scan to him and Mere. They were concerned about your species ability to mate with the Sooul. It was based on body size only."

I on the other couldn't look into his eyes. Hyun is paying far too much attention to my discomfort and motions to my granddad, Steve, and Mike. They come to sit with us and then Hyun addressed the group.

"It is of my understanding that humans don't always mate for life. Have either of you ever mated?" Hyun asks, looking at my friends.

"Yes," Mike replied.

Steve, being the smartass he is says, "Yes, yes, yes, second base, and yes."

I roll my eyes and leave my "No" out of the conversation, because I am absolutely certain Sophee has told her mother we have not traveled down that road yet.

Mike laughs at my silence. "Tough guy."

Steve grinned and gave Mike a cheer with his drink. "But he is a fighter not a lover!"

The pair then burst out laughing at their own wit, causing Hyun and granddad look at each other and smile. They really seemed to enjoy the way my friends harassed me and enjoyed my reactions. They both acted like proud fathers who enjoyed being a part of my life.

"You know, since all the rest of us have mated, maybe we should have a coaching session for you," Hyun suggested with a sly grin.

Crap. I am being made the butt of their jokes. My mouth drops open in surprise as I try and come back with a good response. Granddad and my so-called friends are laughing so hard that I give up on being witty to start laughing as well.

When the laughter is down to a dull roar I said "I am not getting any drunker so that you can abuse my sensitivities, I am going to bed." After standing, I turned and tripped over a chair and landed on my face. So much for lightning quick reflexes and balance, it was not a very dignified exit.

Hyun was good enough to help me to my cabin. He did not to have hold me up or anything silly like that, we just walked together. I may have had a difficult time walking in a straight direction but Hyun did not rub it in. We reached my cabin and I said goodnight but Hyun just laughed.

"I did say I would stay here." Hyun said.

"But it is okay, you can go back to your mate. I will just crash until the morning." I said.

"Caroline told us the bride should never see the groom the night before. I think Shoran, her mom and Caroline are going to stay with Sophee." Hyun says. "You full humans are very funny with all your little rituals, should I call Chandler and your friends to come here?"

I shake my head no. "Come on in Hyun; let's leave it at you and me." I say grateful that Steve and Mike were not here to hassle me. "Please make yourself comfortable. I am going for a shower."

I headed for a shower to clear my head. "Vicky, have the nanites remove all traces of alcohol please." I instructed. By the time my shower finished I was clean and sober. I dried off then dressed in a pair of shorts. With the towel around my shoulders I walked back into the main cabin to find Hyun asleep on my bed. I covered him with a light blanket from the foot of the bed before going over to the lounge and lying down. The temperature in the cabin was warm enough I didn't need the only loose blanket that I had given Hyun.

I rolled the towel up to use it as a pillow because Hyun was hogging both of mine. I sure hope the Sooul don't have any other weird customs because he will not be welcome here tomorrow night.

CHAPTER 13

I woke up at my usual time and stared at the ceiling until Hyun woke up. He decided to go check on his wife and daughter. I thanked him for the information he had given me about the Sooul's bonding announcement the night I got out of the tank.

The mess was fairly full of Sooul families when I got there. Everyone was eating and I realized that this was the meeting spot for families. At the entrance of the serving area I could see several Sooul women helping to wash areas and trying to be useful. The galley crew worked well with them even if they really did not require the help. Shoran's mom poured a cup of coffee for me. "Take this Joshua," she said as she passed me the steaming mug. I accepted the coffee gratefully. "You go sit and I will serve you the morning meal." She ordered pleasantly. I realized that because they didn't have any real duties on the ship the Sooul women were actually acting like waitresses. Maybe it felt better to actually feel like you were contributing. I felt a bit of a warm glow seeing them smiling and obviously happy as they interacted with the ship's crew. Not wanting to intrude on any conversations or family time in the groups of Sooul present I move off to an empty table and sat down. Ankh saw me sitting alone and tugged on his father's elbow to get his attention. I saw them talk for a second then his dad looked up at me. Immediately he stood up and said a few words to his tablemates; they all picked up their food and came to my table. Ankh sat beside me first then the rest just sat down and joined the table.

"Good morning." I addressed them.

Ankh's mother smiled curiously at me; "Why are you sitting alone Joshua?"

"Before meeting Sophee I spent the majority of my time alone. When I came here everyone was in conversations and I did not want to intrude on their family time." I explained.

"You are our family now Joshua, please believe that." She said as the rest of them nodded in agreement.

Shoran's mom then showed up with a huge platter of food and I started laughing at the size of it. "I really hope this is for the whole table." I said at the sight of it. She placed the platter directly in front of me and will a clever smile on her face she said. "We thought you might need extra energy tonight."

Pretty certain my face turned about twelve shades of red while the whole group laughed. Having no proper response I pick up my fork and started eating some of the bacon and eggs. Seeing my red face Shoran's mom patted my arm conveying the joke was in good fun. I smile back, finished the eggs and turned my attention to the fruit on the platter. I answered questions, while I ate about weddings and why we had such elaborate rituals. "Most humans fall in love but do not have anything as spiritually deep as the bond. I think a wedding ceremony allows the announcement of the bond and creates a fine memory to help solidify the union." I took another bite of fruit and chew for a minute. The Sooul at the table are looking at me like I needed to say more so I swallowed and continued. "I have bonded like the Sooul. I would have been happy to make the announcement and bond but since we have the option of a wedding I think Sophee deserves the whole experience. My family is here and the wedding will also make them happy." I looked down at the platter for a second realizing I could not finish it, and then look at every Sooul sitting at my table. "I also believe you need more happy events in your lives." There was no possibility of me finishing all the food so I stood up and picked up my platter to carry it over the recycler chutes. "Too much food, I am going to go for a walk and work some of this off, thank you so much for joining me."

I walked over to dump the tray but was intercepted by Shoran's mom. "I will take that Joshua, you should rest." She said with a twinkle in her eyes. "Thanks," I said keeping my eyes down so she would not see me turn red again.

Then I just walked around the ship for the next few hours. I was thinking about the ceremony, about what married life would be like, responsibilities, if I should get a German Sheppard. Not really sure if I am excited for the ceremony or nervous but I felt a wee bit edgy. Walking keeps me in check and busy so I did my best to wander aimlessly with a calm attitude.

A month ago I was single and heading home; now I was about to be married. I felt like someone who has seen the sun for the first time in my life. I was very grateful for whatever twist of fate took to bring me to this point. I wished that I could just run to the ceremony and get it started. *Calmly Josh, she will be waiting for you.*

Sooul women and kids, every time they saw me during

my walk, had to run up for a hug, I couldn't figure out if it was to congratulate me for the pending wedding or if it was for what I did to the Gham. Either way, it helped a tiny bit to occupy my mind. Give me an opponent in a battle and my nerves are calm, give me a day off for a wedding and I wander around like a lost dog. Would the wedding be as significant to the Sooul as it is to me?

Crap, chill out, Sophee likes what I do, quit worrying about trivial things.

I keep walking to burn off stress until Steve found me outside Engineering. He paused for a second to look for signs of stress or nerves. I guess the outward calm I projected fooled him. "The Chandler sent me to retrieve you. It's time for us to dress pretty."

He watched me closely so I laughed. "Sure pal, you realize that you could have contacted me through Vicky?"

Steve grins; "I wanted to see if the ever-so-calm Josh was a bag of nerves."

"Sorry to disappoint you. I am a little off but nothing worth mentioning." I said because I would never admit to anything that would give my friends ammo for a later date.

We return to my cabin and I am surprised to see that someone has turned it into a honeymoon suite of sorts. The bed is made up with red satin sheets; there are flowers and a fruit basket on the table, plus some honey scented candles on various pieces of furniture. I wonder if these were items from stasis or something my mom had to whip up. Either way I figure Mom and Mere did an amazing job; I would have to remember to thank them later.

Mike enters the cabin carrying a clothing bag. "I took the liberty of having your dress uniform pressed."

"Guess I should have thought of that, thanks Mike, I appreciate it." I said.

My Gunman's dress uniform is a black single breasted tuxedo. The braids, piping are all black as well. The shirt is black silk with a with my 1st Gunman pin on the collar. Other than the pin the only thing on the whole uniform that is not black is the rank insignia on the right shoulder. It is dark grey and simply states; "1st Gunman." I am grateful for my Grandfather's and mother's decision to pick me up after my hunting trip as my uniform was with my gear. The B.N.J. had dropped off a shipment of corn and bio-mass at Mars Colony and had taken on cargo to be dropped at various locations on their journey home. My dress uniform and personal gear was one such item they were transporting. Mike and Steve were not fortunate enough to have their dress uniforms or personal belongs with them. Being Gunmen they always carried battle suits and digital camouflage outfits. Where they got the black shirts and ties to go with them is beyond me.

As I dressed, I had to concentrate on keeping my heart rate low and to outwardly look calm. Those two friends of mine would have rubbed my nervousness in my face for years to come if I was outwardly showing it. I could tell by their demeanor that they were excited to be my best men. They chatted and seemed happy but I could tell that they were a bit nervous by an occasional trickle of sweat that Mike wiped away from his temple.

I just finished dressing when Granddad showed up.

"You clean up nice!" He said as he checked out my dress uniform.

"We should be heading to the mess, Sophee is ready and

your guests are waiting." Granddad said as he put his arm around my shoulder again showing more love and respect outwardly than he ever had before.

Granddad had one of those very satisfied smiles on his face as we walked. Seeing him so happy and relaxed was a wonderful thing.

"It's a beautiful day!" He said.

"Yes the life support on this ship seems to be functioning well." I said knowing he meant the family coming home and marriage; but not cutting him slack. Mike stepped forward and slapped the back of my head. I laughed at him aligning me and stopped in place. Granddad stopped to give me a quizzical look; I put both arms around him for a hug.

"It is a freaking great day, sir."

Granddad looked over at Mike and winked; "Sometime even Gunmen need a whack to make them realize how good they have it."

"Call us anytime, we like smacking him." Steve said.

When we reached the mess Granddad gave me a hug and said; "give me a minute to join your mother before you come in. I am proud of who you are."

That gave me a pause, *definitely not the hardass I remember.*

We gave him a minute to find his seat then entered the mess. I blinked twice at the changes that happened in a few short hours. All the tables had been moved to the sides and rows of chairs had been set up. It was standing room only as small children sat on their parent's laps. The aisle was centered through the rows of chairs. I walked up to Captain Grey who would be performing the ceremony. Captain Grey pointed to where I should stand facing the spectators; Steve and Mike fell in beside me.

Standing in the mess with all of the Sooul and a good portion of the crew, I waited for Sophee. Any stress I felt or nervousness has completely disappeared now the moment was here. My mom already had tears in her eyes. Granddad looked so relaxed he could fall asleep. The Sooul were all wide-eyed and paying attention to everything. Now that I had a minute I could see that the tables had been covered with cloths, the head table was not far from where I was standing almost in the middle of the room. I knew my mother had a lot to do with the set up and meal, I was going to have to owe her big time for all of her efforts.

The music started and I smiled because the first song I played to Sophee at her home was used. She must have listened to the music with my mother and decided to play something she loved instead of the traditional march. Shoran walked in first and I could hear Steve mutter "dibs" to Mike. Shoran turned at Captain Gray's signal and stood to the opposite side of us. Sophee appeared holding her father's arm and walked slowly toward us.

Sophee's simple white gown clung to her like a second skin. The way it shimmered meant that is was made from silk. It had lace around the neckline and on the ends of the long sleeves. Sophee looked more like a fashion model than a bride. Guess I know what mom and Mere were doing all night. The B.N.J. was carrying raw silk but Vicky must have helped to program a replicator for such fine work. Sophee's face was very serene as she walked up to me. By the slight blush on her cheek I could see her excitement. Sophee looked up into my eyes; she lost her calmness and smiled widely. I suspect that my grin was as huge but all I could think was finally she is here, finally this is mine.

When she took my hand a second sense of ease came over me. Her touch, however so soft grounds me. I feel reborn, as a new man, my life has purpose. Not that my life did not have a direction before. Her touch opened my life; it made my existence have a reason. The feeling of completeness is a high and I see Sophee reacting the same way.

Captain Grey performed the service from memory.

Our vows were very simple, to love and to honor each other in sickness and in health, but when I had to give mine I added, "You are the single most important thing in my existence. I worship the ground you walk on and will cherish you forever."

"I am yours," was all Sophee said. Her level of dedication didn't need vocalizing, because with a Sooul the bond means more than simple words.

"Ring?" Captain Grey asked. Before I could say that we did not have any Steve was fishing in his pockets. I glanced over at my mom who was smiling widely when I recognized her wedding ring. My mom must have had it sized for Sophee's smaller finger because it fit perfectly. Sophee did not show any surprise so I was thinking she had already seen the ring.

When Captain Grey pronounced us man and wife the Sooul cheered. I did not wait for the instructions to kiss the bride. I swept her up into my arms and kissed my wife passionately. Sophee wrapped her arm around my neck and squeezed as tight as a boa-constrictor. My heart felt like it would leap from my chest.

The entire ceremony took less than a half an hour, which was followed by the typical receiving line and banquet. The Sooul seemed to enjoy the ceremony by the cheering and happy grins that most of them had. The younger girls paid pretty close attention to all the proceedings. I laughed at them looking at my friends knowing they would be searching for men to have such an event.

We made it to our seat after the receiving line and I smiled when the arrangement were not to the Sooul's liking. The head table was at the point of a fishbone pattern. The Sooul started dragging their tables around and closer. By the time they were done there was no seating pattern, just a bunch to tables pressed close to the head table. At any other wedding I had been to the seating arrangement would have been more formal but the Sooul with their bonds treated everyone like family. My mom and granddad sat with Mere and Hyun. They were closer to the outside of the group.

Most of the Sooul women got up and served the meal to the tables in the tightly packed cluster, which was nice because it would have been buffet style otherwise.

We were just getting close to finishing our meal when Sophee patted my arm to get my attention. "Joshua, you have made me wait long enough, Can we leave?"

"Okay, Sophee," I said with a smile as I slowly stood up. Figuring out that she wanted to be alone now that she had married, it was not a stretch on my imagination. Her people bond then mate or as she calls it share love. The Sooul are safe, we are married, I guess now that there are zero obstacles she wants to complete the bond. I am really okay with that!

Since Hyun was good enough to explain their customs to me I left Sophee with Shoran and walked over to the table where our parents sat surrounded by Sooul. In a commanding voice I speak loudly to Mere.

"By my standards I have married your daughter, by

yours we have bonded and now will mate. Deliver her to my bed!"

As I turned to leave, Steve and Mike rose to cover my six as we walked out of the mess. Good times or bad, my best friends always have my back. Since I don't have a father to escort me to my home as per the Souls customs, if I were a betting man Hyun had told them to walk me to the cabin.

Had I have stayed for a minute longer, the reactions would have been priceless to view. Mom and Granddad looked shocked while every Sooul—including Sophee—had big happy grins on their faces. I bet the cooks and staff manning the buffet would have been surprised as well.

My friends escorted me to my cabin.

"I am not inviting you in for a drink as I have other plans." I said with a smile.

"Congratulations pal, she's a keeper." Steve said.

"Be safe." Mike laughed.

They turned back down the hallway and headed back to the party.

* * *

Mere could see the look surprise on the Chandler's and Caroline's faces when Joshua left. She focused a bit tighter on emotions and feelings—which seemed to be very puzzled at what happened. Placing a hand on Caroline's arm to get her attention Mere looked happily at her new friend. "Our Joshua has obviously decided to do the traditional Sooul announcement of their bond. Joshua has so much respect for our culture, we are fortunate to have him in our family." Mere stood. "Please excuse me as I have a daughter to deliver."

Hyun looks over at the Chandler. "Well, I need another drink; will you join me at the bar?" They leave Caroline at the table with Shoran's mom head toward the bar together.

"It is custom for the father to have a few drinks when his daughter leaves home and mates. Today is a joyous time for her, but a sad time for the parents as their daughter moves out." Hyun says as he picks up a mug of beer. "We would still see her a lot but her bond in now with her mate."

"Hyun, my friend, what you don't know of humanity is that families join when our kids do." The Chandler, picking up his own mug, taps glasses with Hyun.

Mike and Steve returned to the mess and see the two older men standing at the bar. Quickly they moved to join them for a drink. As a joke Steve started sobbing and hugged Mike. Chandler shook his head at the spectacle while Hyun just smiles as all he can sense is humor.

"Josh will never need us anymore," Steve wails hysterically.

Mike pats his back. "Well, they have to leave the nest sometime…"

The Chandler and Hyun burst out laughing so hard they had to set their drinks down so they wouldn't spill them. The Sooul, seeing the two Gunmen making jokes about losing their friend to marriage, smiled as well. It seemed fitting that their Joshua, who liked to laugh, had friends of a similar nature.

* * *

After hearing Joshua announce the bond in the traditional Sooul way Shoran jumped up to grab Sophee in a huge hug. Sophee's joy and happiness radiated from her. Shoran was hugging Sophee tight enough to cut off her ability to breathe, but Sophee didn't mind. She was sensing Shoran's pleasure that her friend had found someone to bond with.

"When you are able to visit me, I want all the details," Shoran whispers to Sophee.

"I don't know how long humans take to mate." Sophee blushes and pauses for a moment. "But knowing Joshua and how he solves all issues I imagine that I will not see you until tomorrow."

"I want details…" Shoran says again. "And soon."

Mere approached her daughter's table, walking past many smiling Sooul. She could sense that everyone found joy in the fact that Sophee found a mate in Joshua. Sophee smiled widely as she waited for her mother to take her and present her to Joshua. Mere moved slowly showing restraint but enjoying the emotions from her daughter. On hearing the end of the conversation, Mere laughed. "I don't expect to see them for at least twelve hours if Joshua is the male we suspect he is."

Sophee ended the hug with Shoran and took her mother's hand.

"I am ready mother." Together Mere and Sophee thread their way past their friends. They left the mess hall at a measured pace. Sophee was quiet and Mere decided that small talk was needed to help Sophee level her emotions and to help relax her.

"Their wedding ceremony custom was nice, and Joshua took it very seriously," Mere said.

Sophee nodded. "My Joshua told me he would marry

me and do things right. I am happy we didn't have to wait until we get to our new home."

"It would seem to me that our Joshua has been talking to some of our people."

"Mom, my Joshua is a planner. He planned on beating the Gham, he planned on bringing us to New Harvest, and he planned on making me his wife. I know he has thought about tonight a lot. I will be very surprised if I am not his only focus for a while."

Mere looked at her daughter's bright red face and smiled. "You would know him best. I give up trying to figure him out."

* * *

I watched my two friends walk away laughing and talking. To be honest I was a bit nervous, not because tonight is the first time but I hoped to make tonight the special time Sophee had dreamed about. I undressed and hung my dress uniform up. Since Mere is supposed to deliver her daughter to my bed I get into the bed and cover up as per their custom.

Sub-vocally I address Vicky, "Weird custom of the male being in bed and having the mother actually tuck her in with him, eh Vicky?"

Vicky sub-vocally communicates with me, saying, "It makes sense a little because the Sooul share a lot of themselves with each other. Sophee's bond will be with you now and Mere will ensure she passes her daughter to someone deserving. If you were not in the right frame of mind as being more excited about mating than the relationship Mere would not allow Sophee to stay with you. You would have to be counseled before Sophee would be brought back."

I chuckled at the thought of being too horny for a wedding night.

"I am now going passive for the next couple days and do not wished to be disturbed." Vicky said, before going silent with a small beep.

Vicky going passive made me feel a little weird but she would be monitoring my health and would know what was going on at all times. It is the burden of Gunmen never to have total privacy. I never wondered if she would be jealous or upset. Either way I would be happy to take some privacy for a few days.

I laid there for ten minutes just chilling knowing that the love of my life was coming to be with me, just me. Sure Sophee is as eager to have love or mate as they call it, but to me this is one of the most important times in my life. I calm my inner thoughts and excitement to a point where I only think of Sophee's needs. By concentrating on the protective emotions and caring I prayed that Mere would sense the profound love I have. I continued to mentally explore our relationship before Mere brought Sophee in. Sophee seemed a little nervous but had a very serine smile. I smile inwardly because her small movements did not seem as graceful as they normally do. Mere's happiness for her daughter is evident by the way she smiles and has tears at the edges or her eyes.

Without speaking they walk to the end of the bed before coming to a stop. Mere unfastens Sophee's gown and helps her undress. When Sophee is naked, she remains standing and her mother picks up a brush off the vanity table. Mere then starts to brush Sophee's long hair. Sophee only looks across the room and doesn't meet my eyes as her mother prepares her. I wonder if this is part of the custom; not looking at the prospective mate while they sense my feelings or emotional content. Sure hope they find me acceptable because I would hate to have to fight Mere if she decided Sophee wasn't in a good place. I think with an inward laugh. Mere finished the back of Sophee's hair and moves forward around the front almost blocking my view. I know the nudity doesn't bother the Sooul but it still seems odd to me that Sophee would just stand there like it is any other day or time. I see Sophee give a slight nod to Mere. I guess the atmosphere is good for bonding because Mere lifts the covers so Sophee can slide into bed. Sophee lies beside me on her back while her mother tucks her in. Mere gives a kiss to Sophee's brow, and with a huge smile she walks out closing the door.

Once the door closes I dim the lights with remote and lay back down beside my wife. Sophee doesn't move, she just patiently waits for what comes next. I decide to start by asking Sophee to roll on to her front. We have the rest of our lives together and I am in no mood to be less of a lover than she deserves. Since she hasn't said a word yet Sophee might need a massage to relax her. She smiles hesitantly and then complies with my request. I also kick the blankets off because Sophee is not shy and I had adjusted the room temperature to a state where we would not need them. Sophee is still dead silent so I rest my hand on the small of her back.

"Nervous?" I ask.

"A bit my Joshua." comes her honest reply. "I have waited

for this my whole life. I never thought I would bond, and to be in this moment fills me with happiness."

"Don't be nervous—" I start rubbing her back in slow circles—"we will take it slow."

"What if I don't want to?"

With that she pushed me over on my back and threw her legs over my hips. I reached up to caress her soft skin while her hands were on the sides of my face; her eyes sparkled as she gazes into mine. Sophee lets out a small sigh as we finally join each other. I wait allowing her to set the pace, and see her grasp at the momentary pain, leaning forward she kisses me. There were tears in her eyes and even though Vicky said we were compatible I wondered if I had made the correct choices. I hold her gently not moving for a couple of minute until she began to slowly rock back and forth. I let her control the tempo, as I didn't want to cause any discomfort to her. The open expressions of pleasure and wonder that flashed across her face were pretty much the highlight of my life. She shuddered twice and fell limply on my chest. Kissing her tears away and holding her close I murmured softly that I loved her. I then started moving slowly and Sophee's eyes widened as she realized that I was still functional.

"My mom did not tell me about the physical pleasure." Sophee said softly. 'Is it the same for pure humans?"

Giving her a kiss as I slowly started to move with her I thought about her question.

"Ask me again in a while my love as I am busy now?" I said attempting to give her serious look. I took some time making love slowly and passionately with my lovely wife and we both finished what she started together.

I don't think the information Sophee got from her mother about making love was anywhere as complete as it should have been. When she climaxed the second time her face wore another surprised expression that was priceless.

Not knowing what she was thinking but seeing the totally happy blissed out expression made me feel that whatever I was doing must be okay. Afterward we lay on our side facing each other with our arms around each other. Sophee had her leg wrapped around mine. We both laughed when Sophee said; "I don't ever want to leave this bed."

"Your mom never told you about orgasms?" I asked hesitantly.

"She told me that the emotion aspect was overwhelming but never said anything about the physical reactions I was having. Do all human females experience this?" Sophee pulled back a bit to look into my eyes as she asked.

Thinking about what I know and have read I decide to not explain that some do, and some don't. Who wants to be a know it all?

"You will have to ask my mom when I am not around because I honestly don't know or care. I only care that you do….." I said with complete honesty.

We snuggled for a bit, spent awhile kissing and just touching each other and then she decided to have more of the same. She pushed me on my back and had her way with me. I asked her afterward if that was the way her people made love with the woman on top or something she wanted to try? Not that I was Mr. Experience or anything but I had never figured that as the go-to position.

"Mother told me it would be the best way to start. It

allows me to be in control, and there was the concern about your size."

"Glad I missed that class," I said with a laugh.

"Would you like to join me in the shower?" I asked

"Try and keep me out." Sophee said with a very serious expression on her cute face.

I scooped her up in my arms and carried her to the shower. Under the warm spray I washed the sweat of from her body and she returned the favor with me. We ended up with her legs around my waist, my hands supporting her back as we made love standing under the warm water. I hoped the water heater in my cabin was on demand type because if it wasn't the rest of the ship's crew and passengers might get upset with us using all the warm water. When we were sated I quickly dried off then wrapped Sophee in a huge fluffy red towel that my mom must have stocked because nothing looked like standard starship linens. The quiet demeanor of my wife and the fact it was past 0300 hours told me that she was exhausted so I gently dried her hair then carried her back to bed and gave her a slow soft massage until she fell asleep.

I lay there looking at her slim back and cute butt for several hours just thinking how lucky I was. How this woman, this perfect soul was mine forever. I knew that I should sleep as well but today's events had me too keyed up to sleep right away. I thought about the family we would have and hoped that I would be a good father to my future children. I pulled a single sheet over my new wife and put my arm over her before I slept.

* * *

I woke to light butterfly kisses peppering my face and neck. Without opening my eyes I say,

"Good morning" to my wife.

Sophee's kisses and caressing continued as she was doing her utmost to evoke a reaction. I opened my eyes to see her smiling face. Again her breath taking beauty strikes me.

"Opening my eyes and seeing you make this the best morning in my life." I said while totally enjoying her method of waking me up.

I would not call her attempts to invoke a physical reaction amateur, maybe inexperienced. Regardless she had me rather ready and if Sophee wants love, Sophee gets love.

"What methods do you like?" her soft voice murmurs in my ear. "Mother told me that you pure humans may differ somewhat from our norms."

"Two things sweetie, first I would rather never hear the term pure human as you are exactly like me other than a few DNA strands, okay?" I get a serious nod from my wife.

"Second, since my experience level is the same as yours we will have to figure that out together."

I laid her back and returned the soft kisses her face then neck. My attempt to simulate a reaction was working because I could feel her pulse quicken. I traveled the kisses down to her chest. My tongue moved slow circles around her nipple before moving to the underside of her breast. Sophee's breathing increased and she started to shudder again so I knew that my amateur methods were having the desired effect. My tongue reached between her thighs and found its goal; with a little gentle movement on the correct spot she was grasping my head, another series of shudders ripped through her body. She was laying spread out on the bed with her arms limp by her side, when I raised myself up and pulled her into my arms.

"That's really amazing Joshua," she gasps, trying to catch her breath, "but what about you?"

I took that as the sign I needed. Making sure my weight was support by my knees and elbows I pulled my wife to me. Sophee's legs locked behind mine and we slowly made love carefully because I wanted to not cause her any discomfort. Sophee giggled at my caution and restraint and gave back as good as she got.

* * *

Our needs were very simple for the next several days; there was no need to leave our honeymoon cabin. Our friends and family had to do without our company as we used the AutoChief in our cabin for meals and spent all of our time together. We made love frequently, slept when we were exhausted. We ate when we were hungry; Sophee enjoyed trying foods from New Harvest, and then we made more love.

I lost all sense of time. I didn't want to leave the cabin; I didn't want Sophee to put clothes on, and I didn't want to share her with anyone. Selfish, maybe, but I didn't know if my desire for privacy and the amount of time I wanted to have with Sophee was a side effect of the bond. As newlyweds we did not have to make excuses, which was good because I just did not care. An in cabin honeymoon was what I needed and I wondered if Sophee would like to go to a really exotic honeymoon on a beach somewhere. When I asked her about her wishes Sophee's reply was quite simple.

"Joshua that seems like a silly waste of time when we could be here making love."

You have to love the simple things. We talked a lot discussing our hopes and wishes. Sophee had no idea what she wanted to do as a job when she got to New Harvest to which I smiled and told her when we got there I would find something appropriate for her.

"By the way Joshua, I get the joke about white dresses now. Caroline told me about brides and as a symbol or purity they wear white." Sophee said when I mentioned again how beautiful she looked at the wedding. I laughed at her shaking her head at my joke.

I had to ask her about the way she always puts her hands on my face or behind my neck when we make love. Not that I had enough experience to know any different but I thought it was something maybe the Sooul did.

She was quiet for a second, and then asked, "You don't like it?"

I smiled. "Quite the opposite, it allows me to focus on you and reminds me I am being loved rather just performing a physical act. I know sex is wonderful, but it is also far more intimate than I ever thought it could be."

I was rewarded with a kiss for my honesty. When we talked I had to ask her more about the Sooul and their customs, needing to make sure that I was fulfilling all of her expectations. It was surprising to find out that woman on top or lying facing each other was usually the only way. Missionary, in the shower standing and what I did with my tongue were things she never heard of from her mother.

When she told me this I didn't laugh, but made more plans for her. I had downloaded the Joy of Sex and although I found a lot of the acts not to be anything that interested me, quite a few more positions did.

"All the Sooul talk pretty openly about love and their mates, but never in my life have I heard about the things you do." Sophee told me with a sly grin. "Who knew that New Harvest could produce such a skilled man?" I felt my face get warm and realize my wife made me blush.

"When I tell my mom and Shoran what it is like to love a non-Sooul--see, I didn't say pure human—they will be very amazed. I am betting Sooul men may come for advice hearing you have all these crazy methods of love making."

The warm flush I felt on my face showed my embarrassment. I would never tell her to please not talk about us because it is her people's way. Even though I am a private person I could never take that away from her.

"Mike and Steve talk about their affairs but not really about such fine details." I said.

"If anyone comes ever to talk to me I will refer them to my copy of the Interstellar Sex Guide." I replied with a twisted grin.

"Oh good, can I read it?"

"Sophee, I was joking, there is no such book that I am aware of. It is just that talking to you is easy, what we do in bed is ours, wherein you can talk about it and share details it is not my way. I would rather not talk about techniques and methods."

"Remember when I said honesty is good for your soul?" Sophee asked teasingly.

I played a lot of music for Sophee as she never tired of hearing my guitar, quite often she would be laying on the bed listening and then attack me when a song put her in the mood. Time was meaningless; our bond and spending as much time together as we could was my only focus.

Knowing that our families would expect to see us someday I wondered when our honeymoon would be interrupted but until then I was busy.

* * *

When the door finally chimed I had to look at the chronograph to find out what time of day it was. Fourteen-hundred, this day was half over and apparently so was our honeymoon.

"Yes?" I ask, after pushing the com switch on the pad by the door.

"Are you ever going to come out? It has been over four days!" my mother's voice says with a hint of amusement.

"Sure, I guess, but we can't be out too long," I reply. Sophee smiles as well at my reply to my mom, like me I bet she didn't care if we went anywhere.

"Your new parents-in-law, your granddad, and your mother would like the pleasure of your company for dinner in three hours." Mother says formally.

"Sure, Mom, we'll try and make it, see you then." I look at my bride. "We have time."

Sophee laughs. "Let's get dressed, so we can go for a walk before dinner."

I put on camo pants and a tee-shirt with regular running shoes while Sophee wore a little sundress with a pleasant little floral pattern, the thin straps allowed her shoulders and neck to be bare. Even though the Sooul did not have any problems with nudity their former clothing style did not show much skin. Before the bond I thought Sophee looked like a young girl, now my perception was that of a very hot young woman. Of course she wore little flat shoes for comfort. Prior to our wedding I had never seen a Sooul wear a dress. I guess my mom and some of the other female crewmembers had the ability to program a replicator to create the wedding dress and the clothing Sophee wore now.

"You look beautiful." I said when she was ready.

Sophee smiled and reached up to give me a kiss; "I will reward your kind words later."

I took her hand and we left the cabin together. We did not hurry or walk with purpose, felling no need to rush we walked the quiet hallways. The ship seemed much quieter than usual with less people around other than the occasional crewman.

"Vicky," I say out loud, "please find out where dinner will be."

"General mess," she answers abruptly.

I almost pause for a minute at that. Vicky has always been polite and talkative. I wonder if she is feeling hurt or a bit jealous of Sophee.

"Vicky, are you mad at me?" I sub-vocalize the question.

"No, this is your time." Vicky says; "Enjoy it sir."

When we eventually reached the mess the majority of the Sooul, my friends, and family were there. Mere rushed up to hug her daughter, asking if she was well. To Sophee's credit she didn't blush but took her mother's arm and walked away whispering away into the older woman's ear.

I would have liked to know what Sophee said that made Mere's eyes go wide and cause her to exclaim, "Truly daughter?"

Sophee grinned, pleased with herself, and walked back to my side as Mere stood looking at me in wonder. Mere then walked over to a group at Shoran was sitting with and sat down. When I saw her talking to the other women I knew instantly that they were talking about us. Pretty soon I saw the ladies start glancing at me and smiling. I could feel my face get warm under their scrutiny. It was obviously happy hour because the food was not ready yet so we went over to get a hug from my mom. Granddad put his hand out for a shake and looked totally relaxed. My mom grabbed Sophee in a really tight hug; I was so pleased to see they got along so well and so quickly. After exchanging a few pleasantries Shoran came over and gave me a hug. She hugged Sophee and then grabbed her hand to lead her away to a group of waiting females.

Steve seeing me standing alone pulled me over to the bar, although his motives were not as inquisitive as that of Sophee's friends. He handed me a glass of single malt and gave me a cheers. He knew I would not be talking about the last several days like the Sooul do. I waited for what smartass thing he was going to say in silence.

"I think your Granddad thought it important to have a meal that you could finish since you left so abruptly at your reception," Steve said. "I was sad because I never got to make my toast."

I laughed and told him, "Sophee just wanted to leave; I guess the Sooul never were told about receptions after weddings. Since she thought she would die before ever meeting somebody to bond with she was tired of waiting."

"Usually the mating would have happened immediately after bonding. I made Sophee wait until I fought the Gham because I did not want to have my mind on anything more than the Gham's destruction and then of course I had to heal. When we had met my requirements she simply wanted to complete the bond." I looked my friend straight in the eye. "And complete the bond we did!" We bumped our glasses; "I am now done talking about the honeymoon."

Mike left the group of people he was talking to and joined us at the bar.

"Four days, Josh, really? Don't you think that raises the bar too high for us mere mortals?"

"Maybe I am trying to set a precedent, this way if you guys get close you may not disappoint any more women in the universe."

Steve laughed at my statement. "I have been talking to Shoran a lot lately, she is nice. I have had really has a hard time getting past the young appearance. Sure she is an adult but dude, if you put a pair of braces on her I would get arrested on Mars if I was with her.

"If you bond, she will not appear young anymore," I advised, "At least in your eyes. I still consider Sophee as petite, but now I see the woman and her beauty rather than her teenage appearance. I find the change odd, but reassuring. Heck, on our wedding night I still thought am I doing the right thing? After bonding and mating everything is perfect."

I look around to ensure our conversation is still private. "If you develop a relationship and get to the mating stage with Shoran remember that they will need a cautious lover because of their body size at first."

An evil grin appeared on Steve's face, I knew I was about to receive a vicious verbal slam. Steve's grin mellowed as my wife joins us and took my hand. He probably tucked his insult into vault for use at a different time.

"Are you telling Steve and Mike how we mated?" Sophee teased.

"No dear, I would never share my techniques with untrained people." I said smiling because I know damn well that they are as curious as the Sooul women.

"Your Grandfather requests we take our seats because dinner is ready Joshua." Sophee says. We move thru the mess and take out place at the parent's table.

Granddad had some more wonderful prime rib cooked with oven roasted potatoes and vegetables. Sophee enjoyed the prime rib and asked the names of the various vegetables. I think she was trying to find out my favorites for future reference. The meal was another amazing success with my new family. I smiled at the realization I was still enjoying the company of a group now. It did not matter if it was just Sophee and our parents or the additional other one hundred and eighty seven.

At the end of dinner Granddad stood up and everyone fell silent. The Chandler raised his glass. "I have few things to say. Sophee, you are an amazing, kind, beautiful person, welcome to our family. Josh you have always been a bit of a loner, now that you have married I can see what a fine man you have become. Treat Sophee like gold or I will give you a clout upside the head."

Even as Granddad said that, he was smiling and not serious, Sophee could read his emotions and knew that it was paternal love.

"Ladies and Gentlemen please join me in a toast to Sophee and Josh, may you have a long happy life and bring me many grandchildren." Everyone took a drink while Granddad waited. "Hyun and Mere welcome to our family, thank you for having such and wonderful daughter to share Josh's life with." Then he took a sip of his wine before looking at all the people from Sooul. A very kind and thoughtful expression was on his face when he addressed the whole crowd.

"I have heard often in the last week how you refer to *your* Joshua. He is mine too, so welcome to my family."

The Sooul clapped loudly because they knew that the Chandler was serious about his feelings, going to this new planet became a bit less of an ordeal when you were with family.

With a wave Granddad sat down. I was surprised that he actually said that much. He was known for being a man of few words; maybe he is getting more emotional as he aged.

Hyun stood, "Thank you Chance my friend, Caroline thank you as well and welcome to our family." Hyun took a long drink before addressing me.

"Joshua, my son, you have delivered my people from the darkness. Sophee is fortunate to have bonded with a man such as you. I am so proud that you have joined our family. My daughter looks no worse for the wear…"

Okay, so I can still blush. My face feels like is a few hundred degrees and I bet it glowed red.

"…so you and I will have to talk about this thing you do with your tongue. The girls can hardly talk about anything else." Hyun then sat down with a smirk knowing he had given me a good hit. It is a great thing when people who had been brutally treated can find humor in life.

With a bright red face I shot a glance at Mom and

Granddad, and they did not look too shocked. Actually Mom blushed and giggled like a schoolgirl with Mere while Granddad simply put his hand over his eyes and bowed his head. Steve and Mike looked at each other and then actually fell off their chairs as they were laughing so hard. If I had not heard them laughing I would have thought they were having a seizure. The Sooul really did not know what was so funny but they could sense my friend's amusement and smiled along anyway. I had to wait a few minutes until they regained their composure and were able to sit back on their chairs. They were as red faced as me. I stood, looking around as I waited for everyone to regain his or her composure.

"Four weeks ago I was alone. Now I stand before you a bonded or married man and I am blessed. Sophee, if I live forever it will not be a long enough time with you. Mere, Hyun; I will always cherish Sophee and protect her and our people with my life. Mother and Grandfather thank you for coming for us and I want you both to know that I plan on a big family and will continue to work on it." I grin wryly at my two friends; "Sex classes start in the afternoon tomorrow."

I reached down to my beautiful wife and pulled her gently into my arms for a gentle kiss and sat down to very loud clapping and cheers. *Hope the cheering for my kiss with Sophee.*

"I was joking about classes Sophee." I said, to ensure she knew that I was joking about my new skills with my friends.

* * *

We had few drinks and talked with almost everyone there. Sophee was always at my side except when Shoran and a few other ladies would steal her away to find out more about our love life. Every single time she talked with her friends I would get speculative glances from the girls and knew I was turning red again. Steve, Mike and Granddad enjoyed my general discomfort.

"You know Josh, maybe if you were not such a stud you would not be the object of such scrutiny." Steve said smiling at the giggling women.

"Bloody chronic over achiever." Mike quips.

"Just be glad they met you first Josh, because I was quite the player when I was younger." Granddad says then gives my friend cheers with his mug of beer. "It's a Garvie thing."

I shook my head at my grandfather, this is the most relaxed I have ever seen him.

Captain Grey came in through the open hatchway and made a beeline straight for us. Slightly out of breath he addressed me.

"We received a call from a mining colony at Bashar. It just got invaded by a small swarm of Screamers. Casualties are high and they are begging for support."

Steve and Mike instantly got to their feet leaving their drinks and moved closer in for an order, which is a typical response for Gunmen. The Sooul went dead silent reading the serious emotions from the three Gunmen.

I nodded at Granddad as a signal to say I have this.

"Plot a direct course, best possible speed Captain. Send a message that there are three Gunmen on board who can deal with it."

I look at Mike and Steve who now had their game faces on. On seeing me study them they come to full attention because the 1st Gunman is about to set a battle plan. In the brief second between them coming to full attention and me speaking you could have heard a pin drop.

"Gentlemen, full combat armor, edged weapons, and be ready by 0600 tomorrow. The briefing will be just before launch."

Steve and Mike throw me a picture perfect salute and leave the mess without a word.

I turn towards Sophee to explain what is happening. Her eyes are wide and tears are rolling quietly down her cheeks. She stammers, "But we just mated…how could you leave me?"

I hate to see Sophee so upset and know that I need to calm her down. Looking to my family I say, "Please excuse us." I gently pick Sophee up in my arms, and I take her from the mess hall. Sophee's arm was around my neck as she buried her face into my chest as she openly sobbed. When we get to the cabin she is still crying. I sit her on the bed and kneel in front of her gently taking both her hands in mine. Tears are still flowing as I look compassionately into them.

"Screamers are only dangerous like small eels, when you are prepared they are not an issue." I said in a very kind voice. Sophee knows I didn't consider the eels anything like a battle or fight.

"We protect humanity. I could not live with myself if people were dying and I didn't help. What kind of man would I be?"

"I am not ready to die yet and need more of your love." Sophee's voice shakes.

"Now?" I ask, "Or before dinner tomorrow when I get back?"

"I have just gotten used to the idea that we are not

going to die. If you die fighting these things...?" She asked breaking off the sentence with a sob.

"Last time a swarm of screamers landed I took them out in two days by myself. I was alone and never got hurt. There are three Gunmen here now; it will be a walk in the park."

"Truth?" Sophee asks with a cautious smile because she can sense the honesty of my statement.

"I cannot hurt myself without inflicting pain on you, and I promised your dad I would care for you. But let's talk about screamers later; I have plans for you now."

Maybe tomorrow before dinner as well?" she asks with what could only be described as a flirtatious grin and raised eyebrows.

I guess I could say that it was a great night; Sophee decided because I was taking control of a difficult situation tomorrow she would take control in the bedroom tonight. I was okay with that.

* * *

Screamers are nasty creatures. Their eggs are launched into orbit to float in large clusters. When a comet or shooting star passes near a pod the gravitational forces can get the clusters moving. Passing starships with a warp fields can also break them from orbit or even cause them to reenter an atmosphere. Once moving in space they continue in a straight line until the gravitational force from a planet pulls the pods into the atmosphere. The heat from re-entry burns off the protective shell causing the pods to hatch when they land. They start life as a small voracious predator and grow quickly to full height when they get enough food.

Adult Screamers are up to five feet tall bipedal, and have

a single arm that comes from the center of their back and curls over their head like a huge scorpion tail. Instead of a hand or a stinger the arm is tipped with a nasty set of claws. Their muscles are very dense which explains why these creatures are so incredibly strong. The bodies are uniformly dark grey in color with occasional darker blotches that allow them to blend in with shadows. As an ambush hunter they need to be invisible until they can trap their prey with the power of the clawed arm. Screamers prefer to eat live animals with their small, viciously toothed mouths. They also emit a really high-pitched noise which sounds like a continuous scream that never winds down. The sound is so shrill and at such a high frequency it causes mammals to go catatonic, which then allows the screamers to feed on their victims.

Regular hearing protection will not stop the sound from incapacitating a person, so Gunmen need to wear a very special type of helmet when fighting screamers. The battle helmet has an organic nullifying frequency absorbent pads which dampens enough of the noise to stop us from passing out. Electrical systems such as weapons also malfunction due the frequencies resonance, so rail guns and lasers or anything with a power cell are useless. My rifle is useless due the low rate of fire. Screamers in groups herd up and try to overwhelm their food sources. An automatic rifle would be fine, but there are only a few hundred rounds of ammunition and not enough time to fabricate some more. My handgun being mechanical will be just fine.

"Vicky, give me an available ten millimeter ammo count please?" I ask sub-vocally.

"Eleven hundred rounds," she immediately says.

I lie in bed with my wife curled up to my side and think; *should I wake her or let her sleep?*

"Vicky, please have Mere and Shoran woken up. Ask them to come to my cabin at 0500 in order to stay with Sophee until I return as she might have a problem staying calm when I have work to do."

I get out of bed quietly trying hard not to disturb Sophee. Once I find my way to the closet I softly close the door before turning the light on. I dress myself in a regular battle suit and then some light combat armor which may help if the screamers try and take a bite out of me. An empty ammo harness goes on over the armor.

I pull my sig and holster off the rack, Steve had returned it to me after cleaning it. Cycling the action a few times to check smoothness of the gun was really unnecessary but I am a creature of habit. The holster clips on my belt then the loaded weapon drops in comfortably. Not knowing an exact number of screamers that await us I then grab my forty one inch Katanna off the wall. Only once before did I run out of ammunition and this sword is one hell of a nice backup weapon. I throw its sling over my shoulder and snap it in place. When I kill the light to come out of the closet I find Sophee sitting cross-legged on the bed watching me. She did not seem as upset as she was last night but I could tell she was concerned.

"Don't worry a bit honey, I have Steve and Mike with me to cover my back. Together we will be fine." I say before her emotions get out of control. Sophee worries but can sense that the screamers don't concern me a bit. If I keep my tone level, relaxed and upbeat hopefully that will keep her calm as well.

Checking the time I grab a long nightshirt and pull it over her head. "I really hate covering you up, but you are having some company." I said with a kiss to the top of her head. Just then there is a chime at the door. I stroll over to the door and open it admitting her mom and best friend.

"You have some visitors," I tell Sophee, giving her a smile. I walk back over to the bed to take her in my arms and give a lumpy body armor kind of hug and kiss. Sophee throws her arms around my neck and kisses me very seductively. At this moment I regret not being able to climb back into bed.

"We will be back before supper." I lower her back to the bed sadly breaking our embrace. "I do have a favor to ask… Can you make those seaweed rolls again? The ones you had made for me back when we were still on Sooul? I really liked them."

Sophee smiles weakly and murmurs, "Of course. It will give me something to do, so I am not worrying too much."

I give Mere and Shoran a quick kiss on the tops of their heads before heading to the door. "Thanks, ladies."

I walk out the hatch whistling and bump directly into Steve. Not sure if he had his ear to the door but knowing him it was a possibility.

"What's up?"

"Is there is still a problem? I saw Mere and Shoran go in and it's very early." Steve asks.

"Because of the mating thing, Sophee has not had enough time to be secure with my leaving. I thought it would be better for her if family was with her when I left." I explain.

Steve nods, and then asks. "Was Shoran worried about me?"

For a tough guy he seems a little needy. As my friend I am not giving him a break. I give a slow shake of my head.

"She knows that there are a lot of men available for her now and she doesn't have to make due."

I walk past him toward the shuttle bay with a grin on my face. I just love it when I can joke around with Steve. Either he is in the beginning of the bond or he desperately wants to be.

Steve follows. "Really, Josh, come on, did she actually say anything?"

As I am walking, I toss back a "No."

Steve sped up to walk beside me and I know him well enough to figure the questioning will continue.

"How did you bond so fast? I have talked to Shoran everyday and we are only just becoming friends."

"Maybe when I saved her from the eel it jump-started her emotions," I say slowly, thinking about what he asked. "I don't know for sure. My friend, I will tell you this Shoran did ask about you and wants to know everything that Sophee knows."

That information made Steve smile, happy that Shoran is trying to find out more about him. We get to the hanger bay and meet up with Mike. He is sitting on a pallet watching the crew prep the shuttle.

He looks at me, checking out my sword and pistol.

"Why can't we have handguns? Mike asks.

"Did you bring any non-electric weapons other than knives and swords?" I notice Mike is holding something that looks odd. "What the hell is that?" I ask.

Mike gives me a crazy grin and lifts up his hockey stick and kisses it.

"It is a carbon fiber hockey stick with a mono-edged blade."

Steve's mouth drops open in appreciation. "Cool! Got an extra one?"

Mike is quick to hand Steve the weapon he had, and then runs back to his cabin for his spare. I know both used to play hockey when they were young, but turning a hockey stick into a weapon is plain weird. At least they will also be carrying standard Katanna swords over their shoulders.

Most Gunmen like different weapons. My first choice is always chemical firearms, because of reliability, Steve tends to grab laser weapons and, usually, Mike likes to have a railgun, but hockey sticks? That is an entirely different thing altogether.

Mike comes running back from his cabin with an extra stick for himself. I wonder when and why Mike had them made. If we were not about to depart I would have asked his reasoning to create such a weapon. Not that there is anything wrong with them, I just wonder where he came up with it.

"All right guys, here is how we will play it," I said to align our battle plan. "I will go straight up the middle of the street with you guys on defense. I will use a handgun until I am out of ammo, and then join you two hockey players at slashing heads with my Katanna."

Both my brother Gunmen have a love of sport and adventure. I hope they are not planning on playing games with the screamers like trying to keep score on each other's kills.

"Let's try and get this done very quickly, so we're home early…That way you can impress Shoran with your battle stories, Steve."

He nods, puffs his chest out and strikes a heroic pose. "Oh, to be a hero."

We walk together to the assault shuttle. Our pilot is waiting by the hatchway.

"Lt. Summer, how nice it is to fly again with you." Mike says pleasantly before boarding the shuttle first. Steve shakes his head at Mike sucking up to the female pilot and boards the shuttle. I nod to the pilot and follow my team into the empty cabin. Crabbing a seat across from my friends I inwardly smile at the happy look on their faces. I know they both like a good fight and are pleased to get off the ship even it is to get covered in screamer blood. We all fasten of safety harness and wait as bay depressurizes. The shuttle vibrates then slowly lifts off the pad and heads out the landing bay. Once clear of the bay into the darkness of space the shuttle circles under the B.N.J. and the acceleration presses us into our seats as we quickly head for the landing site just outside of the town.

I key the the pilot through my helmet. "Lt. Summer, please drop the shuttle in as quickly as you can, if the screamers get a good focus on us you will lose power. When we leave the shuttle we will button up the hatch until the screamers are gone. They will affect the electronics and you may be without power for a while. If you stay inside, you will be safe."

"Yes, sir," she replies, "We will be landing in couple of minutes."

The shuttle swoops out of the sky to fly across the settlement at a high rate of speed. Lt. Summer activated the braking jets at the last possible second in order to draw the screamer's attention. Since they hunt by heat signatures or movement, which instantly made us a large "food" sign. And sure enough, they turned almost as one toward the shuttle.

The screamers who were filling the streets in the town had been trying to get into the closed up buildings, but refocused themselves with the intent of bringing us down. They turned their ugly faces toward the shuttle and directed shrill sound waves at us, but the pilot was able to swing behind a building. Once the blocked by the building, Lt. Summer, had just long enough for the shuttle to land before she lost all systems.

Mike manually bypassed the hatch's mechanism. Both he and Steve pulled the guards off the end of their hockey sticks blades. Mike opened the hatch for Steve to jump out first.

"Lock up would you?" Mike yelled as he bailed out after Steve. Together they started moving toward the oncoming hoard of screamers. I closed the hatch behind me and latched it. When I hit the ground I saw the two Gunmen slashing their way up the street. So much for me taking point I thought. Looks like my guys are having a lot of fun. I follow Steve pulling my handgun out of its holster. The screamers are moving forward in mass making Mike and Steve backpedal as they try to keep the hoard back by slashing through throats. Screamer arms, heads and various chunks mix with the blood which sprays over the entire street. The scene could be described as aliens in a mixer.

"Moving up between you guys." I say on the helmets comm unit. Everything seems to move in slow motion as my battle reflex mode kicks into high gear as I start head shooting. Twenty dead Screamers in twenty shots, a quick reload and I start addressing them again. I manage to reach out a bit farther than my buddies and we start pushing toward through to the center of town. In battle reflex mode my pistol seems slow as the action cycles with every shot. I notice a hockey stick flip out to the side to take the throat out of a screamer as is moves in from a side alley. I move forward of Steve and Mike as I am knocking down far more screamers than their blades are.

The noise of my shooting and our warm bodies brought in another wave of screamers that had been trying to dig their way into the closed up buildings. Our helmets, while keeping us safe from the screamers paralyzing tone, tend to isolate us. We can't communicate with anyone unless they have the same units. The screamers only seemed to be digging half heartedly at the buildings.

I could feel my gun getting quite hot from the amount of ammunition I was firing, so I holstered it and drew my Katanna. The sword would not reach out as far as the boy's hockey sticks but with my enhanced speed I was still cutting through many screamers.

Steve and Mike got a little annoyed with me on lead position and moved forward. Steve signaled they would take the lead and for me to cover their six. They proceeded to slash their way through the swarm trying to kill as many as possible.

I didn't want to encourage their goofiness, but those silly hockey stick weapons worked rather well. They increased the Gunmen's reach and kept them out of danger; at least they did up until Steve slashed through a screamer and got his stick caught on the corner of a building, leaving him temporarily unarmed.

And in those few seconds, dozens of screamers jumped

on him before he could draw his sword. He went down under the combined weight of the screamers and I lost him from view. Mike had his hands full with the amount of screamers that were currently in heading his way so I sheathed my sword and came up back with my now cooled sig. Steve should not be hurt too badly as he is wearing similar armor to me. Although it doesn't protect you everywhere it does protect vital areas of the body. I proceed to blast the living crap out of the pile of Screamers that had buried Steve under the intensity of their attack. I didn't have to worry about hitting my friend with a stray bullet as I crouched to fire above where he was laying.

"Steve is wounded, not severely; his A.I. is dispatching trauma nanites." Vicky said to me to keep me moving quickly.

I picked off the last few standing screamers with headshots. Steve was covered in dead bloody screamers. I saw him with his knife out stabbing the last screamer through its eye socket as it tried to find a place to bite that was not armor. I dropped to my knees beside him pulling the dead screamers off him. He looked like a mess with screamer brains and blood liberally coating every inch of him.

"How bad, Steve?" I ask.

Steve grabs my arm and I pull him up. He leans heavily on my arm and is favoring his right leg. "A couple of bites, I'll be fine." He says grimacing at the pain. He's a tough guy but I don't believe him enough to let it lie.

"Vicky, how bad is his wound?" I ask sub-vocally, examining Steve and looking to see where the screamer blood ends and his starts.

"He has three bites. Large open wounds the nanites are working on sealing off."

Steve turns and limps back toward Mike to start helping with the next wave of screamers. I can see three distinct holes below his belt over his buttocks as he walks away. *That's why he minimized the injury.* I don't laugh at all because it is not funny when your friend gets hurt or at least not until later when we are having a beer and his wounds are treated and healed.

Mike never stopped his attack, still slashing through the smaller group of screamers. I drew my sword again and continued with him. Steve knowing that he would not be as quick drew his sword and covered the area behind us.

An hour later we are thoroughly covered in screamer blood and looked a lot like Steve when Vicky announced, "That is the last bunch of screamers, I am scanning and find no more."

As soon as we finished off the last few living screamers, the three of us actively scanned for more, but didn't find any. I removed my helmet not needing the protection anymore. Mike and Steve were quick to follow. The tangy smell of fresh blood was overwhelming. The ground was covered with the slashed and hacked dead.

"How's your ass?" I asked Steve with a grin.

"Sore," Steve says with a laugh in return.

"Vicky, how many people are left alive here?"

"No human life forms detected in the town," she states out loud.

Mike and Steve look at each other, coming to same conclusion as me. If there are no human life forms on this planet, then who sent the SOS signal? Oh damn, the screamer attack is a diversion.

"Vicky, send a flash to Captain Grey. It's a trap." I turn to Steve, "Can you run?" All three of us simultaneously put our helmets on and activate the scanners.

Mike and I grab Steve and run, half dragging him back to the shuttle. Our pace was slower than we would have liked but Steve's wounds and the screamers bodies slowed us down. We got to the shuttle in a few minutes, the hatch was open and that didn't make me feel better. Lt. Summer was told to stay in buttoned up until we were done and she would not have disobeyed that order.

A male voice comes over the P.A. on the side of the shuttle; "Drop your weapons outside the hatch or the pilot dies."

With no choice I drop my gun belt and sword, I see Steve tuck a knife into his sleeve as he drops his. Mike stands clenching his fists in anger for a second before he complies as well.

Once all three of us are unarmed, we step away from our gear.

As we stand there waiting for further instructions, I hear a fleshy smack followed by a thump and a then muffled curse. Instantly is makes me wonder if our pilot is being abused.

Before we can move on the open hatch Lieutenant Summer sticks her head out. "Ship secure. Sorry, sir."

Feeling relieved that she is safe we enter the ship to find to find the pirate lying on the floor unconscious beside a hand grenade. It took a second for our eyes to adjust to dimmer lighting inside the cabin. Once they had, I could see that the right side of hijacker's head was damaged. He was a fairly large man, heavily scarred, wearing mismatched body armor. His helmet sat on a seat a few feet from him. Good thing he had removed the helmet before talking with us or he would not have taken as much damage when he hit his head on the hatch frame. From his ear to the center of his forehead had a U-shaped groove about and inch deep that was bleeding profusely. Typical for a head wound I thought. There was also blood coming out of his ear which did not bode well for the condition of his brain.

Lieutenant Summer had an angry expression on her face as she rubbed her elbow. "I was not armed when he came in. Had I not thought it would be one of you guys I would have been ready. He had the drop on me, sir; with a gun to my head I could do nothing when he took the ship. After he had taken control he took my personal weapon from the cockpit. He was fumbling with a grenade to throw out the door when he took his eyes off me. I jumped off the command deck and hit him with my elbow. He fell and smashed his head into the hatch frame."

"Thank you, Lieutenant." I said smiling at her verve. "Can you communicate with the ship?"

She pointed at the still knocked out hijacker. "He locked out the com. after he took the shuttle."

"Vicky, scan him please." I order. Hopefully the damage will not stop him from waking up. I need to know how many of them there are. His health doesn't concern me, if he dies so be it.

"With advanced medical aid he will live. If not, the hit will kill him shortly," Vicky reports.

"Can we get him to talk?" I ask.

"Not in his current condition and not without causing irreparable damage to him."

I look to Mike and Steve who both nod their heads to my nonverbal question; yes intelligence is worth more than a pirate's life.

"Vicky, what do we need to do?"

"If you inject him with the beta booster from the ship's aid kit it might bring him out…or it will burst the damaged blood veins in his brain."

The pilot went directly to the First Aid kit and brought it to us without being asked. She opened the case and searched briefly through the drug section. Once she found the proper drug she looked at the unconscious man and then at me. I can tell that even though she gave him a terminal injury she doesn't want to administer the drug that could finish him off. Putting my hand out for the booster let her know that I would take that responsibility. Without expression she opened the end of the pen style injector and handed it to me.

"Thank you." She said sounding a bit relieved that she did not have to do the deed. I gave him the shot to the side of his neck. The pirate's eyes fluttered for a couple of seconds as the beta booster did its magic. He started to focus on us and went stiff as he realized that he was in our custody.

As a Gunman I am sworn to protect people. What is that old line about civilization? People sleep comfortably in the beds at night because hard men stand guard and are willing to do violence on their behalf. Something like that, and it's time to get very hard.

"No threats, where are you from," I say in a voice that is plain and blunt.

I get no answer so pull my knife off my belt and wave it in front of his face. I stick my knife into his arm about an inch and twist it. The pirate's eyes open wider and he starts screaming like a banshee. Those dark spots that Sophee sensed are out in the open now. Neither of my friends would ever do something like this, I guess they have to sleep at night.

I remove the knife and put direct pressure to stop the bleeding on the wound. Once the screams die down I address the pirate again. "Again, I will ask a question once, where are you from?"

"Rockfall," he stammers.

"Mission?"

"To take the Boy Named Joshua and hold it ransom. Kill some passengers to show we are serious about the amount we want," the pirate said with a gasp.

"Why target a New Harvest ship?"

"If we don't do it soon the grandson will be back and—"

His words trailed off as his body arched upward, the seizure that gripped his body took total control of his muscles. The smell of urine followed. When his body dropped to floor of the shuttle his breathing had stopped. Before any of us could do anything his eyes turned red from the aneurism taking place. Not caring if he was actually dead yet I grab his limp body by one arm and dragged him to the hatch. Vicky said without aid he would die, being a Class One healer I accept her assessment and toss him out like refuse.

I will not waste another second with that trash. Lieutenant Summer looked mildly shocked by my action. By the blank expressions on the Gunmen's faces they could have cared a less about him.

"Get us to the Joshua ASAP," I order our pilot.

Mike looks over to Steve and then to me. "Battle plan?"

"Get into the ship, find the fuckers, kill them all, and then destroy Rockfall." I can barely control my fury at these pirates holding my family hostage.

Steve takes a second to think. "One, two, and three I agree with, but four seems extreme."

"Help me with the ones you can, and stay the hell out of my way for the other. You okay with *that*?"

Neither of the guys answers me, but rather looks at each other as if to say "Why's he asking. I say it again, *"Are you okay with that?"*

Steve finally replies, "What do you think, you goof?" He then turns to Mike with a pained smile. "Just because I don't agree with Josh doesn't mean I don't support him."

"I think he is trying to prove he isn't soft from being married and such by getting all tough," Mike replies before turning to me and adding, "You're acting like a knob."

"I agree with all four. They were going to sell the females off to slavers, me included." Lieutenant Summer says through gritted teeth from the pilot's chair.

"Lieutenant, get us to the ship quickly but fly the shuttle like someone who is not used to handling an assault vehicle." I instruct as I take my seat.

The shuttle makes it to the ship quickly. Vicky was able to mimic the hijacker's voice well enough to get us into the hanger bay when the pirates on the bridge unlocked our comm.

"Lasers and edged weapons only, I still have my sig and lots of ammo." I instruct as I move toward the hatch.

Steve seemed to be limping better by the minute by the way he checked his laser rifle and moved toward the hatch without help. I stood in the center of the hatch waiting for the green light above it to signal there was full atmosphere in the bay. I turned to my partners. "Zone attacks with as much violence and speed as possible." It is like a light switch being thrown, their entire demeanor changed and now three Gunmen were in battle mode. Hands tightened on weapons and the safeties were switched, muscles tensed to drive forward.

The hatch dropped and we charged out into the bay to find seven pirates facing us. By the stunned looks of surprise they were not expecting Gunmen to appear. In the second it took to clear the hatch and charge forward it was very apparent that their lives were flashing before their eyes.

Mike and Steve each dropped to a knee on the deck and serviced the majority of the pirates in the bay. With the pirates being headshot by my team I was able to line up on the one closest to me. Since his weapon was not in his hand capturing him was of paramount importance if we wanted any intelligence.

I cleared the ramp with one bound and charged straight at the closest pirate just as he pulled his weapon up to shoot. The pirate was pressing the trigger when I hit him with all my body weight in a running tackle. I felt a quick pain as the laser beam went through the edge of the fleshy part of my thigh, but it did not slow me up at all. With an arm sweep to the left I knocked the gun out of his hand and connected a knee to his groin, driving the air out of his lungs and collapsing him into a heap on the floor of the bay. I knelt with one knee on his chest to pin him. I pulled my knife and brought the tip toward his eye.

"Where are the hostages?"

I could smell urine; this clown was so scared he pissed

himself. The pirate was quick to reply, desperately hoping I would not remove his eye.

"Cargo Bay Two," he gasped, "Cargo Bay Two."

I wave for the other Gunmen to go. By now our pilot had exited the shuttle with her gun drawn. I pointed to the prisoner; she moved closer and aimed at his head. From the look in her eye I knew instantly that she would be okay guarding this scum bag.

"He's all yours," I said as I ran toward the doorway. In my wake, the only sound to be heard was a single bang. On retrospect I should have said; "He is your prisoner."

Tough shit, bad guy!

Each Gunman took a different route toward the cargo bay. Since most bulk cargo bays were directly in the center of New Harvest ships many passageways circled them. With lots of doors or hatches at different locations attacking from many vantage points would ensure that we had clear shooting.

"Vicky, synchronize us for entry, kill the lights one second before." I run flat-out to the farthest hatch. Steve took the hatch closest to the shuttle bay while Mike took the midpoint entrance. As I come to a stop outside the closed hatch I sub-vocally question Vicky. "How many hostiles are there inside?"

"There are twelve pirates spread around the bay. From the monitoring cameras inside the cargo bay most Sooul are sitting on the floor. Shoran is in distress and Sophee is pushing at a man who is trying to remove her clothes. You need to stop running, because your wound opens faster than I can heal it."

My blood boiled at the thought of Sophee trying to

protect Shoran. Vicky's warning about my leg is the furthest thing from my mind.

"Vicky, active Gunman comm; Steve, Mike ready?" I ask.

"Affirmative two." Steve replies.

Affirmative three." Mike answers.

"Go now!" as the hatch opens and I step inside.

"Lights," I say and they flash on.

The pirates are standing around looking confused when the lights blaze back on. The Sooul are mostly sitting with several big tough scary pirates watching them. The weapons the pirates have are all aimed at the hostages and not toward the doors. By the time they realized that they were under attack over half of them were already falling from receiving laser hits to their heads.

The pirate that was nearest to me was trying to rip the clothes off Shoran and stop a very pissed off Sophee. Sophee was trying to push him away and interject her body between him and Shoran which surprised me. Even though I know Sophee could not hurt anyone, I was amazed she would put herself into personal danger. Sophee's love of family and friends put any thoughts of self preservation out of her mind.

Steve entered from hatch to my right and Mike was at the far left entry point. During the first second of his entry Mike dropped to a knee and begun servicing his targets. Being a Gunman and having the training he does shows when he pulls up his weapon of choice. Single shots fired rapidly dropping pirates; I guess it was his luck that gave him the best position and clearest targets. Hearing the repeated whumps from his weapon I knew that he had most targets in the clear. Pirates were dropping like flies except the scumbag that was struggling with Sophee. Not having a clear shot both Steve and I charged the last remaining pirate. Steve's entrance was not as close to the struggling group as mine so I knew that I would be able to get to them first. Sophee continued to push at the would-be rapists face trying to draw him away from Shoran.

I headshot the pirates that were in my view knowing Mike would get the rest. Sophee was still blocking my shot of the pirate as she was now clawing at him. The would-be-rapist finally got hold of Sophee by the right arm and around the waist to partially block her attack. Being a very big man he twisted to build momentum and threw Sophee like a bag of grain toward a wall. I am in no position to catch her or even help but Steve is. Because he was slower getting to the pirate he adjusted his path and dove forward put himself between Sophee and her point of impact. I hear a grunt as he hits the bulkhead and catches Sophee on his chest protecting her from damage and getting the wind knocked out of him.

I see this as my path intersects with the pirate before he can recover from throwing Sophee. The pirate folded in half when my shoulder buried itself into his guts using all my speed and strength.

The tackle carried him a good thirty feet into a support pillar. This pirate was wearing body armor so the impact didn't have the effect I wanted. He is not dead or crushed. The pirate came off the support pillar like a trooper, hands up swinging at me. Since he was a rapist he had no weapons other than a knife on his person. I guess he felt it important to use it because he pulled the knife out with his right hand and silently made a come-on motion with his other hand.

Shoran's attacker held the knife loosely, swinging is

from side to side in very fluid arcs, low with the blade up. He smiled which alludes to him being happy to have the knife.

Knife fighter eh?

I step inside the short arc, my left hand traps his right wrist and I throw my right elbow into his throat. The knife hits the ground as his hand fly to grasp his damaged larynx as the pirate reels back. Having no time for sympathy I swing hard my right hand hard into the side of his face. The first punch broke something in his jaw by the loud crack. I followed up with a bunch more strikes and followed him to the deck as he collapsed.

For the first time in my life, I lost control. The rage at them trying to sell the women into slavery, the hijacking, trying to kill us let alone the attempted rape of a young woman made me into a machine incapable of reason. Mike moved in from my right side and grabbed me in a tight bear hug to check my rage.

"He's dead, everyone is safe buddy." Mike explained as I struggled briefly. With my eyes closed I took a deep ragged breath to calm myself. I opened my eyes and Mike saw my control had returned, tightened the hug for a fraction of a second to acknowledge my control as he met my eyes before releasing me.

What was left of the man's face was no longer recognizable, merely a flattened red and grey pulp on the floor. With blood and brain matter dripping off my gloves I wonder if that now maybe the Sooul will see the darkness in my heart. I have no sympathy for the pirate as he would have died anyway. The Sooul did not need to see me acting like a monster. I pray that they will see a man driven to protect them who will never stop until all enemies are vanquished.

After Mike let me go a few things were very apparent. The Sooul were in shock from the pirates, the attempted rape, plus seeing me lose my mind. Steve was helping Sophee up looking like he had the wind knocked out of him from blocking Sophee's flight. Mike was already covering Shoran with someone's coat.

"Vicky, get medical to this bay, stat please." I order.

Sophee found her feet and rushed to my side. She grabbed me and hung on like a boa constrictor. I peeled of my off the gore cover gloves and put my arms around her, although she was a semi state of shock from trying to defend her friend she did not react to my hands being damp from the blood. I felt relieved that she was safe and her presence touching me calmed the worst of the remaining rage I felt.

"Vicky, how many more hijackers are left on this ship?" I ask as Sophee squeezes a bit tighter worrying that it's not over. I motion with my hands for everyone to stay put and turn so Sophee is behind me, sheltered if any pirates try to retake the hold. I draw my handgun as Mike takes a defensive position covering the hatchway he entered through. From a slight noise behind me I surmise that Steve has done the same. We all had the same training; I need not to worry about them not covering the hatches properly. Vicky must have been scanning the ships entire interior because it took her ten silent seconds to respond.

"There is only one left on the bridge, sir."

Lovely, I think sarcastically, too bad they all were not dead.

"Pipe me to the bridge, Vicky."

The medic had arrived and was checking Shoran and her family. I saw several shots being administered, must be mild sedatives to calm them down. Steve eyes were on his hatch still but he has moved to put himself between Shoran and the entrance. He had recovered from getting the wind knocked out of him when he caught Sophee. The medic tried to check his wounds from the screamer's teeth but Steve was having none of that. You could tell that the pain from the bites bothered him by the way he shifted his feet as he stayed on guard. "Check the Sooul first," he said in a firm voice.

"This is Joshua Garvie, 1ˢᵗ Gunman. You have ten seconds to surrender," I said with a commanding tone.

I counted to about four when I hear my granddad's voice on the comm. "I have his weapon and his surrender."

It was surprising that Granddad was on the bridge and not locked up with the crew.

"I will be there in a minute, Granddad." I said

I looked over to Shoran, who was starting to dose off from the sedative.

"Steve, please take Shoran and her parents to the medical bay please. You stay with her, as you too will need treatment." Steve engaged the safety on his weapon and turned from watching the hatchway and gave me a nod. He dropped to his knees to carefully pick up Shoran. I look down at my wife, and then over at the rest of the women in the bay; "Anyone else needing medical please move forward." No one seemed to need anything more than a tissue for his or her eyes, which was a good sign.

"Do you want to come with me to the bridge Sophee?" I ask realizing she still hasn't let go of my arm yet. Her hand moves to the wound on my thigh.

"Joshua, you are wounded." She said with a shocked voice.

"Sophee, he will need a nanite booster to speed up the healing. The basic trauma units will repair the damage slower without more specialized base units." I smile because Vicky's voice sounds almost like I am being scolded. Leave it to my personal AI to tell on me to my wife.

Sophee's gentle hand touches my bloody thigh. "Mike, would you go the bridge please while we go to medical?"

Mike nodded; "I will go get him." I see him safe his weapon and take off at a jog for the bridge. To which I shake my head, I am his commander yet he obeys my wife without thinking twice.

"Vicky, where is everyone else?" I ask.

"All males are in Cargo Bay One. All female crew are in Cargo Bay 4, including your mother. I have released the lockout on the hatches and they are returning to duty with the exception of a dozen which will a take a bit of time to recover from the beatings they took from the pirates. Luckily the medics had already been treating them. There were no fatalities. Captain Grey was the only one left with the Chandler on the bridge." Vicky ends her report.

Thinking about it for a second we got off remarkably lucky with no loss in life.

"Mike now has the last pirate in custody, sending a medic to the bridge." She says.

"For who?" I ask hoping that my Granddad is okay.

"Mike injured the pirate."

"Seriously?"

"No sir, but you may want him patched up." Vicky surmises.

"Belay that request, let the prick suffer." I said without malice as Sophee's hand on my arm has a very calming effect.

I look at all the female Sooul who are starting to look calmer. The dead pirates spread out in front of them were obviously holding their weapons on them. They were held prisoner while their leader was trying to rape Shoran. What a wonderful way to welcome new people into humanity.

The pain in my heart for my failure to protect them exceeds what my leg feels. I never should have sent a team to deal with the screamers until I had more intelligence. Had we not left or had the shuttle bay been closed the heavily armed pirates would never have gotten on a ship where personal arms are not needed.

Out of the corner of my eye I see Steve start limping for the medical bay with Shoran. It figures that he would let no one else aid him.

"Hyun and several of the Sooul men arrived from Cargo Bay One at a run before Steve made it to the hatch. Mere was walking with her arm around Shoran's mom so both Hyun and her father put their arms around Steve to assist him getting Shoran to medical.

Steve refused to let her go, so they ended up helping to support him from each side which looked awkwardly comical. Shoran's dad could most likely sense that Steve was starting a bond and did not fuss about the big Gunman carrying her. The rest of the males and boys filtered quickly into the cargo bay and embraced their families.

"Would the New Harvest colonists please come with me to the mess?" I asked in gentle voice. I limped to the mess and could feel some blood still running down my leg.

"Not a word about my leg Vicky." I warned my A.I. sub-vocally, the last thing I needed was Sophee being more concerned about my wound. I pull aside the purser as we entered the mess in mass. "Make the mess into a family-friendly party. Music and kids videos; serve pizza, hot dogs, and treats; set up games and when Dr. Cliff is available he will be here as a counselor. Use as much resources and manpower you need."

"Yes, sir!" He gave me a salute, and started off to relay my instructions to the cooks and other people required for the necessary support through his com link.

Most of the Sooul followed blindly to mess not knowing if there was a reason for my request but trusting me. I guess my brief violent encounter with the would-be-rapist did not scare them away.

I clapped my hands to get the Sooul's attention before addressing the group.

"Today I screwed up; going to the planet without full intelligence was stupid. I am so sorry that the pirates scared you and assaulted Shoran and her family. I would hate to see you having to comfort one and another alone. The crew is setting up games, movies, music and lots of food for you to enjoy and to take away the stress from this morning. Dr. Cliff will be here as soon as he can and I know him to be an excellent counselor. If there is anything I can do please tell anyone and they will be able to find me."

Sophee looked up into my eyes; "Is this a human custom, I mean staying together after a bad experience?"

"No, I believe we heal when we are surrounded by love. I need a booster shot and to deal with a few things. Since there are people now arriving to set up the afternoon we can leave for a while. " I said.

* * *

We walked slowly to medical. Dr. Cliff looked up from gluing closed a security officer's eyebrow and shook his head at the sight of my leg. I looked around the open ward at some of the crew who had various bumps and contusions from being beat down by the pirates. I felt very grateful that no one was seriously injured. Shoran and her parents were not in sight and must have been in one of the private treatment rooms.

"Just so you know all the pirates that boarded the ship are dead except one. We have him in custody." I said loudly to everyone who was being treated. Dr. Cliff finished gluing the security officer's wound and bandaged his work. I got thumbs up as recognition from the officer as he left medical. Sophee was quite interested in the severity of the damage to my leg and Dr. Cliff was more than willing to tell her how bad it was before I got my shot of booster nanites. By the time my wound was dressed most of the crew were gone from medical. The suggestion by Dr. Cliff that laying down and relaxation would help my leg heal quicker was not something I was willing to entertain at this time. I got up from the treatment bed and put my pants back on. Sophee and I went to one of the treatment rooms to see Shoran.

Shoran was pretty shaken up, but her slightly bruised body would recover quickly. Her parents also were in a similar mental state. Upset about the incident and feeling that they are not sure they can trust people was written all over their faces.

Steve's ass needed four hours in the tank. Having several large chunks of flesh bitten off by screamer was not something that a nanite booster would quickly fix. The tank he was sitting in was monitored by a medical A.I., which programmed the nanites to rebuild the flesh and muscle structure using the gel in the tank as the building blocks. Had he just taken a booster he would have been healing for at least a week.

"Sophee, I have a few things to do." I said. Responsibility for the prisoner and the mess we made was going to occupy at least an hour or two. Steve looked briefly up from Shoran on hearing I have work and raises an eyebrow in question.

"Mike and I have this. You heal up and talk with Shoran."

I could see that his presence was starting to bring them around. As a Gunman, Steve had typical skills, as a man he was one of the more compassionate and decent people I have ever met. His courtesy for others was the one thing that almost got him rejected from the Gunmen's Element. Although he lacked viciousness when alone, he worked well on defined tasks and was better on teams. Vicky said that Monitor found he had the big brother type of personality, protective and brutal when necessary, but always compassionate to others plights. He was keeping the conversation light and engaging Shoran with his wit. Leave it to Steve to pretend he is untouched by horrific events.

Sophee looked up at me and gave a very tolerant smile. "I will help you with whatever you have to do."

"No! There are things that fall within my job description that you do not need to be a part of." I said firmly. "How about you sit with Shoran and her folks or go help with the kids?"

"Will you be long?" She asks, slightly put off by the firm tone of my voice.

"An hour or so my love. There is a pirate to deal with and a mess in the cargo bay." Being unsure if she was afraid of the pirates or worried about my leg I explained; "There is no danger now, with either the pirate or my leg."

Sophee looked up and gave me a knowing look. "Is this one of those –A Gunman's-has-do-what-a-Gunman-does moments?" She asked with a hint amusement.

I bent over to kiss her on the forehead; "I am frightened that you know me so well." I said with a laugh. Sophee decide to stay and went back into the room with Shoran's family.

Knowing Mike had the prisoner under control I decided to head to the shuttle bay at a jog. There did not seem to be a lot of crew wandering around the ship so I made pretty good time.

The shuttle bay was busy and some crew was just starting to clean up. I helped carry the bodies and load them on a huge cart, then told the cleanup crew I would take care of them. As I walked to the storage bay pushing the cart ahead of me I stopped.

Damn it Josh, get your head out of your ass. It hit me that I should be thinking about how they got here.

"Vicky, open a comm to the bridge." I said out loud as I continue to push the cart of bodies to the cargo bay

"Captain Grey, would you perform an active scan for the Rockfall Ship?"

"Yes sir, scanning now." Grey replied immediately

I only wait for about two seconds before getting the answer I sought. Whatever ship or shuttle brought them here would be armed and still have a crew. I do not want them to get away with this attack.

"Mr. Garvie, there is a small ship maneuvering away from the far side of the planet."

"Signal the ship that if it doesn't stop it will be destroyed. Plot an intercept course and bring us closer."

I pushed the load of bodies on the cart into the cargo bay. There were two crew members loading another cart with the dead pirates. "Gentlemen please leave them, we made the mess and will clean it up." I say to the crewmen. They paused for a second and the short stocky crewman shock his head. "Sir, the Captain ordered us to clean up the bodies."

Who can argue when they have orders from their boss?

"Alright guys, I will help." Together it did not take long to toss the bodies onto the two carts. Both of the crew worked robotically, they must had a lot of experience dealing with gore because they didn't bat an eye here. Once the bodies were loaded the crewman that told me about the Captain's order picked up a hand sprayer and walked over the bloody areas to target the stains. Before I could ask for a mop to help the second crewman walked over to me. "Thanks for the help sir, the nanite solution that we are spraying will clean up all the organic matter and the mess will be gone in an hour. Where would you like the bodies put or do we just jettison them?

"Hang on to them here, for a bit please." I said as I walked to the hatch. I walked calmly to the bridge nodding at several crew members and stopping occasionally to speak with any that looked distressed. I felt it was important to show compassion and steadfastness to prove everything was now handled.

An armed crewman was standing at the entrance of the bridge looking uncomfortable. "Is this the first time you have been armed?" I guessed.

"Yes sir!" He swallowed nervously red faced and took a breath. "We have had very limited training on how to handle weapons and I hope I don't screw up."

"I will speak with The Chandler and get some more training for the shipboard security such as you." The last living pirate was sitting on the floor of the bridge, bleeding from his broken nose. I raised an eyebrow at Mike who smirked.

"I told him to sit down, and you know how I hate giving orders twice!"

"Hear you, brother." I said with a sigh as one would think that a prisoner would know that Gunmen never say anything they don't back up. I knelt beside the bleeding pirate without feeling any traces of sympathy.

"I will only ask a question once." I said very softly. "How many crewmen are left on that ship?"

"One, just one and it is my kid brother!" The pirate practically screamed in a panic. "He doesn't know what we were doing; he is just a pilot."

He started sobbing, which surprised me. I never thought pirates would actually care that much about each other, even for family. Either this guy is a good actor or an anomaly in the pirate world.

"Please don't kill us," he begged, "This was not our choice. We were under orders!"

"My heart bleeds for you," I say, with my voice dripping with sarcasm.

"The ship has stopped and is waiting," Captain Grey informs me.

"Vicky, tie into the other ship's systems and tell me if this scum is telling the truth." I order.

"Yes, sir, one male human on the ship."

"Open comm, this is the 1st Gunman. We have captured your brother and killed the rest of the pirates who attempted to take our ship. Prepare to be boarded." I turned toward the Captain.

"Captain pull the ship along the side of them and detach a docking collar please."

I turn to back toward Mike to give an order, "We need—"

"You need to calm your wife and your people; I have this!" Mike stated bluntly, interrupting me. "Do you have any *specific* orders?"

"Can you take the bodies over to their ship with this scumbag?" I gesture to the bleeder. "I will have Vicky lock their navigation system on the planet Rockfall. This filth can smell their dead until they arrive home."

Mike nodded, and then roughly grabbed the pirate to pull him up off the floor. All the fight or resistance was gone from the pirate and he was pulled toward the hatch.

"Take a couple of ship security guys with you. Disarm any weapons the ship has and confiscate all weapons. If either of them so much as blink, kill them both and we will then destroy the ship." I look at the pirate. "Tell your leaders the 1st Gunman is coming for them at the time of my choosing."

***

By the time I got back to the medical bay things had calmed down. All the ship's crew that needed medical attention were gone. The bay was very quiet except for some soft voices from the private treatment room. I stopped at Doctor Cliff's office to get an update on Shoran and Steve. He informed me everyone would be fine in due time, just some cuts and bruises for the most part. Shoran's emotional distress was dissipating as she talked with Steve and Sophee.

"The Sooul are remarkably tough people, mentally," the doctor said, leaning back in his chair casually. "Their emotional maturity exceeds humans and she will bounce back quickly. I check up on her frequently but think Shoran can leave whenever she feels that it is time."

"Thanks Doc. Would you stop by the main mess and check on the rest of the Sooul. Not sure if they will need medicating to reduce their stress." I said.

"No, I don't believe that is needed," he said shaking his head. "Hyun and others told the medics that I sent that they could stay and eat with them but no one needed anything stronger than companionship."

I smiled at him because I knew how the empaths could be with each other. "Thanks again." Turning I walked out of his office and headed across the empty bay only hearing my footsteps in the quiet ward.

I gave a soft knock on the mostly closed door and heard "Go away unless you're bringing pizza and beer." I gave a chuckle and pushed the door open to find Steve sitting in a pan of green gel beside Shoran. She looked much better and sat on a chair holding Steve's hand as they talked. Shoran's parents had left her with Steve and Sophee to let the rest of the Sooul know that she was going to be fine. The mere fact she felt better around a specific Gunman alluded to maybe the beginning of a bond. I thought about saying something about the mistakes that were made but seeing her holding Steve's hand lightly and not being a bag of nerves or overcome with emotion stopped me dead in my tracks.

"Pal," I say, clapping Steve on the shoulder, "Thanks for catching Sophee!"

Steve smiled. "With my wounded leg, that was the about first thing I could reach."

Sophee spoke up from behind me. "Actually, he is annoyed that you got the pirate first."

I looked into Shoran's eyes. "I failed you. My promise to the Sooul was that they would be safe, but I didn't believe for a second the pirates would hit the ship when we were on board. Realizing that my general perceptions are not reality, I am going to change to ensure you and your people, never have to worry about Rockfall pirates again."

Shoran gave me a brief smile; "Thank you, do not endanger yourself or Mike."

Steve's mouth dropped open in surprise at the hack out of the blue from someone as sweet as Shoran. "But I…." he stammered and then started laughing. Shoran's brief smile came back in full bloom as she reached up to bump knuckles with me. "You two are very mean to Steve." Sophee said between giggles when she looked at us.

"I am glad to see you are felling better Shoran, Dr. Cliff says you can leave whenever you feel comfortable." I said. Her hand tightened subtly on Steve's but I saw it. Whatever happened she is feeling safe with him. Sophee noticed it too and her head tilted a little like she was trying to gauge Shoran's feelings.

"I am going to wait until his wounds are healed so he can walk me back to my cabin. Then we join our parents for evening meal." Shoran looked at Sophee. "You will be there?"

Sophee nodded once and and waved as we left the room. She took my hand and then waved at Dr. Cliff as we casually strolled out of the med bay.

"Shoran's humour is a mix of how close she and I are with the very beginning of exploring the bond process. If she bonds with Steve it will be a slow process because of her forward nature. She always likes to experience things fully before making final judgements." Sophee grinned briefly at thoughts she sensed from Steve before continuing; "I doubt very much Shoran will even sleep with him if there is no bond, you may want to warn him."

"He is an honourable man and if she says no he will whine like most men, I would hate to give him more intelligence than he needs." I grinned at the thought of Steve getting shut down by a girl; "A little frustration is a good thing for ones heart." I said.

"Well I did not like it!" Sophee said as she pulled me to a stop. She lifts her arms up around my neck so I wrapped my arms around her and picked her up. After a few kisses we continue on our way to the mess.

* * *

Granddad was pretty pissed at Rockfall, but didn't know if destroying the planet was warranted. I thought long and hard about the repeated piracy attacks that originated from Rockfall and decided after everyone was settled on New Harvest I would pay a visit and hit their leaders hard.

I had Vicky make note to check area reports and flashes from other planets about attacks. Maybe she could find patterns or information to help my mission. Maybe even find out who came up with these plans at least who it was that ordered attacks and intended to benefit from such actions. That particular person would certainly receive a personal visit from me. If Rockfall leaders decide to continue their ways in the future, we would have to revisit their continued existence. But until then, they could wonder when and where a Gunman would show up.

* * *

CHAPTER 14

It took a few more weeks to reach New Harvest. In that amount of time the Sooul colonists came to realize that, although the galaxy was not absolutely safe, they would have a lot of protection. The three Gunmen on the ship were always armed and whenever we had to go into an orbit to drop goods the ship went on alert. Some of the safer planets that regularly got goods from us found out that Gunmen were always at the transfer points and loaded for trouble. Word got quickly around that the New Harvest ship was serious about security.

The Sooul being used to the way the Gham had treated them let the pirate attack fade in their memories once they saw our continued vigilance in regards to ship security. Shoran recovered quickly and did not allow her personal her bad experience to define her opinion of humanity. She did spend a lot of time with Steve when he was of duty. Steve himself was trying to play it cool and not seem like he was smitten. You could tell that even though he pretended to be more concerned about all the Sooul and using Shoran as his eyes and ears with them it was a ruse or excuse to see her more often. Mike was acting the same way as usual, playing the field. Several times I saw him walking and talking with different Sooul. Sophee was surprised when I told her that he would wait until someone made advances on him as personally he was rather shy.

The Sooul seemed to blend in flawless with the crew, but I could tell that the cooks and staff at the mess would like to go back to running their own show. At least they got a break during this voyage with the Sooul women always ready and willing to help cook, serve and clean up. Captain Grey told the crew to catch up on personal studies and certifications in their newly found spare time.

Sophee was attached to me at the hip. She tried to tend to my needs far more than I required. It worried me that seemed to be her only concern and her that she was putting my needs above hers. Sure being taken care of was nice but she did not seem to have any other interests. I approached Mere cautiously on the subject to ask about her dreams and wishes. "My daughter thought she would never live to be where she is now. Since there is no real work on this ship for the majority of the Sooul she is happy putting all her efforts into her mate. We don't know how much time we will have to spend with our mates when we get to New Harvest and have to start working." Mere said. "Unless you are making emergency repairs or in medical most people work around eight hours." I think about it for a second how to explain it. "All Jobs have a value; some jobs have less than more technical or skilled jobs." I shake my head; if both of a mated or married pair works they can make much more money than a single person. This would allow them the travel on starships and explore other places. If one person works you will have a home and more than enough money to take care of all your needs including retirement."

"What about families with children?" Mere asks.

"Most women take time off to have and raise their babies. Usually until they are school age only one in the family works. You will also find that there is excellent daycare that safely watches and educates small children on New Harvest. My Great-Great-Grandfather set that up because he felt it was a right to have good daycare for your kids." I explained.

Mere accepted what I told her and asked me what I thought of Sophee working. "I imagine when we get to New Harvest I will have to explain my thoughts on this." I said not wanting to tell them about my family's wealth. Sophee would only ever work at something she loved and if raising a family was more important so be it.

I got into the habit of checking the progress of our trip and having a coffee with Captain Grey almost every morning. Captain Grey always seemed pleased when I would show up with a couple of mugs and ask permission to enter the bridge. Sophee joined us most of the time but only drank hot chocolate. Gunmen all are licensed pilots and we had many discussions about things we had seen or had to deal with. I always referred to him as Captain Grey on the bridge but Sophee only ever called him Robert. Apparently she had dispensation. As we got closed to New Harvest the mode on the ship was high, the New Harvest colonists were excited to get there and the crew mostly was excited for their cabins back.

Two days before we were due to arrive we talked with Granddad and decided to make an event of coming home. Normally the ship would just park itself in orbit and shuttles would disembark with and hour or two with passengers or cargo. Instead we planned to let everyone see our approach and share in the homecoming.

* * *

"Are all the people formerly known as Sooul here?"

"As requested, sir!" Vicky answers back through the sound system.

The mess hall is absolutely full of happy Sooul. Granddad is talking with Hyun, and my Mom is chatting away with Mere. It has been a long time since Caroline has opened up and it was nice to see. Meeting my wife and knowing not only that I was coming home that I was had given her some happiness. Since she was forming a friendship with Mere, helping her and Hyun to adapt to the new way of life had given something to do beside sit in a lab.

The entire projection bulkhead was free of all obstructions and ready to be used as a huge monitor. The cameras on the outside of the ship would take the images and run them in real time. I wait for Granddad to give the command to show the approach to New Harvest, but he just nods and smiles; "It was your idea, go ahead."

"Vicky, forward cameras please," I order.

Dark space flashes on the bulkhead then lightens and stars come in focus. The lights in the mess hall dim to give the most clarity to the view before us. Reactions from the Sooul were varied, some leaned in closer trying to see New Harvest while other looked at the expanse with wide amazed expressions on their faces.

"Vicky, identify New Harvest."

A white circle appears around a speck of light in the

darkness or space. The speck becomes a dot, and then the dot becomes coin-sized and continues to enlarge as our ship gets closer. As my planet grows in size, colors become focused; the blue of the oceans and greenish-brown of the land are now discernible. The one continent is long and fairly narrow as it circles about half of the diameter at the equator. About three quarters of the planet is water with ice only at the poles.

The Sooul were watching the monitor with wide eyes. The adults were dead silent as they took it all in. I would have been worried about the silence if their smiles and tears did not tell me what they were thinking. The ship continually drew closer to the planet until it ccould no longer be seen as a whole.

"Focus on Safe Haven, Vicky."

Vicky redirects a camera at the proper coordinates and the town of Safe Haven appears as a few dark spots. Once it was locked on the picture zoomed on until we would see the town. Most of the Sooul moved forward to see the town.

Eventually, buildings, their rounded curves and placement appeared making them look very cool as though they flowed up from the ground. The hotel near the beach was in view so I pointed it out. "This is where you will be living until more homes can be made."

It was a very impressive building, the long bell shaped structure had beautiful curves with regular beams inset at the ends and evenly spaced along the entire length. Hyun was looking at the building and took a guess; "The shape is for structural strength?" I smiled at his assessment. "You are correct sir." I said

Some of the kids present are looking at the amount of

waterfront and seemed nervous. Even without their gifts I could tell when they looked at the amount of water they felt nervous.

"There is a mesh shield with smaller openings than the one back on your old planet that protects us from anything big enough to hurt you," I explained. "The water on New Harvest is great for swimming." The kids don't really look convinced. "As soon as we get settled I will come down and swim with you." I said. Ankh smiled and gave me thumbs up. If I can convince him to try it the rest should follow.

"Vicky, please show the homes on the ridges," I ordered. The camera moved until it was near the base of the ridge, and then focused in tighter on buildings that look like pewter set into the rocks.

"These homes are secure and safe. Floor plans and interiors are up to the families, the outsides are metal, the windows are transparent metal and the frames are greater in strength than a starship hull. If the shields failed there are several backups with their own power supplies and generators. If shields were lost, the marauders could bash themselves to death trying to break in. On New Harvest you are safe."

"Everyone will be taken to the hotel where they will be inoculated against planet's growth enzyme and then go through the orientation class. Attending the orientation is a law here for anyone who has been off planet for more than six months. I would like to point out I will also be in the orientation with you, as well as the other Gunmen." I raise my voice. "*Welcome Home!*"

All the Sooul cheered and smiled as Granddad and I waited for the noise level to die down. Granddad addressed the New Harvest colonists as soon as he could be heard. "Joshua will be taking over all duties from me the Chandler effective immediately, so if there are any complaints or problems please feel free to call on him at anytime day or night!"

I gave a small chuckle and then look at Granddad. "Retiring?"

"Yes, I want to work on some new hybrids in the lab with your mom and actually work a bit less," he answers. "I am going to arrange some crabs for a huge picnic and barbeque on Landfall Day and then be ready to spend time with my future grandchildren. My life will be absolutely full." Granddad's smile expressed everything he is feeling.

"Some things might take time, but we will work diligently on the grandkids." I said feeling happy that Granddad felt good enough to pass the reins to me.

Once the ship was safely in orbit the call came to board the shuttles. The Sooul did not have a lot of personal belongs so it did not take long to start moving them to the surface.

The shuttles were meant to transfer about twenty passengers at a time, so the Sooul would have to go down in groups. I spoke with Lt. Summer and explained to her that no family groups or mates were to be separated when being transported to the surface. I know we generally had rules for full capacities and proper use of resources, but I felt it was important for them to be together.

All the Sooul were taken down by the ship's shuttle craft over a period of three hours. The speed with which they organized themselves and boarded was nothing short of miraculous. Leaving a planet where you were being slaughtered and an almost month long journey on a crowded starship had them eager to touch firm ground to restart their lives in a safer environment. There was a landing pad at the hotel and everyone disembarked their shuttles and was guided into the main banquet hall. The hotel staff was kind and compassionate and ensured families stayed together. Sophee, her parents and I went on the first shuttle and greeted everyone when they landed. Mere thought it would be good if I went down first and helped greet our new citizens.

Most of the Sooul stood around in the hotel's banquet hall and looked lost. I walked around with Sophee, keeping people at ease, until the doctor paged me.

"Joshua; Dr. Cliff here, can the medics start distributing the vaccine?" He asked.

"Would an extra vaccine adversely affect me?" I asked. The Sooul had not seen vaccines and if I went first they would know it was safe.

"No it would not, give me a couple of minutes." Dr. Cliff replied.

When they were ready I stood in front of the Sooul and asked for their attention.

"We all know that New Harvest has a natural enzyme that causes plants and animals to grow beyond normal boundaries. When we first came here it took a very short amount of time to see what was happening and develop a vaccine. Dr. Cliff has tested Sooul blood and said the vaccine is completely safe."

I noticed some kids were trying to hide behind their parents, and seemed concerned with the vaccination. Since kids are generally afraid of the unknown because it might hurt, the first thing that happened here should not be that experience.

"I had the hypo-spray first when I was a baby so I don't

remember it. I will go first with Sophee to prove that it doesn't hurt. The doctor gives me a quick shot. I don't flinch or move, but that didn't seem to calm the kids. They still were standing behind their parents and not coming forward.

Sophee went next; the doctor took a freshly loaded hypo-sprayer from the cart beside him and gave her the shot. She smiled when she didn't feel anything. Even if Joshua said it would not hurt it was something new.

Dr. Cliff nodded to her, "Your very brave Sophee, here is a treat." He handed her a chocolate sucker. You really have to love the fact Dr. Cliff was such a people person. I never would have thought to reward some for getting a hypo-spray with candy. Guess that's why I am not in the medical profession. The kids still seemed a little apprehensive, but now are eyeing the bin of chocolate suckers because they remember chocolate from their first taste at home. Before I could ask them to form a line the little guy I helped with the crawler meat walked right up to me. "Hi Ankh." I said. He gave me the second most trusting look I have ever seen and raised his arms to be picked up. I picked him up, and stepped closer to the doctor. Ankh never even looked at anyone but me. I heard the hypo-spray and Ankhs expression never changed. Before I set him down, the doctor handed Ankh a chocolate sucker. Ankh's smile was a mile wide, he showed everyone how brave he was and got a sucker. He was laughing as he ran back to his parents.

There was a rush of children wanting to get a shot so they too could get a sucker, but I had to pick each and every one of them up so the doctor could administered the vaccine. Once the children were done the younger ladies and teens came for their shots, they were quick to have me pick them up too. Even Hyo who was mated to Lian had me pick her up. I am certain my face had to be turning pretty darn red, either the Sooul females trust me and want to convey that feeling or they like seeing me get embarrassed. I wonder if there will ever be a time that I don't turn bright red. The second-last pair to come up was Hyun and Mere. My father-in-law took his shot and then waited for his mate, who had hopped into my arms like the children. Mere gave me a kiss on the cheek then took a chocolate sucker as well.

Sophee's laughter was at my flushed cheeks and sensing my embarrassment.

"I bet mom and all the women were enjoying your blushing." Sophee said as she dried her eyes.

None of the Sooul men thought anything was wrong with their mates jumping into my arms for their needles like the kids did. It's not like they cannot sense the love I have for all the Sooul, my embarrassment doesn't need to be sensed as my red face told them as much as my emotions.

The last couple in line for their shots was Steve and Shoran. They walked up to the doctor, and Steve had that look on his face like he didn't know if he should pick Shoran up or stand beside her. Guess his courage level was good because when he decided to, her arms flew around his neck. Shoran looked at Steve with a smile; "I don't know if you're as well qualified to protect me as Joshua?" Steve's smile never faltered. "I know, but right now it worried me because Josh looks very tired and I was afraid he might drop you." He said

Steve started to walk away with Shoran still in his arms, then turned around and went back. Once Shoran got her chocolate sucker from the doctor they joined us over by the projection screen on the bulkhead.

Sophee was still chuckling about me having to hold every girl and woman, but Shoran. Steve had a smug expression on his face when he put Shoran back on her feet.

"You don't have to settle for him," I said to Shoran, pointing at my friend. "We can ship him off-planet and find you someone smarter?"

Shoran actually gave me a somewhat hostile look with her eyes narrowing and not smiling. I guess it is okay for her to tease Steve but not me, even if she can sense humour on my part. "I'm just saying…" was all I could get out, straight-faced, before I start laughing.

I don't think Shoran understands humanity very well yet and realize the Sooul are going to have to get used to us, but I knew that Steve knew it was teasing. My friend never lost his smile, and nods to me and takes Shoran's hand as he walks back to her parents.

* * *

Orientation was held that afternoon in same conference room, family groups sat together after having their lunch. The tables and chairs were evenly split up facing the huge screen on the stage. The Sooul had a nice relaxing meal and the presenter waited until everyone was well fed before starting his talk. I paid much more attention to the Sooul than the orientation as I thought I knew everything.

The seminar wasn't too bad; just the standard blurb about ensuring buildings were secure before leaving, checking the shield status before going outside, where secure armored shelters were, how to contact security if trapped in a shelter and how to operate food processors. After this was done the presenter explained that there were nasty creatures as bad or worse than the eels from Sooul in the waters surrounding the continent. "On land we have nasty chickens which are contained with shield fencing, but please listen to this closely. Water creatures and chicken are minor threats which can be dealt with fairly easily; marauders are the greatest danger here! Please watch this video to understand how their intelligence and physical size makes them such a threat."

Hyun raised his hand cautiously to get permission to speak. "I have seen how our Gunmen take bad creatures away; why can they not get rid of them?" He asked looking at me when he asked it. I motioned to the presenter that I would answer.

"The wild boars grow very large and taste very good. Almost half of New Harvest's revenue is due to the meat from the animals that we export. They are too valuable to exterminate." I said and sat back down.

They played a video, which started by showing a class four marauder tearing up the town of Homestead. Thankfully, the video was shot off at a distance so the carnage wasn't right in our faces. As it was, the Sooul watched the huge creature smashing and eating everything in sight. Their expressions were one of sadness. I could easily tell that they were feeling sad for the lost people and a bit distressed that maybe New Harvest was not as safe as they thought it would be.

The second video was of an older type assault shuttle that had been filled with sweet corn. It was then left on the plains until a class five found it. This shocked me because, in my life, I have never seen an animal over class four. I didn't think that fives existed.

The shuttle was totally destroyed by the marauder

in about half an hour with the entire load of corn being devoured as well. Sophee read my surprise and started to say something, but I shook my head to quiet her. She knew I would talk about it later, so she didn't push me. For this I was grateful because I knew what the second video that was showing was going to be a problem. Class fives and the possibility of class six, I was going to have to do something about them.

The last video played for us, I liked. It showed one of the newer bunker-style homes being installed out in the wild. A bulk carrier of corn filled the home and left a trail across a long range to bring in some big Marauders. The second time I saw the class five it didn't bother me, or at least it would not have if it were alone. There were three of the damned things tearing at the bunker, trying to dig under it, flip it over, and otherwise destroy it to get to the corn. The video had a counter on the bottom which explained in hours how long the pigs tried unsuccessfully to gain access to the food. I felt a bit pleased with myself because I had used my knowledge of military emplacements with a bit of advice from Vicky to provide the design of those buildings several years ago.

Granddad's voice was at the end of the film stating all homes on New Harvest would be of this style and provided to all citizens. That was going to be one of my major focuses now; ensuring production of these homes was done quickly. The presenter just walked away leaving everyone to look at each other. Since I knew what was going on and what coming next I stood up.

The murmur of voices faded instantly as the Sooul gave me their attention.

"This concludes orientation, we will now get everyone

settled and set up with lodgings until the new homes are finished. Thank you for your attention." I finished.

Porters came into the main hall and joined up with individual family groups fairly easy to lead them to their suites. It was surprising that there were so many staff on hand to perform this task. I did recognize that this hotel did not have that many people working as porters.

"I find it very interesting that the porters can take everyone to their assigned areas with the Sooul not having last names. Is this you're doing, Vicky?" I ask out loud because Sophee was standing beside me.

"Yes sir, by facial scans I can I.D. the family groups." Vicky answered out loud as well. "I assigned proper sized accommodations to each group and then send them a porter to ensure they find their suites."

"Thank you, Vicky."

"I took the liberty of having extra people here to ensure everyone gets a porter around the same time, so no one will feel left out," Vicky continues.

I chuckle when I see Hyun and Mere stepping out of people's way and looking generally lost. Hyun looks like he wants to ask someone where he should be going while Mere just patiently waits for what comes next. I look at Sophee who is watching her parents and probably wondering why they were forgotten.

"Nobody for Hyun and Mere?" I ask Vicky after seeing no extra porters on the hall.

"Your Grandfather had your new home built last year. It is directly beside your grandfather's home. You might actually say it is in the center between your in-laws and your mom and granddad's. It is connected with secure tunnels.

For your information, after you left to join the Element, Caroline did not do well alone after you left. The Chandler has always treated her like the daughter he never had so it worked out well for him too.

Is granddad's new place at the same location on Last Stand Bluff? If so I can find it."

"Affirmative, your new personal shuttle is in Parking Bay Two," Vicky informs me. "Out!"

I grab Sophee's hand and her bag of clothing, while she held on to a small box of trinkets her parents packed for her. We walked over to her parents, both smiled when we stopped in front of them. "I bet you are wondering where you will be staying?" I asked. "Please come with me." I motioned to a different exit so the parents knew they were not staying at the hotel.

I escorted Sophee and her parents to the shuttle pad.

When we get to Bay Two my old shuttle, the one from a quite a few years back before I joined the P.F.F. isn't there. Instead there is a different low slung military looking shuttle. The smooth surfaces flow like water from the nose of the craft back along the hull to the rear thrusters. The reactive adaptable armor has a golden reflective shine. There are no weapons visible on the surface but I know they are under the shielded ports.

I open the hatch to catch that new-shuttle smell. *Yes!* We walk forward. I head over to the pilot's seat and sit, I briefly scan the control panel and grin when nothing has changed from the last time I flew this type of shuttle during my time in the Gunmen's Element. Sophee stops just inside the hatch waiting for instructions so I call her forward, pointing at the copilot's seat. She shakes her head in a vehement no, causing me to laugh.

"You don't have to fly; I can do that on my own. I just want you next to me." As Sophee settles in the copilot's seat, I turn to face her parents. "Mere, Hyun, move as far forward as you like in order to look out the windows. I will take us for a tour."

Turning forward I catch sight of a piece of paper tucked into the flight controls. I open it and realize it a note to me:

Josh,

> *This shuttle is for your personal use. You may want to download the manual and operating instructions on this Warhawk.*

> *Granddad.*

I hold up the note to show it to Sophee and her parents then chuckle at their expressions. "Granddad is being funny because this shuttle is the same type I flew a lot during my time in the Element. I do not need the manual."

Baby! I love Warhawks, they are very well armed and able to traverse long distances. From atmosphere to space, they are pretty much the best operating attack shuttles ever made. Other than the P.F.F. maybe we are the only private civilians who can actually afford these. I push the neural link connection and feel my senses merge with the flight control. The heads up display that normally on most shuttles would be displayed through a visor is now visible to my eyes only as the information on the control systems is monitored by my brain. The system integrates so well that you don't even get headaches like you would with older units.

"Flight Control, Warhawk One leaving Bay Two for free flight," I said.

"WarHawk One cleared to proceed, good to have you home sir. Enjoy your flight."

I apply power smoothly to raise the shuttle off the landing pad and rise it up into the sky. I continue to increase power to slowly gain altitude until we are higher than the shield surrounding the town. I give the shuttle some throttle and move away from the town. Everything I do during this flight has to be smooth and cautious as my family had only ever been on shuttles twice before. My normal flight patterns tend to be direct with fast approaches and departures. This is not a mission but a happy flight which is something I really am not used to. I head toward the cornfields and I point them out to my new family. "That field alone is over two thousand hectares."

"Do humans do anything small?" Hyun asked, amazed at the size and scope of operation.

I laughed; "That field of NewCoRN ™ is one of fifteen. They are mixed with other crops and rotated so the soil is not ruined. We have robotic planters and harvesters so it really is not that much of a big deal. We are not just supplying our needs, food and biomass is shipped to most planets either by us in bulk amounts or from Mars Colony in smaller craft. Would you like to see a wild deer or boar?" I asked.

Mere and Sophee shook their heads almost in unison. A lot of new things happened today and I figured they were tired.

"Joshua, as much as we love traveling with you I would

like to see where I am going to be living. We have to find out what food supplies are in the house and what needs to be done to make it habitable for us." Mere said.

"Sir; your staff has been at your home for over a month. Your home was finished to your design and Caroline ensured everything was set up like you wished. Sophee and Mere should know this to reduce their stress." Vicky said sub-vocally.

"No let them be pleasantly surprised when everything is good." I replied back in the same manner.

I aimed the shuttle toward Last Stand Bluff and enjoyed the sights of the farm as we flew overhead. As we got closer to the bluff several buildings came into view. The homes appeared to be set into the rock with only a portion of the structure visible from the air. I could see a pool behind the structures cut directly into the rock face. Two of the structures are finished and the third one looks about half complete. The structural supports look like a dinosaur's rib cage sticking up from and open grave. The landing pad is between Granddad's and my home on a lower level. Reducing the power the shuttle lands without a bump on my own landing pad.

Granddad's shuttle was not at his pad, so he must have had some pressing business to attend to before heading home. I could call him to see if he needed support now that he was retiring but if he didn't feel the need to ask for help he must have everything under control. Of course knowing Granddad he might just want me to be with my family today.

My passengers didn't know we had landed until I stood up.

Hyun and Mere both shook their heads. "There is so much more to you than what you show." Mere said. "We know that you can fight of course but we didn't know you were a pilot as well." Hyun said to explain their thoughts.

I laughed. "Yes, I can also chew gum and walk at the same time."

By their blank looks I understand two things; they don't know what gum is and they will be researching another weird thing about humanity. I decide to explain about equipment operations.

"That was another stupid joke. Personal shuttles and work equipment training are done by direct downloads. This can be done after you get settled on New Harvest; we have found it generally takes a month after landing before brain wave function is stable enough to be able to be mapped. Once mapped an educational A.I. will tailor training for each individual.

We left the shuttle and entered my new home. Immediately I was impressed with the wood tones and grains in the main entrance. The design had taken several years of thought before I got around to mapping out the floor plan. Between my mom's sense of décor and the base theme that I decided on the overall impression was warm and outdoorsy. Sophee's eyes were wide as she took in the rich wood panels and the overall size of our home.

"The shell of each home is basically the same except this one is slightly bigger because I have a main lodge room that is larger than average to host meetings. The interior design is one that simulates something called an Aspen Lodge. I looked at Sophee; "Had I known about you or even thought that I would be married we would have picked the layout and design together. Any and all changes you want we can have done." I said willingly.

"I like it Joshua, this is much different than our homes on Sooul and I need this." Sophee said honestly. "Quit trying so hard to change things you like for other people. Please continue our tour."

We wandered around checking out the kitchen and the bedrooms. I know we had a staff but no one seemed to be present. "Vicky, did you ask the staff to leave while I checked out the house?" I asked sub-vocally not knowing why it was so quiet.

"Sir, all staff is at your granddads and Caroline's home for a meeting. The Chandler's staff has been training the new people you assigned to you and they are figuring out how many more are required now that you have in-laws here."

"Thanks Vicky." I said staying sub-vocally.

Sophee, Mere and Hyun were very quiet as we finished and it concerned me that maybe they were not as happy with the place as I thought.

"How do you like our home?" I asked casually.

"It's so big," she blurted out in awe.

I tried not to smirk, but being a guy and hearing that line I could not help myself. Sophee sensing my humor got laughing and then her parents did too. I realized that they were just overwhelmed, but did like the differences in our home.

We ended the tour at the main entrance and looked down a narrow hallway that led off to the other building. I thought I could see some uncertainty in their faces on where they were looking and I knew her parents did not feel comfortable leaving. Vicky reminded me that my design had enough room for plenty of visitors. I think she understood how the Sooul would feel about being separated. Good thing my place had five extra or spare rooms.

"Your new home will be through that tunnel." I said, looking at my in-laws, "Which will always be open so we can spend time together, because my house is your house, period!"

Both Mere and Hyun took a second to look down the hall at the doorway at the end.

"But I need a favor," I continued. "I am concerned now Granddad wants me to run the farm that Sophee will get lonely when I am in meetings. If it is not a problem, would you please stay here with us for a little while? It will also give you the opportunity to tour your new house and make the changes you want as it is being completed before moving in. I just think it will help Sophee get used to having me busy sometimes and maybe help you get your bearings here."

Hyun nods. "As long as we are not causing any problems, Mere and I will stay until Sophee feels more comfortable."

"I will let the staff know you are staying. Tomorrow you can meet them all and decide what changes you want done."

Mere looks puzzled at me then Sophee.

"A staff?" Sophee asked. She looked down at her hands and, with a sad and slightly shaky voice, she then asks, "What if I wanted to take care of your needs?"

I didn't laugh or even chuckle at her misunderstanding.

"Come with me my love and I will explain. Mere and Hyun please come as well because this involves you."

It is very apparent to me they have no idea of the change in lifestyle that is being thrust upon them. The responsibility of managing a planet can wear a person down. Having some of the domestic chores done allows you to focus on what is important and ignore the little noises in life. I guide the trio across the main hallway away from the entrance into the open lodge room.

This building is based on a design I had waiting on my computer with the intent to eventually build when retired from the Element. I designed the protective structures with input from Vicky to make New Harvest safe for its entire people. A few years ago when I gave the design to granddad he started replacing all the homes with these stronger and larger structures. My mom being the busiest person I know contacted me frequently about the décor and furniture. I really have to do something special to thank her besides coming home with a wife.

It is a recreation of a typical hunting or skiing lodge that would have been found in Aspen back on old Earth, but with all modern amenities. I could never see myself living in a house that was not decorated with wood or one that had a modern appearance.

On entering the main door you step into a different time, the natural panels covering the walls resemble a dark cherry wood, even if it is not from earth. The kitchen borders the right side of the main room or the lodge room as I call it. The master bedroom is off the back end of my lodge room. The spare rooms are above and to the right of the master bedroom. The only rooms without wood paneling were the kitchen, the bathrooms and my vault or panic room. All the floors are all done in natural stone tiles taken from local quarries. The staircase up to the guest bedrooms is made from thick timber beams with the stairs cut into them; the handrails are sealed and polished branches. Walking past the staircase is a set of wooden doors that are actually two inches of blast steel with a thin veneer of dark wood over them.

What I call 'the lodge room' essentially equates to large cathedral ceiling living room and office. A round table has room for about twelve and sits off to side. I figured it could be used for dining or meetings. At the other end there is a full wall fireplace with sunken floored area that had low comfortable chairs and couches. I could see a lot of relaxing or conversations happening in this area. The bar is almost between the table area and the living area so I head there first.

"Let's get ourselves a drink and sit near the fire." I poured everyone a glass of the Riesling from our vineyards.

"I hope you like this," I say. "This is white wine made here."

I pick my girl up and sit on the comfortable couch with Sophee on my lap. Sophee calms when I hold her and takes little a sip of wine. She can tell by my emotions that I am concerned with her feelings and that things will be alright.

"Mom, Dad, pass me your glasses. I think it is poison." Sophee is starting to smile a bit as she relaxes trying to joke with her parents.

They all laugh and Hyun makes a big show of drinking while he shields himself with an arm so she can't steal his wine. I put my hand on the side of Sophee's face softly and kiss her.

"Did I over react Joshua?" Sophee asks because she can read the thoughts of compassion and respect that emanated from me.

"Yes, but don't ever hide what you feel. Your only job on this world is to be my mate, nothing else. We are wealthy, and the people who work for us are very well paid. They will clean, they will wash clothes, and they will ensure we have everything here to live. If you wish them to have dinner ready at a specific time, they will do it. If you wish to have friends over, they will pick them up and ask you what kind of food you want them to make? If you want to make our supper or any meal they will make sure you have the ingredients here, or they will take you shopping to get them. This staff is here to make our life easier."

I take a breath before addressing Sophee's parents. "Mere, Hyun, you too have a cleaner and a cook, so neither of you ever need to worry about anything again. You will never need to do anything that doesn't fulfill you…Make your life a happy one."

"Will all Sooul have this? Hyun asks as he tries to figure out his place here.

"The rest of the Sooul are going to learn they can take their time finding a vocation they enjoy; they will have safe homes and good jobs." I look at Mere. "Maybe you both could help find what makes the rest of the Sooul happy? And, Hyun, I know you have a keen interest in the farms and the equipment."

"I will enjoy helping the newer New Harvest citizens find work that makes them happy." Mere said with a happy expression.

I give a little evil grin. "I have what I want, which is your daughter." I rub my hands together like an evil scientist, causing the others to laugh.

Sophee eyes widen when she smiles. "I feel that I now have everything as well."

"If you are unhappy, if anyone or anything bothers you

and any of the former Sooul, I need to know." I look to Sophee's eyes. "When I am having normal work days, not days when a Gunman is required, you can travel with me if you wish or you can stay home. I may be on call every day, but I will take the time to have days off in order to spend them with you. Like naked day, stay-in-bed day, barbecue-with-friends day…"

When I finished my talk to my very attentive family I took a sip of wine. They still looked stunned that they have entered into a life that has options for not just survival but one where they flourish and pursue careers.

"What do you think about this entire new way of life Mom?" Sophee asked.

Mere shook her head. "I don't truly know. Truth and kindness rings out with every thought, but I am afraid we are going to get spoiled." By her smile I could tell Mere was not too concerned about being spoiled. From what I have seen of the Sooul they are a rather hard working people.

Hyun, who had been listening half-heartedly, was examining the clarity of his wine. He raised the glass so the light from the fireplace's flames could be seen through the wine. With a wide smile he got up and refilled our almost empty wine glasses.

"I for one would rather first learn about making white wines. I can tell this is made from fruit but I don't know what kind." He took another tiny sip before continuing. "Making wine was a something we each did. I would like to learn how to make this and work at the place that this is produced. If you like we can plant some of the seeds I brought and make our wine for you to sell as well."

To this I laugh. "In a couple of days I will take you to

the Winery and introduce you to the manager. I know that the wine we had on Sooul was very different from what I was used too but it would sell. Are those fen fruits hard to grow?" I smiled at the thought of a new wine with a different taste from the fen fruit. The wine on Sooule was totally different than what we make here.

"They grow on small bushes and we planted them everywhere." Hyun said; "Nice sandy soil is best, they are quite resilient."

"Mr. Garvie?"

I turn to look at one of my new staff standing in the kitchen's doorway. "Your supper is ready, may we bring it in?" I felt bad not knowing her name so I sub-vocally asked Vicky if she knew it.

"Yes, it is Jules," is her immediate reply because of course she checked everyones security reports.

"Thank you Jules, please serve dinner at the table." From the stunned expression she did not expect me to know who she was. I see Mere nod at Sophee and instantly knew they were ensuring each of them heard it clearly so they could remember it.

"Has Jules worked long for your family, Joshua?" Sophee questions; I can tell she is about to scold me for not telling her about the staff's names. I shake my head with a smile; "She is new here and I had to ask Vicky her name so I would not feel like a goofball. When she comes back with the food I will introduce us."

"We are glad you don't feel like one of your goofballs, but mom and I think you a bit of one." Since Sophee said it with a smile I chuckled out loud.

Jules set the table and then brought the food out. She

seemed pleased when Sophee and her mom helped her set the table and served the food.

We had some really nice rib-eye steaks, baked potatoes and salads for our dinner. Hyun was impressed with steaks. He ate his and was able to finish off what Mere couldn't as well. I had no problem with mine and half of Sophee's.

"If I had to have a favorite steak this would be it. Rib eyes to me are the best." It will be interesting to see what food you like the best in the future."

"It will not be coffee." Sophee said with a twinkle in her eye.

"Saturday is five days away and I would like to barbeque dinner for family and friends. Maybe we should also have Shoran with her folks over too because it make Steve happy." I said

"What about Mike?" Sophee asked; "Does he have a potential mate?"

"Invite anyone you like that is single; with their parents over as well." I said knowing Sophee would pick acceptable possible mates for my friend.

When dinner was finished Jules quickly cleared the table. She made it clear that Sophee and Mere did not need to help her. Jules put all the dishes and cutlery on the cart she pushed out from the kitchen and disappeared for a brief second. When Jules returned she had a small platter with slices of pie which she placed on the small coffee table in front of the fireplace.

"Mr. Garvie, we did not know what deserts your family would like so you're A.I. suggested this."

"Thank you Jules, I don't generally eat deserts but I will enjoy this. In the future please call me Josh."

She smiled when she went back to the kitchen. I passed pie to my family and sat back with a smile. "There are thousands of deserts or treats at the end of a meal. I normally only have them when I am at my mom's or during holidays. Thank you Vicky for telling the staff what my favorite desert was."

It was still fairly early in the evening when Hyun and Mere said they would like to get some sleep, which I didn't believe for a second. I bet they just wanted some alone time.

After they left Sophee and I walked to the master bedroom. Sophee examined the room and was smiling at the décor.

"I like all the wood." She said. "Our previous home never felt as cozy as this."

There was a freakishly huge, super-king sized bed made out of dried and polished corn stalks rather than the expected wood. They looked like logs and were very sturdy. Other than a trunk at the foot of the bed and a few small lounges under a window the room was bare. My thoughts were that the complex wood grains and the overall visual effect would be tainted if there were dressers or too much furniture. The accompanying walk in closet for this room had more than enough storage for anything we needed.

Sophee was looking at the bed when she asked, "How many families will be sleeping here?"

"Only ours, meaning you and me when we are not sharing love." I said

She blushed. "Starting when?"

"Soon, very soon." I said

I showed her the master bathroom and huge closest.

Sophee was surprised that clothing in her size was already on hangers and that some was in the drawers.

"What kind of wood is this?" She asked, as she touched the set of drawers.

"It is called cedar; trees were planted from old earth stock. It has a nice smell and back on earth they lined closets and trunks with it to save clothing from moths. We don't have moths here, but if anything I am a traditionalist." I said with a wave at my hand at the cedar lined closet.

"Vicky?" Sophee queried.

"On line Sophee, how can I help?"

"By the amount of clothing in this room I believe I have you to thank. Thank you." Sophee said."

"Caroline had me send your specific measurements ahead to New Harvest to have clothing fabricated and stocked in your home while Joshua was still in the induced coma. She hopes it would be enough variety for you until you had time to pick out clothing that suits your personal style." Vicky fell silent after telling Sophee my mom again was thinking ahead and looking out for her.

"I will have to thank Caroline tomorrow." Sophee said as she ran her hands over some of the garments.

Then I opened the door that exited off the bedroom to our private hot tub. The tub itself is fed from geothermal springs. It is very private with cut rock walls surrounding the sunken tub with a small alcove that leads through a gate to the family's heated pool.

"I don't know how to swim," Sophee slowly says as she takes in the tub and pool.

"I will be more than happy to teach you." I said as we walk back into the bedroom.

Sophee seemed a bit tense by her quietness and it made me wonder if everything is just overwhelming. I decided now would be a good time to teach her about relaxing. After all she is home, married, safe and loved. I need to be helping Sophee to put her life into perspective and seeing that she understands the overall changes that have happened.

"Sit here for a minute please." I point to the bed. Silently Sophee jumps to get on the high bed and then looks to see what I am doing. The linen closet in the master bath had some huge soft towels on the middle shelf so I grabbed a few. Sophee smiled when I returned and said nothing as I undressed. Misunderstanding my intentions she stripped down quickly as well. To her surprise I held out my hand to pull her gently off the bed. She came willingly with a smile not knowing what I was doing. We walked together out to the hot tub area and sat down with our feet in the water. I stepped in and then take her hand and pulled her to my chest as I lower myself to the seats built into the side of the tub.

"This lesson is called '*How to Relax*'. You my love; have had enough stress in your life from the Gham." Sophee is sitting on my lap in the water so I gently put my hand under her chin and raise her face so I can kiss her. "My new goal in life is to see you smile every day. Your only job on this world is to do things that make you happy and help me start a family."

Sophee kisses the side of my neck before speaking, softly. "If you continue to love me the way you have been, I will smile and the family will happen."

We sit in the hot water for a while cuddling and just enjoying holding each other. I let my mind go blank and just kiss my wife and go with the moment. A slight beep from Vicky startled me out of my happy fog.

"Joshua, remember Sophee's body mass is a lot less than yours and the hot water could affect her sooner than it would you." Vicky sub-vocally warns me.

"Thanks, Vicky. Please determine what nice and warm but safe for someone Sophee's mass, and set the tub for that," I answer back in the same way.

"Vicky warned me that the tub could be too hot for you to stay in very long. Next time it will be safer by being set to an appropriate temperature." Sophee smiles when I picked her up and wrapped her in a huge towel. She gives me an impish smile and heads to the bathroom. I finished drying myself off. Within a few minutes she was back, so I try to take her in my arms but she stops me with a raised hand.

"I am your wife, not a child. Are you always going to pick me up and carry me everywhere?" Sophee asks. I stop dead for a second because she never seemed to mind before. I study her expression and realize from the smile on her face it is a playful scolding.

"Not when we are dressed up to go out or are at a public function, but I like holding you close and will do it whenever I need you." I lower my voice; "I have spoken!" Sophee grins wider at my serious man voice. I know for a fact that she is sensing humor and that I have accepted her scolding.

"Besides the things I want to do to you are nothing that would ever be considered childish." I elaborate.

"Okay then," Sophee decides it is time to return a massage and I laugh when she tells me her job is to take care of me.

When she hears me chuckle she asks, "What is so funny?"

"That I need taking care of." I rolled over and pulled her gently to my chest. A few hours later we were pleasantly tired and totally relaxed from the love making. Sophee was snuggled up tight against me when she said; "Your mom told me that thing you do with your tongue is something a woman can do as well."

I feel my face heat up; it embarrasses me that my mother would be giving my wife sexual advice. Since Sophee, her parents, and all the Sooul are so very open about all things, there is nothing I can do but laugh awkwardly.

"Some things should stay private." I said knowing Sophee would laugh at me being a bit uptight.

"Joshua, your mom is very proud of you and appreciates the way you make me feel. Is it not fair for me to make you feel the same way?" Her green eyes look deeply into my eyes searching for understanding.

"I never expected my mom to know so much about my actions and our personal life. I don't know why it bothers me but hey I would never ask you to stop talking to her." I smile at my beautiful wife because she only wants me happy.

* * *

"Joshua! Wake up!"

Vicky's voice sub-vocally blares in my mind. My eyes snap open and after a few blinks I check the security indicator light on my alarm. Everything is green and the alarm itself is at only 0230 hours. I check quickly on Sophee, and nothing seems amiss. With a concerted effort I stay sub-vocal so as to not disturb Sophee and politely ask. "What's up?"

"The gravity is much higher on New Harvest, and the Sooul's' bodies are not built for it. I have scanned Sophee several times and can see that her joints and organs will start to suffer micro-tearing and fractures very soon."

I stiffen up at the thought of Sophee and all the Sooul feeling pain. Damn it, why now when everyone is safe. These people cannot get a break.

"What do we need to do?"

"Upgrade with nanites to make their tissues stronger in this heavy gravity," Vicky answers. "Standard repair nanites will kick start slightly heavier bone mass and muscles. Their weight should not even increase more than a few pounds."

"Will this be a permanent fix or will the Sooul need ongoing treatments?" I ask.

"It will be a onetime treatment because the nanites will bond genetically to the individual and be passed down to any offspring. Joshua the treatments should start immediately before much damage occurs."

It is a simple solution but the Sooul need to be aware that they need this. The Gham had taken away all of their choices and who am I to make a medical decision on their bodies? I slide quietly out of bed taking care not to jostle Sophee and disturb her sleep. After putting on a robe I walk to the room her parents are in and knock softly. Hyun comes to the door after a few minutes.

"Joshua, is there a problem?" he asks, looking concerned.

"Yes, Sir. Have you noticed that the gravity is stronger here and it is slows you down and makes you tired?"

"Yes," Hyun answers, "but won't we get used to it?"

Mere walks over to the door naked which doesn't shock me anymore. Still being who I am I look into their eyes only. Hyun looks briefly at his mate then together they both look at me for an explanation of why I am at their door this time of day.

"Vicky just informed me that your joints and organs will start to see micro-tearing if something isn't done quickly."

"So we have to leave this planet?" Mere asks interrupting me before I can explain the fix.

"No, we can have nanites programmed to make you stronger to avoid this." I said.

Mere motions me down to her level and gives me a hug. "Maybe you should worry about the big things and continue to solve the things like you normally do. Fix us please"

"Your body, your choice, I cannot in good conscious do anything without your permission." I said a bit overwhelmed by the absolute trust they have in my judgment.

"Now that we are up, I am going to try your thing tonight," Hyun smiled and closes the door in my face.

Way too much information. With a mental shudder, I turn to head back to my room to find Sophee standing at our bedroom door.

"Getting advice from my father?" She asks raising a cute little eyebrow.

"No," I say with a smile. *Like I would need advice from someone else.*

"*Giving* advice to my father?" Sophee asks with a slight tilting of her head.

"No…." I say grinning widely because I know a scolding is coming.

"If you aren't getting or giving advice, then you have to learn to stay in bed with me until morning." Sophee says

"Okay." I say realizing I like it when she scolds me.

Sophee turns to head back to bed so I walk behind her. The way Sophee walks is fascinating because her hips don't sway from side to side like most women. She takes short steps and almost glides as she moves. Since she hasn't dressed her bare butt gets more of my attention than her stride.

"What was so important to leave me alone in this big bed?" Sophee asked.

"The gravity is much higher than your body is built for and you would need a nanite booster to stop having health issues. I wanted to ensure that Hyun knew and would be okay with our people getting shots." I explained plainly.

"You worry far too much; just make it right." Sophee said.

* * *

What Sophee said is true. Instead of just thinking about what should be done, I need to take action and do whatever is necessary to ensure the wellbeing of the Sooul. It's not like they have not accepted nanities or vaccines before. My way of thinking is that the Sooul lost all long term choices because of the Gham and I would absolutely hate to take away any free choice they would have. Still they trust me with all their hearts and maybe leaders should lead for the good of their people. Sub-vocally I instruct Vicky to get the shots done tonight before they start seeing the damage physically.

"Will any of the Sooul need to be unconscious or in a tank for this?" I ask Vicky.

"No, they can have nanite injections that will start the process and they will just think the gravity is making them sore and tired for a couple of days."

"How long would it take to complete the upgrade if they were asleep?" I ask.

"Eight point five hours sir."

"Ensure everyone knows that option, please." I said

I glance at Sophee who is lying on her side waiting for me to settle, completely unaware of my conversation with Vicky. I want her to sleep thru the upgrade because I would not like to see her in discomfort. "When Sophee falls asleep put her out for the time it takes and make the upgrades."

"Yes, Sir."

I lay down and Sophee takes that as her opening to put her head on my shoulder and say; "Now that we are awake, whatever should we do?" It was her turn to lead in bed. For a woman of limited sexual experience I would have to say that she leads the curve. I must admit her attempt at my thing was an epic success. After awhile the late hour took its toll on Sophee and she fell asleep in my arms.

I sub-vocalize, "Vicky, please put her out and make the changes."

"For direct transfer of the properly programmed nanites you need to put your hand on her and wait until I can transfer nanites."

I carefully place my hand on Sophee's back, hoping my touch won't wake her. She sleeps on without knowing I am taking her choice away. Unmoving, I wait. It feels like forever but it is really only about twenty seconds before Vicky releases me.

"All programmable nanites have been transferred. You will now need a base level nanite import, though, to replace the nanites that you lost."

"Yeah, yeah. I know how worried you are when I have

less than the ideal amount of protection, please have them sent over with her parent's shots, too."

I lay for a while with Sophee and then decide to review the farm logs. Since Sophee will be out for eight and a half hours, I get up, dress then head to the kitchen to make a pot of coffee. Vicky informs me that a medical shuttle has arrived with a medic armed with nanite booster shots. When I open the door Steve is standing with the medic and looks at me with amusement. He has no idea why the medic is here but probably figures I hurt myself. The medic steps forward and pulls out a rather large hypo-spray and shoots it into my arm.

"Come in pal." I said with a wave.

"Upstairs, second door on the right," I say to the medic. "Please knock, first."

The medic nods as he reset the empty hypo-spray and heads up toward my in-laws room.

"You know about the gravity, Steve?" I ask.

"I know the gravity is stronger here than earth standard, why?"

I explain Vicky's report to him, and that it only affects the people from Sooul.

"How does you're A.I. know this?" Steve asks.

"My A.I. is different model than yours. The good folks from Asthran felt they owed my grandfather for saving them from possible starvation and gave me a Mark II. I did not know what type she was until after she was installed."

Steve rubs a hand across his chin and stares up at the ceiling as he obviously thinks for a minute. "Correct me if I am wrong... but there are only two of those units in existence. "Nope, you're way off," I reply with a grin. "I know there are three. One for planet defense and one for advanced engineering on Asthran."

I have to give Steve credit, he did not ask anything more about Vicky and her capabilities. Most people would ask endless questions on how advanced someone else's system was.

"Josh, would you please let Shoran and her parents get the shots right away for me?" Steve asks with his head down. I smile inwardly as his demeanor, only someone who is starting to bond would get care enough to ask this for someone else. Steve is embarrassed that he asking for special favors.

"Vicky, please send the medic to give Shoran and her parent the shots as soon as possible." I order out loud.

"The medical shuttle will head directly there shortly, sir." Vicky immediately responds.

"Done, pal," I say with a smile. "They will have the shots within the hour."

Steve looks humbled as he says; "Sorry to ask, but I don't think I could bear Shoran feeling pain."

"They would have had their shots today with everyone else, but you're my friend. Why would I not do something to put you at ease?" I put my hand on his shoulder. "The bond sucks sometimes, eh?"

"It's funny, I am bonding faster than her. She *is* bonding, but her process is slower." Steve said.

"Actually I think the bond happens faster with non-Sooul. Hyun told me that bonds can take a year or more sometimes. You're what three weeks in?" I said.

Steve looks surprised. "I always wondered if I would live long enough to marry, because of my career choice."

I never even considered that I would not live through

my services in the Element, was I so sure of myself that the possibilities of death escaped me? I think about for a bare second and realize that the way I harshly deal with threats and obstacles a positive outcome is usually the result. I never considered losing. Why would any other Gunman feel that way? Maybe the reasons I became 1st Gunman are the same as why I never considered dying.

The medic walks back from Hyun and Mere's room, and looked at me. His face is bright red and he shakes his head before addressing me. "Do they always answer the door naked?"

I burst out laughing at the look of shocked embarrassment on his face. "Welcome to my hell." I joke as I try to catch my breath. "Is there a schedule for the rest of the Sooul's treatments?"

The medic nodded. "Every single Sooul will have the basic shot sometime today."

"My A.I. will have sent directions on whom to start with, but after you do that family group the rest can be completed in whatever order you like. If it seems like too much work for one person, have your supervisor put more medical people on duty."

After I thank him and turn to my friend who had standing quietly waiting; "Come on."

We walk into the lodge room from the front entrance. Steve's eyes take in the layout of the great room.

"Nice!" he says appreciatively. "How long ago did you design this?"

"About five years ago, Mom and Granddad took my plans and since she knew how much I love wood this was the result. I am quite happy with everything they did."

Steve follows me over the bar and I pour us each a cup of coffee.

"I don't like you staying at the hotel." I said honestly. "This place is large enough that you and Mike can move in until your own homes are finished. Probably do Sophee good to have Shoran around since they are such good friends. She likely wouldn't object if you're worried about that."

"My bags are already in the shuttle bay; did you really get that new WarHawk?" Steve asks.

"Yeah is was a costly gift from Granddad for coming home alive. There also are two type-three attack shuttles painted in Element camouflage. One is for you, the other is for Mike."

I hear a slight beep and am interrupted by Vicky going active.

"Mike is at the bay door." Vicky says sub-vocally.

"Let Mike in and send him here please," I instructed her.

Mike strolled in, seeing us with coffees in our hands he automatically grabs a mug from the rack and pours one.

"Can I stay here, too?" Mike asks. I laugh; leave it to Mike to notice Steve's bag out in the bay and make an assumption that is correct.

"Sure, until your place is done or you bond," I tell him.

Mike looks sad, dropping his eyes and voice. "I tried to pick one out, but her dad said not for another five years. Guess you both got lucky, huh?"

We start laughing at his joke; it is rather hard to tell the young Sooul from the older ones before you bond.

"Sophee will invite some young ladies here this Saturday for the BBQ I am throwing. If you clean yourself up and dress nice maybe she will introduce you to them." I take a sip of my coffee and motion them over to the seating area. "Sophee is like most women I have ever known; the idea of setting up someone she likes makes her all excited."

"Vicky; how long until Sophee wakes?" I ask trying to decide if I want to go back to bed.

"Six hours and fifty-five minutes," she replies.

"Being really late or very early do you guys want to get settled and get some sleep, or would you like to get an overview of your duties and what I expect?"

Mike just raises his coffee cup; Steve just keeps looking in my eyes. Knowing my friends I take this as the signal to continue.

"Here is what I would like to do. Gunmen should be highly visible to everyone, travel everywhere at random, and provide aid when needed." I said. Both these guys have the same training as me. "We protect the people and crews of New Harvest. If a marauder breaks through the shield and attacks homes or the town, engage and kill it as fast as you can. Use railgun rounds from the shuttle or rifles, because handguns and lasers will only piss them off. If we hear of marauders in the fields, we will hunt them as a team to salvage as much meat as possible."

"Remember, guys, be armed at all times. Kid's gloves with our people, but knock the crap out of anything or anybody else." After pausing to gauge the two are still with me, I go on to tell them their wages and details about the houses that will be build soon from an orbiting fabrication ship sent from Asthran. Both Steve and Mike look happy at the news as it means they now have a stable life with good honest work.

"As for housing, as soon as the homes are finished for

the Sooul your places will be next in line to be completed. I imagine they will be somewhere on the slope below this place." I finished.

"Steve turns to Mike and asks, "Have you ever heard him talk so much?"

Mike replied, "Only when he talked to the M.P.s."

I grinned, "Well I am not done yet." I leaned back in my chair and studied my two friends as they gave me back their full and undivided attention.

"I do have a concern, though. Marauders at class four are really bad, class fives will be a horror show, and, if Vicky is correct about the sixes, they are about the worse thing ever born. We are going to have to spend some time thinning those down."

"Great!" Steve says sarcastically, "Monster pigs."

"I want to chase them all the way home." Mike says grinning like a fool.

Steve and I groan.

I am still shaking my head at Mike as I say, "Vicky has been asked to get the fabrication ship to produce some more rifles in heavy calibers. We will need to use amour piercing warhead rounds for effective shots. You both will need some range work, as these types of weapons shoot with ballistic curves. Vicky, class four hologram please."

Vicky puts a holograph of a class four marauder over the table with a human in front of it for perspective.

Steve asks, "The shock is that bad from a railgun?"

I have to laugh. "We are farmers and will only wreck a pig if there is danger in the towns. Large caliber railguns will blow even something this large into fragments. I have seen it happen. Shooting them from any position other than thru the eye will not result in a brain kill. When you only destroy the brain we have a lot of meat left over that can be sold at good prices."

Mike looks and the size of the human compared to the creature in the image. "The marauder could swallow us whole. How do we clean it...with swords?"

I smile at that. "Vicky, please insert a harvester by the boar please."

In front of the boar a holographic machine appears that is about twice the size of the boar. "Fully automatic processor ships will clean and section the meat before locking it into stasis storage for shipment off planet—We use the same machine for deer."

I stroll over past my desk to a simple door set in the wall. "Vicky, give armory access to Steve and Mike only."

Vicky replies, "Have them touch the pad beside the door for the DNA key."

After they both touch the pad, the door swings in on silent hinges. Even Mike and Steve, who have seen armories, were impressed by the thickness of the door and the walls.

Mike shakes his head and asks, "KEW certified?"

"No, with the orbiting security we have no one is going to be able to drop anything on us. I like to think of it as a safe place for my wife no matter what happens." I pause to gesture at the walls within. "It also keeps my guns and scotch in a safe place."

There are two racks of firearms with shelves underneath them holding ammo and power cells on two of the walls. There are folding bunks, tables, and chairs along the third wall. The last wall has an electronic view screen, communication equipment and a single door. Through the door is a small alcove with two more doors. To the right is ration storage; to the left is a washroom.

"Nice setup," Mike finally concedes, while Steve just nods in agreement.

"Within a month or two you guys will have a similar home with your own vaults."

Steve waves a hand casually at the inside of my bunker and asks, "As nice as this?"

"All the homes external sizes are the same except mine. My lodge room addition is the only thing different. The vault will be exactly the same, you will have stock your own scotch and wives. What you do with inside of the home is your business, this place is my design."

Mike is quick to ask, "Really, we can pick floor plans? I thought you would just issue generic homes and have people paint as needed."

I laugh at them being amazed they have choices. "When it is time for your units to be produced the fab ship will contact your A.I.s to either provide floor plans or select ones already designed.

"Cool, we never expected to be this well taken care of." Steve said looking over at Mike. Mike is quick to smile and nod at Steve, "We discussed what it would be like here but this is more than we thought.

"Look at it from my view, if you make good people comfortable with good jobs they will want to stay. New Harvest needs you." I give my friends a sly smile, "This is only because there were no trained monkeys available."

With a shake of his head at my hit, Mike turns his attention back to the hologram of the boar. "What's the plan?"

"After my wife wakes, we will take a casual flight in the Warbird to check out how big the Marauders are in this area. I would not like to leave Sophee alone yet. Tomorrow we will have some range practice."

We spent a few hours checking out the various rifles and having Vicky show ballistic tables on the screen. Since killing boar could be dangerous they both decided firepower was needed and picked out some Remington ARs in .308 calibers. The thing that makes them effective for boar hunting is their ability to have a fast follow up shots.

I hear the door from the kitchen area open and turn to see Jules pushing a cart toward the table. "Mr. Garvie, breakfast is being served." Before I can tell her that we have extra people to feed Vicky spoke aloud. "I warned your staff that there would be two extra guests staying here. They promised to stock bananas."

Steve and Mike almost knocked me over in their haste getting to the round conference table. They sat down like little hungry kids and dug in to the plates of ham, eggs, and potatoes. I took my time getting to the table and thanked Jules for breakfast. The boys were stuffing their faces like they had not eaten in a month so I grabbed another coffee and a glass of orange juice. Steve passed the plates of eggs and meat to me. I filled my plate and slowly enjoyed my meal which was contrast to their eating style.

"Man this is good, is everything grown here?" Mike asked when he paused from stuffing his face enough to reach for a coffee.

I pause from taking a bite of ham; "Not the coffee, because we don't have enough volcanic soil to grow those plants. One of my plans is to lift several hundred kilotons of the proper type of soil from a different planet, then drop it on the slopes, and plant coffee bean plants for our use."

"How will that pay for itself, will you export coffee too?" Steve wonders.

"It is a Garvie trait that New Harvest be self sufficient, if we do well enough and have a great product we will eventually sell off planet."

"May I enter?" Hyun asks from the door

"Anytime," I answer. "This is your home as well."

"Would you like some breakfast?" Jules asks as she brings out a pot fresh coffee.

He walks to the table and sits down. "Mere decided to sleep until her nanites were done the upgrade. I would rather be sore for a day or two and not miss anything. This is such an exciting time for us." Hyun smiles at Jules when she brings him a plate and a mug of hot chocolate.

Jules, would you have the staffs join us for coffee, please? I politely asked her as she cleaned up the empty plates. She came out with the rest of the staff a few minutes later. When they were all sitting down at the table looking nervously at us I introduced Hyun and the boys. I explained that they would meet Sophee and Mere later.

Most of the staff was from Vaughn, a planet that had poor job prospects and a very lousy economy. We generally tried to hire people from planets that did not have decent economies. I remember Granddad saying they were very loyal people. The home manager then asked what I needed.

"Set these two gentlemen up with rooms please." I gestured at Steve and Mike who both waved at my staff. "They will be staying for awhile. Also, my wife and her parents are to be given every courtesy. Mere and Sophee will want to cook, so let them."

The cook's eyes widened in concern so I thought I had better let her know that her job wasn't in danger.

"Even if my wife decides to cook supper meals often, you will still have jobs. Breakfast was excellent, and my home is clean and well organized. I am very pleased." I grinned and pointed to the two Gunmen sipping their coffee. "You are allowed to throw rocks and sticks at Steve and Mike. Thank you."

When the staff left after finishing their coffees but they were smiling. We were off to a pretty good start.

Vicky gives me a little mental nudge that Sophee will awaken in half an hour. I stand up and stretch. "My wife's upgrades will be done shortly. I wish to be there with breakfast for her when she awakens. So gentlemen I will talk to you in a few hours."

"Did the upgrades make her taller or more adult-like?" Steve was quick to ask.

"My daughter is a mature woman who deserves respect," Hyun says with a very serious tone, "I just hope Joshua will quit getting her to dress like a cheerleader."

Steve's and Mike's jaws drop in surprise at Hyun's joke, who knew that Hyun would be studying humanity enough to get the nuances of such a joke. Mike starts laughing at the look on my face and gives Hyun a pat on the back. "That's a classic Hyun!"

It amazes me that the amount of knowledge Hyun and the Sooul had acquired on the B.N.J. They must have been studying very hard.

Great, how long before this gets old? I wonder. By their

amount of laughter not for a long time, so I head to kitchen. I could have had Vicky drop the order to the kitchen, but I would rather talk to our staff as well. If no one is there I'll make Sophee breakfast, if the cook is there I will ask nicely for it rather than order it.

I walk into the spotless kitchen to see all the staff working away at their chores. The cook is quick to ask if she can prepare something. "Sophee will be awake soon and I would like to surprise her with breakfast. Could I please have poached eggs, crisp bacon, and toasted English muffins?" Having a mission she started grabbing the correct ingredients and got to work. I wandered around checking out the kitchen's appliances, there was a touch screen on the stasis unit. I decided to check out what was in storage and I'm amazed by its storage size. One of the neat things about technology like the stasis storage for food is that you can cook a meal, put it in stasis, and then call it back six months later just as hot and fresh. Most of the bulk carriers we have to ship goods off planet are just huge stasis tanks. I remember studying about them in school in electromechanical engineering class. Feeling useless and not wanting to be in anyone's way I reached for a coffee cup. Jules was quick to grab a pot and pour me one. I sipped on my coffee and watched Cook do up the meal. Our cook's first name is Cook. It wasn't planned, but it's funny as hell anyways. When all the items were ready Cook made up the plate and put it in a covered warmer. She added a glass of juice to the tray along with the food and handed to me.

"Thank you Cook, this smells terrific." I say before leaving the kitchen. I walked to our bedroom and turned the light on before setting the tray down on the end table before climbing into bed as Sophee wakens.

Sophee's eyes open widely and she looks into my smiling face. She stretches for a second before throwing her arms around my neck. A couple of very nice minutes pass before a grumble in her stomach gets her attention. "I feel like I haven't eaten in a long time." Sophee said raising her eyes in question to me.

"That's weird." I said smiling as I get out of bed.

I fluff some pillows and ask Sophee to sit up. When she gets comfortable I pick the tray up and lower the small legs and place it across her lap. I open up the warmer and hand her the cutlery.

A puzzled look crosses her face as she looks at the food on her lap. "Is eating in bed a custom of yours?"

"No," I tell her, unable to help laughing a little. "Breakfast in bed is a treat every once in awhile whenever a lover wants to spoil their mate. It is meant to be a relaxing way to start the day."

I lean in to kiss her brow. Then watch as Sophee pauses just a moment to look at the food before digging in. I sat and watched her enjoying every little bite. Sophee tries a small bite of everything and then starts working on her favorites. She likes eggs and cheese more than bacon but definitely likes bacon more than hash browns.

I tell her that sometime I throw all the things on the English muffin and eat it like a sandwich to which she calls me a barbarian.

"Why did you get out of bed and eat Joshua?" Sophee asks when she realizes that it is later and I don't appear to be hungry. I take the time to explain that she was sleeping for more than eight hours and it was now almost midday.

I paused a moment before deciding I would rather come clean than not admit what I had done. "Vicky put you out so we could do med nanite transfer. It not only repaired your body from the damage our gravity has done, but will also prevent further damage… I did not give you the option of staying awake, which would have left you feeling sore for several days." I admitted sheepishly because I took away her free choice.

I watch her expression closely, wondering how she'll feel about my making the decision rather than letting her decide. A soft smile crossed her face and she put her hand on my arm. "Next time ask me please." She said softly, "I would rather spend more time with you even if I felt sore." I give her a nod and am rewarded with a nice kiss. "Are my parents up?"

"Your mom decided to sleep at the same time as you, plus Shoran and her folks were done as well. Your dad is trying to prove he is a tough guy and accept the discomfort."

"You worry too much, and spoil me so much." Sophee put the tray on the bedside table and snuggled into my side happily.

"I need you healthy in case I need to have my way with you." I try my best to give her a smoldering look, but probably failed based on her giggle.

"Not now," Sophee tells me primly as she sits up. "I want to meet our staff, and then we are going on a tour to see the rest of the new colonists. They need to know we are okay, and it will allow me to visit Shoran as well."

"I Hope you don't mind that I invited Mike and Steve to

stay here as well until their places were done" Sophee smiled and gave me a kiss for being so thoughtful. "Steve asked me to make sure Shoran got her upgrades immediately because he didn't want her to have any discomfort either."

"What are your plans for today?" Sophee asked as she dressed.

"Most of Harvest's managers handle the day-to-day stuff. I was going to drop in and meet some of them over the next few weeks but had planned on being your tour guide and escort." I said plainly. The smile I got would have warmed the heart of the coldest person in the world.

"Vicky, is Mere up yet?" I asked aloud.

"Affirmative, she is with Hyun in the kitchen."

Sophee finished dressing and was ready to leave so she picked up the now empty dish and tray and carried it to the kitchen.

We found Mere in the kitchen talking to Cook who was smiling. Mere introduced Sophee and they all decided to work on supper tonight together. At least there were no problems with them sharing the kitchen.

It felt very comfortable to sit in this kitchen as Mere had a light snack. "What are your plans?" Mere asked Sophee. "We are going to check on the rest of the Sooul colonists and see if there was anything they needed. Would you like to join us?" Sophee offered.

I smiled on the inside because the rest of the Sooul are in a really nice secure hotel and they were being catered to. I could have told them that all the Sooul were being treated as very special guests but it is better to let the girls find this out on their own.

I decide to fly down to the shore and land on the pad

beside the hotel. We could have taken a ground vehicle but I just did not want to take the extra time to travel. The pad is raised slightly and overlooks the nearby beach. There are Sooul kids playing in the sand and splashing around the shallow water. I look to the lifeguard tower, but don't see one on duty at first. Looking closer I finally see a young lifeguard at the water's edge within yards of the kids. It is so good to see the Sooul children acting like children and just playing without worry.

The diligent life guard must have noticed our attention and looked in our direction before turning her full attention back to the kids. I give her a nod in return and then continue into the hotel. Sophee and her parents head directly towards a group of Sooul that were standing around some data screens just off the lobby in the visitor's center. I see that the Manager's office door is open and he is at his desk. He sees me approaching and is quick to jump to his feet and rush out to greet his new boss.

"Mr. Garvie, I am your manager here." He puts his hand out for a shake. "My name is Wynn sir. How can I be of help?"

I wave him back into the office and follow him in. "How are the Sooul?" I ask without preamble.

"The kids are very reserved, but starting to show some activity. The adults are coping very well. I have seen some of the vids the Chandler forwarded to all managers, and the fact that the Sooul are even out of bed is amazing." He shakes his head almost to himself at the thought of what he had seen. "Most of the adults are searching our databases to find out where they can be of the most use. They clean up after themselves, and actually go down the kitchens to try and help set up the buffets. They seemed a bit unhappy to find the dishes were already cleaned and they had nothing to do."

"Are there any problems at all?" I ask with a smile.

"None sir, they want to work, they need to contribute and it weighs heavily on their minds. My opinion is that they will be much happier once they are able to work; they will have something productive to focus on rather than what they have been thru."

"Are you a mind reader as well?" I asked with a laugh.

Wynn smiles; "Most hotel managers are a little bit sir."

"Would you please continue to assist the Sooul colonists until they are moved out? There will be no reviews on revenue and profitability this year, only customer and staff satisfaction." I explained.

Wynn smiles because he is not being held accountable for things out of his control.

As I rise to leave I find my hand being shook again by a pleased employee.

I head over to the visitor center to find my wife taking notes and talking to a rather large group of people. Large meaning quantity not the size of the people since they were all Sooul.

"Vicky, patch me thru to Human Resources." I say as I stop briefly at entrance.

"Pat here." Is the quick response from the H.R Manager.

"Pat, this is Joshua Garvie." I stay sub-vocal. "Please have a bunch of information here for the Sooul and arrange tours immediately to show them the farms and job prospects. I don't care what it takes. They get jobs, no one losses a job that they already have, if we are over staffed consider it extra manpower until we reach the desired levels."

I then play the boss bit with a firm, "Are we clear?"

Pat is quick to agree and will set up for tours tomorrow in the mid morning. I walk up beside my wife and smile at the Sooul. They go silent, Sophee knowing they are looking for guidance or direction asks me to say something.

"The Human Resources Manager, Pat Embry, is having shuttles bought here tomorrow to begin taking family groups out to the farming, harvesting areas, manufacturing, repair areas, labs and processing areas. Please take the time to ask questions and find something that interests you. I would prefer everyone to take his or her time to see everything before selecting an area in which to contribute." I take a second for everyone to realize that I was getting the ball rolling for them. "One thing you may not realize is that New Harvest is very lucky to have such wonderful new citizens and we know it. Now, is everyone okay or are there any problems that I can help with?"

"This list of questions I collected was just answered." Sophee said.

Sophee reaches up and pulls me down for a kiss before whispering in my ear. "If you could sense the joy the Sooul feel when you call them citizens you would be in tears."

Mere steps forward from the group of Sooul. "I will stay here with Hyun to help organize the groups. You can take Sophee for your tour now. Tomorrow Hyun and I will go with the groups." She smiles at us both happy to have something to do.

"We have great staff that will bend over backward for the Sooul, but I imagine having you two helping will put them more at ease. Thank you." I said to Mere as I pulled Sophee's hand to lead her away. "I am now going flying with my wife."

So, being me, I pick Sophee up and carry her off to my shuttle. Sophee's eyebrow rose a bit at me. "Remember when I said you did not have to pick me up all the time because I am an adult?" "Really? I remember no such conversation." I did say it with a grin and Sophee could sense that I was really excited about showing her our farm so she let it ride. I gently set her back on her feet and took her hand as we walked to my shuttle.

We board the shuttle and I point to the chair beside me for Sophee to take. Once she is seated she reaches forward and keys the restraint switch. The automatic seatbelt crossed her lap and tightens to hold her snuggly in her seat. She has seen this function once on our way here, it will not be long before she is flying and driving. Again the intuitiveness of my bride and most of the Sooul I have met amaze me. I key my restraint and hit the neural link. With a mental thought I close the hatch and start the engine. I grab the joystick, pull back and raise the shuttle as I throttle it forward. The shuttle gains altitude as I swing it away from the hotel.

"Do you mind if I pick up Mike and Steve for the tour?" I ask my smiling wife.

"My friends Steve and Mike are always allowed." She says with a grin.

"Vicky, can you locate Mike and Steve for me?"

"They are in the hanger bay familiarizing themselves with their new shuttles."

The shuttle flies past the resort and crosses a slight rise cruising over green crops as it approaches the high ridgeline where my home is placed. As the landing pad comes into view the two new shuttles that were delivered this morning shine brightly in the morning light.

I pull the Warhawk into a hover over my landing pad and slowly reduce the power until it softly settles to the ground. Before we can leave our chairs Mike sticks his head out of shuttle two and waves. Steve comes out of shuttle three with a smile. Sophee waves back through the canopy at our two friends. Disconnecting from the neural link I stand and take Sophee's hand. We leave the shuttle to meet Steve on the landing platform.

"Like the shuttle," he says with a grin, "short of your Warhawk these are some of the best-armed and armored shuttles I have ever seen."

I would like to take the credit for having these here but Granddad and I discussed what we needed for better security and to deal with the marauders. Hiring two more Gunmen got the talent here to do what we needed. Having good equipment for them to use was also important. Being the 1st Gunman, security and the ability to cover my people was one of the most important things I wanted to work on. When I told Grandfather that having good shuttles would allow the hired Gunmen to have the immediate ability to respond to any threat or problem he agreed.

"We are going past the shields to see some of the deer and a marauder or two if we are lucky. You guys wish to join Sophee and I?" I ask.

"Joshua, I need a couple of minutes." Sophee stated and walked into the house without waiting for a response.

"I am going to get something larger than the handgun I carry for our tour just in case." I say. Mike and Steve both take that as a signal they need to up arm themselves. I headed to my vault and grabbed my trusty Remington rifle and an ammo pouch. I headed back to the shuttle and enter it to find Steve and Mike already sitting in their seats. I place my gun into the bulkhead rack beside the other weapons.

Mike looks at me. "Glad you got married, because sleeping with thing that is just sick."

"Happiness is a warm gun." I say smiling.

"Hope Sophee doesn't get jealous of your relationship with that weapon." Steve also joins in to harass me.

I shake my head at my friends then brief them. "I don't plan on landing outside the shield area, but if we end up having to due to mechanical problems, please use warhead rounds and shoot for the eyes." I tell my friends. "And think a happy thought like this is a joy ride starting now. I would rather not scare Sophee with the wildlife, as these are the equivalent to dinosaurs to the Sooul."

I look over my shoulder through the open hatch and see Sophee carrying a large basket. I quickly step out the hatch and take it from her. I can smell fresh bread so I know she wanted us to have a snack on our tour. As Sophee takes her seat next to the pilot's position I smile. She looks so darn comfortable and is adapting to everything we do.

"Thanks for bringing a snack honey." I said.

Sophee glances over at my friends; "I did not think you would mind. Back on Sooul we went hungry a lot of the time and I was worried that three Gunmen could not protect me if they were weak from hunger."

Steve being the chow hound he is laughed out loud. "I knew you were a very smart person."

I activate the neural link and close the hatch as I apply power to lift the shuttle slowly from the pad.

I saw Mike poke Steve in the arm to get his attention. "See now that he is married he is beginning to drive like an old person."

Sophee looks back at them while they chuckle, tightens her seat belt and gives me a small nod. I stomp on the gas and throw the shuttle through several quick barrel rolls.

Sophee had wide eyes and a smile. "That was fun." She said.

Mike and Steve both had to grab on tight to their arm rests because they didn't tighten their seat belts as tight. Pretty certain they bumped heads too. Neither or my friends complained though, because they had baited me into responding.

We cruised over the miles of winery, the green vines responded like most plants on New Harvest and the rows or vines were easily fifty feet tall.

"How big are the individual grapes? Mikes asks as he stares out the window. Before I can answer him Steve responds.

"Wine grapes are about six pounds, food grapes are two pounds." Steve said with a smirk. "We have been studying what we produce." Mike laughed at the obvious, "We drew cards, I got animals and he got plants. We decided that we both had to become experts in the whole operation to be able to know what dangers were inherent with each area."

"Yeah, I thought I did well at a Jack then Mike drew a King." Steve shook his head at the thought of losing a card draw because he likes to gamble and Mike doesn't.

I banked the shuttle to send us over different areas

of the farm. Sophee was pretty quiet as she took in the scope of our farm. Steve and Mike talked a lot about the animals and basic crops showing that they had an excellent overall familiarization with our operation. After visiting the various areas we turn east and headed out to see corn and the pumpkin fields. A harvester is working a cornfield, so I lower the shuttle from two hundred and fifty feet down to about a hundred feet and hover to watch the process.

"That harvester reminds me of logging machines from my home." Mike is quick to point out. "But I think it is at least four times bigger."

"It is because the corn stalks can reach up to ninety feet high so they have to be treated like trees. Not to mention the fact that the corn kernels take up a lot of storage as well." Steve says to show that he has been studying.

After watching a few corn stalks get processed I slowly add altitude until the harvest shrinks in size and the corn field looks like a forest. I swing the nose of the shuttle north an speak aloud as I add power to the rear thrusters.

"Warhawk One to Flight Control," I say into the open comm. "Flight Control, I am requesting permission to pass the shields for a flight over open territories."

"Warhawk One, permission granted. Stay at minimum altitude 250 feet."

"Affirmative, Flight Control."

Steve raises and eyebrow. "A Warhawk with a minimum altitude?"

"Standard protocol, over flights outside the shield must maintain minimum altitudes to avoid anything that could jump."

Mike laughs. "Jumping pigs, this I've got to see."

Sophee was looking a bit nervous, so I smile and steered the conversation to deer. She had seen the videos of the large marauders and like most of the Sooul they had a healthy fear of large vicious creatures.

"Have you ever seen a Canadian Whitetail deer?"

She shakes her head as I continue, "If you forget their size, just look at how delicate they appear. We will find them first. Since they are not mean or vicious you will enjoy their beauty."

"Vicky, please switch us to stealth mode on my command." I look at Sophee and smile. "If we did not let them know we would be dropping off their radar a rescue mission would be on its way." After explaining I initiated the com and spoke again. "Flight Control, we are going to stealth mode, so we don't scare the deer. Minimum altitude will be maintained, but we are going off your screen for thirty minutes."

"Flight Control acknowledges."

"Here we go. Stealth mode, Vicky."

From the outside, the Warhawk appeared to pop out of existence as the shield activated. The shield simply bends light and radar around it, rather than reflect signals or colors back. Nothing can penetrate the shield or even target the space the shuttle is in. "Vicky, active scan to find me some deer."

Vicky ties into the ship's scanner to stretch her abilities, "Heading 24.3 at six miles."

I slowly bank the Warhawk and aim the shuttle at the desired heading. I keep the shuttle speed down so our approach would not disturb the wild life.

I cut the speed further as we crested over a small rise

arriving at the location of the deer herd. There was an open slope that leads down to a small lake. On the slope was at least a dozen feeding deer. It must have been a seeded slope because the forage was half way up the deer's legs. Most of the deer were does with a few fawns frolicking around them playfully. Near the top of the slope was a magnificent buck with a huge rack. By the way it was watching the herd it was on protection detail.

I brought the ship into a hover at about three hundred feet directly above the lake, and ask Vicky to set the autopilot so I can watch the deer without having to pay attention to the shuttle. Sophee is quickly retrieved her basket and passed out snacks. I think Steve and Mike must have seen vids of deer before as they seemed far more interested in the cheese and crackers than the deer. We sit and watch the young deer take milk from their grazing mothers. "The fawn or baby deer is less than a year old." Mike explains to Sophee. "If the fawn was over a year it would be weaned and on a grass or foliage diet." I added to prove I knew the animals as well.

They are huge but very beautiful, I thought they would be more scary because of their size." Sophee said with amazement. One of the feeding mothers quits nuzzling it's fawn takes a few steps and raised her head with ears pricking up to look midway up the slope at the tree line. The trees are old growth and have a very dense cover, so we are unable to see what she is looking toward. I look away from the view port and hit a few keys on the sensor array control panel. The heat scanner goes off scale in a second revealing large live heat sources rushing the opening.

"Watch this," I said. "Here comes a pack of marauders."
The buck on high sentry lets loose a huge snort which

carries far enough we can hear it over the external sensors. Two with fawns start bounding toward the far side of the clearing when the first boar clears the bush. The rest of the mature female deer follow. Their jumping strides take them almost a hundred feet with each bound. Before the huge boars can get within range of the deer they are gone from sight.

"Holy shit!" Mike gasps taking in the size of the boar

It is definitely a class 4 and at least six tons. The coarse black hair doesn't stop us from being able to see that the animal is heavily muscled and built like a tank. The tusks from the front sides of the marauders mouth overlap and look razor sharp.

"Vicky, rate the boars please."

Vicky activates the scanners and immediately responds. "The small one in view is six tons and soon will be class 5. The other two that have circled the meadow and are staying in the heavy brush, are class 5. The lead boar is about nine tons."

"Thanks, Vicky." I share a look with my friends, and keep myself mentally calm. The absolute last thing I want to do is worry Sophee when I think about how dangerous marauders are. This is going to be one of the first things I do, get rid of the very large boars. I take the controls away from Vicky without using the neural link to manually fly the shuttle and gently bank the shuttle on a southerly course toward the fish factory.

"Stealth mode off." I say to Vicky to deactivate our camouflage.

I put all my energy into feeling happy and seem to think

that I have hidden my feelings from Sophee until she puts a hand on my neck.

"You're not that good at hiding your concern," she says. "Are you afraid for the deer?"

I realized that even trying to keep my emotions and thoughts from my wife is not doing our relationship justice. I should not be hiding things like I believe she can't handle it.

"I really *hate* big boars," I growl. "They are vicious, nasty creatures. I would like to reduce their numbers down to class three or less."

"Was that so hard Joshua?" Sophee asks

"Yes, it was. My life is about making you happy and not giving you anything to be concerned about. My dislike of the boars is because they killed my father and continually try to get inside the shields. When they do people die. I know they are an important resource for this planet and a valuable food source to other worlds." I look over at my silent friends who are listening nodding to them.

"I am going to organize big hunts and get it done," I decide. "So, while you make supper tonight, Mike, Steve and I will have a meeting to start planning the logistics and do a safety review."

Sophee gives me a kiss on the top of my head and said, "I will be a part of this meeting, if you're going to be in danger. I will need more information before you are allowed to go."

Steve and Mike started laughing when Sophee finishes telling me that I have limits. In our world as Gunmen nobody ever has the gall to second guess our tactical decisions. I see them bump knuckles and continue laughing at Sophee's control over their boss. Sophee smiles at the reaction I got from my men.

"Don't laugh. I am almost as concerned for the both of you too," Sophee claims as she turns to look at them. A sly smile appears on her face to lets me know the axe is going to drop. "But, then, Joshua is very popular and can always get more friends."

Slam. Now I am the one laughing at the looks of shock on their faces. Mike's open mouth expression made Sophee laugh. Steve and Mike both took a second to realize that Sophee's humor was a reflection of what I would have said given the chance. By that time Sophee had dropped the sly smile and laughed out loud. Steve reached up with his fist to touch knuckles with her.

"Good one, dear." I said as I keyed the comm.

"Flight control, Warhawk One clearing the shield," I call out.

"Welcome back, Warhawk. You're heading?"

"Flight Control, we will be RTB, out."

* * *

Sophee decided that she could trust me to make safe decisions, I guess and she left to organize supper. I decided to have a meeting with my Gunmen, I left Jay out because his area of responsibility was geared more to shield security. We met in my main lodge and decided to discuss the problems of the larger boars. Vicky put holograms of their bone structures over my main meeting table.

"They have a very heavy bone structure and are incredibly hard kills." I started to explain. "Eye shots with warhead rounds are the most effective for dropping them with minimal damage to the salvageable meat."

I see my friends nod in agreement.

"Let's take one shuttle out so you can see how hard they actually are to drop." I said openly without putting forth a challenge to their abilities.

"Hunters used to take down the class threes and only had to use armored personnel carriers. Sure sometime the drivers and shooters got knocked around some but they were okay." I paused a minute to take a sip of my drink.

"The class 3 marauders were the largest before you left?" Mike asked. I nodded to him. "The shuttle full of corn that we saw the class four tear apart was as large in mass and armored the same way as APCs. So we will we take the WarHawk and stay in the air?" Steve asked as he was putting the overall danger from the large animals into perspective.

"If two class 4 attacks the APC it would be destroyed." I confirmed

Mike asks, "Who will drive?"

I laugh at Mikes attempt to get to fly my Warhawk. "My bird, you guys can target the eyes with warhead rounds from your rifles."

"I can't believe Sophee is allowing us to go out without an army around you," Steve pokes fun at me.

"She knows how much firepower the Warhawk has. I had the manual out, reading about the weapon systems and maneuvering capabilities, of the ship when Sophee came in to ask what I was studying. After a brief review of the Warhawk she asked me if there was any better platform for our safety. When I told her no, she sensed the truth and felt much calmer." I finished my explanation and leaned back for their reactions.

"I find it curious that a Gunman would actually need to study a manual on a Warhawk." Steve slowly shakes his head. "Mike, didn't you get a download about them in basic?"

"I sure hope Sophee never finds out that he was reading it for her benefit—" Mike says looking up at the ceiling like he has something to hold over me.

"Come on, guys," I said trying not to smile at their mockery. "If you're ever man enough to marry you will need to make your wife feel better, you know this."

"—and, like I said before, he is getting all soft," Mike continues, ignoring my protest.

I should have hired strangers

* * *

Early the next morning we board my shuttle and I strap into the pilot's position. "Gentlemen, warhead rounds can only be active if the barrel of your weapons are outside of the hatches. If the end of your barrel is inside the shuttle a dampening field will engage. It will stop all rounds from being anything more than just a bullet." Vicky announces thru the shuttles P.A.

"Vicky, you don't trust me?" Steve asks.

"No."

I laugh at the look on his face, and Mike joins in but is not dumb enough to ask Vicky about himself. Vicky has never put a damping field around my weapons ever and I think she is just being overprotective. Still it is nice that she takes care of me and I can tell Sophee about the extra level of safety which in turn will make her fell better.

With no civilians on the shuttle I engage the neural link and add full power to the thrusters. I get clearance to leave the shielded area and launch the shuttle into the sky. I keep the shuttle below the speed of sound so I don't disturb the farm animals and people on the ground. I look back at my friends and get thumbs up from Mike. "That's better; at least you can still fly like a Gunman when Sophee isn't with you."

We clear the shield and I initiate the heat scanner, set the size for class 4 and start a search pattern. At two hundred and fifty feet altitude, we don't see much else but trees and bush. Steve and Mike visually scan out their hatches looking for signs of boars. The dense foliage below shows nothing of what could be hiding underneath.

"Maybe hunting during the heat of the day makes the body heat scanner less effective." I said to Steve. "Reprogram for a layered scan and see if the heat is being reflected off the canopy." Mike suggests.

Damn he's right. "Good call pal, the top surface is actually warmer than the body heat settings." I said thinking we may have to come back when it is cooler. Vicky suddenly takes the flight controls and raises the shuttle with a burst of fire from the altitude jets. Knowing that there has to be a reason I manually start to pull the nose up with the stick. Before the shuttle can get more than ten feet higher it is struck from below with a hammer-blow impact.

"You guys still buckled in?" I say aloud.

"Affirmative." Steve responds

"What the hell was that?" Mike asks in a pissed off tone of voice.

The Shuttle noses over and starts to lose altitude as warning alarms begin to sound.

"I have flight control Vicky." I say so she will not try and take control. As much as she is a fine pilot in the time of multiple failures a skilled human pilot performs better.

I bleed off the forward speed by pointing the nose of the craft at the sky and hit the altitude control jets. It was like a kick in the ass with a large boot. The shuttle shot up to five hundred feet in altitude very quickly. Checking the indicators for damage I found out that we lost a few thrusters.

"Is there any other damage, Vicky?"

"Pressure loss indicated that the hull has been breached; no water landings and you must stay suborbital." Vicky informed us.

"What hit us a missile?" I asked while trying to check for and smoke trails.

"A class 5 hairy missile would be my bet." She said.

I look over to my crew and shook my head in disbelief. "Guess the big ones can jump pretty well, eh?" I asked my friends. "So you know this is a new development, I had never seen a marauder jump like that before."

Steve looks calm but Mike looks pissed off. Steve has always been the person to reflect on things and make plans where Mike would be happy to turn around and strafe the area with railgun rounds.

"Let's burn some foliage to get that pig into the open and blow its frigging head off." Mike suggested.

Mike's attitude is funny; I respect the absolute dedication in protecting human life but, like me, he doesn't like to be pushed around by anything.

"Stealth mode, please Vicky." I command. The shuttle turns almost invisible, as we glide over the open areas toward the wooded area again. Steve unbuckles from his chair and moves forward to the copilot gunner's position. Once he was buckled in and connected via the neural link he activates the laser and the heads up display.

"Overlay the heat signatures to the HUD please, Vicky." Steve said.

"Don't actually hit the boars when you drive them out, Steve. Remember that we are here to harvest not toast the animals." I said being unsure if he is thinking about the target or just moving his target. The laser pod rotates out of the nose of the shuttle and starts tracking the heat sources. Steve puts the laser canon on manual and aims it away from the body of the animal.

The forest was thinner below us so Mike opens the window hatch and pushes the barrel of his rifle out the window. He strapped himself into the pivoting shooters' chair. Mike inserts a magazine, chambers a round and flips off his safety.

"Starboard side is ready." Mike announced. Steve targets the area around the boar with a burst of laser fire. The green beams pass close to the boars without moving them from their hiding place.

"Can you move toward the back end of that heavy brush?" Steve asks as he points right. I bank right as Steve moves from the copilot's seat to the seat beside Mike so he can cover the port side of the shuttle. Steve fastens his seat belt, reaches down and pulls some concussion grenades from the pack tied to the side of his chair.

Concussion grenades wow. I never thought to pack any as I generally hit what I am shooting at. I don't use peripheral weapons.

"Nice call, Steve." I said with a nod at the grenade in his hand.

Steve sets four grenades for extended delay to allow them to fall through the canopy to the ground. A simple adjustment to the proximity fuse setting ensures they will explode at zero feet. This way, when they hit the trees, the explosive will detonate under the foliage and drive the animals out to an open area where they can be targeted.

Steve dropped one grenade with no results; the second grenade went off with the same results. After the third explosion, I could see the trees being knocked sideways as the huge animals pounded their way thru the brush.

As the class 5 came clear of the forest I hear Steve whisper; "Wow! Here piggy, piggy…"

Mike watched the animal turn slightly to the left through his riflescope. I added some lateral thrust and swung the shuttle sideways to give him a clear shot. Three more massive boars break free of the covering foliage and came into view. The first class 5 was obviously the alpha of the group because it turned slowly with the shuttle as the other circled behind it.

"It appears the stealth mode has a malfunction." Mike muses seeing the marauder spin with the circling shuttle.

"I am glad they are not armed." Steve quips.

"Damn, with the way they jump they don't need weapons." I said.

Shooting the huge eye from a thousand feet was not as easy as either of the Gunmen thought it would be. The boars have small dark eyes that blend in with the black hair on their face. Mike leaned over and seated his rifle into his shoulder. We watched as he fired once, then twice and heard him muttering to himself. The two warhead rounds exploded harmlessly in the ground well behind the marauder. "Damn," he said, "it moves fast." Mike knew he was beat and dropped the magazine from his rifle and unloaded the chamber. "Josh, spin the shuttle to the port please." Steve asks.

One down, one to go, I think with a smile knowing that shooting at this level might be a bit beyond them.

"Let a real Gunman try," Steve teases as he shoulders his weapon.

Three shots later the boar was still slowly turning in circles watching the shuttle with a piece of one ear missing. Steve's face was red in embarrassment for his failure at this task. "Maybe it is your planet and you should show us how." Steve challenges.

"You are shooting at a five inch target that is moving in several axis's from a moving platform." I said to dampen their frustration.

"Vicky, plot a course to the hanger," I instructed out loud. I removed my hands from the controls to address my friends as the shuttle accelerated up and away from the boar under her control.

"Sorry, guys, I should have been smarter about this. Without stealth there is no way you could hit an eye. The boar would keep us directly in front of its nose and the eyes would be a very small, hard to hit target. We will need two shuttles, one circling to give the boar something to watch and the other in stealth stationary for a shooting platform.

"Really, you should have been smarter?" Steve said. Mike is quick to join in. "Why didn't you just laugh at our expense and then say I have an idea after seeing this?"

"Yeah, we are not your wife, so quit treating us like kids."

"I have a question; could you have hit it?" Steve asked with a raised eyebrow.

"No comment. Let's go have a few cold ones, a good meal and maybe come back tomorrow loaded for action. We could drop one to see if my plan works."

I turn back to the controls and manually take control.

"Vicky, connect me with Sophee please," I say sub-vocally.

Sophee is fairly quick to answer. "Hi, are you okay? I can't sense your emotions at this distance."

I never thought that not being able to sense me would cause her distress. That is something that can be easily remedied here. I will have to instruct Vicky to monitor Sophee's location and connect to me anytime she is feeling anxious.

"We are fine. We need more equipment and a better plan to safely drop the big ones. Right now we are going to come back for a swim and dinner. Do you want to be alone tonight?"

"Our moms, Shoran, her mom and Kee with her mom are here." Sophee's voice comes back sounding a bit relieved. "We are trying to plan a dinner for this Saturday."

"Great ask the staff to prepare something for tonight if you wish."

I felt a small shutter through my feet followed by metallic screech. Red lights started flashing as shuttle started to shake hard, an alarm sounded.

"STRAP IN!" Vicky's command was so loud she hurt our ears.

Sophee heard everything. "What is going on?"

I interrupted her as I cinched my seatbelt tighter; "Call you back in a few minutes."

"What's happening, Vicky?"

"The hull breach is widening as we speed up. There is nothing on the sensors because they are out. Warhawk's have no internal cameras to tell me how bad the damage is."

"That just sucks!" Mike said as he giggles.

I throw a glance back at my friends; Mike is giggling away and Steve has no look of concern. "I bet we beat everyone to the scene of the crash," he said with a deadpan expression.

Why me? I am certain somewhere deep inside I had a chuckle brewing at our predicament; however Sophee would be upset if I don't call her back soon.

The bottom of the shuttle peals away as the gravity field starts to fail. We are only five hundred feet in the air so I react quickly and point the bow at the sky and start the thrusters. The shuttle points up like ballistic missile with weak engines and slowly starts to lose height. I try to control the rate of decent but the shaking is increasing as we drop lower. The shuttle's wobble overcomes my control and it starts to flip over. Losing our only upward thrust the Warhawk stalls out and crashes loudly to the ground. We are lucky that we did not land in the heavy canopy but in an open meadow a thousand yards from a high rock bluff.

I still hear Mike giggling like a madman.

"Well that was unpleasant." Steve said comically.

I unbuckled my harness and reached for my rifle. "Grab your rifles and ammo, we need to clear the shuttle quickly." I order loudly.

Both Steve and Mike were already loading ammo clips into their combat harnesses. I grabbed a harness with warhead rounds in my weapon's caliber and start climbing out of the fractured hull.

"Vicky," sub-vocally I ask, "what is the crew's health status?" I had to ask Vicky because neither of them would admit to any wound that doesn't affect their ability to fight.

"Mike has a minor wound to the leg, and Steve acquired a couple of scrapes. Their base nanites will fix them up quickly."

Great, anytime you can walk away from a crash it is a good thing.

"Scan the area. How long do we have?"

"Minutes; you need to get away from the shuttle and get to cover."

"Gentlemen, those marauders we saw will be heading here within a few minutes. Our crash was loud enough to call them in. Load up." I feel my pulse calm and that old pre battle chill invades my soul.

I open the bolt on my rifle and put one round in the barrel and four in the box magazine.

"All rounds fifties from now on, Vicky." I instructed as Steve and Mike got out of the destroyed Warhawk. I saw Mike had a large blood spot on the front of his thigh while Steve left pant leg is half torn off. On closer inspection his shin looks like someone ran a cheese grater. Neither of them will have the speed required right now.

"You guys head for the rocks, I'll run interference!" I said over my shoulder as I ran toward the oncoming marauders.

Identical twins could not have had the same annoyed

expressions that they showed but they realized I was unhurt and was right. They made a beeline for the rocks.

I sprinted toward the open area we just came from to intercept the boars before they would overtake my friends. The pounding of the marauders feet could be felt through the soles of my combat boots as the biggest of the class five marauders appears in the opening running straight toward me. I throw the rifle up, seat it quickly on my shoulder to target the marauder. At eight hundred and fifty yards there is no way to target an eye so I readjust my aim and squeeze off a round.

The bullet flies true and hits the only place it can do damage at this angle. The largest boar's front leg directly above the knee takes a penetrating warhead round and, while the explosion was not too large, the results were spectacular. The boar performed a beautiful summersault when its nose hit the ground. Rolling to a stop the Boar ended up facing slightly away from me and I could see part of its eye. Not wanting it to suffer of get up and chase me on three legs I fired another round at its head. Through the soles of my feet I can feel the other boars running toward the crash site. Their feet echo as they clack on the rocks and hard ground. Taking one marauder out while standing on the ground is difficult, if all three of the other slightly smaller ones appear it would be very difficult without a railgun. There is a time to stand and fight and a time to flee. I made an instant choice and turn back to run as fast as I can to join my friends. By now they would have reached to bluff and hopefully are safely at the top and would be able to provide covering fire.

I reached the rocky bluff and saw Steve at the top of

the steep section pointing to the area they climbed. Mike is laying down aiming his rifle at the area he believes the boars will come through. I start climbing as fast as I can to get higher than the boars can jump. Mike fires his weapon repeatedly to cover me while I climb the last few yards. Close to the top I see a hand to pull me up the last five feet. Grasping that hand, Steve pulled me over the last section of vertical rock. "Nice shot on the charging boar!" Steve said as I try and catch my breath. I turned to look down the bluff. Down about four hundred feet are three more huge boars staring up at us. Mike's shots had wisely been into the ground in front of the animals to stop their attack.

"Thanks for not shooting them Mike."

"Well we are farmers who harvest them; it would be a shame to destroy valuable recourses." Mike said wisely remembering our conversation about not destroying these animals.

"Vicky, go active. How many boars are in the area?" I asked

"There are just the four you see here at the bottom of the bluff and one wounded that you already shot." Vicky answers back.

Damn, I thought I killed that one.

"Are there any behind us on this bluff?" I queried.

She is silent for a second as she scans the area behind us.

"There are no boars within scanning range on this bluff!"

That's not normal! I know the boars are everywhere including near the shore because they lack fear and are the toughest things on the planet that we know of. If they are not up here where there is a very abundant food source there had to be a reason.

"Gentlemen, there may be something bigger and more dangerous on this plateau than the boars. Your rear guard now, I will handle the boars."

Steve and Mike are quick to move apart and watch behind us for hostile life forms. Both their backs are to the bluff, their weapons are ready if they have to cover my back. Mike had managed to grab his helmet and engaged the built in scanner to scan for movement.

"Vicky, contact Jay for pick up! Tell him it is urgent. Also get a harvester in the air on this position."

I fully reload my rifle and lay prone facing over the edge. The big wounded class five is out of my range, but the four marauders are not. The butt of my rifle pounds back into my shoulder with every shot. Warhead rounds require more propellant to get their mass moving and I am certain someone smaller than me would have a bruised shoulder after this. The first three marauders are lobotomized in quick succession by exploding bullets. I had to shoot number four through the leg to drop him as he was really nervous and was jumping back and forth shaking his head like he was suffering from a bad headache. Once I dropped him with the leg shot I had to reload before putting my final shot through his eye.

"Is there anything else down there, Vic?" I ask as I turn to face the possible threat behind us.

"Just the big wounded one."

That boar is not an issue because the broken leg and the huge head wound but he needed to be finished off.

"Climb down guys, I will cover you." I said watching the forest behind us.

Mike shook his head no. "You first, pal; because there is no way we are going home without you."

The top of the plateau behind the bluff had really heavy old growth cover. Anything that wanted us would be able to get in close. Mike turns his back to me and continues watching the tree line.

"Maybe we should all climb down at once?" Steve suggested.

"There is something unnatural about the lack of boars in this area and I would advise leaving until this area can be fully investigated." Vicky quickly agreed with Steve.

I walked to the edge waited a second to ensure Steve and Mike were with me. I smile when they walk up to the edge of the escarpment and waited for me to take the first step down. Together we take turns climbing down in pairs with the last person covering the other two with his rifle. I can feel the hairs on the back of my neck rising every time I look down and take my eyes off the top of the bluff. Being unsure of what the possible threat is but knowing tough animals are afraid just gives me that uncertain feeling that I don't relish.

Mike and I reached level ground first, he covered the top of the bluff with his rifle and I watched for additional marauders. When Steve reached the bottom I suggest we jogged back to the first to the first marauder. It needs to be put down and it might be smarter to be away from an unknown element. All three of us break into a comfortable jog but we keep our weapons ready. When we finally get the badly wounded boar I walk wide until I can see the remaining eye, I felt bad that my snap shot missed killing the boar earlier. I do not like to see any animal suffer. The warhead bullet merely glanced off it skull exploding on the surface of the tough skull bone.

The warhead round flies true and detonates as it enters the marauder's eye laying waste to the animal's brain. The head doesn't blow off as the skull is too thick and strong but the other eye which was ruined sprays out in a glorious fashion. The massive head drops and the boar rolls over as it dies.

"You sure it's dead?" Steve asked needlessly.

"If a boar was lying on its feet it is alive and dangerous. When they roll over in their sides they are dead." Mike says smiling because he could use his knowledge.

"We should climb to the top of the dead boar to get us off the ground with a better vantage point." I say grabbing a handful of the boar's hair so I can pull myself up. The view from the top of the dead boar was darn near twenty feet higher that the ground. "Mike, please watch the bluff with a scope, Steve watch the flat land in case of more boars." I instructed. I walked a few feet away toward the boar's head to call Sophee in peace.

"Vicky, connect me with Sophee." She linked me up to Sophee.

When I hear the connection open I started with; "Hi, Honey…"

All I can hear is crying from my obviously frantic wife until my mom takes the comm away from her.

"Are you boys okay?" Mom askeds with concern in her voice.

"Yeah, Steve got some scrapes and Mike cut his leg, while I have a bruise on my elbow." I reply downplaying the crash. "We had some bad mechanical problems with the Warhawk. Did granddad get it at an auction?"

Steve walks six feet from his watch and whispers to Mike; "What do you think his grandfather will say when he returns the keys to the shuttle?"

They both laugh quietly. I can picture my mother frowning and shaking her head because I know she heard. Keeping my tone light for Sophee's benefit I continue.

"Vicky called Jay to pick us up and for a harvester to grab the five marauders we harvested." I said to make it sound like any other hunting trip. "Is it possible to get a recovery crane for my Warhawk? I lost the keys."

Mom isn't dumb and I can hear her fingers keying something on a pad. I know she is sending quiet instructions to Flight Control. They will vector the crane to our position.

"Sure, honey, Jay should be there in ten minutes can you wait that long?" My mom is not that good of an actress and I can still hear the concern in her voice. I had better make light of the whole situation for Sophee's sake.

"Absolutely. We are fine and there is nothing around to bother us." I clarified hoping Sophee was still listening. "The only danger we have is that we might fall off this dead pig we are standing on."

"Caroline, I am better now. Why are you standing on a pig?" Sophee asked sounding like she has got a grip on her emotions.

"We didn't know if there were anymore marauders around and thought this would be the highest, safest place." I explained like it was an everyday occurrence. Steve and Mike still watch their assigned zones but are moving their feet, dancing like two maniacs. "Can you delay supper for an hour or so? We would like to act as over watch for the harvester until the meat is picked up."

"Really, there are no other problems?" Sophee asked.

"Mike and Steve are dancing around the top of the marauder like a couple of goofballs. I would rather not see any of the meat get wasted by having other marauders feed on the dead ones." I lower my voice to a whisper. "Please don't tell Granddad I put a dent in the Warhawk."

"I am certain he will forgive you."

"I will see you soon, honey." I shake my head at my friends. "End transmission."

Steve and Mike both look at me like I am a liar. If they were married they would know that our significant others need to be sheltered from the brutal aspects of life.

"There is a dent in it!" I said loudly defending myself.

We are still laughing when the shuttle Jay was piloting in screams overhead. The shuttle comes in very fast looking for danger then banked to land beside the dead pig. Jay has the same shuttle as Mike and Steve but his looks a little more used. The door opens up and Jay steps out holding a railgun rifle with my grandfather right behind him. I walk down the rear hip and jump off the boar's back leg. Neither Steve nor Mike took their eyes off the bluff or the flat lands.

"Okay guys, were good now." I said to allow them to follow me to the shuttle.

"We were monitoring your transmission to Sophee and that," Grandfather said, pointing to the totaled Warhawk, "is more than a dent."

"She doesn't need the stress of worrying about me." I shrugged. He should know I was making it easier for her.

The harvester was only another few minutes behind the

shuttle. It was quick to slide over the first marauder and start to tractor beam it inside for processing.

"Thanks for the ride." I spoke casually to Jay trying to act like it was another day in the park. I could tell Granddad was not very happy with me as he pulled me aside. Red faced and shaking he looks like he's about to blow his top.

"Do you think you are the best person to lead these little excursions?" His unhappiness is more than his anger which surprised me. "Have you thought about your wife? About your mother and everyone here who depends on you? You're a new husband with no kids to carry your name on. I will not live forever, what happens to New Harvest if your gone because of stupidity?"

I start to stiffen up and bite back a less than kind response. My impulse was to act defensive and blurt back that he is not my father. As a grown man and the First Gunman I need to control myself because he is only showing his love and concern. If my father had been as thoughtful and cautious he would still be alive. I see the edges of his eyes are watery and he is close to tears. This is what love is all about; worrying about the safety of your family.

I look Granddad in the eyes. "Yes, I am the best person to lead these hunts." I made my voice sound a quiet and calm as I could to show my respect. "My crew is alive because of the way we work together; I now know what needs to be done to ensure these little excursions are safe. Don't worry, Grandfather, I will be more cautious in our future endeavors."

I step closer and give him a hug before walking into the shuttle. Before joining the Element he and I clashed a lot and my first thought was to respond as a kid would have.

Granddad deserves my respect and I am glad that I showed it to him.

We all boarded the shuttle. I took copilot seat beside Jay. Granddad sat in the middle while the boys took the side gunner seats

"Jay, please fly overwatch until the boars are picked up. I will get Vicky to continually scan for marauders. Mike, Steve, please man the railgun mounts; Steve cover the harvester, Mike the bluff."

Jay took the controls and lifts the shuttle off the ground and up to double the minimum altitude. This put us slightly above the harvester ship to watch for marauders. Although Vicky is scanning for the huge boars and would let us know if any were approaching we still fly overwatch anyway. The harvester finishes with the first boar and flies closer to the bluff to pick up the next one. I see Mike engage his helmet scanner as he watches the top area of the bluff where there are no marauders but something unknown.

Granddad got out of his seat and took a couple to steps to put his hand on my shoulder. "Josh, sorry, for giving you hell. I was worried about you."

"No problems, grandfather. Who knew a marauder could jump that high? Come out with us next time as our hunt will be so safe it will bore you."

He nodded at me in acceptance then pointed to the top of the cliff that Mike was watching.

"Jay said that you're A.I. is concerned about the lack of boars up there? Have you found out what was scaring them out of that area?

"Whatever it is, it was close and it gave us the willies

sir." Granddad looks at me with surprise. *A Gunman got an uneasy feeling from something?*

"If it proves dangerous to the settlements I will end it."

The first boar was finished and the second was being processed by the harvester, when Mike asked me to take his weapon while he went to the head. I stepped back to his post and grabbed the gun to start scanning the bluff.

Mike stopped by my grandfather's chair. "Sir, I was with Josh when he wrecked the Warhawk and will drive carefully if you get me one."

Having made his point or hack Mike happily replaced me at the gun mount.

Steve, having overheard Mike, is snickering at my expense. I shook my head not in anger but amusement as my best friend is trying to downplay the day's events with humor. I sit back down in the copilot chair and watch the scanners. Granddad smiles and actually doesn't look as upset as he did. *Good job Mike.*

"The crane is here." Vicky announces as it appears over the trees.

"Open a channel to the pilot, Vicky." I instructed as I was watching the scanner for more mauraders. "Stay above five hundred feet when traveling over the wilds, apparently class 5's can clear two hundred and fifty. Please take the Warhawk for salvage but not to my home."

Steve and Mike both start grinning at each other so I ignore them, "You coming for supper tonight Gramps?"

"Got room for an old fart, do you?"

"Of course, who else will add some maturity to the group?"

Granddad looked over at Steve and Mike before answering. "Yes, I can see that you will need some maturity."

The Warhawk was lifted slowly by a blue tractor beam. Then it deposited on the platform behind the pilots cab, automatic curved arms deployed from the sides the hold the shuttle to the platform. The arms looked vaguely like a spider grasping prey.

"Crane Two, returning to base."

"The pilot of the recovery vehicle is Ensign Adam McGillivray." Vicky says sub-vocally.

The crane slowly spins on its axis to aim toward town.

"Thank you Adam, see you later." I said as the recovery crane disappeared out of sight.

The harvester pilot, having processed the last boar, says, "Returning to stasis area for drop off. Good haul, guys." The harvester raised itself higher and headed towards its base as well.

Seeing everything complete and the area safe Jay directed the shuttle away from the harvester and raised us up to over a thousand feet to return us home.

"It is rather surprising that the five's could clear two-fifty in this heavy gravity." Jay stated

"Want to come for supper too, Jay?" I asked realizing that I had left him out.

He merely nodded and hits the Autopilot engagement switch to fly us home. He is a man of few words.

Mike and Steve did not leave their gun stations until we crossed the shield into the protected section of the farm. Once safely over the shielded farm land they unloaded their weapons and took their seats

"Whatever we do, make light of it. Today was no big

deal." I said not wanting Sophee to get anymore stressed out about our little adventure.

Mike, forever the smartass, chirped from his position. "Yep, no one lost an eye, nothing serious happened."

The shuttle was much faster than the crane so we landed at the family pad well before the crane returned. The girls came out of the house to greet us and check us over. Even though they knew we were not hurt my mom and wife just had to check on me. Shoran and her mom came out as well to check on Steve.

As a rule I have learned not to leave anything to chance. My stupidity was I didn't think about where I was going and what was happening around me.

Sophee walks up to me, trying to read my emotions, which were a bit clouded and then resigned when out of the corner of my eye I could see the crane flying by with my wrecked Warhawk in the open for everyone to see. Mentally I kick myself for not having the crane take a different route to the salvage yard.

Sophee turned to see at what I am looking at and then she shook her head. The smashed Warhawk was lying on its side looking very much wrote off. Based on Sophee's ragged breath and shaking shoulders I saw that she was about to emotionally lose control. In order to prevent her feeling embarrassed later I swooped her up in my arms and walk inside with her to go directly to our room.

Sub-vocally I ask Vicky to tell my friends and family the bar is open and I will be out shortly.

I climbed on my bed with Sophee lay down facing her with my arms around her.

"I am fine, honey." I said putting as much love and

honesty into my thoughts. "A jumping marauder dinged up the Warhawk and I crashed it, that's all. We climbed a ridge to be safely away from them and shot the boars from four hundred feet high. No major problems. Look at me!"

I opened my arms to show her I am perfectly fine. Sophee was finally able to get her emotions in check and looked up into my eyes. I wrap my arm back around her and tried to kiss her but sensing my feelings she decided there was enough truth and hugged me tight.

"When will I ever be sure of what you do?" She asked with a puzzled expression. From the way you behave and talk you could be sitting in a chair talking to someone or fighting for your life and I cannot tell.

I thought a few seconds about it.

"I screwed up, we need more ships and to be smarter regarding our flight patterns. From now on, three ships will go out when we hunt—two shuttles for decoys, and one shuttle to shoot. It would make it much safer and faster."

I kept looking into her beautiful eyes as we spoke so she could see and feel my sincerity until she finally smiled.

"Okay," she replied calmly, "But I need to be at your planning meetings so I feel more comfortable with your hunting trips."

"Agreed, my love." I answer in a tone that lets her know I will fully comply with her request. "Now that I have you here in this bed what should we do?" I raised my eyebrows and give her a silly grin.

"I should be making dinner with the rest of our friends and family. You should sit and relax with your friends. I will give you the evening off because of your stressful day.

Tomorrow you can make me a typical New Harvest meal on your barbeque."

I decide to change out of my Gunman gear and dress in shorts and a very loud surfer shirt. It is the little things like not dressing like a Gunman all the time I do to relax Sophee and the people around me. Sophee waited patiently for me while I changed and smiled at the bright out of character colors of my shirt.

When we come down the hall out to the lodge room a round of applause greeted us from Steve and Mike. They both had changed while we were gone and are both wearing hockey jerseys now. I give a slight bow and lead my wife to the bar. She is quick to take a couple of open bottles of Riesling white and grab some glasses then disappear into the kitchen.

I decide to open a third bottle of wine when I see that no one had a drink yet. I pour Granddad, Jay and Hyun each a glass. Shoran's and Kee's father nodded at me when I wiggle the bottle at them. I poured them both a glass and handed them over.

"I prefer a glass of single malt, gentlemen?" I said looking at my friends.

"Please." Steve responded.

"Oh yeah, me too. Mike said.

I dropped a few cubes of ice into each cup and poured a healthy sized shot into them.

"I am glad you did not spend four days in your room this time." Mike said. "We all would have got very thirsty." He smiled like he had just made an epic funny.

"Sophee was a bit upset with me and I thought it better

that we talked about today privately. And she shot me down and said that she had to help with supper." I explained.

While I took a sip of my drink Vicky sub-vocally announces, "if you wish to update your grandfather twenty-four tons of meat are in stasis ready for shipment."

"Grandfather, twenty-four tons of meat is ready for shipment." I said to give him good news.

"It is not worth the cost of a grandson." Granddad replied letting me know he was still a little upset. Hyun reading Granddad's concern looked at me seriously as well.

"Joshua, what happened that has everyone so worried about you boys?" Asked Hyun.

"I'm sorry; I need to check on my wife." I shake my head at being questioned and let them know either of my friends could tell them what happened. As the 1st Gunman my decisions are generally not questioned and I find that it is not fun explaining myself over and over again.

I entered the kitchen to see the women in a cluster around a small view screen all talking and intently looking at the images.

Sophee looked up and, on seeing me in the doorway; she motioned for me to come over. When I get to the group, my mother is in the center of them showing footage of the boars being pulled into the harvester on her data pad. I imagine that the footage was shot from the shuttle we were in by Jay. It did not show anything more than us standing on the dead animal and then the harvesters picking them up.

I back the pad up and zoomed the view out to show them from where we were shooting from. This I knew would make Sophee and our moms feel better.

"I made the mistake of taking into consideration that

class five animals could jump that much higher than a class four could. They dinged up my shuttle and wrecked it."

"Do you know the amount recovered yet?" Mom asks.

"Twenty-four tons." I said and watched her smile at a full three-month supply.

I put my arm around my beautiful wife and get a hug in return so I know she felt a little better about today's hunt.

"Is there anything I can do to help?" I ask.

"No, what are you avoiding my Joshua." Sophee asked with slightly tilted head.

I have to chuckle at her being able to read me so well. "Granddad and your father are being all parental and causing me to feel grumpy and having to explain myself again."

Sophee pulls me down to put her arms around my neck and give me a gentle kiss.

"I suggest you treat them with as much thought and honesty that you do to me. Remember they love you as well." Sophee's sweet voice always makes me think and I can do nothing but smile at the great truths that come from her. I returned the kiss and simply walked back out to the main lodge room to join the men.

I saw Hyun staring at me as he talked with my granddad and it made me feel like I was letting them down.

This can't be good. I poured myself a fresh scotch. I sat on a stool with the data pad from behind the bar and started making some notes. They included everything that I remembered about the animals and their behavior during the hunt and how we could safely take them out.

I could feel by the footsteps someone was behind me. I just waited for them to speak knowing who it was.

"Chandler and I are not going away," Hyun says.

"You sure?" I ask smiling as I turn to let him know I was joking. "Steve, Mike, Jay I need some backup."

Not to be left alone Shoran's and Kee's dad joined us as well.

"Running towards the boar?" Hyun asks in disbelief.

It is obvious that my boys were updating my Grandfather and Hyun in my absence. I looked to my friends; "Who was the best person to stop the lead boar?" Neither said much, *great hang me out to dry.*

"If Mike and Steve don't admit it out loud, one person had the ability to make the shot at the range it happened. As for that case closed, I have a new plan. As soon as I get a new shuttle it will happen."

I decided that being second guessed by my friends, grandfather and father in law was not something that I liked.

"Class five marauders need to be harvested in a different manner to be safe. The shuttles would fly around acting like decoys and get the boars to spin in circles. This will give the shooter who will be in a shuttle in stealth mode a clear shot at their eyes.

"Minimum height for this hunt would be five hundred feet. Should one ship go down or crash the other two could use railguns to protect it. I am going to kill any marauders class three and up." I pause for a minute to see if the other Gunmen agree and are satisfied when then give me a nod of their heads.

"I am also going to find out what lives up on the plateau."

Jay smiles, which is weird because I have only ever seen

him smile a few times, and says. "Good plan if you have the resources."

I nodded almost to myself. "We would have if I didn't wreck my new shuttle."

Chandler and Hyun look at Jay for further comments. It is only because he is older than me that they actually believed he might have more insight.

"As 1st Gunman Josh is my commanding officer and knows exactly what is best for this situation." Jay is quick to point out showing the proper deference. "I would not second guess Josh because he is absolutely correct in almost all his judgments."

I raised an eyebrow at that. "Explain, please."

Jay grins at Granddad. "See, Josh is willing to listen whenever he thinks someone may have more data or information. Let's have a mini debriefing right now."

We all grabbed data pads and headed to the main dining table. I gave an overview of today's hunt based on my view point and what our successes/failures were. I could see Steve and Mike making notes on several of my points. Steve gave his overview and made a couple of points that I did not. Mike followed with his and he too echoed Steve's points. Jay nodded a few times at them for their thoughts and beliefs. Granddad and Hyun did not seem too happy with several of the points made by them.

Everyone listened openly without making any interruptions. From the frowns on my Grandfather's face I could see he might have something to say but refrained until he had all the data. Then, surprisingly, Vicky spoke up with her review. It was different because her review calculated success of each action mathematically. Her numbers did not disagree with my actions too much.

"There are a couple of points where I disagree with you guys." I said when each of us had finished our review.

"On top of the ridge I was not going to leave or lose a man. On the plain with the charging marauders I was the person with the most accurate high-powered weapon. Even if my two wingmen do not admit it, I am the fastest too."

Granddad notices my men nodding and relaxed a bit.

"I would rather you used railguns and came home alive, than salvage a few pounds of meat." Granddad said.

"Sir, New Harvest is successful because we ship meat, produce and biomass." I ensure I met his eyes when speaking to show him I am acting like a leader not careless. "Wasting good meat would be an unwise thing, had we carried railguns we would have stood our ground and slew the marauders. We had a little run and a wee climb which harvested over twenty tons of saleable meat." I finished seeing my guys looking like they wanted to say more but holding back. "Steve?" I asked.

"You did not address the fact you would not leave us at the top of the bluff." He said with a firm expression. "Your life is far more valuable to New Harvest than Mike and mine together."

I smiled at his reasoning and saw Mike nod in agreement to Steve.

"Not to me." I said softly. "Now that I think about the issues we had with aggressive marauders, we are going to make some changes. We could get some regular domestic pigs from the pens at Mars colony or one of the worlds in the belt. Let's raise some up to class two. Hunt and store class three to five marauders. Introduce a larger shielded area for the domestics to run and eventually we will have no big marauders left and can fully release the domestics afterwards, breed the meanness out of the bloodline."

"The area above the bluff will need some investigation." Grandfather added in to remind me of that additional task.

"Whatever it is up there, it scares the marauders. Maybe even eats them. We will find out what it is and, if it endangers the citizens, it will have to go." I smiled at the simple answer.

CHAPTER 15

Several months later, Landfall Day was upon us. The biggest holiday on New Harvest, Landfall Day was first celebrated by the colonists who successfully travelled from earth when they had a huge party the day they landed. Over time it became the family holiday on New Harvest.

I had already caught a few of large crabs, and tried the Sooul method of cooking them. Hyun, with the help of the other Sooul, were manning the crab pots for the big picnic. It is not as fast as using laser heaters to flash the strips of meat, but it works just as well on our crustaceans. This was going to be an epic barbeque, as I decided to host an open event that everyone was invited to, and I think we were going to feed almost five thousand people during the day.

The meat was cooked in two shifts to ensure there would be plenty of food so whoever had to work got the ability to join in after they were done. If I had to guess, about half the existing citizens and all of the Soul were present. The Boy Named Joshua was also in orbit, so a lot of the crew got shore leave. All passengers were invited down to the surface as well. The crews from the fabrication ship that had been in orbit were also included.

It was a very bright and warm day when Sophee and I

left the lodge. The barbeque and picnic area was set in front of the hotel facing the beach since it had the most open ground near the water. The live band was playing a variety of music and had a pretty good sound. Children were running around and everyone seemed very happy to mix and mingle. Huge canopies provide shade for picnic tables. All in all it was an excellent looking event. I knew the men from Sooul were quite excited to be cooking the crabs for everyone. Their good mood was actually infectious.

The Sooul had a dozen pots cooking on heating elements very similar to the ones they had back home. The smell of cooking crab made my mouth water. Some of the cooks from the B.N.J. were helping the chefs from the hotel with the roasting of several piglets on spits. Most of the crew from the fabrication ship was gathered around the outside bar. Their light blue coveralls made them stand out compared with the shorts and tee shirts of the New Harvesters.

I left Sophee with Shoran and her father to go find Steve and Mike. I saw them away from main picnic almost behind the hotel in a heated discussion with Jay who was shaking his head. I made my way toward them, Steve's red face told me all was not well with him. The only time he ever has a red face is when he is laughing or mad. He does not look amused today.

"Problems gentlemen?" I asked calmly.

"Some of the people who were traveling on the B.N.J. are dirt bags." Mike said watching Steve's reactions. Instantly I know that Mike and Jay are acting like the voice of reason talking Steve down. To have someone who is as generally calm as Steve this upset is not normal.

"I see a lot of rage in you Steve, why?" I asked carefully

because he is my friend and I want him to understand that no judgments are being made.

"I slugged a guy that groped one of the Sooul." Steve said.

"Who got groped?" I asked losing my smile as my pulse quickened.

"It was Kee," Mike said with disgust. "I wasn't here to hit him, Steve stepped up for me."

The expression on Mike's face would be almost funny if abuse of a woman was not involved. I could tell he was glad Steve defended his new girlfriend but annoyed that he never got to throw the punch. Also the fact he was calming Steve down when he was pissed off was mildly amusing since he generally was the hothead.

"Vicky, connect to the B.N.J. in order to find out who the passengers are and upload their info to our A.I.s." I ordered now that I have an understanding of what happened.

I see Steve, Mike and Jay close their eyes for a second as they downloaded the information. Both Steve and Mike lost their red faces when they have the data. Now they have the information they needed their focus is absolute. They took a step closer to me for orders.

"It may be a holiday here, but you gentlemen will have to spend some time away from your girlfriends..." I said to them in the serious voice of their Commander.

"I see you both are armed, good let's get to work. Stay loose, move around, and watch these people. Anymore problems, arrest them and we will hold them until the B.N.J. departs."

Steve turned away and moved toward the outside bar

while Mike headed for the beach. Jay pointed toward the hotel then headed that way.

I slowly wandered around looking for the strangers; people that don't fit in-predators. I only got a hundred feet from where we had out meeting when Vicky contacted me.

"Joshua, one of the armed passengers from the B.N.J. has taken Sophee hostage by the cooking area."

NO NO NO! My mind screamed as Sophee and the Sooul are supposed to be safe here. Who would have the guts or the lack of brains to attack innocents? On my planet? *Rockfall…* I turned and sprinted in full battle reflex mode toward the cooking area.

"Connect me to the boys, Vicky!" I order. An immediate beep indicates they are receiving me. "Gunmen, go hot on alert. These visitors are most likely from Rockfall and have taken Sophee hostage. I will rescue Sophee, capture or if they resist, kill the rest."

I ran past the bar and toward the barbeque area and see a group of people in front my wife and the guy who holding her around her throat. Shoran is pleading with the terrorist holding Sophee to release her.

I drew my sig as I slowed down and approach the group. "What do you want?" I asked loudly with my command voice.

The terrorist turned slightly toward me trying to hide behind my wife and tightened his grip to pull her closer. He has a knife pressed firmly against her carotid artery with his right hand. Sophee looks pleadingly into my eyes and I saw her fear. I studied the person holding my wife to come up with a plan or method to take him out. I realized whatever he is here to do he is also upset and nervous. His face is flushed and he is shaking. A sheen of sweat glistens on his forehead. I worried about the amount of shaking he is doing and that he may actually cut Sophee without intending to. He is not answering me with demands which worries me. I lowered my voice to calmly try and reason with him.

""Please let go of my wife and we can come to a peaceful agreement." To show my seriousness and to seem less threatening I holstered my pistol. Both my hands moved up into the air showing that I am no threat.

"Sir, he is wearing a vest with Tri-Fusion explosives under his coat and has a detonator in his other hand," Vicky informed me sub-vocally. Good information to know, I wish we had knew this before they left the B.N.J.

"Tell the boys and Jay," I replied sub-vocally, before addressing the man again. "What's your name?"

I saw his knife hand twitching and he answered, "Doug."

"Well, Doug, you don't want to die today do you?"

"I am already dead." Doug said as tears started to run down his face.

Bomb vests are only effective if used, this guy would have no idea he grabbed a Garvie. I realized that he is here for a reason. If they came on the B.N.J. it is not like that hostages was their goal. Is the vest wired so it would explode if tampered with? Is Doug a pawn to be used as a suicide bomber?

"Not by me or mine if you let go of my wife," I promised. "We will help you remove the bomb and then I can help you with whatever is bothering you. You have my word as a Gunman."

Doug's eyes didn't change at my offer, nor did he relax. It is very obvious that he is not even considering accepting help. His powerful bomb vest will shred the entire area and the knife at my wife's throat is not necessary for his mission. Will he try and kill her before he detonated?

"Vick, if he stabbed her through the neck could we save her?" I asked sub vocally.

"No, the trauma would be too severe for someone with her body size.

A feeling of despair and a cold chill invades my soul. Sophee's new-found happy life can't end like this. My heart would not be able to survive either.

"My A.I. informs me that your vest is made of Tri-Fusion explosives. It would take out the whole surrounding area. Please release my wife, you don't need her." I pleaded.

Sophee remained silent as she read his emotions. She looked up and tears pour out of her eyes as they meet my gaze

"I loved you." She said voice filled with sadness saying goodbye.

Since Sophee obviously believed it is over I decided instantly to act. Before I can move, Doug's arm twitches and he drove the blade through Sophee's neck.

Sophee's eyes went wide as the blade severed her spinal column and carotid artery. Her body started to convulse violently then her muscles relaxed as she started to die and sagged in Doug's grasp.

I screamed in uncontrolled rage and my mind goes into slow motion as a bunch of things happen. I draw my sig and shoot the murderer high in the right shoulder. Doug is flung backwards from the force of the anti-personnel round and, as Sophee collapses unsupported. I dove to catch my falling wife and cradled her to the ground.

"Save her!" I yell, panicking as I placed my hand on her neck wound. "Transfer all my nanites to her!" I screamed at Vicky. I sat on the ground, holding Sophee, waiting for the miracle that never came. Her blood was warm on my hands as I felt her pulse stop.

"I am sorry, sir," Vicky said quietly sub-vocally. "The wound was too severe."

* * *

Shoran put her arms around Sophee and me. Tears ran down her face as she absorbs her friend's death. Mere and Hyun both stood back in each other's arms, shocked that a human would murder their daughter.

I gave Sophee a gentle kiss on the forehead and closed her sightless eyes before laying her on the ground. Shoran let go of us to collapse sobbing uncontrollably. Burning hatred fills my being as I slowly stood up.

It took four steps to reach the downed terrorist who was lying flat on his back alone. Doug was gasping for air as he bled out from the blown apart shoulder. I looked down at him coldly without any trace mercy. His knife removed all of my humanity. "Hope it hurts." I said to him when I looked into his pain filled eyes.

Without thinking twice about my actions I raised my boot and, with a quick movement, I stomped down on Doug's throat causing his windpipe to collapse. His body arched as he fought a losing battle trying to bring in air.

"Choke on your own blood, you piece of crap." I said as I watched without emotion, as his face turned blue and he stopped moving.

I turned away from the dying murderer. There are other

possible attackers here with him that will need dealing with. My emotions flat lined because there is no time to think about Sophee. If there is one bomb maybe…

"Vicky, scan the bomb and ensure it is inert." I said hurriedly.

"Bomb is live and will detonate if moved or touched," she reported out loud.

Clearing the area and sharing the intelligence is the main thing that had to be done. "Vicky, open comm." I said as I notice some people starting to head to safety after hearing about the bomb. I took a few steps past the cooking pots looking for other terrorists. Before Vicky can finish connecting to my men a sledgehammer blow hits from behind and darkness takes me.

The shockwave from the bomb obliterated everything in a several hundred foot circle. The force alone would have killed hundreds of people but unknown to us was that the bombs were biometrically linked to their leader's heartbeat. Five more vest bombs spread around the gathering went off simultaneously. Everything that was set up for the Landfall barbeque and celebration was destroyed in an instant. The hotel which was armored to resist a marauder attack rocked on its foundation but stayed intact. After the massive explosion there was silence for a few seconds until the debris fell back to the ground with some rocks rattling off the hotels outer shell.

CHAPTER 16

There was small light at the end of a long tunnel which beckoned ne closer. What hit me in the back? The darkness starts to fade as ny senses sharpen. My ears start to process the sound of liquid running down a drain.

My body registers warmth as a warm spray as the dead nanites gel is rinsed off me. I feel fine but something nags at the back of my mind until I open my eyes to see Jay. He is standing alone outside the reanimation tank at the medical facility on New Harvest. Suddenly it all comes back and I feel like a hollow shell. My Sophee is dead. Murdered, when I could not save her. I wish that I was dead too. My heart pumps without reason; there is nothing just blankness or a void where my soul used to exist. I robotically stand as the door opens and walk out. I take the towel off and dry myself in silence. Jay doesn't speak giving me time to deal with my feelings as he hands me clothes.

Once I am dressed I look at Jay's sad face. He looks like he has aged ten years and his normally tough and confidence demeanor is subdued. As long as I have known Jay he has never looked as weary, as if life has placed a great weight on his shoulders.

"How long was I in the tank?"

Jay's gaze searches my eyes for some signs of life that I would be hard pressed to have. In return all I see is compassion and caring which not normal things for Jay to be showing.

"Seventy-four days, Josh."

By the lack of family or friends here when I was awoken it would seem that the losses were high. I am unsure how many of my friends and family died. There is no way I am ready quite yet for the update and I decide not to ask the questions right away. A simple thought crosses my mind. *What about Rockfall?* I take one deep breath and instantly I have a target.

"Let's go to my lodge room, because now I am declaring war on Rockfall," I said.

Jay slowly shook his head, which seems odd knowing how Gunmen think.

"Josh, there are six Gunmen on New Harvest, including the Commander of the Element" Jay says. "You have no enemies left living."

"Vicky, connect me to the Commander Harris," I order.

"Connected, sir." Vicky answers.

"Are you able to meet me at my lodge for a war council, sir?" I say not just as his 1st Gunman but also as the owner of this planet.

"Captain Garvie. I have been using your lodge as an office and we are all here waiting for you."

All the Gunmen that Jay said were on New Harvest? I thought. Does he think he needs backup?

"Good. See you in twenty minutes, sir. Garvie out." I respond.

I follow Jay like a zombie through the mostly empty hospital. Is it good not to see many wounded or healing people? Or may this be a sign that a lot of citizens are dead. I will wait for the briefing with the Commander to find out. Sophee's loss is mind numbing and I have not had enough time to process my feelings.

Jay led me to his personal shuttle and opened the hatch. Without asking he drops his ass in the pilot's seat upon entering. Protocol is that the higher-ranking officer says who flies but he ignored it. I could care a less at the moment so I just sat in one of the passenger seats. Before Jay takes off after doing his preflight checks he turns back to look at me.

"Josh, I am sorry for your loss." The grief Jay feels shows on his face by his watery eyes and in the tone of his voice. I look rather blankly at him, as I am too messed up too say anything back. I tried to say thank you back but choked on the words. Healing time in a reanimation tank is timeless. Time stopped when I was unconscious; to me my wife has been dead to me for only minutes.

When he turned back to the controls I could see Jay's reflection on the windshield. The tears that welled up in his eyes as he spoke to me ran down his cheeks. Jay took a second to wipe his face then punched a few buttons and lifted the shuttle into the sky.

The rest of the ride was quiet; Jay didn't need to be empathic to understand loss and gave me the gift of quiet time. I didn't look out the window as we passed the hotel, not sure if I could stand the sight of it. The flight was mercifully short and we arrived at the landing pad outside my house.

As we landed I could see that Granddad's place and Hyun's are both dark. Not surprising, I think as him or mom would have been waiting for me if they were able. Jay shut down the power to the shuttle and opened the hatch. He waited outside for me to join him. I sat still for a second before I could muster the will to move. Silently I stepped out of the shuttle and walk past Jay.

Bury your emotions and act like a Gunman. It was hard, but I took a deep breath and tried to focus on my duties pushing my grief back where I could function as a leader.

I walk normally without broadcasting my feelings into my lodge room. Commander Harris got up from his chair and shook my hand without speaking. The rest of the Gunmen just gave me a nod. It was easy to discern by their somber expressions that they didn't want to put me under any more emotional stress. Jay stepped over to the bar and grabbed a couple of bottles of water and motioned to my regular chair. I sat down and accepted the drink from Jay. Commander gives me a minute to take a sip before speaking.

"How do you want the briefing?" He asks kindly.

"Brief," I reply succinctly. "I need to know who I lost and the status of New Harvest. After I learn if everything is stable I am going to go kill every terrorist I can find at Rockfall. You can call them pirates if you want; I don't and I am going to kill them all."

I can feel my blood boiling with every word and, as I finish speaking, I look at the other Gunmen. Even though they are trained like me and think like me, not one of them nodded in agreement. Jay, who supported my grandfather for years sat stone faced. I find this a bit odd. Gunmen know why we don't leave enemies alive. The mere fact that no one supports the 1st Gunman in a time of crisis pissed me off.

Screw them. I will go alone!

"It has been taken care of." Commander Harris said with the utmost respect. "We glassed the planet over a month ago, and there is no life on Rockfall anymore. Beacons have been placed in high orbit and are set to warn anyone of the surface radioactivity. We had let you, your family, New Harvest, not to mention other planets, down and that was remedied."

Damn, I wanted to kill them by hand and then hit the planet with nukes to leave nothing but slag on the surface. Shit, why did they have to take that away from me!

I see one of the Gunmen sitting across from me give a small tight smile. I have to think for a second to remember his name, ah yes Chad Anthony.

"Were you involved in that Chad?" I ask

"Sir, I did recon and found that Rockfall was empty of civilians and heavily fortified." He made a small gesture at his data pad and a hologram if Rockfall appeared over the table. A red dot approached the holograph and hit the small brown planet. An orange wave radiated out in a circular pattern from the impact point. The wave continued to circle the entire planet until it had consumed the entire surface.

"The entire planet is void of life and the surface is melted to glass which is over a hundred feet thick."

"Jay, what were our losses?" I ask quietly.

"The bombs were all synced to the leader's heartbeat and, in total, six bombs went off. Your wife was the only

Sooul not killed in the explosion; eighteen hundred and nine New Harvest people including the all Sooul died. Your mother and grandfather, Hyun and Mere, were less than twenty feet from one bomb. All the Sooul and your parents were buried in the Garvie family cemetery together." Commander Harris looked down not wanting to see my reaction.

Steve and Mike?" I asked.

"They were included in the eighteen oh nine."

The loss of almost everyone I know hit me like a freight train. My chest was constricted and I couldn't breathe for a minute. When I was able to drag oxygen into my lungs, emotions I always tried to avoid bubbled to the surface. My tenuous grip on any sort of control failed, and I wasn't able to hide my feelings anymore. I hung my head and cried.

Jay motioned for the other Gunmen to leave and opened the door. Silently they moved out of the room while their 1st Gunmen, now a shattered man dealt with his sorrow. None of them had ever suffered such a loss and the sight bothered them. Jay and Commander Harris waited quietly for me to get myself together both standing close but not trying to comfort or console me.

The Commander gave me time until I pull myself together. It took a good ten minutes before I could even control my ragged breathing. Once that happened my eyes stopped watering and I was able to focus.

"The Gunmen will stay here to provide support for New Harvest."

A medic came in through the open door and raises his eyes to Jay who slowly gives an uneasy shake of his head. I catch this out of the corner of my eye and wonder who sent him. Did Vicky or Jay call for him? Damn, I don't generally lose control like this.

I look at the medic. "Thank you, no. If I need a tranquilizer I will have my A.I. contact you." I said.

The medic in turn looked straight at Jay again and waited until he also gave a nod before leaving. Jay was watching me closely I guess to see if his boss was getting his act together. Or because of his guidance and closeness to my grandfather he feels that is now his job to help me. Either way I don't care, I am infinitely grateful for his support.

"Vicky, please contact my managers and ask them to come here in two hours for a business meeting. Also tell them I do not wish any condolences." I say out loud so Commander Harris and Jay will know that I am back on track.

Jay sits back down and slightly tilts his head. "Maybe you need some time to deal with your grief, Joshua." He phrased it like a suggestion.

He is only trying to help, but I would rather not think about my losses now. Getting back to running New Harvest would give me something to focus on. I need anything to focus on but my friends and family for I am not tough enough to do both.

"I must ensure the farm and my people are safe. Will you stay on Jay? Are there other Gunmen who will need jobs?" I ask.

Jay thinks for a bare second before answering. "Yes to both."

"You are authorized to hire three more retired Gunmen

and be their supervisor. How about we get together tomorrow and go over the details?" I ask.

Jay gets up from his chair and walks toward the door; "If you need me, call."

The Commander walks by me and touches my shoulder. "Call if you need me as well Captain Garvie."

Commander Harris joins Jay and together they walked out speaking quietly to each other. "Joshua, I can only imagine what you are going through. Please accept my heartfelt sorrow. I too will miss Sophee, your mother, and grandfather." Vicky sub-vocally said.

"Thank you, Vicky, but no more discussing Sophee please."

As I stand up and realize how broken my soul is, my heart is cold, and the feeling of completeness I had is missing. There is no joy and I feel there never will be any in my life ever again. God, I wish that I had died too. I briefly consider eating a bullet from my handgun but simply will not do anything that lets down my dead family. Will the sense of loss ever be less or will I someday feel better?

I know the answer in the ball of ice that once was my heart: I will be forever alone.

I walk out my front door and pick a few of the flowers that Sophee loved. The Garvie family plots are only a few hundred feet away. I head there, as I really need to say goodbye. From a distance I can see a new black shiny headstone that is surrounded by bright flowers. The gravestone was a huge block of local black granite that had been polished to a high sheen. Sophee's name, along with my mom and granddad's names, was on the top row. All the rest of the Sooul were listed below as Hyun Garvie, Mere Garvie, and Shoran

Garvie and so on. To me it seemed fitting, as the Sooul who had no last names were now Garvies.

"Who made up the grave stone, Vicky?"

"The survivors from on the fabrication ship did it, when they asked about the names I thought it fair because of your love for the Sooul and how both of you adopted each other."

"Well done." I said as I leaned over the flowers to press my forehead against Sophee's name. "And the flowers, who planted them?"

"Your staff did it because of how Sophee loved the bright colors in her garden."

"Where is my staff now?"

"They all are either at the lodge or at the hotel."

"I will need to thank them later. Please remind me."

I sat down on the new sod feeling that I needed to be near my loved ones. The polished black stone was easy to read from where I sat. My eyes sought out Sophee's name near the top edge and I sort of lost control again. Drying my eyes with my sleeve I took the time to read every name. Trying to put a face to everyone was not easy. When my gaze got close to the bottom the flowers came into view. I just watched a few bees move from blossom to blossom for a while until Vicky spoke.

"Your managers are now getting to the lodge."

I use my hands to push myself up. Standing in front of my friends and family I take a deep breath.

"I will be back." I said to the people who were ripped from my life. I walked out of the family cemetery and headed back toward the lodge. I can't think of it as a home anymore; that ended with my family. I have tucked all my sorrow and grief away so that anyone who sees me will just see a guy going about his business. Most of the people on New Harvest will think that the time I spent healing in the reanimation tank has given me time to deal with the loss of my loved ones, but in truth it feels as though my wife and family died a mere three hours ago. The pain I feel from their deaths will be mine to live with forever.

I arrive back at my house and walked into the front lobby where a dozen men await me. They greeted me with silence unsure as what shape I would be in. Quite a few of them are in work clothes but no one is dirty. I motion to the main lodge room and ask them to find a seat at the table.

Once they were all sitting I addressed them "I am sure all of you have also lost friends or family, my condolences." A couple of the men nodded as if to say; "Yes we did." and a couple looked down as if they were having problems still with their loss.

"My focus now is the farm and business, ensuring we are on the right track." I look to Wynn first. "Status of the hotel?"

"Fully repaired and taking customers. We are at 40% capacity with no issues. You will find the tourist numbers are still down due to the attack."

"Thanks Wynn." I said as I looked over to my winery and brewery manager.

"John, status of winery and brewery?"

It did not take long to realize that granddad had excellent people filling the top positions. They had gone about the business of New Harvest and deferred any hard decisions until I was awake. I made a couple of calls about some delayed shipments and then told them what I thought.

"I am pleased with the way all of you have conducted

our business in the wake of the attack. I would like all of you to stay in the job positions you now have and only rotate out when you feel the need for change. You may contact me through Vicky, anytime there are issues. Thank you."

Taking it as a dismissal they got up and quickly left my meeting room.

CHAPTER 17

A few months passed and security on our ships was better, covered by scanners that checked everyone before they boarded my ships. We had rudimentary customs inspection now as well. I know that is like closing the door after the cat got out, but no one ever thought wholesale terrorism would ever happen since the earth was destroyed.

The Boy Named Joshua was renamed and became The Sophee and all other ships were named after deceased Sooul. I did not cause that to happen but did not stop the wave of loyalty and remembrance that the people of New Harvest thought were necessary. The Winery was named after Hyun. In the short time he worked there people quickly learned to love my father-in-law. It was surprising to me but an honor none-the-less.

I think my staff worried about me far too much. They were very good at preparing my meals and ensuring I was always well fed. If I had a day with meetings nice clothes were laid out. Everything they could do to make my life easier was done quickly and efficiently. Sometime I would never even know they were around. Even if I had a day where I would be traveling to different sites they would pack a lunch and have it in the mini fridge in my shuttle.

I imagine Vicky was involved sharing my travel plans and calendar.

Jay had a habit of showing up at my place with a few cold beers or a bottle of scotch from time to time. I think he was trying to bring me out of my funk. It is not like I was sitting in the dark brooding or crying. I generally worked late and threw myself into the day-to-day operations of the farm. Jay did not realize there was nothing that ever could repair the damage to my soul. Even when I was in a group of people I still felt like a ghost wandering alone. I could see the people of New Harvest moving on with their lives, they got better and their mental anguish over the attacks faded.

Jay and the other Gunmen who worked for me made sure I was never alone when hunting or doing anything considered dangerous. I didn't go to any functions or social events ever because of the way people looked at me. Their sympathy made my heart hurt all the more.

* * *

I was lying in bed about three months after awakening in the reanimation tank when it occurred to me that the entire event was recorded. Most likely stored on a drive from the cameras that watch for creepers. Do *I want to relive that day?* I can't hurt anymore than I always do so yes.

"Vicky?" I ask out loud in the dark.

"Online Joshua." She answered immediately. Since Sophee died Vicky always addressed me by my full name, just like Sophee did. I never asked her to stop but my heart lurched in my chest every time.

"Show me the terrorist event." I ordered.

"The video has been locked out by Jay."

"I outrank him; play the video Vic, please."

There is a pregnant pause. "Download or on a screen Joshua?" Vicky voice has changed to one of concern.

"Main screen in the lodge please." I said as I roll out of bed and grab a robe. Vicky turned the lights on so I walked without smacking into anything out of my room, down the hall into the dimly lit lodge room. Not knowing what I would see I moved over to the bar and poured myself a triple. I moved one large chair into the center of the viewing area and sat myself down. I took a solid hit of scotch before saying; "Play it please."

Dispassionately I watched the whole video several times from different angles. That animal named Doug had Sophee in his grip and if I had shot him over her head she would have died instantly. After watching the magnitude of the explosions it was very apparent that there was no suffering. I can only imagine how everyone else feels. So many families destroyed, torn apart by my failure to ensure their safety. How I survived at all is very surprising, the worst of the explosion was slightly defused by one of the crab pots I had moved behind. I watched as medical staff arrived and picked up the lump of broken meat that was me.

As I sat thinking about my failure as a husband and as New Harvest's leader I heard a voice in my head, almost like a whisper. "Come to me"

"Vicky?" I ask.

"Yes, sir?"

"Did you hear that?"

"Hear what, sir?"

"I don't know, a voice in my head." I said puzzled. Vicky would have found mental instability during one of her med scans. So if Vicky is not the cause of the voice who is? Does someone have the ability to use his or her mind and broadcast a message to a specific person? Not that I have ever heard, but however improbable it seems to be happening.

I get up out of the chair to investigate and walk outside of my house. Standing by my landing pad the whisper "Come to me" is stronger here. It is repeated every few minutes. Returning to my room I dress in a battle suit. There is an unknown element and nowadays I take every aspect of security very seriously. Deciding that weapons may be needed I head to the gun vault and pick out my sig and rifle. I load both weapons and safety them as I am heading out the door. Stopping to listen for the voice in my head I wait. Once I heard it I walk slowly in large circles to try and get a bearing from the source. After walking for about half an hour and making marks in the sandy soil at the clearer sound a direction was clearly outside of the shielded area.

"Who are you?" I ask mentally trying to put as much form into my thoughts as possible. Either the person or entity trying to communicate is very strong at non-verbal or I succeeded because the answer was immediate.

"A friend," whispers the answer. "Come to the bluff where you crashed your shuttle."

I wonder at this for about half a second if someone can survive up there they could be a threat. We could tell that something was scaring the marauders away; even Vicky thought it was not natural. Deciding on a course of action I return to my house's landing pad and board my Warhawk. I sit in the pilot's seat and activate the neural link. Vicky has not heard the voice so she is not in the loop as I begin start up procedure on my shuttle. Once everything was in the green I apply power and lift the Warhawk off the pad into the air. I open the comm channel to Flight Control.

"Warhawk One leaving for free flight. Clear me over the shield."

Flight Control is quick to respond to my request. "Alone, sir?"

I smile at that; Jay has everyone trained to look after me. "Not hunting, Control. Please clear me. Over."

"This is Flight Control; you are cleared to proceed."

I raise the shuttle up until I am clear of all shields and set the navigation control for the bluff. The shuttle accelerated towards our destination. I leaned back and tried to listen for the voice but did not hear it. I am still going to investigate the area even if the voice in my head is silent. The shuttle had just cleared the shielded section of the farm when I hear the beep of an incoming call.

"Problems, Josh?" Jay asks casually.

"I don't know," I answer honestly. "As soon as I have an idea what is bothering me or if this is a wild goose chase, I will call you back."

"Why don't you swing back now and pick me up?" Jay suggested.

I have to smile again at the tone of Jay's voice. "I am okay, really, and I am not going to off myself. Stop worrying. Out." The dark thoughts I had originally when I got out of the tank only lasted a few seconds. I could never do anything to disrespect my dead family or the Garvie name. I close the comm and watch out the cockpit as the light pre-sunrise starts to appear on the horizon.

The bluff where we shot the large group of Marauders

appears just ahead so I bring the shuttle in slowly and land at the base of the bluff.

"Vicky, please scan for marauders. Are there any in the area?" I query.

"Scanning indicates none within twenty miles Joshua."

"Thank you Vicky, I winder if whatever scares them from the top of the bluff is increasing its territory." I said speculatively.

"Joshua, you should ask Jay or the others for backup. It is not very prudent to be taking this action alone." Scolds my concerned A.I. in a very paternal voice.

Grabbing my rifle from the rack I open the hatch and step out into the pre-dawns slightly damp chill. Down below the bluff where I landed the slight brightness on the horizon is hidden from view. The air is still with no hint of a breeze. Slinging the rifle over my shoulder I take a few steps from the shuttle toward the bluff and calmly wait. It only took a few minutes before the voice was back. The voice seems more powerful now that I was closer to the suspected source.

"Come up to see me." The whisper in my head ordered.

"Why?" I ask. "I am here and can hear you clearly. Who are you and what do you want?"

Receiving no answer I address my A.I. "Still can't hear the voice yet?" I ask.

"Nothing registers on the Warhawk's scanner." Vicky warns. "So this is either mechanical or possibly a shielded life form. Either way sir you should be calling for backup."

I briefly consider Vicky's opinion. Nothing seems overtly threatening and I do not feel like the voice bears me any malice. If jay or anyone else had heard the voice they would have reported the contact. No, this is something that I should do.

Guess I will go up and say hi.

I pull my rifle tighter on my shoulder and start climbing up the bluff. The climb is slower than last time without marauders giving me the adrenalin rush. It gives me time to think about what kind of mechanical device could communicate mentally with a single individual. There is nothing I know of with this capability because even Vicky had to be implanted in my body to use sub-vocal communication.

I make it to the top of the bluff almost exactly where Mike and Steve covered me last time. The voice has not spoken yet, so seeing nothing close by I slowly start moving further inland. Once I push thru the dense undergrowth near the top of the ridge it thinned out a bit. Not a good area if you needed to fight off a marauder because it would be on you before you could get time to shoot. Oddly enough I don't fell as creeped out as I did last time I was on this bluff.

"I am here!" I announce and paused to wait a minute until I hear a response back.

The voice in my mind is much stronger now when it spoke. "You came alone; no harm shall befall you. Leave your weapons, and move forward."

Sure I will leave them. I wonder what Vicky will say to that? Whatever or whoever it may be is afraid of an armed Gunman. Wise choice but even unarmed we can still be deadly. If weapons scare it then maybe it is not all that powerful.

"Vicky, any idea who I am talking to?" I ask wondering if her sensors are picking anything up

There is no answer.

"Vicky!"

"You're A.I. is shut down, and it will not reboot until our conversation is done."

I think for a second. In the time I have owned Vicky only tachyon radiation shut her down and only once. She was then able to shield herself and avoid that again. I placed my pistol and rifle on a flat rock. My knife goes with them as well so I am truly unarmed. There is a large open tunnel leading deeper into the dense brush so I walk into it. After a few hundred feet I come to a ramp that leads down into a large cave. The opening is small enough that a marauder class two would have a hard time fitting through. The cave doesn't appear dark, but was dimly lit from inside.

I pause at the mouth; "In the cave?"

"Proceed," comes the reply.

"Not very talkative are you?"

"We will converse shortly."

"I figure Jay will be mounting a rescue mission shortly since Vicky and I are now off the grid. Can you sense that from here?

"Yes, and by the time they restore power to the shuttles you will be gone or returning home."

Gone? That's scary. Since I do not live my life with fear in my heart I stay silent and head towards the light I see down the cave. The cave changes gradually from coarse rock to smooth rock walls. The dirt floor also turns to bare flat rock and the passageway looks more like a built tunnel than cave. Just ahead thirty yards I can see that the cave opens up in a well lighted area.

As I approached the open area it is very apparent that

someone has been doing some technical work here. The walls changed again to a dull metallic material and floors look like they are made of something poured like cement. The walls arch overhead to form a very high cathedral ceiling. The light comes from the very peak of that roof and is not as bright as daylight.

At the far end side of the roughly circular room is a pool of unnaturally dull dark brown liquid that looks thicker than water. I hesitate on approaching it and wonder if it would splash if I tossed a rock into it.

Rather than touch anything, I stand and just visually inspect my surroundings as I wait. There is no way to know if that brown pool is alive or poisonous. Nothing else seems to be of any interest in here. It is about five minutes before the voice says; "You have patience, human."

"My name is Joshua Garvie, not human. What's your name?"

"I am Ejhs."

"Show yourself then, if you want to talk to me." I said.

Ejhs gives a human like sigh, before replying. "Brace yourself."

Brace myself? Whatever it is has a very high opinion of itself. Taking a slow measured breath I mentally prepared to meet this Ejhs.

A single bubble works its way through the brown liquid popping in slow motion as the surface starts to move. A dark head slowly rises from the depths. I try to step forward for a better view but realize my feet and legs are immobilized. Ejhs never said that was going to happen. Had I just walked into a trap?

Good thing Ejhs did lock me into position somehow

because as the Gham rose out of the pool of liquid I would have been either running for a weapon or straight at it. This Gham is easily two times larger than the drones that I killed. My heart is beating like a drum in my chest as I thought they all were dead.

I take a few breaths to lower my heart rate and wait. Since my feet are immobilized I should be a pretty easy kill. Hopefully I can block the attack to get a few shots in. Wonder if this is the Queen, its size alone tells me that it is not a drone. The Gham finishes rising and takes a step toward me.

"I regret freezing your feet and shutting down you're A.I." Its head tilts oddly to the side as if it is studying my reactions. "I wanted to talk to you before you tried to kill me."

"Wise choice." I said while keeping calm.

The Gham paused. "Was that a joke or serious?" Ejhs asked.

It was not making any move to attack so I said; "Yes." *Let it try and figure that out.*

"Ah," it said, with a nod of its head. "I thought I would have your species figured out by now."

"Why, so you would know how to kill and eat us?"

"Not all of us were like my daughter." It stated. "Your feet are free now, but please don't try to kill me yet. We must speak."

I take a step back and realize that I am free. So she is a Queen Gham and wants to talk with me before we kill each other. Odd, I would have figured she would want to destroy the creature that killed her daughter and all her drones.

"Are we going to sit in this creepy cave, or do you want

to sit in the rising sun while we talk?" I asked. Inside the cave she would have the advantage in a fight. Outside I could acquire weapons and have the room to move around in a battle. Still she froze my feet without mechanical aid and probably could kill me outright. Either way I would rather die outside than in her cave.

"Lead the way out, Joshua Garvie."

I turned and walked out of the cave with the Gham Queen following me. The hairs on the back of my neck stand on end at the thought of having such a creature where I couldn't see her. I couldn't quite trust that Ejhs wasn't like the Gham I'd met on Sooul and, not knowing if I was going to be attacked, it left me in a slightly uncomfortable position.

I refuse to walk out looking like I am scared. Calmly I lead her outside.

"Are you somehow keeping the boars away?" I ask trying to understand the abilities of my possible advisory.

"Correct." Her black talon tipped hands waves at the general area. "You are safe here."

I walk past my weapons desiring to get them but not sure she would let me. We find a group of rocks that are flat and I sit down facing her. The Gham squats and waits for a second to catch her breath then speaks.

"My daughter had illusions of grandeur."

I almost smiled. "You must have been studying us for a while to pull that term out of your hat."

Ejhs looked blankly at me. "Since humans moved onto this planet I have monitored and studied them. I understand your society and history by monitoring your networks." She paused. "The fact your people came here to create a farm as you call it impressed me enough not to destroy you. Your people are feeding whole other planets and helping to ensure your species survived. This I did not understand until I investigated humanity. My grasp on your people is now good." Ejhs shifted slightly before continuing, I could hear her joints creak with age.

"My daughter lived for the rush associated with collecting life energy. Once collected, she was able to feed herself to create drones and expand her population base. She was the first to ever do this in several of your millenniums. I have never had more than two drones at any time." Ejhs shook her head as if she disagreed with her daughter's life. "She made her choice and left. I had no contact or desire to intervene in her existence."

"Even though she was killing millions of sentient beings?" I asked.

"Sentient beings come and go. Truly smart ones would have been able to defend themselves, not laid down like your sheep. When you ran into her drones, your action was her downfall." Ejhs said. "For this I am grateful."

"Why do you want to talk with me then if it is not for revenge?" I asked openly.

"You may have noticed, I don't kill. Not you, nobody or anything." Ejhs states. "With discipline, you can take small bits of energy from plants or life forms without destroying them. When your ancestor released marauders, their general rage and anger provided a major source of energy that I had never seen before. This high-energy food source has revitalized me. Even though my energy is at a very high level after five millennia I grow weary. Since I am the last of my kind there is no reason to continue. If I do one noble thing before I pass on, human history may not look at the Gham and judge us based on my daughter's actions."

"What noble thing do you wish to do? Living here and not killing is great but that will not make up for your daughter's crime in most of humanities collective minds." I said honestly wondering how she could do anything good enough to overcome that history.

"The reason you are here now is because of the injustice that has befallen the Sooul and the people of this planet."

I shrug. "And the people responsible paid with their lives."

"As I said, I have monitored you humans since you have come to this planet and feel a kinship with your way of life. Your people here are very peaceful and they treat each other decently." Her clawed hands spread wide as she gestures past the bluff towards the main farm. "Creating food for others is such a noble lifestyle. The fact your relatives have helped so many by sending ships of aid where it is needed also struck a chord with my thoughts. The peace I feel since your people arrived has made me respect humanity very much."

Ejhs paused to look at my reactions. I find it oddly pleasing that I no longer hate the Gham. Here I sit still saddened and feeling the loss of my people but I no longer could put the energy into hatred.

"You did not run to your weapons to try to kill me, which also speaks volumes about your humanity Joshua Garvie." She continued, "I have a proposal for you."

I look into her featureless black eyes and wonder about it. Do I offer her a job at the farm? What does a five thousand year old being need? Or more specifically what is her point.

Knowing hold old she is makes me wonder if there were tech advancements she wants to share.

"Would you like the Sooul to have a second chance? A chance to live their lives fully?"

"More than anything," I answer honestly, but remain skeptical as to where her question is leading.

"When one has lived as long as I have, one begins to understand the similarities between energy and time. I could send your consciousness back to any point in your life within the last cycle of this planet… if you trusted me to do so."

Oh, let there be a God! I sit up straighter upon hearing this bit of information, but unsure how such could truly be possible. My heart feels like it just turned on again and I wonder if it will burst through my chest. The chance of undoing the past mistakes and crimes is more like a dream. I try to calm myself before asking if she was serious.

"Really?"

I don't want to seem too eager, like I need this, so I say nothing more and wait. Ejhs hasn't moved, just continues to look at me with those deep black eyes. She tilts here head again doing that weird assessment of me for a minute.

"Your pulse has increased and your body temperature is rising, sending you back would also benefit me as I said I grow weary. You avoid the attacks and return to the way your life was."

"Seems too good to be true," I say. *God, please, God, make this true.* I find myself praying that this is not an elaborate game she is playing.

"This is not without risk," she states. "I will die doing this, as will you in this timeline. You awaken back when you wish and will just be yourself. You will retain all the knowledge you have now when the transfer is complete."

"If we both die in this timeline and I am able to return to six or seven months ago will you not do the same?"

She does a fair imitation of a human shaking her head. "No, my energy will not return and my time will be over."

"As much as I miss my family, I can't ask you to die to make my existence better," I said painfully.

"That is why you are going back; a noble life should be rewarded. And maybe history will not think as poorly of the Gham as they do now."

"What happens to this timeline? Does it affect everyone here and now?"

"It never existed."

"How does this happen?" As I was asking all I could think was *'please, please let this be possible, please…'*

"Think about the time you want to occupy, focus on one thing in that time."

I decide doing my wedding over would not be fair to my wife, as I would know everything and that would change the intensity of our love. However, the dinner party after our in-cabin honeymoon would be the right time. This way I would know about the hijacking attempt when we receive the call about the Screamers. That would be a great time to have an advance warning.

"You will not be forgotten and I will ensure all humanity knows of your heart." I promised.

Ejhs looks into my eyes and its talons feel warm as she places them on my head. A shudder runs thru my body as I feel a current of sorts.

"Concentrate on the time you wish to return to—"Ejhs voices sounds even raspier, more distant.

"—As if your life depends on it."

I think about the moment before standing to talk. Sophee's warm hand was in mine. My thoughts are about the memory of her touch. Just her hand, giving mine a squeeze as I rise to thank Hyun. I can picture Steve and Mike still laughing at Hyun's comment. Mom is giggling with granddad who is covering his eyes.

My eyes closed on their own accord and a point of light forms in my brain. There is a burning pain, a pain I could not ignore. The light got hotter and hotter until it seemed as though my brain was expanding to explode. There are no rational thoughts as I feel my consciousness spray out of my skull and I lost all control over my body. I collapsed and all my senses went into a white fog of nothing.

CHAPTER 18

"Joshua!" Sophee cried out as she tries to stop me from collapsing. I was just starting my thank you to Hyun and Mere when the fog that surrounded my mind simply disappeared. I hear Sophee's voice yelling for help and I feel my heart come totally alive. My entire soul is awakening and it takes me another couple of seconds before I can open my eyes. Steve and Mike have jumped across the table and are holding me down before I can even move.

Laying flat of my back with Sophee, blessed Sophee holding my face and my friends holding me down in case I am hurt or sickly makes me grin happily up at them. "Darn it is good to see you, my friends. I am fine now, so you can let me go."

Mike and Steve shared a look before hesitantly letting go of me. I stand up and grabbed Sophee with a huge hug. After a second I sit back down with her in my arms. I didn't speak; it was like I could finally breathe again so I just held Sophee close.

Vicky had called a medic, when he arrived and pushed his way through the worried group of Sooul. He had an open scanner and was trying to find out what had caused me to collapse. I waved him off feeling better now than I have in half a year. Vicky has class one healing protocols, maybe she wondered if she was broken. More likely she was unsure and wanted a second opinion, silly A.I.

"I know what caused my collapse." I said with a huge happy smile trying to erase the worried looks from my wife and family. "I am not sick or ill; please do not worry. It will never happen to me again. I promise."

There is no way I am going to ever fail Sophee or my people again. I look over at my mom and granddad as well as the Sooul around me who all look greatly concerned.

The smile that was erased from my life previously is now in full bloom.

I give Sophee a kiss. She looks confused, but can easily sense the joy in my heart. The warm feeling of love and joy start to affect her and the Sooul nearby. When I see her slowly relax I motion to my friends with a finger.

"No more booze, you both are back on duty," I order.

Mike and Steve both look at me oddly, but nodded and put their drinks down. Granddad and Hyun also had odd expressions on their faces after hearing my order to the other Gunmen. I have to be ready regardless knowing that we are about to get a distress call.

We talked and enjoyed the evening even though my family was concerned about the collapse. The Sooul knowing that I was an odd man by their standards took a very short time to feel better. They realized I had told them a truth and was showing nothing but love and happiness to my wife and family. Caroline and Granddad were keeping a pretty serious eye on me and I figured I would have some explaining to do later. Captain Grey came in the main entrance of the mess and approached our table. Steve and

Mike were immediately on their feet knowing I had put them back on duty for a reason.

"We received a call from a mining colony at Bashar. They just it just got invaded by a small swarm of Screamers. Casualties are high and they are begging for support." Captain Grey reports to Granddad. Granddad just waved his hand at the two Gunmen and me.

Wow, just like before.

I nod at Granddad accepting that it is our duty.

"Plot a course best possible speed to Bashar. Send a message to the P.F.F that there are three Gunmen on board who can deal with this." I turn to look to my pals, continuing to speak. "Gentlemen, we need to have a briefing."

Steve cocks his head and looks at me like I am holding something back. Sophee looks like she is going to panic. I smile and kiss her.

"Can you give me ten minutes with the boys, please? I am not going anywhere." I told the love of my life.

Sophee reluctantly agreed, and hugged me. "I need more time with you."

"Talk with my mom or tell the Sooul women how awesome I am. Be happy and then we can go back to our cabin." I stand up not feeling embarrassed at all. "Grandfather, Captain Grey, Steve, Mike, join me for a few minutes please, in my cabin."

* * *

We walk out of the main mess and down to my cabin. I ask them all to take a seat at the table.

Steve looks dubiously at the table. "You didn't have sex on it, did you?"

Mike laughs, while Granddad and Captain Grey shake their heads at Steve.

Granddad has no patience for joking and gets right to the point. "What the hell is this about, and why the hell did you collapse?"

"Forget about the collapse right now, sir. You will know more when I am able to tell you." I meet granddad's eyes and hold them in my gaze for a second until he gives me an almost tiny nod. "Captain Grey, I am fairly certain the Screamers are a trap. Have a shuttle remotely sent to the surface. This will allow the pirates to believe we have left the ship. Leave the shuttle bay open and we will deal with them."

Not telling my brother Gunmen that I know what is going on is hard. This timeline will need to be maintained as close to nominal as possible. I turn to my brother gunmen to give them their orders.

"I figure about twenty pirates will attempt to take the ship. If we are hidden in the open bay we can surprise them before they cause problems. Once the pirates are in the hold, we will cut them to ribbons. Captain, I will need you on the bridge and, when Vicky gives the word, you will need to perform an active scan to find their ship and blow it all to hell."

"How long have you known this was going to happen?" Steve asks me knowing my intelligence was far too good to be luck or speculation.

"Need to know, buddy, need to know," I reply. "I will see you at oh six hundred. Be dressed in battle suits, armed with lasers or low power projectile weapons. Meet me at the main bay doors." Orders given I rise from my chair. "Let's go back to keep our people at the dinner from worrying."

Steve and Mike look oddly at me. My calmness doesn't fool them. While knowing I have serious intelligence they are perplexed that I did not share it earlier. As their 1st Gunman normally they would had known of such an event as fast as I did.

"Yes?" I pleasantly ask my friends.

"We will take some stimulants from medical and patrol the ship." Mike informs me. "At least one of us will be in the bay all night."

I think it is unnecessary, but agree to allow them to do so. They are Gunmen after all, and being such cautious people they will ensure the ships safety.

"Captain, could you please get Lieutenant Summer briefed quietly so she can program the shuttle with no one else knowing?" There is no way of knowing if the pirates are not receiving information from aboard the ship already.

"Yes, sir," he said as he left the cabin.

I look to back my friends. "I know you're wondering about all this and I am sorry I cannot tell where my head is yet but the time will come when I can explain. Sorry guys."

Steve and Mike accepted my apology it even if they don't understand my reasons.

"If we didn't trust you with our lives, we would think you were crazy," Mike admits, walking toward the door.

"Go and be with your new wife," Steve adds. "We will watch the ship until morning."

I grabbed granddad's hand to pull him to his feet. "Come, old man, let's get back to that party."

With a shake of his head he followed me out the door.

"You know, Josh, it is not just Mere that has difficulty figuring you out."

"I am coming home with a wife, I am going drop grandkids at your feet, and I am going to protect all the people of Harvest. Hope your okay with that?"

Granddad put his hand on my shoulder in a maternal gesture. We walked back to the main mess and joined our families.

Sophee's face lights up with a very happy smile when she sees us enter. Moving over to where my mom is I bend over and give her a kiss on the cheek. Mere is beside mom looking up at me as well so I give her a kiss too.

"Thank you for everything you did to make the cabin up for our wedding night. Sophee's dress was also beautiful. I owe you ladies a big one." Mere and my mom smiled at my thank you. I quickly grabbed my wife up for another kiss.

"My wife needs some Joshua-time and I am dying for some Sophee-time." I explain as I carry my wife toward the door. I stop at Shoran's table where she sat with her parents. Steve has decided patrolling and security is more important at this time than trying to woo his girlfriend. I am happy that he has priorities but try and lessen the impact.

"I had to put Steve on a task with Mike." I keep my emotions guarded but open. This way Shoran will know there was a need for him to be away from her side. "He will be free tomorrow."

She gives me a pouty smile so I figure Steve will not be in too much trouble with her. I nod at her parents and we leave. Heading back to our cabin, as I reach the doorway I see a fully armed Gunman come around the corner on patrol.

"Hey, pal, you might want to stop by the party. Tell your girlfriend that I felt uneasy and because you work for me you had to go back to work."

"Don't think so, Josh. I will tell her there is a security issue, so Mike and I decided to pull voluntary guard duty. You're not being responsible for me missing time with my girlfriend."

"I've missed you, brother." I said causing him give me another puzzled look.

Sophee never said a word as I carried her into the cabin and over to the bed. I climbed in and then pulled her tighter. I was so happy to have her back stupid tears leaked out of my eyes. I am glad it was in the privacy of our cabin, as my brother Gunmen would have mocked me mercilessly for being emotional. Feeling of relief and gratitude to the Gham queen came easily. For the time now I needed to hold Sophee and feel her heart beat against me.

* * *

Sophee could not understand why Joshua collapsed or why he was just holding her and not getting undressed. Normally when they are in the bed, clothes are not any kind of option. Her hand reached up to his face and, to her total surprise, she felt tears. His emotional state was love as per usual, and something else... maybe relief? There was also joy, which was not a new emotion, but it was at a level that far exceeded his norms.

"I love you," I said in a very gentle soft voice to see if he would talk about what he was feeling.

Joshua smiled with that happy with life grin that he wore generally. He started undressing then helped me with my dress. Loving Joshua is nothing like loving a Sooul man from what I hear. He has what he calls his fore love or was it play? Joshua gently turned me on my stomach and started giving me of those gentle massages starting at my feet. He continued upward ensuring my leg muscles were taken care of. When his hands touched my buttocks I almost lost control. My Joshua knows what I like and finds every single tense spot on my back and neck. His kisses liberally pepper my neck and shoulders. When he rolls me over to continue I have just enough of this and wrap my legs around him. I pulled him to me not needing anymore of his play. His eyes open wide when we join. My hands cradle his face as I feel his emotion of grief, which not something I've felt before. Then the relief and love he that he feels takes over and it is stronger than the emotions he had at the dinner after he fell. As he slowly loves me his emotions of love seem to get stronger as the time passes. He kisses me deeply and I pull myself harder to him. This time of love has gone on longer than any time before, there is no urgency just overwhelming emotion. My heart and soul belong to this wonderful man and the power of these thoughts brings tears to my eyes as well.

* * *

Her musical voice stirred me to action.

I didn't say anything, merely started to undress Sophee, which made her very happy. The smile she wore outshines anything I have ever seen. I feel no reason to madly couple and decide give her my best efforts. Warming her up with a slow massage is one of the things Sophee loves. When I finished and rolled her over she attacked me like a boa constrictor. To say the loving-making was gentle was an understatement. It was very slow and intense, downright magical. Sophee emotions showed in tears on her face, I never wanted this moment to end.

I picked Sophee up and carried her to the shower. We enjoyed the warm water slowly washing each other as lovers not rushing and going with the moment. When we got back to bed I gathered her up into my arms and held her till she fell asleep.

"Vicky?" I ask sub-vocally.

"Yes, Sir?"

"Could you please have Mere and Shoran woken up around five a.m.? Please ask them to come spend a few hours with Sophee. This way she will not be scared and alone until this pirate business is finished."

"Joshua—" Vicky practically sighs "—I am worried about you."

"Don't be. I am alive and well. I am better informed now than I have ever been."

I don't want to do anything but watch Sophee sleep. To me I cannot get enough of the sight of her.

Maybe because I was watching her, or maybe she could sense feelings, my beautiful wife woke and realized that I was fully awake. Sophee stretched like a cat before placing her arms around my neck. Her beautiful greens eyes had everything my soul needed to be complete. She could not understand how relieved my emotional state currently was.

"My husband, are you going to tell me what has happened?" Sophee's gaze is full of unconditional love but questioning.

"No, I think not. Would it be sufficient to say I love you and will ensure you are safe always?"

"I knew that." She said as she leans closer to kiss me gently on the lips.

"I have a problem that needs dealing with and I need your understanding."

Sophee knew there was some problem or security issue from earlier in the evening when Captain Grey reported on Bashar. She also knew it was severe enough Steve and Mike went on patrol duty. If the problem was critical Joshua would be taking care of it. This must be the issue.

"Joshua?" Sophee ended speaking after saying my name waiting for the axe to fall.

"Some pirates are going to attempt taking over this ship. We can stop them, deal with the attack in a very quick manner, but I will have to be a part of the fight." I slide my hand up to under Sophee's chin and return a kiss. "I do not want you to be worried."

Sophee's smiles sensing that everything I have said it true and honest.

"I am not in danger and it will only take a few hours at most." I explained. "Then we should spend the rest of the day in bed or just being together with our friends. I really don't care what we do as long as you are with me."

"Maybe you should sleep." Sophee suggests knowing I have some work to do in the morning.

"Kind of hard to sleep when my eyes haven't seen enough of you."

Sophee's eyebrow rises at that, and I again remember that I tell her more by trying to be silent. We snuggle for a few hours, her lying on my arm with one leg over mine. We talk softly about New Harvest and what our home will be like. Both of us must have dosed off because I heard a chime at the door and jumped. I hop out of bed and throw a robe on while walking over to the door. When I open it Shoran and Mere are waiting as requested.

"Come in, ladies, and thank you for your willingness to spend a little time with Sophee while this tiny issue is dealt with."

Mere raises her eyebrow at me but cannot sense anything more than my total happiness. I stand to the side while they enter. Shoran runs over to the bed and jumps up beside Sophee to watch me get ready. Sorry to disappoint her but we have a large walk in closet.

"Do you have time for one of your coffees?" Mere asks as she stands by the AutoChief.

"Please." I say as I head to the closet and put my battle suit on. I put on the reflective body armor suit, which is a bit different from my normal suit. Before leaving I grab a long shirt for Sophee. Leaving the closet I walk across the room to where Sophee is sitting on the bed and pull the shirt over her head.

"Sorry, honey," I say as I gently lift her to her feet. Shoran looks at me with a smile and holds her arms upward so I would lift her off the bed as well. When I put her on her feet both her and Sophee giggle at my red face. I key in the security code on the pad beside the headboard, which raises the bed. Underneath is an array of personal weapons.

I grab my sig and some magazines. I then open the compartment at the rear or the cache and pull out my modified AR15. Four clips of ammo go into my harness and I am ready for a fight.

Sophee looks a little worried, by the serious look on her face. So I give her a big kiss. Out of the corner of my eyes I see Mere scrunching up her nose at the smell of the coffee in her hand. I casually take the coffee and sit down at the table. Sophee moves beside me and sits on the chair beside me. I take a sip of the hot bitter fluid and give an overly theatrical "AHHH." Since I have their undivided attention it would be a good time to explain what's up.

"Pirates suck, and they are not very good people. They are however stupid and mean. Mike and Steve could handle this easy without my help. The only reason I am helping is because I am their leader and it is what I do. Please don't worry." I take a few fast gulps of my coffee to finish it and stand after giving Sophee a kiss on the head.

"Remember my love for you always will bring me home."

I turn away and open door to almost run into Steve who has his ear against it. I started laughing as the door closed and we walked away. Steve's face turned a bit red in embarrassment for getting caught but he didn't make excuses or apologize. He looks at me and then started; "I saw...."

Remembering this last conversation before I interrupted him.

"Steve, Shoran is here to help keep Sophee calm while we attend to business. Yes, she likes you and is asking Sophee questions about you." His mouth dropped opened at me having the answers before he asked the questions. I continue to mess with his mind.

"I think the bond was quicker for us because of me saving her from the eels."

I keep walking as Steve stops dead at that comment. He is trying to put together that I know details of things that have not happened. As a Gunman he knows we are all awesome in our own minds but having me know everything is freaking him out a bit. Personally I think it is fun to knock him of his game.

"I have asked you those questions before haven't I?"

"Need to know, buddy, need to know."

* * *

Back in the quiet cabin Sophee glances at her mom and her friend.

"Last night my Joshua brought me here and crawled into bed clothed. He just held me quietly for quite a while. When I touched his face there were tears mom, tears! They were tears caused by relief and then all I could sense was joy and love, but it seemed at a different level—much higher, if you could believe it." Sophee smiled at the memory of their shared evening.

"Really, even more love?" Shoran has wide eyes trying to believe that Joshua could up his feelings.

Sophee's face turned thoughtful. "We also had the gentlest, slowly intense act of love, better than any previous time."

Mere even raised an eyebrow at that, especially after the story Sophee shared about their relationship during their honeymoon.

"So what are Joshua and the boys doing this morning?" Mere asks deep in thought. Yesterday Joshua was relaxed and calm when he showed up to the meal. After he collapsed everyone could feel the change in the amount of emotions he had. What was changing about this man?

"Stopping pirates or some such… I am going to have to

look that up and see what they are." Sophee said moving to the data pad.

"Last night, Steven was dressed like Joshua is now," Shoran said, waving towards the door her friend's husband exited through earlier. "Same type of armor and with weapons. When he stopped to see me, Steven said both he and Michael were going to be patrolling the ship. They were staying awake all night, so it must be a bit serious."

"Joshua never slept much either; I woke up to him watching me with a happy smile on his face. He could not tell what he was thinking so we snuggled and talked about New Harvest." Sophee frowned; "He was not worried but still did not rest."

"Curious, as it seems that life off Sooule is not as safe as we hoped," Mere says. "I hope these pirate people are not like the Gham. We need nothing more in our lives like them."

Sophee, still curious, moved her hand over the data screen to activate the ship's library. "I want to know what a pirate is." She said starting her search.

* * *

Steve and I meet up with Lieutenant Summer, Mike and Captain Grey in front of the closed doors of the shuttle bay.

"Because of the screamers ability to take down a shuttle, I will have to fly it down to the surface and wait until you come to clear them out." Lieutenant Summer wisely said.

"The screamers can only disable the electronics, I will be safe inside."

It makes sense to me but there will still be a hijacker on the ground. I remove my sig and instruct her to strap it on.

"What a nice gift. " She smiles as she tightens the belt around her waist.

I get a little more serious. "Land a couple of miles from town so the screamers can't affect the ship, and stay buttoned up until someone opens the hatch and comes in. It will be a hijacker trying to take your shuttle." I point at the pistol on her hip. "Every bullet in this gun is an anti-personnel shock round. I know you have been trained in weapons, so be ready, aim center of the mass, and shoot him until he is dead. No talking or asking for surrender, that's an order!"

Lieutenant Summer's eyes turned hard as she lost her smile. Her right hand came up to her brow with a perfect salute. "Yes, sir." She turned and when through the opening hatch to the shuttle.

"Captain Grey, please be on the bridge and be ready for our signal to vaporize the other ship; make sure you use several gravity missiles." He nodded once and left for the bridge.

I turned to Steve and Mike. "I know they are going to enter the shuttle bay in suits, but I do not know if it will be *en masse* or single file. Make sure you have good cover and shoot to kill. I would like to knock them out before they can spread the word to each other or back to their ship."

Both Steve and Mike know that I somehow have the inside track on how the scenario is likely to be played out. Being the warriors they are, fine details on how to work together in an ambush are not necessary. They have a mission and tools to perform it. I smile at the fact they don't question me and accept the need-to-know. Their trust and obedience is absolute.

"I know what is supposed to happen, but not the results.

Cover each other and treat this as a battle for our lives... Are you ready?"

"So treat this as an average Tuesday?" Mike said with a smirk.

"Yeah," Steve agrees, as he checks his rifle, "Just another day at the office."

We move into the bay and set our suits to shadow camouflage. Mike and Steve selected areas with good cover. This will allow us to have a clear field of fire over the shuttle bay's door. As soon as I see them take cover I contact the shuttle.

"Lieutenant Summer, free to launch."

I close the comm and wait. The shuttle bay depressurized and the main bay door opens. Gravity automatically shut down. The shuttle rose a few feet and is pulled outside the ship by a tractor beam. I remain in place because my boots sensing no gravity locked themselves to the deck magnetically. I crouched and aim myself toward my target across the bay.

"Unlock my boots anchors Vicky." I command as I pushed off the deck.

I soared high and straight as an arrow toward my target. When I reach the far wall and planted my feet the boot magnets activated again. I walk up the wall into the shadows of the air recirculation vents. Once I am hidden from view to any approaching ship from outside the bay doors I remove my rifle from my shoulder.

I check my AR15 and chamber a round. It doesn't take very long before Vicky sub-vocally says, "Be ready."

I aim at the open bay door and wait. Through the secure comm I can hear the breathing of my team, slow and steady. Ambushes are not like a fight or battles; you have to wait for the enemy to appear. Seconds take minutes and those minutes seem like hours as I wait.

In the vacuum of space everything is absolutely silent, which only adds to the eeriness. The first hijacker appeared in the blink of an eye gliding in on his thrusters. He lands and aims his laser rifle at the hatch. Behind the first hijacker a line of hijackers appears as if on a string. As they land they don't split up and cover different areas like Gunmen would have done. They start slapping each other on the shoulder as if to say; "Good job we are onboard". Poor training makes them cluster near each other, which will make our job much easier. I wait until all the hijackers are well inside the bay before attacking.

"Vicky, close the outside bay door." I said. This was a signal to the other Gunmen, for when the external hatch slammed shut we began our attack.

I target the first pirate and give him two rounds in the chest. I must have unconsciously switched to battle-reflex mode, because everything slowed down the moment I started firing. I could feel the rifle snap back into my shoulder with every squeeze of the trigger, and actually had to wait for the action to cycle twice before I could move on to the next target. I swept my fire over the group of invaders as fast as I could, the force of the bullets hitting their chests blowing them back toward the closed bay doors.

With a minute the firepower we put on the group of hijackers had worked its magic and I was out of targets. Dead pirates hovered in a haze of frozen bloody fog only stuck to the deck by their magnetic boots.

"Vicky, please go active. Status of team?" I ask.

"One hundred percent sir."

Seeing no movement from the hijacker but not wishing to endanger any Gunmen I issue another command; "Scan them for survivors."

"One survivor near the bay door's manual override; he is wounded and will need medical aid." Vicky says aloud over the Gunmen's net.

I try and see the survivor thru the fog but cannot spot him from my vantage spot. Before I can ask my team if they have a visual I see Mike raise his laser rifle. He fires and then stands up from behind the refueling station he was using for cover to sling his rifle. To me that is a clear indication of a fatal hit.

Vicky sounds smug. "All invaders have been eliminated."

It's just that easy. With the knowledge I had nobody got hurt and Shoran did not get assaulted. I feel pretty good about this. Do I feel bad about killing all the hijackers without warning them? No, they were a hostile force performing an illegal action. There had been no declaration of war, they are not soldiers. There would be no reason to ask them for surrender. Peace by the destruction of our enemies. Even though we are done here the job is not complete.

"Vicky, message to the Captain. Destroy the other ship." I said it aloud and both Steve and Mike heard the order.

"Missiles away!" Vicky responds within four seconds.

I release the magnets manually and glide to the deck of the shuttle bay. Steve lands beside me and Mike lands closer to the far side of the bay probably to check his target out.

"Open the bay doors please, Vicky." I watched as the huge hatchway opens again and see bright stars for space twinkling off in the distance.

"Gentlemen, nice shooting!" I pointed at the dead

hijackers. "Help me gather the trash up, please. Vicky release their boot locks."

Once the magnets on the boots were released the bodies started floating. This made it easy to grab a body and move it. It doesn't take us long to collect up the remaining bodies and jettison them out into open space. They will either float away forever or get drawn into some planet by gravitational forces. I don't care, as they are nothing more than garbage to me. We float over to the airlock and sail in. Once we orient ourselves, it cycles and fills with air as gravity returns. The inside lock opens and we walk into the ship. I punch the hidden keypad on my sleeve and the helmet I was wearing folds back leaving my head bare.

"Vicky, connect me to Sophee, please." I order as I notice Mike and Steve removing their helmets as well.

Sophee answers pretty quick, "Joshua?"

"Hi, dear, we're all done and safe. I have to go see the Captain and Granddad, but then I'll be back to our cabin."

"Okay." Sophee answers.

I turn to Mike and Steve who are simply waiting for any further orders. "Do you guys feel like going down and cleaning out the screamers?"

Mike shrugs, before giving a sly little grin. "Sure."

"No hockey sticks!" I say as I mime taking a slap shot.

His mouth drops open. Sputtering, he asks, "B-but *how*?"

I completely ignore his surprise. "On the other shuttle are two more ARs and plenty of ammunition. There are a couple thousand of Screamers, so be smart, shoot them, clear the swarm. Retrieve Lieutenant Summer. When all this is done join us for supper. Bring the good Lieutenant as well."

Steve and Mike saluted and head directly back into the

airlock. I head to the bridge to have a quick discussion with the Captain. I am very curious of the status of the missiles. Actually since they did not tell me they missed I am really going to the bridge as a commander. Ensure all tasks have gone perfectly and show that I care about the orders I gave. It will also show Granddad that I am fine and in control of this situation. When I reached the bridge the Captain was talking with my grandfather. I joined them and asked how the missiles attack went.

"Ensign Sills; replay the missile attack." Captain Grey orders the young woman sitting at a control console. On the main screen there was a radar image showing two fast moving yellow blips and then after a few second a third blip leaving the B.N.J. as well. They were tracking toward a red icon near the outer edge of the screen. The view changes and we can see that two missiles strike the other ship. The expanding explosion draws us into it and the screen goes blank.

"Quite the nice view from the rear tracking missile Captain." I said, "That satisfies me. Thank you."

The Chandler, on the other hand, looks less than impressed with me. "Can you tell me how the hell you knew this was going to play out?"

I looked at him for a second giving him a nod that I recognized his frustration before addressing the captain.

"Captain, when our people get back on board, please set a course for New Harvest. Can Lieutenant Summer be freed from duty tonight?"

"Absolutely," he answered.

"Thank you. She will be joining us for a private dinner tonight. If you have time please come as well. Come on, Grandfather, let's talk."

We left the bridge together and walk toward our cabins. I think I need to be careful about coming clean with my knowledge but really do not want to endanger the future. Changes to the timeline must be avoided.

"Can you wait until my boys get back for an update?" I ask my Granddad.

"How about you come clean *now*?" He said slightly exasperated with me.

I stop walking recognizing his frustration. Granddad stopped as well in the empty corridor and raised and eyebrow at me.

"I have found out that time and energy are similar. This has given me firsthand knowledge of some events. I don't know if I should protect the timeline but I am unwilling to take that risk. There is only one more major event that will need different handling. Until then sir I would rather keep this quiet and will only be able to fully update you after everything has transpired."

Granddad listened carefully to what I said and processed the information. To give him credit he did not play twenty questions. The amount of trust he showed me proved instantly that he has accepted my position or finally sees me as a leader.

"Was that so hard?" The frustration that I saw disappeared to a slightly pleased smile. He motioned down the corridor and we continue walking together. When we reach his cabin he briefly stops.

"I believe I need a nap Josh, call me if you need any support or advice." With a smile he went into his cabin.

I called after him. "Are you coming to dinner? I am grilling steaks in the small galley!"

"Wouldn't miss it," he said as the door clicks shut.

"Vicky, make sure mom knows the invitation is for them both please." I said as I approached the door to my cabin.

I walk into my cabin to see three women huddled around a small monitor. Sophee and Shoran are in the front row with Mere looking over their shoulders.

"Ladies, if you push the icon that looks like a box in a box it puts all the data on the bulkhead like a large screen." I advised.

Sophee's hand reached up and a picture of an 18th century pirate appears on the bulkhead. She takes one look at it before she turns to inspect me, checking me out from head to toes. I know she is looking for wounds or damage to my battle suit.

I raise my arms and slowly turned in a circle for her. "Satisfied?" I ask pleasantly.

"Pirates, Joshua Garvie?" She asks sounding a little miffed.

Sophee using both my names caused me to smile. *Wow, I must be in trouble.*

"Not anymore." I say.

"You need to quit smiling, quit acting like everything is good." Sophee said to show me how serious she thought pirates could be. Her research must have been pretty thorough because she is pretty annoyed. Maybe I should tell her to research Gunmen and see what is thought about them.

I walk over and pick her up and kiss her; "But everything *is* good."

"Put me down this minute, Joshua." Sophee's voice is only slightly annoyed when she gives those orders. Maybe it is the love I am feeling for her or the total amusement at the pirate research she was doing. The exasperated look on her face is about the nicest thing I could ever see. God I missed her when she was dead. She could be punching me in the face and I would be happy to take it.

"Never." *Never, never, never* I thought. I will die before I will let go of you.

I give Sophee another kiss as I carried here over to the lounge. I pull my AR off my shoulder and lean it against the wall. I sit down with Sophee on the lounge. Mere and Shoran watched our entire little conversation like flies on the walls, as they can easily sense my happiness.

"Pirates are small-time criminals who feel they can steal other people's hard work. They also believe if they scare you badly enough, you will roll over and allow them to own you. The one down on the surface is dead by now. The large group of them that were going to try and capture this ship is dead. The ship they came in has been destroyed." I explained it very bluntly with no sugar coating any details. "This ship and everyone aboard is totally safe and these bad guys no long exist. Whatever you were looking up about pirates was not in this day and age, those pirates were not dealing with Gunmen. Besides, that pirate on the wall is Jack Sparrow an actor." I laughed out loud at the image on the wall.

Sophee looks at me and I know she senses the total lack of concern over this day's events. Her arm rises up and comes around my neck as she returns a kiss.

"I am thinking about taking over one of the grills in the small galley tonight. Grilling some steaks would be fun after the boys return from cleaning out the screamers on the surface. Shoran would you and your parents come? Mere and Hyun will come too I hope."

Vicky interrupted. "Joshua, flash from the surface: Mission accomplished, one non-life threatening injury."

That's odd because changing the Gunmen's weapons should have changed the outcome of the day. Or does fate predetermine what happens? It can't in all cases because the pirates here are dead. Does Steve sitting in the medical bay getting treatment lead to something greater? Not likely because they all could die in a terrorist explosion in six months. Maybe the screamers just like the taste of Steve's ass.

"Please tell Steve that a bite on the ass is quite funny. He should only have to be tanked for a few hours and still able to make supper." I look to Shoran. "Steve got bit in the butt again by a screamer. Lost a chunk of flesh, so why don't you meet him in the shuttle bay and make sure he gets to medical? He would enjoy your company while he sits in the tank."

Shoran can sense that nothing too serious has happened to Steve by the way I don't show any concern.

"Please excuse me, Sophee." She says as she headed for the door.

"I will walk you to medical." Mere says like a mother trying to ease Shoran's worries. They left immediately, which was perfect because I want Sophee to myself for a while. The day did not weigh heavily on my mind but I was glad it was over or at least the pirate hijacker parts. Sophee still looks puzzled at my knowledge and put her hand on my cheek. "You are acting like you know everything, and it is disconcerting."

"I only know some things, trust me on this sweetie."

"You were not the same last night," Sophee said. "The love we shared was different. Your love was so intense I almost felt unworthy of it." She smiles at me. "I may need some more."

"I never will be the same as I was." I said looking into those mesmerizing eyes.

"Oh," I said. "There is one other thing."

Sophee is still holding my gaze; "yes?"

"I will need more Sophee." I say breaking here gaze to pull her in tight. "Do you feel like helping me cook supper tonight for our parents and friends?"

"Isn't it generally the women who cook?" She asks.

"On New Harvest there is generally a sharing of household duties. My father used to cook and much as my mom when I was a small child. Do Sooul men not usually cook?"

"No they usually work the fields or clean. When they did the grull and crawler back on Sooule it was under the female's supervision." Sophee said. "Are you a good cook?"

"I only grill stuff well. Granddad is a better cook. He does these fish fillets stuffed with crab meat and baked in a wine sauce that is plain amazing." I explained.

"Females generally cook because they will not leave their children. I hope you will not mind but I like cooking for you. Seeing you eating and happy makes my life feel complete." Sophee gets a cute little mischievous smile. "It could also be that if I know how much you are eating I will know how much energy you will have in our bed…."

Ok I blushed at her straight forwardness. I realized that cooking makes her happy and will not interfere but will always try and help when I can. She is going to find things very different when she gets to New Harvest.

"I am going to change out of these clothes into something

more casual." I lifted her off my lap and gently sat her on the lounge. Stepping into the huge closet I remove my battle suit and retrieve casual clothing.

"Would you like to have some fun at Steve's expense?" I ask stepping out wearing jeans and tee shirt.

"He is going to be sitting in a tank with no pants on, so let's go grab some snacks and get a whole bunch of people to go visit him. His face will turn red, and it will throw him off his tough-guy game."

Sophee didn't take any convincing because of the humor I was feeling. She would rather that we were laughing and having a good time rather than dealing with pirates and such. We went down to the small galley and made up some finger foods together. We prepared small sandwiches, vegetables and other different foods from New Harvest together. I was pleased to see that Sophee and I worked well together in the kitchen. I hope I didn't do anything stupid that would make her kick me out.

"That was different making food with a man." Sophee said in a teasing manner.

"I am not just a man." I replied. "Quit treating me like a piece of meat."

By the amount of laughter that came from my wife she knows when I am joking and actually loves the happy banter. We loaded up a cart with all the snacks and went by the main mess to gather a few dozen Sooul to join us. By the time I called Mike on the comm to tell him the plan Steve had been sitting in the gel for over half an hour. Mike also thought it was one of the funnier things anyone had ever done to Steve. We had Vicky to call the doctor to get permission to take over the infirmary. Luckily for us he was the only patient being treated at the time.

When we opened the door to medical and walk in, it was quite funny to see Shoran holding Steve's hand from the side of the short tank he was sitting in. Steve was sitting pantless in the slightly opaque gel while nanites sealed his wounds. Sure enough, his face went bright red when we all walked in. The Sooul of course walked right up to Steve to check on his well-being.

Shoran jumped up and thanked us for the kindness and support we were giving Steve. He, however, knew perfectly well Mike and I was taking great enjoyment out of his predicament when he sent a glare our way. Steve cringed every time someone came near him, he was more uptight about nudity or specifically his, causing us to snicker. Mike pulled a bunch of chairs over near to Steve's tank for the Sooul to sit on. Others sat happily on beds nearby. Playing the gracious host I wheeled the cart around to everyone seeing that they had food and would stay for a while.

I decided to go for the jugular. "See, honey—" I point toward Steve's groin. "—That's why he would be good for Shoran."

I thought Mike was having a heart attack the way he gasped for air. I've seen him laugh so hard he feel off a chair and this was pretty close. Steve sputtered trying to defend himself before he too started laughing as hard as Mike. Once Steve has a good laugh he seemed to relax in everyone's company.

"But the gel is cold!" he claimed.

The Sooul laughed along with us sensing that we were

having a grand old time. Sophee whispered to Shoran about why the joke was funny.

"I sure hope its shrinkage." She said deadpan.

This time Mike fell off his chair. Shoran let go of Steve's hand and stood to give him a kiss and whisper something into his ear. Steve's embarrassment left him and a very serine smile appeared on his face. After all the laughter was over and the food was gone we packed up the cart and said our goodbyes. Steve only had another hour or so before he could dress and we could do some grilling.

We used a portable grill in the galley to make steaks for the group. Sophee helped me but allowed me to do the steaks. I took orders for how everyone liked their steaks and work diligently to see that they got what they wanted. Sophee's mom tried to help but gave up when she Sophee and I were having such a good time cooking together. Mom and Granddad sat with Hyun and Mere. Steve brought me a drink and gave me a fist pump for today's joke. Mike was happy to chat with everyone and had a rather nice time. I did get a bit nervous when Lieutenant. Summer got into a conversation with Sophee but since I had nothing to hide I just let them talk.

* * *

Sophee was getting a beer for her husband because he would not leave the grill. She also decided on a glass of wine for herself when another woman touched her on the shoulder.

"Sophee? I am Anne Summer."

Sophee looks over at the nice looking woman recognizing her even though they had not met formally. "You're the pilot right?"

"I am," Anne answers with a slight nod. "Did you know I have known Joshua for over seven years?"

"He never mentioned it." Sophee said. "But I don't know everyone he knows."

Sophee can sense that Anne is very forward but honest. Anne knowing her husband doesn't even threaten her a bit. Joshua is faithful and loyal and did not know love before her. All the people on this ship are good people, maybe this Anne wants to share something about Joshua with her.

"Yeah, when he first traveled on this ship I hit on him."

Sophee's eyes go wide remembering that Joshua told her what hitting on was; "Really? What did he do?"

"It was amusing. I didn't know him and thought he was cute, so I thought I'd hit on him maybe for a date. He turned bright red and walked to the other side of the serving line to get away from me. For all his embarrassment he still was very polite."

Sophee looks thoughtful for a moment, but could not help giggling. "He does blush a lot and was a bit repressed when I meet him."

"You take good care of him, Sophee, he is a really good guy." Anne said pleased that she met Sophee and was able to tell her that she had married a good guy.

"I will." Sophee gave Anne a hug and then added, "Please make him blush anytime you want."

"Okay," she replied with a mischievous grin, "But not tonight. He gave me a really nice sig, and I would feel guilty for it today."

* * *

I worked very hard not to pretend I knew what was

going on. For day-to-day business I would listen to staff and not make immediate decisions like I knew what was happening. Sophee was pretty easy to deal with, as our strong relationship grew much stronger. The small changes I made in some respects made me look a bit wiser. When I took my WarHawk to harvest the large marauders we stayed much higher. The idea of having one shuttle backing up a two-shuttle hunt team seemed excessive but was really safe. When my fellow Gunmen asked why we were staying so high I had a great answer.

"Marauders in the class three range and jump about a hundred feet, class four around one hundred and seventy feet. If we plot the curve five and sixes may jump over the minimum safety height of two hundred fifty feet. Life is dangerous enough, why take dumb chances?" *I nailed it.* We never crashed my shuttle and still took most of the really large dangerous animal down.

* * *

The night before the Landfall holiday I called for a meeting with Jay and the boys to discuss the security arrangements. Trying to be smart I had a few people over from the hotel resort to give the girls a spa treatment, but I don't think I had Sophee fooled. She could tell I was not sharing something. Tomorrow was a day that could never be repeated and I think my emotions may had showed my concern.

I passed a round of scotch out to my friends. We all sat down, I took a sip of my scotch. Explaining that unless our actions are changed dramatically they would die was not easy. As my staff, Gunmen or my best friends it was even harder. I should have dealt with it and left my staff alone.

If I don't allow the scumbags from Rockfall to at least step on my home planet with the bombs I will have no reason to nuke them.

"Tomorrow, over eighteen hundred citizens will die unless we act. I'm not just talking about the people of New Harvest, but all of the Sooul as well… Plus you two, Mike and Steve."

Steve and Mike put their drinks down very abruptly. Steve's face took a hard turn while Mike bowed his head and rubbed his temple to keep calm.

"Do we at least die well?" Mike asks in a tone that quivered with rage.

"No, terrorist bombs from Rockfall kill everyone." Giving them a moment to let that sink in, I address Vicky. "Connect me with Captain Grey on the B.N.J."

As I waited the couple seconds for the connection I notice Jay staring intently at me because he knew I had a plan. Steve is sitting tensely keyed up while beside him Mike continues to try and calm himself. I hear the tone of the connection.

"Captain Grey, how far out are you?"

"Twelve hours until orbit, sir." He answered back immediately.

"I want you to disembark the passengers only on the first shuttle load. Claim there is a problem with the landing area and have Lieutenant Summer land three miles out of town on the auxiliary landing site. When the passengers are off the shuttle, she needs to return immediately to the ship for your crew." I paused for breath. "This is a matter of life and death, do you have it clearly?"

"Yes, sir. Is there anything else we could do?" Captain Grey asks willingly.

"No, we need your passengers to step on the planet. Do not approach them or take any precautions other than landing at the auxiliary sight." I replied, "Brief Lieutenant Summer in private about the landing site and what we want please."

"Affirmative. Grey out," the Captain said in a clipped tone as he broke the connection.

I punch a key on the table and a 3D holographic map appears over the table. I had spent a fair amount of time figuring out my plan and mapping ranges.

"Jay, I want you at the midpoint between the shuttle's auxiliary landing site and the hotel with a rocket launcher." I punch a few keys and the position where I think he should be lit up green and an arrow hovers over the exact spot for him to be. "If the shuttle doesn't land at the right pad and heads for the landing pad on the hotel roof blow it out of the sky!" Jay nods accepting the fact that he might have to end up killing the pilot as well as the terrorists.

Neither of my friends said a word yet and waited for their assignments.

I point to a spot east of Jay's place. "Mike, you're here. If anyone makes it that far, kill him. Steve, I need you west of Jay, here. Same thing; kill them all." The spots where they were to be positioned lit up. Vicky sent the coordinates to their AIs.

"You sure you don't want us closer?" Mike asked judging the distance to the landing pad.

A dot one hundred yards from the landing site lights up and a yellow arrow points down at it.

"No! I am here. And will actually deal with the bombers. You guys are backup incase they don't land where I want them or get around me somehow. We do this my way, okay?"

"When will you let us in on what is happening?" Steve asks, knowing because I have given orders without input from them this has to be one of those *'He knows something'* moments.

"More assholes are coming to kill as many of us as possible," I growl, pounding my fisted hands to the table and causing the map to wobble for a second.

"I am not going to let it happen again. Full disclosure after tomorrow, but for now it is the most important day in our lives. I cannot cover every possible situation alone."

Pausing, I take a deep breath, trying to calm the hammering of my heart.

"Please help me?" I ask expressing my absolute need for their support.

Steve and Mike both stand slowly pushing their chairs back. Coming to full attention they give me perfect salutes. I rose and returned the formal gesture.

"Secrecy, until tomorrow guys." I said to them. "Dismissed, be in position by oh eight hundred hours."

They both were quick to walk by me leaving their drinks untouched.

"I bet they are checking their weapons, and then going to spend some quiet time with their girlfriends." Jay said when he and I were alone.

I examine Jay's expression and watched him take a slow sip of his drink. His hands are steady as a rock. Even though he was not told that he would die he is cool and focused.

"You okay with the launcher orders?" I ask knowing

the possible death of an innocent would be a burden on any Gunman's mind.

"I am surprised you just don't take the shuttle out of the sky without waiting," Jay said.

"The passengers would know something was up if there was no pilot and the good Lieutenant deserves our protection as well."

"Does the Chandler know?" Jay asked before finishing his drink.

"I will tell him after. At his age he does not need the additional stress." I said.

"Be safe Josh." Jay said putting a hand on my shoulder as he passed me heading for the door. After he left I just sat and looked at the full tumblers of scotch sitting untouched on the table. It must be a fair shock to Steve and Mike find out when they would die. They will be better tomorrow once this is over. Hopefully we will all be around to talk about it.

* * *

"Sophee?" I addressed my wife to get her attention in a soft manner trying to hide the dark spots again.

"I need you to do something for me."

"Anything, Joshua," She replied, just as seriously.

"I need you to stay here in the armory instead of going to the Landfall party until I come for you."

"Alone? But why, Joshua?" Sophee can read my concern and stares into my eyes try to fathom the reason for my request.

"There will be danger tomorrow and I am concerned I may not be effective enough in my preparations to ensure you are safe," I said slowly, trying to hedge around the topic.

Sophee knows how much I worried about her back on Sooule, which made me decide to hold off on completing our bond.

"If you stay here I will not worry and will be able to stop what could happen." I paused before continuing. "Remember pirates? Well, some become terrorists and, instead of trying to steal, they kill for no good reason. More are certain to be coming, and I beg of you to stay here where I know you are safe."

"If you were worried about everyone, the Landfall day celebrations would not be happening." A very soft smile appears on Sophee's face, as she understands my reasoning.

"I worry more about you then anyone else. Believe this. If the Landfall day party was not happening we could tip off the terrorists and not defeat them. I have been given a chance to make things right. Your being safely here with whoever you wish would put me at ease. Do this for me, my love?" I ask.

"Are my parents and our people going to be safe?"

"Like you said, if I didn't think it was safe I would have canceled the Landfall Day celebrations. Regardless, what I am asking from you is what I need."

"How will it look if I hide, Joshua, while everyone else is exposed?" Sophee asks. "You show everyone you are fearless, but I am so frail I need to be protected?"

I smile at her bravery and draw her into my arms. I knew she would be like this, brave to the end and wanting to not be treated special. Pulling her close we share a wonderful kiss.

"Vicky, put her to sleep!" I command sub vocally as my hand caresses her bare back.

Instantly, Sophee slumped in my arms and her head drops to my shoulder. I carried her to the bunk in the armory and gently laid her on the bed.

"Ensure she remains out until after this crap is finished." I ordered Vicky, as I covered her with a light blanket. I gave her a final kiss on her forehead and then stride across the armory, only to pause in the doorway for one last look. My eyes slide over every inch of her body, branding it into my memory, before turning away. She *will* be safe.

* * *

I went looking for her parents and found them in the kitchen putting some finishing touches on a picnic basket. They both looked surprised to see me appear without their daughter.

"Can we speak with privately?" I asked them.

Mere sensing how serious I was took one look at her mate and followed me out of the kitchen. We walked in silence over to the security vault and stood by the open door.

"Sophee is sleeping, and she would not wake until later." I said.

Mere peered into vault to see her sleeping and her eyes widened. I feel regret for taking away Sophee's choice and realize she will be smoking mad at me when she is awakened. I know our love is more than strong enough to weather it but I still have a lot of guilt.

"Those pirates from Rockfall are returning today to kill in an act of terrorism against our people. I have good plan to take them out before they succeed." I said feeling confident in my plan.

Mere's eyes watered and a few tears fell when I explained

what could happen. Being safe, they had finally had become comfortable with their lives. Hyun's reaction was very different than anything I had ever seen from him. His eyes narrowed a bit at the information and he stood a bit straighter. He waited until Mere was giving me a hug before pointing to his wife and mouthed the word *'Please'*. When she too slumped into my arms, Hyun stood the door when I carried her inside the armory and laid her beside Sophee.

"It is best we don't tell the rest of the Sooul." Hyun said. "I trust your plan but do not want them feeling like Mere was."

"There are no Sooul, only vertically-challenged New Harvest people," I reminded him trying to add some humor to lighten the mood.

Hyun managed a chuckle, before sighing. "How do you plan on dealing with their anger when they wake up?"

"Straight on. I will hand her a stick and she can lay a beating on me if she wishes," I said honestly. "I figure her love will eventually overcome her anger… or that is what I am hoping."

"I don't know if I can take that kind of beating." Hyun said as he shook his had at the thought.

"I will give Mere a smaller stick for you," I promised, straight faced. Then, my eyes grazing over the women in our lives, I drape an arm around Hyun's shoulders and give him a squeeze. "I realize you do not love Mere any less than I love Sophee. You will be safe when I succeed. He smiled to let me know my respect was appreciated but said he didn't know how he was going to explain the girls' absence at the BBQ.

"Don't lie," I advised him. "Just say: *Joshua had some other things for them to do, and they should be here later."*

The 1st Gunman

I had Vicky inform the house system to wake up our wives and open the armory when this nasty business with the pirates was over.

I left Hyun at the house to go meet the other Gunmen at the agreed upon location before we were set to disperse. We all stood silently for a minute, then, with a simple nod to each other, headed directly to our assigned positions. Each took cover when and got comfortable as we waited for our foe. We were several hours early but well prepared to wait because we didn't know if the bad guys stuck to schedules.

"The shuttle is preparing to leave the landing bay now Joshua." Vicky said sub-vocally.

"Plot their course and if they are not heading to the auxiliary platform notify Jay." I ordered.

The sound of the shuttle was the first indication that the plan was good. With a roar it came in and landed on the auxiliary site. The first step was successful and we are in the proper position to ambush them. Within a minute, the hatch was open and six men walked out. Their long shirts covered the bomb vests well. If we did not know of their plans I don't think I would have been able to tell that they were wearing them.

Doug looked around, confused, and then addressed the rest of this merry band of terrorists. He was likely saying; "Crap, now we have to walk a couple of miles to town." They began moving toward the town. Lieutenant Summer, bless her heart, was quick to raise the shuttle and head back to the ship before the pirates could take more than a few steps.

Since Landfall Day is the biggest event on Harvest, the six bombers could hear the crowds already and could see their destination. Not having people around the landing site didn't seem to put them on their guard. They just moved forward towards town on their deadly mission.

I sat back in the small pump shed that was just off the roadway the pirates were using. It would work well as a hunting blind while I waited until they cleared the landing site. I pick a programmable warhead round out of my ammo pouch and set it to explosive tip. It doesn't need to be armor piercing for this shot. After loading the rifle, I pulled the weapon up to my shoulder and sighted down range toward the terrorists. It is much easier to think of them as terrorists rather than pirates because then their deaths would then be justified. At three hundred yards I figured they would step slightly higher when they crossed the slight rise in the road. When they did the view was clear and they were alone on the roadway. I saw through my riflescope at the man who had murdered my wife.

I know he has not done it yet, but he will if left to his own accord. With the crosshairs on the center of his chest I pause for just a second. He doesn't know what is coming and, by not giving him any warning, technically this is murder… but I am okay with that. I pulled the slack on my trigger and sent a bullet down range.

The explosion from my round was dwarfed by the power of his vest's bomb. Of course his vest ignited the other vests and the entire group of them blinked out of existence. The resulting shock wave hit the pump shed, blowing it to pieces and flinging me a good thirty yards. I was wearing Level II ballistic armor, but the force of the shockwave still knocked me out.

When I regained consciousness I asked Vicky for my status. I tried to move, but was pinned by the debris. I don't feel crushed but there is a solid mass of material pinning my chest to the ground. I was able to slightly turn my head to see the blast site that was now a ragged pit fifty feet deep and twice wide.

"Soft tissue damage and a concussion; dispatching all trauma nanites to repair it," Vicky informs me. As I try to shift some of the debris, she then adds, "Why don't you wait for help?"

Steve, Jay, and Mike were coming at a dead run upon hearing the detonation. Mike and Steve quickly pull the debris off my back and help me to my feet. Jay stepped forward and hits the side of my neck with two shots of nanites. Silently, he reloads one more and shoots it into me as well.

Passing me his canteen, Mike says, "Drink the whole thing."

My hands were shaking as I took it from him. Was it from the injuries I had sustained or because everyone I love survived? The water was nice and cold, but has a slightly metallic taste to it that meant it was full of nanites as well.

"Enough, you boneheads, my weight is going to go up ten pounds because of all the nanites." I said with a painful grin.

"You're bruised and scraped from head to toe. You look like shit." Steve with a look of concern didn't abate much.

"Feel like *mashed* shit," I said, grinning crookedly. "Vicky is clearing up the concussion, but I had better wait a while before heading to the party."

I raise my hand up to wipe my brow and realize that my battle suit is tore to hell. My hand itself is covered in scrapes and bleeding in several places.

Mike puts his arm under my elbow and helps hold me up.

"Thanks pal, do I look as beat up as my hand is? I ask trying to be humorous.

"You wish the rest of you looked that good." Mike said just as seriously as Steve's tone was.

I realize how truly sore I really am. "Let's head to the lodge and have a drink… but, please, get me a ride."

Jay had called for pick up after shooting me full of nanites. The wait was only a couple of minutes but in those couple of minutes I finished the canteen and was really starting to feel the pain of my injuries. The shuttle landed less than ten yards from my position. I limped into the shuttle with Steve and Mike supporting me from both sides. When I sat down there was a question in my mind if I would be able to rise.

When I got to my home Sophee, who Vicky awakened after the explosion came running out. I think she was going to give me trouble for putting her out until she caught sight of us. She froze when she saw me painfully limping slowly up the path. When she took in the bruising coming out on my face and arms along with the blood smears, her demeanor changed from slightly annoyed to greatly concerned. "Steve, Mike, help him to bed. I will call a doctor." Sophee spun on her heel to head back to house. I tried to laugh but it hurt, calling after her; "I have already been given four hits of nanites, and will surely live."

With no more than a turn of her head, she gives me one of those looks that lets a husband knows he better step in line. She then turns on Steve, saying; "Help him to our room please."

"Sophee, I need to call the Commander of the Element first." Once through the door, I let go of my buddies and stagger slightly to my desk. Sophee pauses to gauge my determination, and decides to let me remain where I was. I am fairly certain that if she thought my health was in any further danger, she would have somehow had me on the bed before I could blink.

Vicky connected me to Commander Harris and I proceed to update him on the failed two attacks. He asked a few questions so I had Vicky download reports and send them to him. At the end of my report I said, "Rockfall needs to be taken out, either the fleet does it or I will."

"From the condition your in now you may be unable to make good on that." Commander Harris smiles as he assessed me. "I agree and will put out a set of orders. Rockfall needs to be eradicated"

I thank him for the support and close the comm.

Sophee, standing just out of the camera's sight line, has finally lost all patience and demands that I rest so as to allow the nanites to finish their repair work. I realize that she is of course totally right but I cannot get out of my chair. The short time sitting has frozen me up. Steve and Mike grab an arm and help me to my room. Sophee has them hold me up while she helps removed the tattered battle suit. I sit on the bed when my friends lower me down. Steve reaches down to my feet and lifts them into the bed. I repressed a painful groan.

"Thanks pal." I said when I caught my breath.

"Vicky says short of dropping him in a tank for a few days nothing will fix him better than rest. You know how much of a baby he is about going into regeneration tanks."

Steve grinned at Sophee. "The doctor will be by shortly to confirm everything. Call us if you need us."

Sophee reaches up to give my two friends hugs and walks them to the bedroom door. When she returns she tucks me in and gives me a kiss on the least scraped section of forehead she can find. She cleaned up my battle suit and came back with a cold wet cloth for my head. The nanites were in full repair mode in my bloodstream and the pain was fading a bit. Sophee turned from the bed and walked to the door.

"Where are you going?"

"The doctor is coming and I was going to wait by the door for him. You, my Joshua also need rest." She said kindly.

Being stuck in the bed for a couple of days at the doctor's and Sophee's—orders, I entirely missed the Landfall Day barbeque. Hyun and Mere were kind enough to bring me a huge plate of steak and crab, and they sat with me while Sophee spread word as to why I wouldn't be attending.

Steve and Shoran, Mike and Kee also came by to visit, but I felt guilty they were missing the BBQ and told them to go enjoy their day so I could sleep. Sophee wanted to leave me in peace as well, but I told her I needed her close to keep my heart strong—*if* she didn't mind missing the party. That made her smile and, once she was convinced she could not hurt me, she snuggled into bed beside me happily.

Sophee was quiet as she could again sense the relief I felt. After hearing about the original Rockfall attack I could tell she was thinking about everyone dying. After a few moments she said; "I died?"

"You, all the Sooul, my friends, Mom, Granddad, and

a lot of regular citizens too," I explained. "My heart was taken."

I then explained about the other Gham queen and what she did. How she lived without killing and that her daughter was so unlike her. I also told her how she thought we humans were noble creatures feeding most of the galaxy. By studying us she had grown fond of our lifestyle and attitudes. More so that she wanted us to not suffer. When I told about which point Ejhs sent me back to and the reason for not wanting to redo our wedding night I got a beautiful smile and a kiss.

Sophee thought about Ejhs actions for a bare instant. The Gham were not Ejhs, and her life story should be told. After all she gave life back to our people.

"We will need to tell the story to the rest of the colonists from Soule."

"I totally agree… but could we wait until I feel better?" She just smiled.

The End

JOSH'S PLAYLIST IN ORDER

The Power Of Love by Frankie Goes to Hollywood
More than Words by Extreme
Thinking of You by Ed Sheeran
It Ends Tonight by The All American Rejects
Gives You Hell by The All American Rejects
Lay Me Down by Sam Smith
Cinderella Man by Eminem
Marry Me by Train

CPSIA information can be obtained
at www.ICGtesting.com
Printed in the USA
BVHW090115030620
580577BV00004B/12